## "DO YOU KISS ALL THE WOMEN YOU'RE

He

She _____ on the
floor, a _____ ensive
posture _____ have
kissed me because I'm so beautiful." She watched a
frown appear and rushed on. "No, I thought not. You
kissed me because you felt sorry for me. Well, I don't
need your pity, thank you very much." She whirled
away from him, choking back tears.

"Pity?" Luke got to his feet, grabbed her arm and
swung her around to face him. Before she could
react, he yanked her close and crushed his mouth to
hers.

His mouth devoured hers and his arms molded
her body to his with a ruthlessness just barely held in
check. He drank from her, deeply, thoroughly, and
finally felt her stunned response.

Just as abruptly, he wrenched his mouth away
and let her go. "Did that feel like pity to you?"

## Praise for Pat Warren's Wonderful,
## Award-winning Novels

"Ms. Warren melds chilling suspense and passionate romance into a marvelous amalgam of reading
pleasure."
—*Romantic Times* on *'Til Death Do Us Part*

"Captures the drama, action and passion that one
has come to associate with the Montana Maverick
series."
—*Affaire de Coeur* on *Outlaw Lovers*

Also by Pat Warren

Forbidden

Published by
WARNER BOOKS

# BEHOLDEN

## PAT WARREN

WARNER BOOKS

A Time Warner Company

WARNER BOOKS EDITION

Cover design by Diane Luger and Rachel McClain
Paper Sculpture by Don Broda
Book design by Elizabeth Sanborn

Warner Books, Inc.
1271 Avenue of the Americas
New York, NY  10020

W A Time Warner Company

Printed in the United States of America

First Printing: May, 1996

10 9 8 7 6 5 4 3 2 1

For Frank; first, last and always

# ACKNOWLEDGMENTS

My sincere thanks to Gerald Shur, Senior Associate Director, Office of Enforcement Operations, Criminal Division, U.S. Department of Justice, Washington, D.C., for invaluable information regarding the U.S. Marshals Service Witness Security Program. And my heartfelt gratitude to Officer Mark Ruffennach, Community Affairs Unit, Scottsdale Police Department, for patiently answering my many questions about police procedure.

Additional thanks go to the ER staff of Scottsdale Memorial Hospital, North who so generously allowed me to question and observe. And specifically to Dr. James E. Roberts for sharing a small portion of his knowledge of reconstructive plastic surgery.

In all cases, I followed their recommendations as closely as fiction would allow. If there are errors, they are all mine.

And last, but certainly not least, to Chris Flynn and Jane Kidder, writing friends extraordinaire, for encouraging, editing, and for always being there, both personally and professionally.

# BEHOLDEN

# *PROLOGUE—*
# *CALIFORNIA—MID-FEBRUARY*

A cold winter wind rearranged snowdrifts in the large fenced yard, but the man wearing a ski mask, sturdy parka, and heavy boots scarcely noticed. Squinting, he glanced up into a sky sullen and gray though it was only four in the afternoon. But the stark whiteness of endless snow that covered the rugged mountain area kept visibility decent. He stepped closer to the protection of the cabin's sidewall, taking a moment to catch his breath.

Removing his leather gloves, he shoved them into his pockets and bent his head to light a cigarette, drawing deeply. The trek up the mountain road hadn't been easy, even for someone as physically fit as Nick Russo. How the old man had managed it, he'd never know. Driven on by adrenaline, Nick guessed.

He took another drag on his cigarette, pleased with his own cleverness. He'd sensed days ago that the old geezer would lead him to the girl, and he had. Some people thought Nick was irresponsible and a hothead. Today, he'd prove them wrong, prove he was cool and in control. Sam would be proud.

Nick glanced toward the gate he'd had to shove open after shooting off the lock. The old man lay there a few feet away, as still and lifeless as the two German shepherds Nick had wasted. Thank God he'd slipped the silencer on his .44 Magnum. Even in this howling wind, he knew that sound could travel. And the man guarding the girl had sharp ears and keen instincts.

For all the good it would do him this time.

Turning his attention to the cabin, Nick hoped the old guy hadn't led him astray. There were no markings, no number plate or mail box. Still, he'd marched to it like a homing pigeon. Nick could see a light on in a small high window, probably the kitchen. Neither the commotion at the gate nor the barking dogs had alerted the two inside. Good. He'd have the element of surprise on his side.

Taking a final pull on the cigarette, Nick tossed it into the snow. His fingers tingled as he reached inside his jacket for the Magnum, and it had nothing to do with the cold. At last, he was going to even an old score and at the same time get rid of the woman who was standing between his brother and freedom.

With a dark smile of anticipation, Nick made his way to the cabin's back door.

# CHAPTER ONE—
## ARIZONA—*the previous October*

The day had been much like any other, Terry Ryan was to remember later. A bit hot for autumn in Phoenix with the sun spreading warmth since dawn, then around six silently slipping behind Camelback Mountain to the northeast of the downtown area. There'd been not the smallest sign throughout the busy workday to hint of what was to come when she stepped through the double doors of the *Phoenix Gazette* onto the sidewalk.

"It's the sort of story that can make a reporter's career," Don Simon said as he pushed his small, rimless glasses higher up on his nose.

"That's great, Don," Terry told him. "You've worked really hard."

Don took his friend's arm, guiding her across busy Van Buren Street toward the parking garage they both used. "Can I help you carry some of that?" he asked, indicating her armload.

Terry held her two art folders and a zippered case close to her chest as she adjusted the strap of her leather bag more comfortably on her shoulder. "Thanks, but I can manage." A light evening breeze tossed her long, blond hair about as she hurried across.

"I stumbled on this almost by accident, you know," Don

went on. "And here I thought the police beat was for rookies. Talk about being in the right place at the right time." Impatiently, Don shoved a lock of curly hair from his forehead, a habitual gesture. "But you could have blown me away when Cy told me to follow through. I was sure he'd want to put someone more experienced on such a hot story."

Terry knew that Cy Werner, the managing editor, could be difficult at times. "You've been with the paper five years. That sounds like a lot of experience to me." She stepped up onto the curb as a city bus rumbled by, spewing dark fumes. "You discovered it, you deserve it."

Terry both liked and admired Don Simon. He'd gone to school with her oldest brother, Sean, and had hung around the Ryan house since their high school days. Last spring, when she'd mentioned that she was thinking of trying for an interview at the *Gazette*, Don hadn't hesitated in arranging an appointment for her and giving her a glowing recommendation. Though he modestly denied it, Terry was certain Don was at least partially responsible for her becoming the youngest political cartoonist on staff.

At the elevators, Don pressed the button, then checked his watch. "I'm meeting with my source at nine tonight. I sure hope he hasn't changed his mind about talking."

Terry glanced over her shoulder and saw no one else around, but lowered her voice nonetheless. "Aren't you a little worried, getting involved with underworld characters, policemen who've taken bribes, setting up clandestine conversations about money-laundering schemes?" She'd been shocked when Don had confided earlier some of the details about his possible big scoop. "These are dangerous men. Maybe you shouldn't be meeting one of them alone."

Don followed her into the empty elevator and waited until they were moving before he spoke. "We're meeting in a public place." It was a seedy bar in South Phoenix, but Don saw no reason to mention that. "And he's a cop."

Terry's eyes widened. "What made this man decide to

blow the whistle on his fellow officers?" Years of listening to her policeman father talk about loyalty within the ranks had her wondering if Don's informant wasn't fabricating the whole thing. Cops ratting on cops rarely happened. "I mean, what's he going to get out of it?"

"Immunity, he thinks. Of course, that's not up to me." Don checked the area to make sure no one could overhear them. It was after seven and the place was almost deserted. "I hesitated mentioning the whole thing to you, because of your dad and all."

"Dad's been retired from the department over a year. But he's got a lot of friends still on the force. Lord, I hope none of them are involved." Terry sighed, knowing how awful morale would be around the Central Precinct when all this hit the fan.

"Yeah, me, too. This guy swears he's got proof positive tying the mob to several top cops." His eyes shimmering with excitement, Don stopped behind his red Nissan and smiled at Terry. "Wish me luck. I may get a bonus for this one."

"Let's not count our Pulitzers before they're typed," she said with a smile. "Good luck, Don. And please, be careful."

"Thanks, I will. Catch you later."

Terry walked on to the last space against the wall, where she always parked her tan Volkswagen. The car was only three months old and she hoped to keep it from getting banged up for at least the first year. She'd noticed that people drove like they were trying out for Indy on the sloping garage ramps.

Shifting her bundles, she dug around in her jacket pocket for her keys. Just as she reached her car door, the pile she was balancing in one hand slipped to the cement floor. "Damn," she said aloud, then smiled as she bent to retrieve her things. Her father hated hearing her swear and made her hand him a quarter every time she let loose around him with a four-letter word. Last time she'd visited her parents, John

Ryan had collected three over the course of the evening and told her his penalty jar was getting full.

As she reached for her folders, she heard the squeal of tires from a vehicle roaring around one of the bends. Not Don, she was certain, for he tended to drive like a little old lady out for a Sunday outing.

Terry slid the second folder onto her pile as she heard the approaching car screech to a halt nearby. She stretched to retrieve her zippered case from beneath the car. Before she could straighten, car doors flying open froze her in place. Then the sound of a gruff voice sent a warning shiver up her spine.

"Simon, this is for reporters who stick their noses where they shouldn't." The remark was followed by two dull pings, which, to her horror, Terry recognized immediately. The unmistakable sounds of gunshots muffled by a silencer.

Heart pounding, blood roaring in her ears, Terry flattened herself, then peeked beneath the Volkswagen and down three car widths. What she saw nearly had her gasping out loud.

Don Simon lay in a twisted heap with three sets of legs standing over him. Scooting lower and peering upward, she didn't recognize the short, swarthy one holding the gun or the well-dressed taller man beside him. But the third man was as familiar as her father: Police Sergeant Fred McCarthy, better known as Mac, a man who'd been a life-long friend of the Ryan family. Dear God, Terry thought, afraid to breathe.

Shocking her further, the gunman leaned down toward Don's dreadfully still body, checked his pulse, then straightened wearing a cold, satisfied smile.

"He won't be writing anything ever again," the man said. He turned then and looked around. "Where's the girl he came in with?"

The sound of a car traveling overhead had them glancing up. "That's probably her now," Mac said. "Let's get out of here."

The bitter, metallic taste of fear clogged Terry's throat. Unable to look away, she watched the three men climb back into a waiting gray sedan with tinted windows. Just before the doors closed, she caught a fleeting glimpse of another man inside the car, but only from the knees down. The next sound she heard was the sedan taking off, wheels squealing as it turned the corner on its way out.

Terrified beyond belief, Terry lay where she was, wondering if her legs would hold her. She saw no one else, heard nothing else. Quickly, she scampered upright and found her keys. It took three tries before she managed to unlock the door. She tossed her things in, climbed behind the wheel, and shoved down the lock. Again, she had difficulty inserting the key, this time in the ignition, with her hand shaking so badly. At last, the motor turned over. Her system cried out for a cigarette. She dared take the time to find one in her purse and light it. Inhaling deeply, she backed out.

Where the hell was everyone? she wondered, changing gears. The garage operated on a monthly basis, drawing on office personnel in the busy downtown area. How was it that not a single soul had happened by and witnessed what she had?

There had to be a watchman around somewhere, or did he only work nights? Maybe there was an office with a phone. No, she'd be better off getting far away and then calling.

Cruising to just behind Don's red Nissan, she stopped, staring out the window where his body lay sprawled on his back, his white shirt bright with his blood, his broken glasses beside his head. Minutes ago, he'd been so excited, so alive. And now . . .

Fighting nausea, Terry started toward the exit ramp. Please, God, she prayed, don't let the gray sedan be anywhere in sight.

Flipping on her lights, she emerged onto Van Buren into light evening traffic. She paused, checking in both directions. No gray cars. The trembling was back or maybe it had never left her. What should she do? Call the police? But Mac *was* the police, at least at the nearest station, Central Phoenix Precinct. Stopping at a light, looking about fearfully, Terry considered her other options.

She could call Andy Russell, a friend she'd dated sporadically awhile back. Andy had recently made detective and worked out of the Mt. Shadows Precinct. Or maybe she should call her father, tell him everything, and see what he'd advise. John Ryan had instincts she could always trust, especially about police matters. Yes, that's what she should do, Terry decided as the light changed.

Impatient, she couldn't wait until she drove to her parents' home. Up ahead on the right, she spotted a Circle K convenience store. Lights, people, safety. Terry drew on her cigarette, trying to calm herself as she pulled into the small lot. Her eyes scanned the area, but she saw nothing threatening. She grabbed her bag, stubbed out the cigarette, and hurried to the outside pay phone.

Her mother answered on the second ring, but when Terry asked to speak to her father, she told her he was out.

"Have you forgotten? Dad bowls on Fridays," Emily Ryan said in explanation. "Is something the matter, Terry? You sound out of breath."

Terry swallowed hard, ordering herself to sound cool and collected. "No, nothing, Mom. I . . . I just had something I wanted to ask Dad."

"You could come over and wait for him. He'll be home in about an hour. I've got pork chops made."

The thought of food had her stomach roiling. "Thanks, but not tonight, Mom. I'll call back later." She hung up as a man wearing a grubby shirt and soiled jeans came out of the store tearing open a pack of cigarettes. He glanced over, gave her a tobacco-stained smile, and started toward her.

Terry hurried to her car and climbed in as the man gave a throaty chuckle.

"Where you going, honey? I just want to use the phone."

Jumpy with nerves, Terry carefully backed out into traffic. In the right lane, she cruised along, considering where to go. She had to get to a place where she felt safe, where she could figure out who to call about Don. The picture of him lying in his own blood swam into focus in her mind's eye, and she struggled with another wave of nausea.

She'd go home, Terry decided, to the apartment she shared with her cousin. Lynn Hartley was solid as a rock, as sensible as her widowed mother, Julia. They'd figure out what to do together. That decided, she felt better. She turned on her left blinker and checked the rearview mirror before changing lanes. And her heart leaped to her throat.

The gray sedan with the tinted windows was right behind her.

Sandra Porter stepped off the second floor elevator in the Van Buren parking garage and smiled up at Curt Gervaine. Tall, dark, and French, he intrigued her. Finally, after working together at the Arizona Bank for six months, she as teller and Curt as assistant manager, he'd asked her out. Dinner, dancing, and who knows what to follow. It was only seven-thirty. She took his arm. "Why don't I follow you to the Hyatt?"

Curt walked with her toward their cars on Row Four. "That'll be just fine." He paused as they reached his sleek Infiniti and squeezed her hand. "See you in a few minutes."

"Mmm hmm." Still smiling, Sandra hurried on. Her Toyota was parked just on the other side of a red Nissan. But as she walked, she noticed something dark red and wet trailing down the walkway. Glancing to the right between her car and the Nissan, she saw the man lying on his back, one leg twisted under his body, blood trailing from his chest onto the cement floor.

Sandra let out a piercing scream that echoed through the high-ceilinged building.

*** 

Almost dizzy with fear, Terry tried to focus on a plan as her eyes darted from the windshield to the rearview mirror. Was that the same gray sedan? Where had they come from? How had they spotted her? Was it really them or was her imagination on overtime? Damn those tinted windows that kept her from seeing inside. Her damp hands clutched the steering wheel as she found a break in the left lane traffic and scooted into it. If the gray car wasn't the right one, it wouldn't follow her.

Just past the next light, the gray sedan moved into the left lane, leaving only a white Buick between them. Terry felt nervous sweat trickle down her spine. Where the hell was a police station that wasn't Central? But would they even believe her if she accused a sergeant from Central Precinct of being involved in a brutal killing?

Up ahead, she saw the signs indicating the approach to Papago Park and a maze of roads that led to the Phoenix Zoo. The area was well lighted and usually filled with people, residents and winter tourists. Without signaling, she bided her time, then quickly turned left. Holding her breath, she watched the rearview mirror. The gray sedan followed, about three car lengths behind.

Her Volkswagen couldn't outrun the more powerful sedan, Terry thought. She'd have to outwit them. She knew this park well, having picnicked here often with her family over the years. Squaring her shoulders, she stepped down on the gas and swerved to the right.

For long, frightening minutes, she zigzagged around the winding roads, the sedan following like a patient predator wearing down its prey. Finally, luck smiled on her as a busload of tourists returning from a day's sight-seeing moved to their respective cars in the zoo parking lot. Terry managed to maneuver her VW between a truckload of teenagers and a family of six in a station wagon.

Eyes shifting every which way, she spotted the gray

sedan stuck behind an older couple in a staid Lincoln ambling along. Adrenaline pumping, she stayed with the cars, noticing the sedan falling farther behind. Finally, she saw her chance at Hayden Road, hung a quick left, and pressed the pedal to the floor. She was in Scottsdale now, another police district, and if she got picked up for speeding, so much the better.

No cops in sight when you need them, she thought as she switched lanes and whipped through an amber. She was nearly to Chapparal now and couldn't see anything resembling a gray sedan behind her. If she could make it to her apartment, she would have a fighting chance. She felt so vulnerable in her car. Even if, as cops, they learned her identity from her license plate number and therefore her address, surely Mac and his companions wouldn't storm her apartment. She'd feel better there. She could call 911, her father, someone.

She drove as if her life depended on it, and it very probably did. At the same time, her mind raced like a runaway train. Had they spotted her in the garage, after all? If so, why had they waited till she'd left to go after her? Had Mac recognized her car? The VW was new. Maybe not. If Mac had been a party to killing Don, would he stand by and watch the gunman shoot her as well?

Too horrible to contemplate, Terry decided as she swung into her parking space. Cautiously, she looked around and saw no cars that didn't belong there. She also noticed that Lynn's space was vacant, meaning her roommate wasn't home yet. Damn.

Gathering her things, Terry hurried up the stairs and made it inside the apartment. Quickly, she closed the drapes over the picture window, then collapsed on the couch and lit another cigarette. She had to do something, had to. But what?

She reached for the phone and dialed her parents' number. The answering machine came on. Great. Now her mother was gone, too. She hung up without leaving a message, not wanting to alarm whoever arrived home first. She'd call when she got some place safe. Feeling desperate, she searched her memory and finally recalled the name of the bowling alley her father frequented. She looked up the number and dialed, only to be told he'd left ten minutes ago. Frustrated, she slammed down the receiver. Be calm, she told herself.

She needed to think, to get away. Mac knew where she lived. He might lead them here. Where could she go where he wouldn't follow? The idea came to her, a place away from people where she could lock herself in and decide what to do.

But where was Lynn? Terry rubbed her forehead where a headache was pounding. The cigarette wasn't helping and she snubbed it out. At her mother's, most likely. She dialed Aunt Julia's home and nearly sagged in relief when Lynn answered.

"Hi. Listen, Lynn, I need a serious favor," she said, trying to keep her voice even. "I need to go away for the weekend and I want you to come with me. Right now."

"Right now?" Lynn's voice was hesitant.

"Yes, please. I'll explain everything later."

"Okay," Lynn finally answered. "Is everything all right?"

No, nothing was all right. "I can't go into it now."

"Where are we going?" Lynn asked. She knew her cousin almost as well as she knew herself. Though Terry could be impulsive occasionally, there was an edge to her voice tonight that had Lynn frowning.

"I'll tell you when we get going." Actually, she'd thought of a place, the cabin in Sedona. The house was jointly owned by the Hartleys and Ryans, a place where her father and Lynn's often had spent weekends fishing, taking Terry's two brothers. The two-bedroom place was tucked into the woods near Oak Creek Canyon and well stocked with staples, the perfect retreat. If he were intent on pursuing her, Mac probably wouldn't think she'd go there this late in the season.

"You sound strange. You're sure you're all right?" Lynn wasn't crazy about secrets.

"I . . . I really need to get away, then I'll be fine. Please don't ask any more questions right now. I'll explain everything later. I'll throw some things for both of us in a bag and pick you up in twenty minutes. Just tell your mom we're going to meet some people. Okay?" She held her breath, needing Lynn to agree, afraid to be alone tonight.

Something was very wrong, Lynn thought. Terry was not an alarmist. Whatever it was must be terribly important. It never occurred to Lynn to refuse. "Sure, Terry. I'll be ready."

Relief flooded Terry. "Thanks." She hung up, ran into the bedroom and hauled a suitcase from her closet. Eight minutes later, she was ready to go. But first, one more call.

Quickly, she looked up Andy Russell's phone number and dialed. Another answering machine. Still, he could return any minute, Terry decided. At the beep, she spoke into the phone. "Hi, Andy, it's Terry Ryan. I really need to talk with you. It's eight-fifteen and I'm leaving for our Sedona cottage right now." She rattled off the number. "Please call me there as soon as you can. It's really important. Thanks." She hung up and stood looking at the phone, wondering if she should have said more. No, Andy would call.

At the corner of the window, Terry moved the drape aside and peeked out. Her car was exactly where she'd left it and no one was around. Drawing in a deep breath, she left to drive to Julia Hartley's.

"Why this sudden trip?" Aunt Julia asked Terry, her round face showing annoyance. "Lynn and I were going shopping together tomorrow."

Terry's face felt tight with nerves, but she forced a smile, not wanting to alarm her aunt unnecessarily. "There's always next weekend, Aunt Julia. Or why don't you ask Mom to go with you? She loves to shop." The two women were sisters, but while Julia was quiet and serious, Emily was open and fun-loving.

Julia walked out onto her front stoop with the girls, wishing young people weren't so given to changing plans. "What did Emily say about you two going off like this so suddenly?"

"I couldn't reach her. Would you please let her and Dad know? Tell them I'll call sometime tomorrow or Sunday." Anxious to be on the road, Terry rushed toward her VW.

"I don't like this," Julia went on. "Where on earth are you going? It's already dark." She touched her daughter's blond head. Ever since her policeman husband's death five years ago, Julia had this irrational fear about her only child's well-being.

"Mom," Lynn said, opening the car door, "it doesn't get any darker. We're big girls now. Will you lighten up?" Her mother was as overprotective of her as Uncle John was of Terry. Nice to be cared for, but Lynn found it smothering at times.

You couldn't keep children with you always, Julia knew, but it was so hard to accept. "All right, dear. Will you call when you arrive wherever? You know how I worry."

"Sure thing, Mom." Lynn kissed her mother, then got in since Terry was already revving the engine impatiently. She could hardly wait to find out what in the world was bothering her cousin. She'd never seen Terry so fidgety.

"Drive carefully, Terry," Julia called after them, waving as the Volkswagen disappeared from sight. They were so alike, those two. Both blond, blue-eyed, just a bit taller than her own five-five. Lynn was a little heavier than Terry, yet they could wear each other's clothes and often did. Born only two months apart, they weren't just cousins but best friends who looked after each other.

As she slowly walked back to her house, Julia hoped they would do just that on this unexpected trip.

***

She'd thought she'd calm down once they were on the way, but Terry couldn't shake the feeling of being followed. Noticing that her hands held the wheel in a white-knuckled grip, she forced herself to relax her hold, finger by cramped finger.

"What's wrong, Terry?" Lynn asked, studying her cousin's profile. Terry was acting so out of character that her behavior was beginning to frighten Lynn.

How could she tell Lynn that less than two hours ago she'd witnessed a cold-blooded killing and that the men who'd done it had methodically followed her? And worse yet, that Mac, the man who'd been like an uncle to the Ryan children and Lynn, was involved? Lynn would think she'd lost her mind. Maybe when they got to the cabin and safely behind locked doors, she'd think of a way to explain the unexplainable. "Lynn, do you trust me?" Terry asked, rubbing her forehead where the headache was sending shooting pains throughout her entire system. Absently, she lit a cigarette.

"Of course I do. Why would you even ask?" They'd been inseparable since childhood, roomed together in college, and now shared an apartment. Lynn couldn't imagine *not* trusting Terry.

"Then please, let's wait until we get to the cabin in Sedona and I swear, I'll tell you everything." Her eyes scanned the rearview mirror, then the traffic ahead, the headlights making the ache behind her eyes increase. "Right now, I need to concentrate on driving."

"You have a headache, don't you? And I'll bet you haven't had anything to eat lately." Always the more sensible one, Lynn wished Terry would take better care of herself.

Food was the last thing on her mind at the moment, Terry thought as she took a swallow from the can of Coke Lynn had handed her. She cracked the window and drew on her cigarette.

Lynn watched Terry's hand tremble. Whatever was wrong had certainly shaken her friend. Suddenly, the Volkswagen swung erratically as Terry changed lanes too quickly, then overcorrected, causing the small car to sway. This had definitely gone on long enough. "Pull over, Terry, and let me drive. I don't know what happened to you today, but you're in no shape to drive for two hours."

Terry let out a shaky breath. Maybe Lynn was right. Without a word of protest, she angled to the right and pulled off on the shoulder. She got out to change places, her eyes examining every approaching car. "Hurry, will you?" she told Lynn as she climbed into the passenger seat.

Careful, as always, Lynn eased back into traffic. She was fidgety with worry over whatever was bothering Terry so she had to concentrate extra hard on her driving. The seat wasn't right, but she didn't want to adjust it until the next light. And the ring on her right hand was driving her nuts.

She slipped the silver ring off and held it toward Terry. "Would you hang on to this for me until we get to Sedona? This darn rash on my hand is itching like crazy."

Terry slipped it onto the ring finger of her right hand, then rolled her head around, rubbing her temples. If only the pain would ease she might be able to think more clearly.

"There's Tylenol in my purse," Lynn said, glancing over.

Terry reached into the backseat and grabbed Lynn's purse. With the Coke, she swallowed two pills, dropped Lynn's purse on the floor, then leaned her head back, closing her eyes.

"Fasten your seat belt," Lynn said. "We'll be on I-17 in a minute." When Terry didn't move, she glanced over at her. "Are you all right?"

"*Please* stop asking me that. I'll be fine as soon as my head stops hurting like hell." And even better when she reached either her father or Andy Russell. She wanted to hand over this burden of witnessing a murder to others, to be free of it. Brushing back her feathery bangs, she opened her eyes and turned to check the traffic behind them. It was dark, but she couldn't see a car that resembled the gray sedan. *Please, God, let it be so.*

Still concerned, Terry peered around Lynn out the driver's window. Was the car in the far lane gray? The windows were tinted and . . . No, there were only two doors and the one at the garage had been a four-door. Why hadn't she had the forethought to get the license number?

"Terry," Lynn began again, "what are you looking for?" She'd been craning her neck in every direction since they'd set out.

"Nothing. Just drive." She ground her cigarette out in the ashtray, leaned her head back and closed her eyes.

It was going to be a long trip, Lynn thought as she swung onto the sloping entrance ramp to the highway leading north. She turned into the curve, then stepped on the brake to slow their descent. That's when she noticed that the pedal went all the way to the floor, yet the car was picking up speed on the downward loop. The first rush of panic had Lynn gasping. "Terry, the brakes won't hold."

Terry jolted upright, her eyes wide. "That can't be."

Lynn tried to pull out of the curve, but the car was going too fast and the wheel wouldn't straighten. She could see the cement retaining wall just ahead of them. Gripping the wheel, she cried out. "Oh, my God, we're going to crash!"

The tan Volkswagen grazed the retaining wall, spun completely around, carried along by the momentum of the curve, then smashed into the wall with a shattering crunch of metal. The engine mounted in the rear of the vehicle hit cement, sparking a violent explosion.

Fingers of fire engulfed the small car as black smoke swirled up into the peaceful evening sky.

# CHAPTER TWO

He'd never seen anything like it. Officer Charley Drake took out his handkerchief, wiped his damp face, then held the cloth to his nose. The heat was so intense, the smell of metal and plastic and gas burning vile enough to threaten his dinner. His partner was in the patrol car radioing for two ambulances. Charley was sure that when they managed to extricate the driver's remains, one ambulance might as well head for the morgue.

They'd been cruising along Bell Road about a mile from the I-17 turnoff when they'd gotten the call that a civilian with a car phone had reported an automobile out of control and crashing. Four minutes later, they'd arrived and the fire hadn't yet burned itself out.

Charley circled around the smoking wreckage toward the woman lying motionless on the ground about twenty feet from the burning car. She'd been tossed free, but he wouldn't bet much on this one's chances either. Who'd have thought that not wearing a seat belt would give her a fighting chance? The older couple who'd witnessed the accident huddled together near the squad car.

The veteran cop stooped alongside the unconscious young woman, his frown deepening. Her blond hair was badly singed, but that was the least of her problems. Her face was the worst, with shards of glass from the windows embedded in her skin, probably from the impact. She was lying at an odd angle, but he knew better than to move her. Her hands were cut and bleeding almost as much as her face, indicating she'd probably raised them to try to protect herself.

It hadn't worked.

Carefully, Charley touched two fingers to her throat again and found her pulse, still weak but definitely there. From the slender shape of her, the poor kid looked to be young, in her early twenties, he'd guess. Probably been pretty at one time. She may never be again, he thought wearily as he straightened.

"Ambulances are on their way," Officer Greg Tompkins said, walking over. He glanced down at the girl. "She still alive?"

"So far." Squinting at an object off to the side, Charley walked over and picked it up. "A handbag. Wonder which one of them it belongs to." He opened the zipper and removed a red wallet. "Lynn Hartley," he read from the driver's license in the glow of the squad car's headlights.

Officer Tompkins glanced up at the sound of approaching sirens. A fire truck and two ambulances came racing down the ramps, pulling off on the shoulder. "Might as well wait until we get them to the hospital before notifying next of kin." His gaze took in the smoldering inferno that had killed one girl and badly injured another. "They were probably going like a bat out of hell and lost control."

Charley watched the fire truck hoses begin spraying the burning wreckage immediately. It was their second accident since the evening shift began. "Yeah," he agreed. "Damn shame." A rumble of thunder sounded in the distance and the first raindrops fell as both officers looked up. Just what they needed.

It was going to be a long night.

***

Nights at the ER at Phoenix General Hospital were usually long. Rainy nights seemed even longer. It was definitely not a place for the squeamish. Dr. Noah Grayson, a third year resident, was in charge when the EMS attendants wheeled in the two accident victims. It took him only moments to pronounce dead the woman who'd been removed from behind the wheel, burned beyond recognition, and move on to the next cubicle. The living had to be attended to urgently. "What do we have?" he asked the ambulance attendant.

"Accident, I-17. Volkswagen spun around and hit the retaining wall. This one wasn't wearing her seat belt. Got tossed free, but apparently hit her head."

"What're her vitals?" he asked.

Jane Amelio, a ten-year veteran of the ER, rattled off the numbers from the attendant's chart as they transferred the woman onto the table. "Vitals steady. Pulse 110. BP ninety over fifty and falling. Apparently glass severed an artery in her neck. They were able to close it off, but she's lost a lot of blood."

"Who's the surgeon on tonight?" Noah asked, leaning closer to examine the glass shards in the woman's face around the cervical collar. There were at least half a dozen fine slivers that he could see, and several were in pretty deep.

"Dr. Renfree," Jane told him. "Shall I page him?"

"Yes, and tell them to prep the OR."

Jane signaled the triage nurse to take care of the page.

"Let's get a CBC and a Chem 7." Noah checked the woman's eyes, then saw that a cut on her head had begun bleeding through the bandage that EMS had put on. "Inspect that head wound for traces of glass, then clean it up before she loses more blood." His practiced hands moved over her shoulders and found that her clavicle was broken. A floating piece, yet. She'd need surgery, probably a permanent screw.

He lifted one of her hands, then the other. "Cut this ring off. Pick out the glass particles you can reach, then treat the cuts and burns."

Jane was already at work on the worst of the patient's head wounds as she glanced up at the monitor. "Her pressure's dropping."

Dr. Grayson stepped aside and spoke to the younger nurse, Amy Stowe. "Get a cross-check on her blood and get her to the OR, stat." Wearily, he stripped off his gloves. "Come on, people, let's move it."

"She's going to need plastic surgery, poor thing," Amy commented.

"If she makes it," Grayson said. "Has anyone notified the family?"

"They brought in a purse with ID," Jane told him. "I believe the desk's already called."

The doctor turned to Rodney, the first year resident holding the clipboard with the chart he'd been jotting instructions on. "Get an orderly to take the burn victim downstairs. I don't want some parent or husband rushing in here and seeing that poor soul like that until we've had a chance to prepare them."

"Right." Swallowing hard, Rodney went to round up an orderly, wishing he'd never had to look at that charred body in the next cubicle. He hoped the girl's relatives were made of strong stuff.

Outside the hospital, the rain continued to fall.

In a rundown area of South Phoenix, Willie Morrison squinted up at the sky, cursing the rain. He hated getting wet, he thought as he turned up the collar of his light jacket. He was a little drunk, he knew. Not falling down, but with a nice buzz on. But he'd had the good sense to leave Mickey's Bar at ten, just like he'd promised Thelma. Maybe tonight, she wouldn't yell at him and make him sleep on the couch.

It was six blocks to their apartment down Washington Street. Grabbing the front of his pants, Willie knew he'd never make it. He should've gone back in Mickey's, but he'd been in a hurry to get home. He walked somewhat painfully past the adult bookstore, turned into the alley alongside, and unzipped his pants.

Moments later, with a sense of relief, he zipped up again and turned to leave. But something caught his eye, a pair of shoes sticking out from behind an overflowing trash can. Squinting in the pale glow from the streetlight, Willie saw they looked new. A bit unsteadily, he leaned down for a closer look.

"Jesus H. Christ!" Someone was wearing the shoes, someone who wasn't moving. Nervously, he glanced over his shoulder, but could see no one. The guy was probably passed out drunk, he decided as he circled the can. Maybe he had a fat wallet in his pocket. A little extra cash might make Thelma smile.

The man lay on his side facing the dirty stucco wall. Gingerly, Willie reached to turn him over. As the man flopped onto his back, Willie saw the badge on the inside flap of his jacket and the bullet hole in the center of his forehead.

"Sonofabitch," he whispered, then turned and ran back to Mickey's Bar.

Julia Hartley's open raincoat billowed out as she hurried down the corridor of Phoenix General Hospital, her lips moving in silent prayer. "Holy Mary, Mother of God, please help me. Let my baby live."

The telephone call had come only half an hour ago, but it felt more like an eternity had passed. The voice on the phone had been calm as she'd said that there'd been an accident. Julia's worst fears confirmed. The caller had asked her questions: When had the girls left? Who was driving? Where were they headed? But when she'd asked just how badly hurt Lynn was, the caller had instructed her to come to the hospital right away, that she couldn't tell her more.

For the first time in her life, Julia had driven like a madwoman. Downstairs, they hadn't been very encouraging. Critical, they'd termed Lynn's condition. She'd already lost her husband. Surely God in his mercy wouldn't take her only child.

Julia reached the nurse's station on the fourth floor, out of breath and heart pounding. Running a trembling hand through her dark hair, she stopped in front of a uniformed nurse making notes on a chart. "I want to see my daughter, Lynn Hartley, please."

The nurse checked the admittance sheet. "I'm sorry, Mrs. Hartley, but you'll have to wait. She's in surgery."

Julia's hand flew to her chest. "Oh, my God. What's wrong with her?"

"I really couldn't tell you. If you'll have a seat in the waiting room across the hall, the doctor will be out to talk with you as soon as he's finished."

Julia read the nurse's name tag. "But can't you tell me anything, Nurse Andrews? I'm . . . she's all I have."

Sympathy filled the nurse's eyes. "I'm afraid I can't."

"What about Terry? My niece was in the car with her. Terry Ryan?"

Nurse Andrews knew exactly where Terry Ryan was. The police officer who'd been up earlier had explained the accident. She worked to keep her expression even. "I believe the police officers who were on the scene are still downstairs. Let me see if they'll come up and talk with you." She picked up the phone.

Feeling helpless, Julia stuck her hands in her pockets and waited. Lord how she hated hospitals, the antiseptic smells, the muted pagings, the soft-soled shoes marching on spotless floors. She'd spent days at Tom's side after he'd been shot in the line of duty, leaving only for meals she didn't want, dozing in the chair for endless hours. And she'd lost him anyhow.

The double doors at the end of the hallway swung open

and she looked up. John and Emily Ryan were hurrying toward her, their faces filled with the same fear she knew was on her own. A thunderclap overhead startled her momentarily, but she had no time to worry about the storm outside.

With a sob, Julia rushed to meet her family.

Ninety miles to the north of Phoenix in Sedona, lightning streaked the sky as a man sat on his newly laid flagstone patio drinking coffee from a mug. He liked watching storms, enjoyed the excitement and drama of it. The danger. Even as a young man, he'd been drawn to danger.

But not so much anymore.

He wanted out. Perhaps not permanently, but for several months more anyhow. Then he'd see how things were, decide if he'd go back or not.

Taking another swallow, Luke Tanner watched the rain fall all around his small wood frame house and onto the new roof he'd finished installing yesterday. A damn fine job, if he did say so himself, especially for a man who hadn't worked with his hands in years.

But he'd surely made up for lost time lately, Luke thought as he drained his mug and bent down to pick up a stick. The big yellow Labrador who'd been dozing at his feet jumped up excitedly. Luke threw the stick and Yuma took off after it in a game he never tired of, rain or shine. He'd run across the abandoned dog on his wanderings through the small town of Yuma near the California-Arizona border awhile back, and had fed him a time or two. After that, the dog had leaped into the passenger seat of Luke's white pickup and they'd become traveling companions.

They had a lot in common, he and Yuma. Luke had been abandoned, too, more than once. Rainwater dripping from his coat, Yuma returned and dropped the stick at Luke's feet. "Good boy," he said, patting the big head. The dog was

exactly what Luke needed for company. He was *all* he needed.

Off to the right, he gazed at his dilapidated barn with a
critical eye. Now that the house was in decent shape, he'd
get started on repairing the outbuildings. Fix the barn, turn
the carport into a garage. Then a fenced corral so he could
bring home his horse. He'd put a deposit on a black stallion
with white markings named Domino. Like Luke, the stallion
was a little shopworn around the edges, but he had some
good years left. The redrock country of northern Arizona had
dozens of riding trails along Oak Creek Canyon and up into
the low mountain ranges. A man could be alone with his
thoughts up there, think things through, let the tension seep
out of him.

And Luke had plenty of tension stored up. It happened to
most of the guys who worked for the Justice Department.
His job as a deputy U.S. marshal was demanding, risky and
often life-threatening. In twelve years, he'd had more close
calls than he cared to count. It wasn't any one incident that
had triggered the need for time off, but rather the feeling that
if he didn't straighten out his head, he'd be facing serious
burnout.

Not that he'd want a desk job like his immediate superior,
Bob Jones, had settled for after a decade of working in the
field. Perhaps that was why Jones had understood Luke's
request for this leave of absence. He had weeks of accumulated vacation time and plenty of money set aside. What he
no longer seemed to have was peace of mind.

A damp breeze ruffled his dark hair as he propped his
booted foot onto the railing that fenced in two sides of his
patio. Luke was a tall man, slim-hipped, broad-shouldered,
in excellent physical condition. In his line of work, he had to
be. He'd let his hair grow shaggy, tired of the regulation
haircut the department required, and he hadn't shaved in several weeks. He also hadn't climbed into one of his dark,
three-piece suits since he'd driven away from the Phoenix

office three months ago. The casual clothes and careless grooming were a welcome change.

The first month, he'd just drifted around in his truck, stopping when the mood moved him. He'd holed up at a friend's cabin for a while, fished a lot, and read every book in the house. Then one day he'd spotted an ad offering a run-down ranch for sale on ten acres just on the edge of the mountains. He hadn't been aware he'd wanted a place of his own until he'd driven up that day and seen the spread. The cabin was secluded, surrounded by evergreens, cottonwoods, and saguaros much older than he with a crystal-clear stream running along the back property line. He'd made an offer on the ranch on the spot.

Luke heard a night bird perched on a low limb of the palo verde tree alongside the patio loudly protest the rain, and smiled. His place, his land, where he could do as he wished and answer to no one. He liked the new feeling of owner-ship, the isolation, the solitary life. He'd always enjoyed being alone.

Because of the way he'd grown up, because of his work and his personality, Luke Tanner was a private man, unwill-ing to share much of himself with others. Perhaps unable to, he'd often thought. He'd turned thirty-eight yesterday and hadn't received a congratulatory card or call from anyone. The price of seclusion and a secretive job.

To be fair, he hadn't had a phone installed, and only Jones knew how to reach him. With only Yuma for company, there were no pressures, no demands, no lags in the conver-sation.

The storm seemed to lessen, the thundershower turning from a downpour to a drizzle. He liked the sound of the gen-tly falling rain. It soothed his nerves. He was regrouping mentally, slowly but surely. Speed wasn't important; healing was.

A man could get used to this life, Luke thought. He liked his job and he was damn good at it. But he wasn't anxious to go back. Not yet. Maybe not ever. He'd hinted at that very thing the last time he'd talked with Bob. His friend hadn't been pleased, but he'd understood. How many years can a man put his life on the line daily protecting others before he makes a serious error in judgment? Some agents who burn out and fear they're on the brink of losing it make the transition to a desk job. Others just retire. Luke wasn't sure where he fit in.

Yuma sat by the screen door leading to the kitchen, whining to be let in. Luke glanced at his watch and stood. "Almost eleven. I guess it's time we locked up, boy." With a last glance at the rainy night, he went inside with his dog.

In downtown Phoenix at the Central Police Station, Sergeant Fred McCarthy sat back in his desk chair, stroking his full mustache and listening to Detective Earl Bates's report on the discovery of *Phoenix Gazette* reporter Don Simon's body in a parking garage on Van Buren. McCarthy was a short man, stocky and somewhat barrel-chested, with a fondness for fast sport cars and imported cigars. Around the station, most called him Mac, except for the few who referred to him as "Bulldog" because of his tenacious nature.

Tonight, the sergeant was tired and wished the slow-speaking Bates would get on with it. The long meeting with the Russos together with Sam's insistence that they had to take Simon out tonight had taken its toll on his nerves. It was already past eleven and he had a lot to do. He wasn't crazy about working the night shift, but it was usually quieter than days. Tonight was one of the exceptions.

"Time of death approximately seven, two .38s to the chest. Killer likely used a silencer since the watchman on duty heard nothing, or so he said. Body found about seven-thirty by a couple of bank employees. I've got both their statements, but they saw no one suspicious and heard nothing odd." Earl ran a hand over his balding head, carefully smoothing the little hair he had left. "What do you make of it, Mac?"

"Hard to say." Mac picked up his gold Cross pen and swiveled it between his fingers, working at keeping his face expressionless. Russo had insisted he go along for the hit. From the beginning, Mac hadn't thought he should, but the crafty mobster wanted to drag him in deeper and deeper. Some days, Mac felt he might never surface. "A reporter makes enemies occasionally. Simon wasn't exactly high-profile, though."

"I've got a call in to his managing editor. Maybe Simon was working on a story that someone didn't want printed."

Mac frowned. "Wasn't he on the police beat?"

"Yeah, I've seen him around here quite a few times. He'd hear things, get leads, run 'em down."

"Ever read a story he wrote that he picked up around here?"

Earl nodded. "There was that land fraud scheme a year or so ago. Remember, it involved a couple of builders who hired someone to discredit that land developer?"

Mac knew it. "Yeah, that's right. That's still pending, I believe. Maybe you should check into those guys, see if they're still carrying a grudge over Simon's involvement."

Earl shrugged, then got to his feet. "I guess I will. Not much else to go on. Looks like a hit by a pro to me."

The desk sergeant walked over as Earl left. "Mac, I just got this report in. There was an accident on I-17 tonight. A Volkswagen went out of control and crashed. John Ryan's daughter died, burned to death, and his niece is critical. Tom Hartley's daughter."

Mac's fingers tightened on the pen as the blood drained from his face. "Terry's dead?"

"Yeah, that's what it says here. Patrolman on the scene called it in. John's over at Phoenix General. Pretty tore up, I guess. You and John and Tom go back a long way. I thought you'd want to know."

"Okay, thanks." Alone, Mac sat back, loosened his tie and undid his top button. He took several long breaths, then leaned back and closed his eyes. This wasn't supposed to have happened. What had gone wrong?

When he'd stepped out of Sam's car a couple of blocks from the parking garage, Russo had promised to forget the girl, that she probably hadn't seen a thing and it would only arouse suspicions to go after her. Had Sam changed his mind and tracked Terry? Or was it a coincidence that Terry Ryan's car had gone out of control this same evening?

"You all right, Mac?" Earl asked from in front of his desk.

Mac straightened. "Yeah, just tired. What is it?"

"Talk about your nutsy night, listen to this. Black-and-white just called in. Officer found shot in the head in an alley on Washington near Mickey's Bar. Some drunk found him. No sign of a struggle and his gun still in his holster."

"What's his name?" Mac asked, trying to sound casual.

"Jerry Foster. Ten-year man. He was off duty. We've got a couple of uniforms down there questioning the bar regulars. Chances are, no one will talk, as usual."

Mac scrubbed a hand over his face. "You're right, Earl. It's turning into a bitch of a night. See what you can get on that for me."

"Will do."

Mac opened his desk drawer, took out a package of Rolaids, and popped two in his mouth. Damn, but he'd tried to warn Foster, tried to tell him he was playing with fire threatening to blow the whistle on Russo. The young idealistic punk hadn't listened to the voice of experience. And now he was dead. Mac sighed heavily.

Checking to make sure no one was nearby, he picked up the phone. It took three rings for the party to answer. Swiveling his chair around, he kept his voice low. "You promised you wouldn't go after the girl."

The voice was silky smooth and unrepentant. "Things changed, Sarge. Relax. It was rigged as an accident. Brake failure."

Jesus! They'd taken a hell of a chance being seen messing with her car. "I don't like it."

"You don't have to. Just do your job and I'll do mine." The phone landed on the cradle with a thud.

His mouth a thin line, Mac hung up. Things were getting out of control. Losing control always meant trouble. Rising, Mac grabbed his jacket from the back of his chair.

There was no question about it. He had to go to Phoenix General, though it was the last thing he wanted to do.

Detective Andy Russell glanced at his watch as he entered his Scottsdale apartment. Midnight. He and his partner had been on a stakeout for forty-some hours, watching the condo of the girlfriend of an escaped convict, hoping he'd show. He finally had and they had him in custody. But the long hours had Andy feeling stiff and sore, his eyes red and grainy.

Sliding home the dead bolt, he shrugged out of his jacket and shoulder holster, stretched until his shoulders popped, then walked into his kitchen. The blinking light on his telephone answering machine indicated two messages. He punched the Replay button, then reached into the refrigerator for the container of orange juice.

He drank deeply as he listened to his mother's voice, asking him to dinner on Sunday, wondering where he was, hoping he was all right. The poor woman would never get used to his hours or his job. The second message began and, recognizing Terry Ryan's voice, Andy moved closer.

She sounded upset, which wasn't like Terry. In the five years he'd known her, the only time he'd seen her rattled was when her father had had his heart attack. Quickly, he jotted down the phone number she gave him for the Sedona cabin where she was heading.

She'd be there by now if she left around eight as she'd said. Midnight wasn't too late to call if someone was having a problem. He hadn't seen or heard from Terry in probably three months. Odd that she should call him now. He dialed the number.

Eight rings later, Andy hung up. He finished his juice, then rummaged around in the drawer for his address book. He checked Terry's apartment phone number and called. The answering machine clicked on, and he swore. No point in leaving a message at this hour. He'd try to find Terry tomorrow.

He glanced out his kitchen window and saw that the rain had stopped and the sky was clear. Tomorrow should be a nice day. Yawning, Andy moved toward his bedroom, hoping for twelve hours of uninterrupted sleep.

Five days and her daughter was still in a coma. Julia Hartley sat alongside the hospital bed, her thin lips moving in prayer. *Dear Lord, please bring Lynn back to me.* She looked so small, so pale, whiter than the hospital sheets. Her beautiful hair all shaved off, her head bandaged. Her face was loosely bandaged, too, with just her bruised eyes and swollen lips visible. Julia wondered how bad the scarring would be. They'd told her about all the glass particles they'd had to remove and some that were in so deep they'd have to work their way out in time.

Julia didn't care, as long as Lynn lived. Plastic surgeons could work wonders, once she recovered. The machines behind the head of the bed flashed on and off, red, yellow, and green lights, the numbers changing. The automatic blood pressure cuff tightened at timed intervals, registering on still another monitor. Tubes were hooked up to needles inserted in both her arms, and a catheter trailed under the sheet, the bag hanging from the side of the bed. The oxygen cannula ran beneath her nose.

Modern medicine, Julia thought. So much she didn't

understand, yet she had to believe it all would work for Lynn. Shifting her attention, she carefully picked up one of Lynn's hands. It, too, was heavily bandaged, as was the other. Glass cuts and burns from the fire, they'd told her. They'd had to cut the silver ring from her finger, the one Julia had given Lynn years ago that she always wore. She touched the cold metal in her jacket pocket, as if the gesture might somehow bring her daughter back.

Gently, she smoothed the skin on Lynn's left arm, one of the few sections unbandaged and unhurt. Her hand felt a small ridge, and she leaned closer to examine it. An old scar, by the looks of the blemish. Odd, she couldn't recall Lynn having a scar on either arm.

No matter. She'd take her, scarred and marked. Any way she could. At least, there was a chance that her daughter would recover. For Emily and John, the hoping had ended that dreadful night. Even family at their side, the boys and Mac who'd rushed to the hospital to be with them, hadn't eased their pain. Their Terry was gone, to be buried tomorrow evening. Julia grieved for her niece, for all of them.

From her other pocket, she removed her rosary. Lowering her head, she began again to pray.

Emily entered her house through the back, her steps slow. Try as she would, she couldn't seem to rise above the grief that sat in her chest like a fifty-pound weight. Her sons, Michael and Sean, and their families had been over almost constantly, trying to comfort while dealing with their own pain. Still, nothing helped.

Emily wanted to crawl into the casket where her daughter's body lay burned beyond recognition, and be buried with her.

In the kitchen, she set down the bag of groceries on the counter. She had no interest in cooking, yet she knew they had to eat. Life went on, Father O'Malley from St. Timothy's had said only last night. He'd told her the same thing twelve years ago when their oldest daughter, Kathleen, had been killed at age seventeen driving home from a party after drinking illegally. It had taken her years to adjust to that, and she was older now. Emily wasn't certain she'd make it through Terry's death.

Swiping at a quick flash of tears, she walked into the living room, then stopped at the archway. John was sprawled in his lounge chair, the near-empty bottle of bourbon on the table beside him, the glass tipped on its side in his lap. Passed out again. Emily felt a rush of anger, then a wave of sympathy as more tears filled her eyes.

John had never been a drinker, not like this. Oh, he liked an occasional beer and his holiday bottle of Jamison's, as most Irishmen did. But since the night they'd been called to the hospital, then asked to identify Terry's body, he'd scarcely drawn a sober breath. Just what she needed while trying to cope with her own loss, a drunken husband. And him with a heart condition.

Terry had been her father's girl, more lately than before. John had taken Kathleen's death very hard, working longer hours to pay off the debt her accident had left them with, escaping from his memories that way. And, though he loved his sons, he'd drawn closer to Terry after losing his first daughter.

And now she was gone, too.

John was making her nervous though, Emily thought. His drunken ramblings didn't make sense. He mumbled about vague suspicions, blaming himself, wild discourses that went on and on until he fell asleep. Later, when she'd question him about what he'd meant, he said he couldn't remember what he'd said or why.

Who could blame him for drowning his sorrows? Emily thought as she turned to go back to the kitchen. She'd do it herself if she thought it would help. She'd put away the groceries and make some dinner, then wake him and get some food into him.

They had the rosary at seven tonight at the funeral home to get through.

Father Timothy O'Malley had the look of a man who should be wearing the brown robes of a monk, with his round face and balding head with its fringe of gray hair. But instead, he was the sixty-two-year-old pastor of St. Timothy's and a priest who was close to many of his two thousand parishioners. The Ryans and Hartleys were two of the families he'd seen through several weddings and far too many funerals.

Seated alongside Lynn Hartley's bed at Phoenix General, he checked the date on his watch and calculated that it was nearly two weeks since the accident. He'd conducted Terry's funeral last week and visited Lynn regularly, often with Julia. Today, he'd stopped in alone before going to the rectory for lunch, and he found himself marveling at how far the young woman had come.

Her head was still bandaged some, but at the hairline, some new growth of blond fuzz was beginning to show. Her face had patchy bandages, but was still quite swollen, with dark smudges around both eyes. She was wrapped heavily around the shoulders where they'd operated on her broken clavicle. Her hands were discolored and puffy, but healing. Yes, he could see progress, and the doctors he'd spoken with earlier sounded more hopeful.

Touching her arm, Father Tim began to pray over her, which was his habit just before leaving. As he finished the short prayer, he felt movement under his fingers. Suddenly, her eyes blinked, as if trying to focus in the bright light.

Hope rising in him, Father gripped her arm. "Thank God. Can you hear me? It's Father O'Malley."

Clearing her dry throat, she strained to see him. "Yes," she managed. Her hand moved to her face, finding bandages. Noticing the tubes, the condition of her fingers, she frowned. "What happened?"

"You were in a terrible automobile accident." He squeezed her arm gently. "Your mother will be overjoyed, Lynn. I should call her right away."

The blue eyes looked back at him, puzzled. "Father, I'm not Lynn. I'm Terry Ryan."

At the same moment, on the second floor of the Central Precinct of the Phoenix Police Department, Captain Ed Marino hung up, struggling with a juvenile urge to hurl the phone across the room. The mayor had chewed his ass but good.

Remember your blood pressure, his doctor was always warning him. If he were to check it right now, the reading would probably shoot off the chart. Deliberately, Marino took in a deep, calming breath, then walked to the glass door of his office and opened it. "Phil, come in here, will you?"

Sitting back down at his desk, Marino reached into his desk drawer and removed a cellophane-wrapped cigar. Longingly, he fingered it, then held it to his nose and inhaled. Damn doctors always limiting a man's pleasures. What did they know?

At sixty-four, he was ten months from retirement and looking forward to moving to Seattle to be near his son and his family. Things hadn't been the same since Beth had died two years ago. He'd lost his enthusiasm and most of his energy when he'd lost his wife. All he wanted now was to ride things out until next June, retire with pride and an impressive record that spanned thirty years.

But both daily Phoenix papers were demanding answers on the killing of one of their own, reporter Don Simon. And now, the mayor had yielded to pressure, asking what exactly his department was doing to find the murderer.

Marino tossed aside the cigar and watched Lieutenant Phil Remington come into his office, close the door, and settle his long frame in the chair across from him. The captain envied Phil his full head of sandy hair only slightly gray at the temples even though the man was in his forties. And he didn't carry an extra pound but rather was tan and fit, dressing like someone right off the pages of *GQ*. Leaning toward comfort rather than fashion in his own attire, Ed knew he could never again look like the urbane Remington, if he ever had. However, the man was vain to a fault and snobbish to boot. But Phil's saving grace was that he was always on top of things, which was why Marino relied on him more and more lately.

"How are you feeling, Captain?" Phil asked.

"My prostate's the size of Cleveland. How the hell do you think I'm feeling?" Annoyed with his own shitty mood, Marino shifted on the chair cushion, trying to find a more comfortable position. "Tell me what's happening on the Simon case. The mayor wants action, like yesterday."

Phil adjusted his pleated trousers as he crossed his long legs and began his recitation. They were interviewing everyone who parked regularly and even occasionally in the garage where the killing took place. They'd talked with the reporters who worked with Simon and were running down leads on the stories Don had been working on. They'd spoken with downtown snitches, checked out area vagrants in case anyone had spotted something suspicious, and hauled in a few known underworld characters for questioning. So far, they had nothing positive.

Calmly, Phil met Marino's eyes. "I wish I could tell you I expect something to break momentarily, but this one's got us puzzled. It smacks of a professional hit, but we can't pinpoint why Simon was set up."

"I see." Regretfully, Ed pocketed the cigar. "Just what would you tell the mayor if you were in my shoes?"

"The truth, Captain."

Ed checked his watch. He had a doctor's appointment in an hour. He'd have just enough time to grab some lunch if he left now. If he didn't leave soon, he'd probably explode. He stood. "Fine. I'd like you to handle this. Call the mayor and explain all that your men have done so far, and all that you're planning on doing." Some would call Marino's order a copout. He called it delegating responsibility.

Skirting the desk, he reached in his pocket for his keys. "Stay on top of this, Phil, and report to me as soon as you know *anything*. I'll check with you later." With that, he grabbed his jacket from the wooden coat rack and walked out.

Lieutenant Remington sat for a long moment staring after the captain as he wound his way through the bull pen desks. Marino had once been a very fine officer, concerned about his men, fresh and innovative. Slowly, Remington got to his feet. He'd never allow himself to get like that, he vowed. He'd quit the department long before he gave up and gave in to complacency, fear, and the weariness of age. He had too much pride to allow himself to become a laughingstock.

Leaving the captain's office, Remington walked to his own desk and dialed the mayor.

# CHAPTER THREE

Father O'Malley handed a tissue to Terry Ryan as the tears continued to stream from her eyes. He was still in shock, trying to adjust to the fact that they'd buried the wrong girl. He needed to tell the Ryans and Julia Hartley. But Terry was so broken up over the news of Lynn's tragic death that he couldn't leave her yet.

Terry's mind whirled round and round. Dead. How could her innocent, fun-loving cousin be dead? She wiped at her eyes with the tissue, then studied her bandaged hands. The story Father O'Malley had told her, of the accident and all that followed after, was as if it had happened to someone else.

She remembered driving, then switching places with Lynn. They'd been on their way to Sedona for the weekend because . . . because . . . "Oh, God!" she whispered, as the memory slammed into her.

Concerned, Father took her hand in his. "You're going to be all right, Terry."

It all came rushing back, walking into the parking garage with Don, the shots, the men in the gray car, trying to outmaneuver them, picking up Lynn. A horrible thought, an incredible fear, hovered at the back of her mind. "Why did my car go out of control like that? It was almost new."

"They don't know, dear," Father told her in his kind voice. "The police haven't told us anything."

She knew. Someone had to have tampered with the brakes or something. And, because of that, because of what she'd witnessed, Lynn was gone. It was her fault, all her fault. She should have told someone, should have gotten help instead of running like a scared rabbit. Choking back a sob, Terry clutched Father Tim's hand, ignoring her own bruised fingers. "I need to make a confession, Father."

"Certainly, dear." It wasn't unusual, a person who'd escaped death, needing to reaffirm her faith. "But shouldn't I call your family first? And the doctor, to let him know you're awake?"

"No, please. I need to confess, right now." She simply had to tell someone, and Father Tim was someone she could trust, bound by his vows not to repeat her story. As he bent his head to her, she closed her eyes and began.

Listening, Father Tim could hardly believe his ears. This poor child who'd nearly died had witnessed a murder and, as if that weren't enough, had seen an old family friend apparently involved in the killing. Father knew Sergeant McCarthy nearly as well as the Ryans, and thought him a fine man. Was Terry to be believed, or was she hallucinating? Still, he'd read in the papers about that reporter's terrible death happening the same evening that Terry had been in her accident. She wouldn't have known about it if she hadn't been there, since she'd just awakened.

Father Tim gave Terry absolution, then sat back. "I'm so sorry, my dear," he said, wishing he could remove the pain from the young woman's eyes. "Let me call your family now."

They'd been after her, Terry thought. She was sure of it. The men she'd seen at the garage, Mac and his friends, the ones who'd followed her in the gray car. She couldn't allow them near her family. She couldn't let them know where she was. Even though they thought she was Lynn, they might want to kill her, too, just in case she knew something. "Does . . . does everyone think I'm dead?" she asked Father Tim.

He hesitated, then decided there was no way to keep the truth from her. "Yes. We had your funeral last week." He leaned forward. "Terry, your parents will be so relieved that you're alive." He rose. "I'll just go call them."

She reached for his hand, caught his sleeve, and moaned at the slice of pain that shot up her arm at the sudden movement. "No! Please, Father. I just told you what I witnessed. Those men mean business. I can't jeopardize Mom and Dad."

"Come now, Terry, surely they wouldn't . . . "

"Yes, they would." It hurt to speak with her throat so sore, but it would hurt more to keep still. She had to think, to find a way. She knew someone who might be able to help. She had trusted Andy enough to try to call him that night. She had a strong feeling that he wouldn't let her down. "Father, there's a man I need you to call for me. He's a detective out of Mt. Shadows Precinct. Andy Russell. Please, look up his number and be sure no one can overhear you. Tell him where I am and to come to me right away. He's a good friend. He'll come. Try the station and his home both."

Father O'Malley looked skeptical. She'd been in a coma for many days. Was she rational? "Are you sure, Terry? Your father was an officer. Why don't we . . . "

"No, please, please. Do as I ask. And hurry. Talk to no one else, promise me." In her anxiety, her voice fell away into a sob.

He patted her arm in a gesture of comfort. "All right, I promise. I'll be right back. You rest." Reluctantly, he hurried off.

Terry sank deeper into the pillows, praying Father Tim would reach Andy and that her friend would come, that he'd be able to help her. She was too tired, too weak to plan her way out of this alone. She had to get somewhere safe. If word got out that she was alive, they would come after her again.

She felt the tears flow freely, unable to stop them. Sweet, gentle Lynn, a helpless victim. Don Simon shot down in cold blood. Her life in danger even in a hospital bed. Where would it all end? When would she ever feel safe again?

Closing her eyes, she prayed Father Tim would hurry.

Detective Andy Russell stood in the hospital elevator riding up, his mood impatient. He hadn't been terribly surprised to get a call relating to Terry Ryan. When he'd been unable to reach her the morning after that odd message she'd left, and then had learned of the accident, some sixth sense had warned him that something wasn't right.

Terry was a careful driver, someone he'd ridden with often and had never seen take chances or use excessive speed. Of course, she could have lost control somehow, gotten distracted by something. But then there'd been that mysterious message on his machine where she'd sounded frightened and anxious. Andy's suspicious nature had had him checking out the police report the following day. And he'd learned plenty.

And now he'd learned from a priest that Terry was alive and her cousin had been the one who'd died in that fiery crash. The elevator doors slid open and he stepped out, checking the signs with directional arrows before turning left and heading down the corridor. He passed the nurses' station, where two heads were bent over a chart, a third person was talking on the phone, and a fourth was writing on a wall blackboard. He moved along, finally spotting Room 410. The door was slightly ajar. Cautiously, he pushed it open.

A bald-headed priest looked up from the chair pulled close to the bed where a heavily bandaged woman lay with her eyes closed. "Yes?" he asked hesitantly.

"I'm Detective Andy Russell. Are you Father O'Malley?"

Father Tim relaxed, smiling as he rose. "Yes, indeed. Come in, please."

Terry opened her eyes and let out a shuddering breath. "Andy. Thank God you've come."

He moved to her side, frowning at the bandaged head, the gauze dressings on her swollen face, the wrapped hands. "Terry. I can't believe you're alive."

"I'm having trouble believing it myself. Father, would you please close the door?" A nurse had looked in earlier, but she'd feigned sleep, needing them to believe she hadn't awakened until she'd had a chance to talk with Andy. "Sit down," she said to him. "I've got quite a story to tell you." She spoke slowly, her voice low and raspy, sore from tubes that had been inserted earlier.

While Father Tim pulled over a second chair, Andy settled his six-four frame in the one the priest had vacated, a frown on his face. "Are you in any pain?"

"Not much." She glanced up at the tube carrying liquid into her arm. Fear overrode any pain she was feeling. She touched the largest bandage on her right cheek. "I'm worried about my face, but there's a couple of other things I'm more concerned about right now. Father Tim told you what happened, about the mixup and Lynn dying?"

Andy had met Lynn a couple of times, but hadn't known her well. "Incredible. Do you remember the crash at all?"

"All too clearly. We were going down a curving ramp onto I-17 when suddenly, the brakes wouldn't hold. We kept gaining speed and then the steering wheel wouldn't straighten. Lynn yelled that we were going to crash. We bounced against the sidewall and the car spun around, then zoomed backward. I felt the impact just before the fire broke out. My door flew open. Glass was flying everywhere and then there was an explosion and I felt myself being thrown out. After that, I don't remember anything." She sucked in a painful breath.

"You weren't behind the wheel?"

"No, Lynn was driving."

"The police report said you were driving, that Mrs. Hartley had seen the two of you leave her home and you were definitely behind the wheel."

"I had been when we left Aunt Julia's, but I had this really bad headache so we switched places." She had another headache today, far worse than that one. Terry made an effort to ignore it, knowing medication would only dull her mind and memory.

"And there was a ring, one Mrs. Hartley said Lynn always wore," Father put in.

Terry glanced toward him. "The silver one, yes. But Lynn had a rash so she'd given it to me and I'd slipped it on." She looked at both hands. "What happened to it?"

"I understand they had to cut it off your finger," Father said.

Terry drew in a shaky breath. "Lynn told me to put on my seat belt, but I didn't get around to it. I . . . if we hadn't changed places, Lynn wouldn't have died." The tears, so close to the surface, filled her eyes again. "It's all my fault. They meant for me to die, not Lynn."

"They? Who is this *they*?" Andy asked.

"I need to start from the beginning." Terry raised a hand to her throat, hoping she had the strength to tell it all again. She was so very tired. "Could I have some water first?"

Andy held the glass to her, guiding the bent straw to her mouth while she drank. "If you need to rest for a while . . . "

"No, I have to tell you, because I need your help." She took a deep breath and recounted everything she could recall from the minute she and Don Simon had left the *Phoenix Gazette* offices until she'd awakened here a short time ago, including an explanation of her anxious message left on his answering machine.

Andy brushed back his longish blond hair as he listened intently. "You're saying that Don's story was to be an exposé of high-ranking police officers who allegedly are on the take, being paid to look the other way regarding certain underworld characters working some sort of money-laundering scheme?"

"That's basically what he told me, yes," Terry answered.

"And he didn't tell you the name of the cop he was to meet that night?"

"No, only that he, too, was in on the scheme and hoping for immunity in exchange for his testimony."

Andy leaned forward, his mind racing. It all tied in with some things he'd heard. The rumor mill between precincts was semireliable. Terry, unfortunately, had been in the wrong place at the wrong time. "And you say your family knows Sergeant McCarthy quite well?"

"Very well. Father O'Malley knows Mac, too."

"He's one of my parishioners," Father Tim added. "I've seen him at the Ryans' at family gatherings." Not all that often in church, however, he thought.

In his eleven years on the force, Andy'd seen many an atheist who was honest and many a devout man as crooked as a hairpin turn. "What about the others? Did you recognize either of them?"

Wearily, Terry shook her head. "I'm sure I've never seen them before."

She was tired, he knew. He would have to handle this carefully, for Terry's safety, and so as not to tip off the wrong people. But first, he'd have to convince her of the seriousness of her situation. Leaning closer, Andy touched her hand. "Terry, I need to tell you something upsetting, and I'm not sure I should."

She gave a small, bitter laugh. "Look at me. How much more upset can I get? Just tell me."

"After getting that phone message from you and then hearing about the accident, I got suspicious. I went nosing around and finally got a copy of the police report of your accident. The conclusion was that the witnesses noticed excessive speed, so drinking is always suspected. Your blood level tested zero for alcohol content. Despite her burned condition, apparently they were able to check the driver and the report indicated alcohol was involved."

"Alcohol?" Terry was furious. "That's impossible. We hadn't been drinking. After the way my sister died, you know I'd never drink and drive, or get in a car with someone who had. Certainly Lynn hadn't had a drop, either. I'm telling you, Andy, something happened to my car. Suddenly, the brakes wouldn't hold and . . . "

He held up a hand. "I know. I know because I checked it out myself. At the time, I thought you'd been the driver and I know you're too responsible a person to get behind the wheel after drinking. I just told you what the report indicated."

"Then someone altered the police report."

"That's possible, but there's more. I went to the police garage and got to talking with the mechanic who'd checked over your Volkswagen. Sure enough, he'd found a hole in the brake line and another in the steering column. A small hole allows the fluid to leak out slowly, so the victim drives for a while, not suspecting a thing. Then, suddenly, there's a loss of control."

"But when could someone have tampered with my car?" She tried to think. "It had to be those few minutes I was in our apartment trying to call Lynn. But I didn't see anyone around."

"These guys are pros, Terry," Andy told her.

The truth, what she'd been suspecting, sank in and Terry's eyes grew wide with fear. "That means that someone . . . tried to kill me, right?"

"That would be my guess."

She closed her eyes for a long moment before questions came whirling to prod her. "Did the mechanic put all that in his report?"

"That's what he said, that he sent it over to Central. So I went over there and found that Sergeant McCarthy personally had initialed receiving the accident report. It took me awhile, but I got a copy. No mention of the mechanic's report, only that the accident was consistent with a drunk driver losing control of her vehicle."

"Two fudged reports." Terry was scarcely aware of her fingers gripping the sheet in frustration. "So my parents think I'd been drinking, lost control, and caused the crash?"

"Basically, that's what Mac told them, yes."

"This is so unfair. Can you get that mechanic to dispute the report and include his findings?"

Andy sat back thoughtfully. "I can try, but I don't know how much help that'll be. If what you say is true, that Sergeant McCarthy was in that parking garage alongside the man with the gun, he's got good reason to cover up the cause of your Volkswagen going out of control. But more importantly, I don't think we want the sergeant to suspect that you're alive. He's probably feeling safe again, thinking you're gone and Lynn's the one in the coma."

Rising, Andy paced the room, wondering which of several possible directions to go. Finally, he returned to her bedside. "Can you describe the other two men you saw?"

Terry frowned. "I'll try." She closed her eyes, concentrating. "One was quite tall and younger than the second one. They were both dark, not fair. The tall one had a mustache like Mac's, quite full, and he was wearing a suit. The shorter one had on a white shirt with suspenders and he had something in his mouth."

"A cigarette or cigar?"

"I don't think so. More like a toothpick." She shook her head. "I can't remember exactly."

"If I brought in some pictures, could you identify them?"

"I think so. Do you think you recognize them from what I've said?"

Andy sat down again. "I'm not sure, but if they're the

ones I suspect, they're involved in drug smuggling. From Colombia, through Mexico and across the border into Arizona, Texas, California. Big business. Lots of money to be made, and they need to sanitize it, to have some dummy companies or legit businesses they can filter the profits through. That's a lot easier to do if the cops look the other way, and the way you get them to do that is to grease their palms."

"You think that's what Mac is into?"

"Yeah, I do. And Don Simon was about to pull the plug on their cozy little operation, so they had to shut him up. Did you know that that same night, a cop was found killed in a downtown Phoenix alley? Two .38 bullets, just like with Simon."

Terry sucked in a breath. "Oh, God. He was probably the man Don said he was meeting. Andy, you've got to help me. You've got to tell someone you trust so they can send someone to guard my room or whatever. I . . . I'll never be able to go to sleep, even here, thinking that they could find out I'm alive and try again."

He touched her arm. "I'm going to do better than that. Money laundering across state lines is a federal crime, so the best thing to do is call in the feds. No one can protect you like they can." He got to his feet and turned to the priest. "Stay with her, Father, while I go make a couple of calls. But first, I have to talk with your doctor. I don't want *anyone* outside this room except your doctor to know you're awake or your true identity."

Terry's eyes held his. "Are you sure this will work?"

"Don't worry, please. I'll be just down the hall at the phones where I can see your door. I won't let anything happen to you, Terry. Just hang in there, okay?"

Wearily, she closed her eyes.

The man who entered her room, awakening her from a light doze, had light brown hair cropped so close to his head that he reminded Terry of a soldier in the first week of basic training at boot camp. He was around six feet tall, quite slim, and wore a brown suit with a buttoned vest, an incredibly white shirt, and a conservatively striped tie. Intelligence and a sort of resigned patience commingled in his brown eyes.

Protectively, Father O'Malley rose from the bedside chair.

Following the newcomer in, Andy closed the door and walked over to introduce everyone. "Father, Terry, this is Chief Deputy Bob Jones from the Phoenix office of the U.S. Marshals Office, Criminal Division, Department of Justice. Bob, Terry Ryan and Father Tim O'Malley."

Jones smiled at Terry, then shook hands with the priest. "Please, sit down, Father."

O'Malley checked his watch. "Almost midnight." He'd been at the hospital a full twelve hours. "Actually, if I can be assured that Terry's in good hands, I should run along."

"Father, I'm sure you've had a long day, from what Andy tells me, but I think it best that you stay while we go through this." Jones had dropped everything after talking with the young detective, made numerous phone calls before meeting with him, and been briefed further as they'd driven over. "Terry's situation must remain strictly confidential and you're a vital connection to her family. I'd like you to hear what we have to say."

"Well, of course, if I'm needed." Father Tim sat back down.

Jones pulled a chair over and again smiled at Terry. "How are you feeling?"

"Tired, hurting, frightened out of my mind. That about covers it." She couldn't believe that a government agent was here at this unlikely hour. The fact that he was indicated that the situation was possibly even more serious than she'd suspected.

"We'll let you rest in a short time, and I hope the things I'm going to tell you will take away most of your fears. As to the healing, that will take time. I've spoken with your doctor, as has Andy, and he updated us on your condition. He was in earlier to check you over, is that right?''

"Yes."

"He gave us your complete records." Jones indicated a briefcase Andy had set down against the wall. "All your X-rays, test results, charts, list of medications, everything."

Terry frowned, wondering if she'd missed something. "Why?"

"Because we're going to have to move you out of here."

She glanced at the needle still taped to her arm, the monitors blinking away. "Move me? Can I go like this?"

"Your doctor has given us permission to take you to another facility." Not without protesting mightily, but after Jones had shown his credentials and reassured Dr. Renfree just how they planned to handle the move, he'd reluctantly agreed. Renfree had also agreed to thoroughly examine Terry Ryan once again, then release her to Jones's custody. Even doctors caved in to federal authority.

"I don't know," Terry said, her voice sounding weak and skeptical.

Bob unbuttoned his jacket and leaned forward, keeping his voice low, though he'd positioned Detective Russell at the door in the unlikely event they were interrupted. "As you've undoubtedly figured out by now, you're in danger if you remain here, especially if your true identity is learned."

Terry's gaze slid to the door as if half-expecting the three men from the garage to come charging in, guns blazing. "Yes, and it worries me."

"From now on, let me do the worrying." Jones gave her a reassuring look. "Do you have the strength to recite what happened that night, exactly as you remember it?"

She didn't want to, but she knew she had to. Her eyelids felt so heavy, her limbs impossibly weighty. Again, she went through it all and when she was finished, Jones had just a couple of questions.

"I don't suppose you caught a glimpse of the license plates on the gray sedan?"

"It was always behind me and had no front plates."

"Would you look at a couple of pictures we've brought along?" When she nodded, he signaled Andy, who handed him a packet. One by one, he showed her the five-by-seven black-and-whites.

She took her time, squinting despite the bright light. Finally, she settled on one. "I'm pretty sure this is the tall one, although he stood to the side. The man in the suspenders who did the shooting isn't in this group."

Andy stepped closer. "The man you identified is Sam Russo, the Arizona front man for the mob. He's been arrested half a dozen times, but we've never been able to put him away. I believe he's on probation right now. He works with his brother, Nick, who's another slick operator."

Terry drifted a moment, then brought herself back by sheer force of will. "So what are you going to do? When will you move me?"

Bob took over. "Tonight, to a private hospital. Then, when you're well enough to be released from there, we'll need to get you to a safe place, Terry, so you can recover without fear." He didn't think that right now she could handle knowing that Dr. Renfree had said she'd need plastic surgery on her face soon so she wouldn't wind up with permanent scarring. "Meanwhile, we'll build our case and when the time comes, we'll need you to testify as to what you saw."

"A safe place. Where would that be? My father's a retired policeman, but I'm afraid to involve my family."

"And you should be. No one is to know where you are. Once we relocate you, you must stay out of sight until you testify."

"Out of sight. You mean, away from Phoenix? But my family's here, my friends, my job."

"I'm aware of that. Do you want to jeopardize them? You

witnessed a cold-blooded killing and then these same people tampered with your car in an effort to silence you. Do you think they would hesitate to harm others to keep from getting caught?"

Her hands were trembling and a frisson of fear raced up her spine. "No, I don't think they would."

"We're going to move you out of here tonight. Only one other person, a female agent who's also a nurse, and I will know where you are for now. Later, a senior agent will be assigned to you and will remain with you until the trial. He'll help you every step of the way, even help you build a new identity."

Surprise had Terry trying to sit up. "A new identity? But I don't want a new identity. I want to be me."

This was always the hardest part, Jones knew. "You will be, on the inside. But outside, we've got to change your appearance on the off chance that someone Sam Russo knows spots you. He has connections in several states."

"But they think I'm dead."

"Yes, they do, and we're going to do everything we can at this end to keep them convinced you are. But nothing works all the time and we don't take chances. We'll do our best to keep them in the dark as long as possible." He turned toward the priest. "That means, Father O'Malley, that we *must not* inform the Ryans or the rest of her family that Terry's alive and Lynn Hartley died. For their protection, they need to believe it was the other way around. Can we trust you, sir?"

He didn't like deceiving people. It wasn't his nature or his vocation. But he could see the necessity. Father O'Malley nodded. "Absolutely."

"Good." Bob turned back to Terry. "Most especially since Sergeant McCarthy's involved somehow, we need to let your family believe as they already do. You're our only hope at this time of putting these men behind bars, where they belong."

Terry's head was aching mightily by now. "How long will all this take?"

Jones raised a shoulder. "I wish I could tell you. A couple of weeks, a couple of months, maybe longer. Or it could go more quickly. Cases take time to build, evidence has to be collected, court time assigned."

Terry sank back. "What you're saying is that I have to put my whole life on hold for God-knows-how-long."

"Terry," Andy stepped in, "Chief Jones has already stuck his neck out for you. Everybody who goes into the Witness Security Program has to be authorized for placement by the Office of Enforcement Operations. He's not empowered to act until he receives notice that you're approved for inclusion in the program. He's rushing this along to keep you safe."

"What if they don't approve me?"

Jones touched her arm. "They will, Terry. After talking with Andy, I wasn't willing to risk your life by waiting. I know this will be difficult. It's a damn shame you stumbled into such a heinous crime. But think of all the good you'll do eventually by removing these scumbags from society. Think of the kids who might not become addicted to drugs because of your testimony."

He had her and he knew it. Besides, she was too weary to argue any longer. "All right, but . . . can't I at least talk to my father? To let him know I'm okay? He's got a heart condition and. . . . "

"I wish I could say yes, Terry," Bob told her. "We can't risk his life, or yours."

"But won't these men know something's up when I disappear from the hospital? I mean, I know they think I'm Lynn, but aren't they watching, waiting for the person in this bed to either recover or die?"

Jones wished she hadn't asked this particular question right now, but he had to tell her. "They will learn that Lynn Hartley died of internal injuries."

A horrified gasp escaped from Terry. "What about Aunt Julia? Will she be told the truth?"

"Terry," Andy interrupted, "her daughter's already dead. She just doesn't know it yet."

"Oh, God, this is brutal. It's all so damn unfair. Innocent people are going through hell because . . . "

"Because men like Sam Russo have no morals, no ethics, no compassion. Life isn't fair, Terry." Bob stood and looked down at her. "But you can put these particular men away where they won't be able to do this to anyone else ever again."

Her hand with only two fingers unbandaged moved up to press against her puffy lips. "All right, you've convinced me."

Andy leaned down to kiss her bruised cheek. "You're doing the right thing, Terry. I wish I could go with you."

"Me, too," she told him, her eyes damp again. She'd be with strangers, for months, with no contacts. Dear God, how was she going to manage? To whom could she turn?

"Andy, how is it you can't be involved?"

"Because once we call in federal agents, their authority supersedes the local police. Don't worry, Terry. You're in good hands."

"Chief Jones," Terry said as he picked up his briefcase, "who is the agent who'll be assigned to me?"

Bob narrowed his eyes thoughtfully. It would take some fast talking, but he knew exactly who he wanted on her case. "I can't say right now, but you'll know soon enough."

# CHAPTER FOUR

Luke Tanner paused with his hammer in midair, the nail only halfway in the fence board he was attaching to the post. His cabin was some distance from the road, the sounds of traffic usually muted by acres of tall pines, squatty evergreens, older cottonwoods, and pale green palo verdes. The noise from an approaching engine was rare enough to cause him to stop working, his eyes going to the winding dirt path, the only passageway to the main highway. Yuma had heard the car first and was already racing to meet the new arrival.

Luke wasn't expecting a delivery since whatever he purchased in town he hauled home in his truck himself. He wasn't expecting a friend or neighbor since he'd met none since arriving two months ago. The last vehicle that had wandered in a couple of weeks ago had been a Jeep full of tourists who'd gotten lost. Checking to make sure his .38 was tucked into the small of his back at his waist, he let his hands hang loosely at his sides as he walked toward the front porch he'd finished reinforcing last week.

He recognized the car the moment it came in sight, and the man who got out as soon as he'd parked the blue Buick behind Luke's white pickup. A standard government issue vehicle driven by Bob Jones, who removed his suitcoat and tossed it onto the seat before striding forward, Yuma sniffing at his heels.

"Seems as if you're having a hot spell, same as we are down in Phoenix." Bob rolled his shoulders after the two-hour drive, noting Luke's inscrutable expression. The man definitely wasn't glad to see him, but he was too disciplined to show it.

He didn't want to be unfriendly to his old friend, for Luke respected Jones as he respected very few. But he knew exactly why Bob had come. To get a rundown on how he was coming along, the unasked but implied question being how soon before he'd be returning, cutting short his leave of absence. It had happened before. The service was always shorthanded.

Luke wished he knew the answer himself.

"What brings you up my way?" Luke asked as they shook hands. Squinting at his commanding officer, he almost smiled. "As if I didn't know."

Bob ignored the comment and strolled toward the back. "You've done wonders with this place." He'd been up only once before, and then briefly, when Luke had purchased the ranch, surprising Bob. Luke had never indicated an interest in establishing roots. On the patio, he crouched to examine the flagstone inlays. "You have hidden talents."

"Glad you think so. How's the family?" Jones had a wife and two young sons.

"Fine."

Luke flipped open a folding chair, then went to the kitchen and brought back two long-necked bottles of beer. Without asking, he held one toward Jones before straddling the only other chair. Bending his head back, he drank thirstily, then eyed his boss. "All right, let's have it."

Jones took his time looking the younger man over. A bit on the scruffy side, but Senior Agent Tanner looked tan and lean and strong, the restless energy more contained, the fatigue absent from his gray eyes. Those eyes that had had many a subject squirming under their intensity.

Bob took a drink before answering. "Three months is a long time, Luke. I thought you might be itching to get back in harness by now." Actually he'd thought no such thing, but it was a start.

This time Luke did smile, his teeth very white against the leathery look of his face. "Sure you did." He drank again, then crossed his arms over the chairback and waited. "I asked for six months off, remember?"

"I remember." Luke wasn't a man to beat around the bush with, Bob knew. He hated dancing around a subject himself. He leaned forward, elbows on his knees, the beer bottle dangling in his hands. "There's this new case. A special one."

Right on cue, Luke thought, his mind already searching for feasible reasons to decline. "They're all special, Bob." A dedicated chief deputy, Jones had a strong affinity with the silent victims, as he called the people forced into the protection program. Most had few choices as their very lives were uprooted and forever changed over a chance sighting or fateful happening.

"This one really is. A young woman who witnessed a brutal shooting, almost getting killed herself in an arranged accident, her face scarred by flying glass, perhaps permanently." Bob shook his head. "Poor kid."

Luke glanced at the twilight sky above the redrock mountain in the near distance, a brilliant sunset just beginning. What the hell. He'd been about to quit for the day anyhow. He drained his beer and stood. "Why don't I throw a couple of steaks on the grill while you tell me about this poor, special kid."

Bob crossed his legs. "If you really want to hear."

Luke's lips twitched. "Oh, yeah. I'm dying to hear your story."

\*\*\*

The minute the sun dropped out of sight, the air turned much cooler. Luke served the steaks and a big salad at the kitchen table with a second beer, listening to Bob as he ate.

"Before we moved her out of the hospital last week, we brought in a steno and took down her statement, which she's signed."

"You think that's enough to arrest this Sergeant McCarthy?" Luke asked, mildly interested despite his desire to stay uninvolved.

"Along with what I've got in the car it is." It took Bob only a few minutes to get the manila envelope from his front seat, then sit back down across from Luke. "I asked Terry Ryan to look at some pictures to see if she could recognize either of the other two men she saw that night. She picked out one, but we didn't have a photo of the other man."

"Well, at least you've got two IDs."

"Oh, I've got all three. The detective I was telling you about, Andy Russell, reminded me that Terry's an artist with the *Phoenix Gazette*. Her hands had been cut, but they're healing pretty well. She did a sketch for us of the third man." Bob pulled the drawing from the envelope and handed it to Luke. "She's quite good. Artists apparently make note of more visual details than most of us. Look at these."

"I'll be damned. Ozzie Swain, complete with toothpick in his mouth and pockmarks on his face. Mob muscle. He works for the Russo brothers."

"That's right." Bob removed the photo of Sam Russo Terry had identified. "According to Terry, the man she sketched did the shooting while Sam and Mac stood by and watched. There was a fourth person who never got out of the car, but she only caught a glimpse of him from the knees down in the backseat."

Involuntarily, Luke's hand reached to touch a six-inch scar on his right side, a souvenir of his own encounter with Sam's brother, Nick, some years ago. Both Russos were vicious SOBs.

Jones noticed Luke's reaction and thought he knew what he was remembering. "Are you thinking that maybe the guy in the car was Nick Russo?"

"I doubt it. He's more of a participant than a spectator. If Nick had been there, he'd have been holding the gun."

"You're probably right."

"So this is how you figured on getting me back, knowing how badly I'd like to even the score with the Russos?"

Bob shrugged. "The thought crossed my mind."

Luke studied the man across from him as he sipped his beer. The chief wouldn't push; it wasn't his style. Yet Luke knew that they really needed his help on this one or Bob would never have come in person to ask. The other thing that Bob would never mention aloud was that Luke owed him. Out in the field when they'd both been fairly new agents, Bob Jones had taken a bullet meant for him. It wasn't the sort of thing a man like Luke Tanner ever forgot.

Luke cleared their plates, poured two coffees, then sat back down and gazed out the window at his spread. He felt an affection for the place that he'd put his mark on and a genuine reluctance to leave right now, when there was so much yet to do before the snow fell. But a man who hates to flinch when he looks into his shaving mirror knows there are some debts that have to be paid whether the timing is wrong or not.

Besides, when push came to shove, he was aching to put the Russos out of commission for good.

"Okay, I'll do it," he said quietly. "You got Washington's approval, I take it?"

"Not yet, but it'll be here any day. I had to get her out of that hospital. When Terry drew that sketch, Andy Russell looked at it and thought he'd passed a man who looked like Ozzie in the halls of Phoenix General a couple of times. You remember that Swain always wears bright-colored suspenders, and with that pockmarked face he's not hard to spot. Visiting hours are all day long. Security at most hospitals isn't what it should be. The place is like Grand Central most of the time. I wouldn't be surprised if Sam sent Ozzie to keep an eye on the girl until they determined her condition and identity for sure. With McCarthy getting the police reports, Russo knows that one girl was burned beyond recognition. In their line of work, it pays to eliminate all loose ends."

"So where'd you take her?"

"To that private hospital outside San Diego that we've used before. She underwent plastic surgery on her face yesterday. Temporarily, I've got George Everly with her and Sara Baines. Remember them?"

"Yeah, sure." Luke had worked with Sara before. She'd been an RN for ten years before going into law enforcement. She was good, a big motherly woman who knew how to follow orders even if she didn't like them. George was another story. The man was methodical enough to drive you crazy, someone he could never partner with. Privately Luke thought that Everly should have taken voluntary retirement some time ago, or requested a desk job. They really had to be shorthanded for Bob to pull George out and put him on a case.

Luke finished his coffee. "Looks like you're bending a few rules on this one, old buddy, rushing her through before the paperwork's in."

"Sometimes, you have to. I want this under way ASAP. Terry Ryan is a brave young woman who had a good life going for her, until she witnessed that shooting. She's lost a reporter friend, a cousin who burned to death in the crash, and survived an attempt on her life. And now she's been taken away from everyone she knows. That can't be easy."

No, it never was. "How's she handling it?"

"She's not happy, but she's cooperating so far. She doesn't know it, but the worst is yet to come." When the healing was over, loneliness and frustration would set in. Jones glanced at his watch and stood. Eight, and it was a long drive back to Phoenix.

"Looks like you've got a case. When are you planning to issue arrest warrants?"

"Tomorrow. I had to delay until Terry was safe. This morning, I had Phoenix General release a statement that the second occupant in the Volkswagen has died of internal injuries. The longer we can keep the suspicions that Terry's still alive to a minimum, the better off we'll be."

"What about the family? Didn't they want to see the body?"

Jones sighed heavily. "I told them that we had to move the body to do a police autopsy, that they'd get to view her later. They didn't buy it, especially John Ryan, Terry's father. He's a retired cop and he's sure something's rotten in Denmark. Trouble is, he can't prove it, though he's driving everyone crazy with calls and visits demanding answers." Jones shook his head sympathetically. "I can't blame the man."

"You located Russo?"

Bob allowed himself a small smile as he walked toward his car with Luke. "Sam's on probation. He's violated the terms so it's automatic jail, no matter what his expensive attorney pleads. And the new charge is accessory to murder."

"Which is also what McCarthy faces." Luke watched Bob climb behind the wheel, then braced a hand on the closed door. "Let's hope you draw someone like Carmichael." Judge Henry Carmichael was known to be tougher on cops gone bad than anyone sitting on the bench.

"That would be nice." Bob held out his hand. "I appreciate your cutting things short here." His statement left volumes unspoken.

Luke shook hands. "Only for you would I do this."

"I know that." He handed Luke a second manila envelope. "All the particulars are in there—pictures, addresses, bio on Terry Ryan and her family. When can I tell George you'll be relieving him?"

"Give me three days, maybe four. Will she be out of the hospital by then?"

"Most likely. George has a secured place set up in San Diego. Info is in there. I'll activate your checking account."

Luke was thoughtful. George had found a secure place. He wasn't sure he trusted the man. Maybe he'd step up his timetable.

Jones started the engine, slipped into gear. "Oh, and Luke, get a shave and haircut."

Luke waved a dismissive hand. "Yeah, yeah."

It was easy to read the shock followed by cold fury in Sergeant McCarthy's gray eyes as he looked up from reading the warrant for his arrest that had been handed him. "Phil, what the hell is this?"

Seated at Captain Marino's desk, Phil couldn't quite meet Mac's eyes. "Accessory to murder, like it says."

"Whose murder?" Mac demanded.

Remington didn't want to do this, not to an officer in Central where they'd served together for over twenty years. They were more than coworkers; they were friends. He wished Marino hadn't chosen this week to have his damn prostate out, putting Phil in charge as second-in-command. "There was a witness to the shooting of reporter Don Simon. We have a sworn statement that you were present. The county attorney feels he's got a case."

"A witness!" Mac's eyes narrowed. "Who's this witness?"

Phil knew by the silence outside the open door of the glassed-in office that all the cops were listening, most looking stunned. "You know I can't discuss the case further. I advise you to call your attorney, Mac. Your first appearance before the judge is tomorrow morning at eight-thirty."

Mac turned to see two officers step in, moving to his side,

waiting to escort him out. One held a pair of handcuffs. He swung back to the lieutenant. "Do something, Phil. We're friends, for God's sake." He stroked his mustache nervously, hating the tremor in his voice.

Remington dropped his gaze. "I can't, Mac." He picked up the Miranda and read the sergeant his rights.

Humiliation had Mac curling his fists. "More heads are going to roll before this is over. Mark my words. I'm not going down alone."

That was exactly what Phil was afraid of. Why couldn't Mac see that his hands were tied on this? Silently, he nodded to one of the blues who quickly threw on the cuffs and led Mac away. Rules were rules, and if he didn't follow them, if he made exceptions for a friend, word would get back to the captain eventually. And he'd lose the respect of his fellow officers. Leaning back in his chair, Phil scrubbed a trembling hand over his face. He was a man not easily ruffled, but today's events had shaken him.

He was still stunned over an incident earlier. Out of the blue, a deputy from the U.S. Marshals Office had arrived with three warrants in the murder of the *Phoenix Gazette* reporter. The ones for Sam Russo, a man with known mob connections, and his henchman, Ozzie Swain, had been no surprise. The shocker had been the order to arrest Mac.

The feds were closemouthed as usual, but already rumors were running rampant. No one as yet really knew who this mystery witness was. Phil had his own suspicions, and they had him tense. It was hard to remain untainted when one cop in a precinct was arrested. Usually it was only the tip of the iceberg.

And he had other problems.

The young detective from Mt. Shadows Precinct on the east side, Andy Russell, had everyone up in arms over the Ryan girl's Volkswagen, dragging in the mechanic who was ready to swear there'd been tampering, accusing someone in Central of changing his report. The receipt had been initialed by Mac. Phoenix General Hospital had released a statement that the Hartley girl had died of internal injuries. Phil had thought that was the end of that. Terry's father, John Ryan, did not.

John was like a thorn in Phil's side, giving voice to countless ungrounded suspicions, replaying possible scenarios, throwing out veiled barbs. Repeatedly, he'd come to the station insisting on an investigation, demanding answers.

Phil didn't have any.

He leaned forward, bracing his elbows on the desk. He hated to see Mac led off in cuffs, but there was nothing he could do about it. All he wanted at this point was to keep up with the work in the captain's absence, to keep a low profile. The things that were wrong with the department, such as what Mac allegedly was involved in, had happened before he took over for Marino. He wouldn't get the blame. If anyone would, it'd be the captain. The buck always stopped at the top.

When Marino retired next year and promotions would be considered, Phil's record would still be clean. Of course, he'd have to be careful, not make enemies, not step on any toes. Maybe he'd be wise to have a chat with Mac after his hearing, calm him down, tell him to stay cool.

After all, it wasn't over until it was over.

Sara Baines had often been labeled a tough, efficient, no-nonsense woman, in both her career as an RN and in law enforcement. She knew she could not help her patient subjects by being overly sympathetic. Her work called for her to be an odd mixture of detached and caring.

Yet, owing to a strong nurturing streak, her heart went out to the young woman in the bed struggling to recover from a great many recent traumas. Her facial surgery done several days ago was healing well, probably because Terry Ryan was young and had been healthy before her accident. She was sleeping now, the medication Sara had given her after changing her bandages allowing her to rest.

Sara checked her patient's pulse, then quietly left the room. She found George Everly playing solitaire at the kitchen table, his jacket hanging on the chairback, his gun holster strapped on in plain view. Sara walked to the counter and poured herself a cup of coffee from the pot. "Want some?" she asked him.

"No, thanks. I can't handle too much of that stuff."

George looked every day of his fifty years, Sara thought, mostly because he'd inherited a tendency toward baldness and a short stature that made him look beefy rather than solid. He'd been trained years ago and had been quite the boy wonder in his youth, or so she'd heard. Sara found him dull and uninteresting, but no one had promised her excitement on the job.

"She asleep?" George asked.

"Yes. It's the best thing for her, of course. But, you know, even asleep and medicated, she moans and she thrashes, like she's reliving the terrible things that have happened to her."

George placed a black jack on a red queen, freeing a space. "Probably is, poor kid. I've got a daughter about her age. What'd the doc say about her face?" The doctor from the private hospital had stopped by daily per Jones's instructions to check on the patient under federal guard. George hadn't been in the bedroom during his visits.

Sara sipped her coffee. "He said she'd probably need more surgery later. Her kind of injury has to be repaired in stages. In the long run, provided she doesn't develop an infection, she'll do okay." She'd watched the doctor change the bandages, seen the swelling and the redness, and knew it would be some time before all that disappeared. "I wouldn't want to hand her a mirror when she's awake just yet though. Or tell her she'll face the knife again." The present condition of Terry's hair alone, growing back in blond tufts from when her head had been shaved, would surely make her cry, the nurse thought, to say nothing of the condition of her face.

Sitting down at the table, Sara saw George contemplate the cards spread before him. He appeared to be stuck. She waited several seconds, then could stand it no longer. "The six of hearts at the end. Move it to the seven of clubs."

George made a face. "Oh, yeah."

She glanced at the wall clock. "What time did Luke say he'd be here?"

George looked at her from beneath shaggy brows. "Couple of days, Jones said. But you know Luke. He's not one to give anyone his schedule." He went back to his game. "Don't worry. He'll be here when he's good and ready."

Sara had to agree. Luke Tanner definitely marched to his own drummer. She'd worked with him on several cases. The man was unflappable, with nerves of steel and a hard face that revealed nothing. Perfect for his line of work.

A bit difficult to live with, though. And live with him in somewhat close quarters as they watched over Terry Ryan was what she'd have to do, for a while yet anyhow. Sara and Luke Tanner were both the same age and at five-ten, Sara was only a couple of inches shorter than Luke. But there their similarities ended. Beneath her professional demeanor, Sara had a soft heart. She doubted if Tanner even had a heart.

George folded his game. "Want to play double? I've got another deck of cards."

"No, thanks." Boredom was the worst part of this job. "I think I'll make a pot roast. Maybe I can convince Terry to eat some when she wakes up." Sara glanced out at the bright San Diego afternoon before finishing her coffee and rising to check the contents of the refrigerator.

At that moment at Arizona State Prison in Florence, Sam Russo walked into the visitor's room, sat down in the second cubicle, and picked up the phone. On the other side of the thick glass, his brother, Nick, already had the phone to his

ear. "About time you got here," Sam said, his deep voice
low.

"I've been busy, checking out stuff, like you said." Nick
leaned forward, noticing that his hands were sweaty on the
receiver. Damn but even visiting prison made him nervous.
Just turned forty, he was movie-star handsome, with curly
black hair and a muscular build he owed to gym workouts
and daily runs. His clothes cost plenty but leaned toward the
flashy, a fact that didn't seem to keep women from throwing
themselves at him. Nick had never married, valuing his freedom too much. The one person he owed his complete alle-
giance to was his older brother, Sam.

"What'd you find out?" Sam asked, impatience making
his words clipped.

"Hospital says the girl's dead and . . . "

"Bullshit! Who else could be their *special witness*? Did
you see the body?"

"No. Ozzie was working on it with his connections at the
hospital, but he had to get out of town and lay low for now.
He's not going to do us any good if he's in here with you."
Nick could see the sweat on Sam's face, and it scared him.
He'd always admired Sam's cool attitude under pressure.
He'd never seen his brother sweat. But then, he'd never seen
his brother in prison before, either. His hands shook. He
wished he had a cigarette.

"I say she's alive. She's got to be the one. Someone
knows something, and I want you to find that someone."

Nick swallowed hard, sending a glance toward the guard
standing by the door at Sam's back. "The cops are watching
me, you know."

"You know how to get around them. I taught you myself.
Now get going. Check out the girl's family, her friends, people she worked with, old boyfriends. Find out if there really
is a body. You follow me?"

"Yeah."

Sam Russo's philosophy was simple: every man had his

price. "You got money. Pay for information. Find that someone. You got to find the girl, dead or alive. Without her, they got nothing."

Looking into Sam's fiery eyes, Nick nodded. "I will." He had to find her and spring Sam. His brother wasn't handling prison well. Sam had practically raised Nick after their parents had died. He owed Sam, big-time. "You can count on me."

"I am, little brother." Sam dropped his voice even further. "And if you find her alive, you know what to do, right?"

For the first time, Nick smiled. "Yeah, I know what to do."

It was a lovely day in San Diego, even though it was late afternoon and the end of October. Terry sat curled in a corner of the couch leaning her crossed arms on the back, looking out the third story window. It was the kind of day she'd like to have gone wandering down by the waterfront, to feed the gulls, do a little shopping, then stop at Anthony's for lunch. Like she and Lynn used to do when they'd drive to California for weekends.

Terry swallowed around a huge lump in her throat and blinked back a fresh rush of tears. Her grief was like a prickly blanket she couldn't shed. When would her emotions settle down? When would she be able to live with her losses?

She raised a hand to brush over her nubby hair. Her first day up since the facial surgery and she'd looked in the bathroom mirror. That had been a mistake. She looked like a damn scarecrow with frizz on her head and her face bandaged. The pain was still there, but she'd refused Sara's offer of medication after dinner. She was sick and tired of being fuzzy-minded. It was better to be hurting some than be out of it all the time.

Terry glanced through the archway into the kitchen and saw that Sara was baking a pumpkin pie, which Terry had mentioned was her favorite. Sara was awfully nice and even

George, sitting at the table playing his endless hands of solitaire, was kind to her. But she missed her family and her friends. She missed her life.

Turning back toward the window, she noticed a gauzy black witch figure hanging from one of the balconies across the way. Hard to believe it was almost Halloween, four weeks since the accident. She had no idea exactly where their motel was located, just that it was "somewhere in San Diego." Federal agents liked to keep everyone in the dark. After trying to get information from them, Terry decided all of them, from Bob Jones to Sara and George, were obsessed with secrecy.

Just then, she felt more than heard something behind her and swung toward the door. She became peripherally aware of George suddenly in the archway, gun in hand, Sara right behind him. The man who stood in the doorway was tall and tan, wearing a navy three-piece suit, his hair clipped short. Terry blinked at Bob Jones, wondering why he'd entered so stealthily.

But no! Her frantic mind registered subtle differences. The man could have been a clone, but he was younger, leaner, harder. She saw no weapon in his hand, but nonetheless, she sank back into the couch, drawing her legs up close as a silent scream built in her throat.

"For Christ's sake, Luke," George said, returning his gun to his shoulder holster. "Did you have to scare us like that?"

Luke Tanner's cool gray eyes took in the room, the girl with the bandaged face and the two agents by the kitchen. Slowly, he raised his hand and held up a small pick. "I got in with just this. No dead bolt. The chain wasn't even on. I thought this place was supposed to be secure."

George's face turned red. "It's broad daylight and we're both here."

Luke nodded toward the couch where Terry sat, trying to calm her breathing. "And if I'd been the wrong person, she'd be gone by now." He set down the case he'd been carrying. He'd inspected the grounds before entering, checking everything out thoroughly. He couldn't believe George Everly thought the place safe. "Get her packed up. This place is too accessible. Outdoor walkways all around, too easily scaled walls and cheap windows, to say nothing of flimsy locks." He didn't add that an agent who was more than a little careless hadn't helped the situation, but he thought George got the picture.

"I'm not sure Terry should be moved," Sara interjected, coming forward. "Her doctor comes over daily."

"I'll talk to him," Luke said brusquely, settling the matter. "We leave in thirty minutes. Get her ready." He turned to the door.

Annoyed, Sara's mouth was a thin line. "Wouldn't you like to at least be introduced?" she asked him, barely suppressing a trace of sarcasm.

Luke's eyes were calm and as cool as the ocean on a winter day. "What I'd like is everyone's cooperation. Sorry we can't take the time for social amenities just now. George, step outside with me, please. Sara, I'll be back as soon as I make a couple of calls."

Awkwardly, George indicated the wall phone in the kitchen. "You can call from here."

Luke glanced at the older man. "You're absolutely certain that line is secure?" When George dropped his gaze instead of answering, Luke turned the knob. "I'll be back in twenty-nine minutes." He waited while George preceded him outside, then closed the door firmly.

Terry unclenched her hands and released a shaky breath. "Who in hell was that?" she asked.

Sara made a disgruntled sound. She respected Luke Tanner, but she didn't always approve of his methods. However, if ever she had to go into the witness protection program, he'd be the one she'd want in charge of keeping her safe. "That, honey, is the new federal agent assigned to safeguard you."

*Lord help us all*, she finished silently.

# CHAPTER FIVE

She was sweating, anxious, frightened. Her heart was pounding and she could taste her own fear. She smelled gas fumes, felt a searing heat. The sound of metal ripping, crashing, burning invaded her ears, followed by a piercing scream. Was it her own? Then she was being wrenched forward, tossed in the air, landing hard. Sirens were screaming and she was wrapped in a blanket of red-hot pain.

With a start, Terry awoke, jerking upright, trying to escape the images behind her closed eyelids. The seat belt she was wearing stopped her progress, yanking her back, causing her to bump her head on the window. "Shit!" she muttered, gingerly touching the spot. That was all she needed, another bruise.

Still disoriented, she blinked, looking around, absorbing the eerie sensations of darkness and movement. Memory drifted back slowly. She was on the back couch seat of the gray van with tinted windows that was hurtling through the night toward what Senior Deputy Luke Tanner considered to be a safe house. A fortress complete with barred windows, barbed wire fencing, and two snarling dogs in all probability, she thought crossly.

Over her protests, Sara had given Terry her pain medication before they'd set out just as the sun dipped behind the shoreline. She'd struggled to stay awake, but the pill had tugged her under and she still felt groggy.

She saw that Luke was in the single seat behind the wheel, driving the way she'd imagined he would, with steely control. On the bench seat in front of her, Sara was asleep, snoring softly. Terry thought that she was certainly entitled, for in the week or so they'd been together, she'd scarcely seen the woman close her eyes.

Bending to retrieve the bottled water she'd tucked under the seat, Terry moved too swiftly and felt a sharp pain race along her shoulder. A groan she couldn't prevent escaped from her.

"Are you all right?" Luke's deep voice asked.

Terry glanced up at the rearview mirror and met his steady gaze. In the dim dash light, she saw that his eyes were the color of the old pewter candlesticks her mother had on the mantel. The look lasted mere seconds, but she felt the impact throughout her system.

"I'm terrific," she answered. "On top of the world." It was the longest exchange they'd had since meeting, including his terse commands when they'd been leaving.

For several minutes Luke had been glancing into the mirror, watching her struggling with her restrictions and discomfort. She had to be hurting, scared, probably missing her family. He'd half expected tears, but she'd surprised him.

Terry Ryan was feistier than he'd originally suspected. He'd been impressed that she hadn't screamed when he'd easily broken into the motel room. He'd been surprised just now when she'd sworn after bumping her head. Studying Bob's file notes earlier, he'd had her classified as a Catholic school–educated Girl Scout who likely wouldn't say it if she had a mouthful of it. Maybe he was wrong.

The thing was Luke hadn't had much experience protecting young women. He'd had several criminal types in the program, being tucked away so they could testify against the kingpin in return for immunity. Unsavory characters he hadn't trusted. He'd had whole families he'd had to relocate, to set up with new identities since the father in the family was vulnerable because of what he knew. But only once before had he been assigned to watch over a single young woman, and that had turned out badly.

"Why don't you move up here?" Luke suggested, indicating the single seat to his right. He could gain her cooperation more readily if he got to know her.

Terry wasn't sure she wanted to sit up front, close to the windshield, where she'd probably relive the accident. Yet she didn't want to annoy her protector by refusing, either. Somewhat awkwardly, she made her way to the seat and quickly buckled herself in, noticing that Sara slept on.

She could see more clearly out the windshield than through the more heavily darkened side windows. They were on a four-lane divided highway which, she gathered from the occasional road signs, was heading north along the coast of California. There probably was no point in asking Luke exactly where they were going since she doubted he'd tell her. Fog had rolled in from a churning sea and a chilling gray rain had begun to fall. The weather added to the gloomy atmosphere inside the van.

Though he'd invited her up front, it apparently hadn't been for a chat, Terry thought as she surreptitiously studied Luke's profile. Grim was the best word she could come up with to describe his closed expression, his hooded eyes. Not a man one would want to run up against in a dark alley. Or one a person might choose to spend weeks with under what amounted to house arrest.

He'd changed from his business attire into jeans and a denim shirt, the sleeves rolled up. He had a leather jacket draped on the seatback and he wore black sneakers. The better to creep around undetected, she imagined.

Terry decided she preferred dull, boring George.

"You fired him, didn't you?" she asked, still looking at Luke. She needed to talk, if only to occupy her mind.

His eyes on the road, Luke frowned. "Who?"

"George."

"I don't have the authority to hire or fire. That's Deputy Chief Jones's job."

"But you told Jones that George wasn't exactly doing a great job, right?"

Luke let out a long breath. "A federal agent's responsibility in the program you're in is to keep you safe from all danger, to remove all potentially harmful obstacles humanly possible. I think George fell considerably short on that." He sent her a quick, assessing glance. "I take it you prefer to remain alive?"

He had her there. "Yes." But her sympathetic nature still nudged her. "He's a nice man."

"Nice isn't what this is all about. Nice won't cut it if the men who are after you find you." He let that sink in. She had to be made to realize the seriousness of her situation. What she was going to go through before all this was over wasn't going to be a day at the beach.

Terry sighed. "I don't suppose you smoke?" She hadn't smelled cigarettes in the van.

"Not anymore. Do you?"

"I did, before all this." It'd been awhile now, and the doctor had advised her not to start again. But the craving would hit her at the oddest times. "Right now, I'd kill for a cigarette. But I guess it would be stupid to go back to it."

"I can get you a pack next time we stop. With all the changes you've had to undergo, maybe this isn't the best time to quit."

That was the first spurt of human understanding he'd shown. "How long ago did you quit?"

"Six years, five months and . . . eleven days."

"Odd how every ex-smoker seems to remember that time frame almost to the minute." He still wasn't smiling, but with a shared weakness in common, he seemed less formidable somehow. "So now you have no bad habits, I'll bet."

He sent her another quick glance, his hard mouth softening. "Absolutely none."

She checked him out again more thoroughly, noticing his workingman's hands, scarred and callused, and wondered why a federal agent wouldn't have smooth, soft skin. "What about your hands? You bite your nails, don't you?"

"No. I sort of tear them off. Same thing. You caught me."

His admission relaxed her another fraction. "I'm surprised you don't have a car phone in here," she commented, studying the dash. He had every other gadget known to man—a compass, a CB, a fuzzbuster.

"Car phones use the airwaves. Others on the same frequency can listen in. Ham operators can monitor the calls. Too risky."

Terry was sure he was right. She drew in a deep breath, catching the still-unfamiliar scent of the sea drifting in through the window Luke had cracked a bit. The faint moan of a boat's foghorn sounded far away. The wind beat against the palms along the left and the rumble of the tide rolling in could be heard vying for attention with the distant thunder. She shivered and pulled her knees up, hugging them.

"Are you cold?" he asked.

"No, I'm just not fond of being out in storms."

"It's only a little rain."

She watched the windshield wipers slap back and forth, letting their monotonous rhythm all but hypnotize her. But her mind wouldn't be still, the memories attacking her awake or sleeping. A loud clap of thunder seemingly just overhead had her jumpy. "When I was a little girl, my father used to tell me that angels in heaven were bowling when it thundered."

"One just got a strike." He'd read John Ryan's profile in the folder Jones had given him. The retired cop hadn't struck him as a whimsical father, yet the report had indicated that

John Ryan was very close to his daughter. In the shadowy light, he noticed that Terry's skin was nearly as pale as her white bandages. "You miss him a lot, I guess."

Terry swallowed. "Yeah, a lot." Keep talking, she told herself. It's so much better than thinking. "He makes me put a quarter into a Mason jar every time I swear," she confessed, almost able to smile.

"Then you already owe one. I heard you back there."

"If you could read my mind, you'd know I owe far more."

Luke slowed as the highway trailed through a small town, one of many along the coastal road. "You've had a rough month." Pretty dumb, stating the obvious, but it was as close as he could come in trying to let her know he understood.

Odd how kindness made her want to cry. Terry touched the scarf she'd taken to wearing over her patchy hair. "This probably sounds stupid, but even my hair hurts."

"A little nerve damage probably. It'll go away." His quick glance took in her appearance. New white tennis shoes, navy sweatshirt and pants, checkered scarf twisted about her head. She'd had no clothes so Sara must have picked out her outfit at a local San Diego store. He had a feeling Terry would have chosen differently. According to her file, it was the cousin who'd died who'd been the conservative one. "Why don't you take off that scarf? It can't be real comfortable."

"Because I look like a scarecrow trying out for Halloween."

"No one's staring. Besides, I'm sure I've seen worse."

"That's really a comfort." She might have if George had been the driver, but something about Luke Tanner had her feeling doubly self-conscious.

She shifted her gaze out the window. They were going through a small town with low buildings, a church steeple illuminated on a hillside, the influence of Spanish architecture evident everywhere, not unlike some Phoenix neighborhoods.

The dashboard clock read ten after nine as she listened to her stomach growl. They'd missed dinner.

Luke heard the sound and realized he ought to stop for food. It'd be too late to find anything open by the time they reached their destination. Up ahead, he spotted a sign advertising the golden arches coming up in five miles. "I'll pull up to the drive-in window and order takeout. What would you like?"

"I'm not hungry," Terry said, despite her noisy stomach. The problem was that every time she ate, she developed pains shortly after. Chewing made her cheeks ache where delicate stitches had been taken. "Maybe just a milkshake."

If he were alone, he'd have driven through. Long ago, Luke had disciplined himself to hold off on food in order to get to safety first. He didn't honestly think anyone had discovered where Terry Ryan was; nor were they being followed. Still, he had to consider the two women in the car, one young and frightened, the other just waking from a nap. If he wanted their voluntary cooperation, that is.

"You have to eat in order to get well."

The simple, soft-spoken statement was nearly her undoing. She knew he was right, but she was so damn tired—of hurting both physically and inside on a much deeper level. And she was afraid—of more pain, of dying as horribly as Lynn had, of going to sleep because she was sure to relive the nightmare. How could she explain all that to a cop whose main job was to keep her alive, not chase away her fears?

"All right, you order for me and I'll eat it."

This concern for someone's health and well-being was new to him. "Listen, I know what you're going through. I . . . "

"No!" Terry gritted her teeth, feeling altogether fed up and frustrated. "I wish everyone would stop saying that. You *don't* know how I feel, not any of you. I don't have a speck of ID, no driver's license, no money of my own. My purse is gone, all my . . . my pictures of my family. My best friend is dead and no one I love even knows where I am. Someone tried to kill me and may still succeed. I have peach fuzz for hair and God-only-knows what my face will look like after these bandages come off. How can you possibly know what I'm going through?"

Luke listened, knowing she had every right to feel as she did. To have a close brush with death was a reminder that the next time we might not be so lucky, something the young rarely gave much thought to under normal circumstances. He'd had plenty of close calls and each had made changes in him. He wondered if he could make her see.

"I know because I've been where you are. I tangled with one of the men involved. I appreciate your fear and I respect your feelings. You've got to trust me. I'll keep you safe from him and the others, but you've got to put your whole trust in me, to do *what* I ask *when* I ask." He shifted into the right lane, then turned into the parking lot, heading for the lane that led to takeout. He glanced over to see her watching him intently. "Do you think you can manage that, Terry?"

It was the first time he'd used her name, giving a more personal slant to their relationship. God knew she wanted to trust him, wanted desperately to turn her worries over to someone else. Maybe he was the one who could end the nightmare and return her to her world. "I'll try," she said softly. "I'm sorry I lashed out. It's just that my life is out of my control and I hate that. I dislike being beholden to strangers for even the toothpaste I use. I've been on my own for years and I loathe this dependency."

"I'm not good at relinquishing control, either. I'll do everything I can to get your life back for you as quickly as I can."

Terry sat staring out the window, wishing her emotions weren't so raw.

Luke pulled the van up to the ordering menu, then swung

around toward Sara. "Dinnertime. What'll you have, ladies?"

In the city of Phoenix, Officer Neil Manning was on night patrol, his squad car assigned to the downtown district frequented by prostitutes and drug dealers. Since his partner, Jerry Foster, had been found dead in an alley several weeks ago, Neil was traveling with a rookie named Pete Hansen, fresh from eight weeks of training after the Academy. The kid was twenty-six and nice enough. But he talked incessantly about his wife and newborn son, things a single guy like Neil couldn't get into.

He missed Jerry.

"Take a left onto Roosevelt and let's swing along there, see if there's any action," he told Pete.

"Sure thing." Pete licked his dry lips. "Mind if I pull in over at Circle K and get something to drink? Betsy made fish for dinner tonight—fried perch fillets so tender they melt in your mouth. But man, am I thirsty."

"Yeah, go ahead." Neil watched the lanky kid run inside and sighed heavily. Things just weren't the same. He and Jerry had been friends for a long time, and roommates in an eastside apartment they shared since Jerry's divorce two years ago. They'd been on the same wavelength in so many ways. Neil just couldn't figure why someone would off a nice guy like Jerry.

The scuttlebutt around the station was making him fighting mad. Some guys were saying Jerry had been on the take and that he'd been eliminated because he'd been about to spill the beans. Neil didn't believe the gossip for a minute. Jerry had complained a lot after his divorce, saying he was being sucked dry by his ex over child support, but he'd kept up his payments. He'd even managed lately to buy some spiffy clothes and a new Buick. The two of them had put in a lot of overtime and Jerry had learned to handle his money better, that was all. Apparently there were guys at the station who were jealous. Just yesterday, Neil had almost come to blows with Fred Harmon, a loudmouth who suggested Neil didn't know his partner's secret life.

That was crazy. Neil knew everything there was to know about Jerry Foster. Hell, his mother, a widow who'd been blind for years, was depending on Neil to settle her son's financial affairs. He'd even made the funeral arrangements. It was the least he could do.

Pete pulled open the door and got in, drinking through a straw stuck in a huge plastic container.

"How can you drink that sugary garbage?" Neil asked crossly.

"Sugar's energy, my friend," Pete said, backing up, then pulling into traffic.

*You aren't my friend*, Neil thought sadly. *Never will be.*

The stucco house painted a desert brown was so well camouflaged by the surrounding shrubs and trees that a passerby might well miss it, Terry thought as she peered out through the windshield. In the headlights of the van, she could see that the structure was two stories high backing up to a rising hill, the property completely enclosed by a chain-link fence. Luke had jumped out and opened the padlocked gate with a key from his pocket, then hurried back to drive through before relocking the fence.

"Who owns this place?" she asked as he climbed back in.

"The Bureau. Confiscated a while back during a drug bust."

Staring out at the overgrown bushes trailing onto the pebble drive, Terry frowned. "It looks neglected."

"They deliberately keep the yard this way. It discourages visitors." Luke pulled the van close up to the attached garage door. "You two sit tight while I have a look around." Taking his high-beam flashlight, he stepped out into a light drizzle. Once in the yard, he reached for his .38 before disappearing around back.

"He's the most cautious man I've ever met," Terry said to Sara.

"Honey, that kind of caution will keep you alive." Sara stretched her long legs. "I think we'll all be glad to get into a real bed."

Terry felt tired and stiff, but not necessarily sleepy. She'd watched the storm blow off to sea and settle into a light rainfall as they passed through the coastal towns. After they'd eaten, Sara had dozed, but Terry'd been too curious to drop off. She'd asked only one question of Luke, why he wasn't taking the highway instead of the slower inland route. He'd explained that it was more difficult to follow them through the rural roads where there were always plenty of turnoffs. She figured he probably was right.

She'd seen the sign indicating that they were on the outskirts of Carmel, and had sat up straighter when Luke had told her they were almost at their destination. With Lynn, she'd visited the small artists' colony last summer, and they'd both loved the town. Never had she dreamed that one day she'd be hiding out from a killer in the same peaceful area.

"No one asks too many questions around here," Luke had volunteered when he'd seen her interested look. "It's sort of an unspoken rule that people here believe in live and let live, respecting one another's privacy. That's one reason I use this safe house whenever I can."

They passed an ice-cream parlor and an arcade of shops. "I don't suppose we'll be able to come into town?" she'd asked hopefully.

"We'll see," he'd answered in the maddening tone a father might use on a pesky child.

Suddenly floodlights illuminated the yard just before Luke stepped out of the front door. Terry saw that heavy black wrought iron shielded each window and nearly groaned aloud. While the practical side of her knew that made the house even safer, she hated the prisonlike feel of protected windows.

Luke opened her door and helped her down while Sara climbed out of the van's sliding door. He turned on lights inside, then went back out to bring in their luggage. Terry stretched her sore muscles before taking a look around.

It was a surprise to find that the place, though quite old, was far cozier than she'd expected. A stone fireplace in the corner of the living room, a long corduroy couch, deep comfortable chairs, a cluttered bookcase, and several colorful pillows. A narrow archway led into a dining room with a wooden table, and past that she could see the kitchen. The colors were golds and browns with a touch of orange, circa 1970. The only criticism she might have were the heavy drapes covering all the windows. For security reasons, no doubt, she decided.

"It's not so bad," Sara said, gazing at the stairs leading up.

"I've never been in a so-called safe house," Terry said, shivering in the chilly room. "Is this better than most?"

"By far." Sara unbuttoned her jacket. "I understand that the dealer who owned the place had a wife. She probably did the decorating. Definitely a woman's touch in here."

"Can law enforcement do that, take a person's property, furniture and all?"

Sara stifled a yawn. "Sure. For nonpayment of taxes, for fines levied. In this case, I believe the owner's in prison and the wife's been deported." She moved to the stairs. "Let's go up and have a look. I think you need to get to bed."

Luke returned and preceded them with the bags, placing her small suitcase in the room he'd apparently decided would be hers. It was small, sparsely furnished, but done in soothing shades of blue and white, and directly across from a very masculine room with heavy pine furniture. Terry watched Luke set his leather case in there before carrying

Sara's plaid bag to the room at the end of the hallway. The closed door she assumed was to the bath.

So he'd decided to keep an eye on her from across the hall, had he? She wouldn't have been shocked if he'd have dragged out a sleeping bag and unrolled it next to her bed. A sneeze shook her and she reached for a tissue from a box on the nightstand. A man who took protecting very seriously, that was Luke Tanner.

She should probably be grateful, Terry thought as she blew her nose. Not much would escape those cool, watchful gray eyes. However, the loss of her privacy bothered her greatly. Would he wait outside the bathroom door until she finished showering and taste her food before she took a bite?

Fatigue settled over her like an enveloping fog, causing her unfair analysis, she was certain. She heard Luke and Sara having a muffled conversation down the hall and wasn't even mildly interested. After a quick visit to the bathroom, she closed her bedroom door, toed off her sneakers, and pulled the scarf from her head. She'd heard the furnace go on, but it was too chilly to bother removing her sweats. Sighing, she slipped beneath the heavy quilt. The bedclothes smelled fresh and clean. She closed her eyes.

She was just dropping off when she heard a brisk knock on the door, a pause, and then the sound of its swinging open. Raising her head, Terry saw Luke fill the doorway. "Did you want something?" she asked, her voice sounding sleepy.

"You need to leave your door open. I'll be just across the hall with mine ajar as well."

Her head came off the pillow as she scowled at him. "Aren't you carrying things a bit far?"

"No, ma'am." Luke's face was stern. "I need to be able to see you, to know where you are at all times."

She couldn't muster up the energy to be angry. "Fine. Wake me when it's time for our shower." With that, she snuggled down again and closed her eyes.

He almost smiled. Even with her hair chopped off and bandages on both sides of her face, she looked appealing, a small mound beneath the thick covers. A sense of humor might just help her get through the next couple of months.

Pulling the door halfway to, he backed out into the hallway and found Sara studying him, a quizzical expression on her plain features. "Any instructions before I turn in?" she asked.

"I'd like your door left open, too. Another set of ears won't hurt."

Sara pushed away from the doorjamb. She, too, had had a good look around and wondered where Luke was coming from. "I've been in a lot of safe residences. This place is built like a brick shithouse. Do you still think something might go wrong?"

Luke ran a hand over his hair, still surprised at finding it so short. "You've been around long enough to know that something can *always* go wrong."

"Not with you around, Tanner." She gave him a quick wink and disappeared into her room.

He hoped she was right.

The morning sunshine was most welcome after the rainy drive up. Terry stood in the kitchen looking out the window and sipping strong black coffee. Actually, she preferred coffee with cream. Or, more correctly, she preferred flavored coffee, with a touch of hazelnut or amaretto. She supposed she should feel fortunate to have plain Maxwell House brew.

As she'd guessed, Luke was already outside when she'd finally wandered down a few minutes ago. She'd even managed to shower and put on clean sweats with no one breathing down her neck. She'd wound a fresh scarf around her head and walked into the kitchen just as Sara was pouring. Taking another swallow, she squinted, trying to see through the mesh screen on the window and the ironwork. "What's he doing out there?"

"Chopping wood." Sara joined her at the sink. "We've got the heat on in here and he's chopping firewood wearing only a T-shirt and sweatpants in forty-degree weather. Serve him right if he catches a cold."

"A germ wouldn't dare set up residence in Luke Tanner." Terry slid her glance to Sara and caught the smile. "You've worked with him before?"

Sara watched Luke's steady swing, saw the block of wood split and fall from the stump. Patiently, he placed another chunk in position and raised the ax. "Oh, yes. He's interesting, to say the least." Sara jotted another item on the pad in front of her.

"Interesting and about as sensitive as a drill sergeant."

The big woman smiled. "Don't let Luke hear you say that. All agents are required to take sensitivity training."

"You're kidding!"

"Not at all. Cops, too, in most cities. The thing is, you've got to know the book, but also when to set it aside."

Terry finished her coffee. "I think Agent Tanner may have been absent the day they taught that class."

Sara stuffed her list into her pocket. "I'm off to stock up on groceries. Anything special you'd like me to get?"

Cigarettes, Terry thought immediately, then decided to tough it out another day. "I like ice cream," she said, feeling childish at the request.

"Already on the list. Luke likes chocolate. That okay?"

"Sure. Could you pick up a newspaper? I haven't read one in ages." As a political cartoonist, the first thing she'd done each morning was to pore through the *Times*, the *Post*, the *Tribune* and several local papers to get an overview of what was happening around the country in order to get ideas and plan her drawings. "I feel out of touch."

"No problem. In the meantime, there's a TV in the living room."

Terry wasn't a television watcher, but maybe she'd have

to resort to viewing to pass the time. She gazed out the window again, wishing she could go for a long walk.

"Did you take your pills?" Sara asked. When Terry nodded, she picked up her purse and the keys to the van. "Luke's already talked with the doctor we use up this way. He'll be paying you a visit this afternoon. The bandages should be coming off soon."

The thought sent shivers of alarm through Terry. Would there be scarring? Would she look like her old self, even if she no longer felt like that person? Setting down her empty mug, she hugged herself, closing her eyes and wishing she could be back home in her own kitchen, getting ready to set out for a day at the *Gazette*.

Sara frowned as she studied her young charge. "Are you all right, Terry? Anything you want to talk about?" Physically, she was healing, but Sara had been a nurse long enough to know that the mental anguish of what Terry had gone through would take far longer to overcome.

"I've been better." She hated the quivery sound of her voice.

Sara touched her shoulder. "Give it time, honey. In a way, you're like a rape victim. Your life was forever changed by an act of violence. It takes time to recover. However, you can look at yourself as a victim, or as a survivor. Survivors heal more quickly."

Terry glanced up. "How long are we going to be here, Sara? How long before I can go home?"

"I wish I could answer that, honey. Not one day longer than necessary, I promise you." She gave Terry's arm a quick squeeze. "I'll be back."

Terry watched her leave, promising herself she wouldn't cry. Tears won't solve your problems, Dad had always told her. It's a tough world out there, he'd warned. She was finding out just how tough.

Moving back to the window, she looked out and found Luke leaning on the ax handle as his eyes scanned the yard.

His shirt was stained with sweat, and the pile of split logs was impressive, but he wasn't even breathing hard. Strong, disciplined, always in control.

And attractive. Instinctively, her hand touched the scarf covering the half inch of hair on her head. She couldn't believe how slowly it was growing out. Impatience is your worst fault, Theresa Anne, her father had often said. Right again, Dad.

By contrast, she imagined that Luke Tanner was as patient as a monk in a monastery. She could see that he hadn't shaved this morning, and found herself picturing him with a beard. It would add a hint of mystery to a face that was already difficult to read. It was a strong face and he had such a solid body. He scared her to death. She didn't want to react to him as a woman, yet as she watched him toss the split logs into a box as easily as if they were toothpicks, she felt an unexpected sensual tug.

Ridiculous, Terry told herself.

What she needed was to breathe in some brisk, cold air. She walked to the kitchen door, shoved it open and stepped outside.

Luke swung around at the sound of the door opening. Instantly, his face registered a fierce scowl. "Get back inside," he snarled. *"Now!"*

# CHAPTER SIX

Luke closed the kitchen door behind him, then turned to Terry. "I'm sorry. I didn't mean to yell, but you have to understand that you can't be outside. Not yet." He saw her hands trembling and wished he hadn't had to frighten her. "The men who might be searching for you know what you look like, your height and build, that you've got bandages on your face, that your head's been shaved. Looking as you do, you're a dead giveaway to any passerby."

Terry jammed her hands into her pockets. "How could anyone see through those thick shrubs alongside the fence? Besides, who knows we're here?"

"No one, I hope. But it's possible. An innocent tourist may be a paid informant."

Her heart was still pounding. "That sounds like paranoia. Surely you don't suspect everyone."

"To those of us in law enforcement, *everyone* is a suspect. Someone with a high-powered rifle up on that hillside could pick you off from quite a distance."

Terry felt a shiver take her. "Thank you for sharing that. Do you have to scare the hell out of me?" Crossing her arms over her chest defensively, she glared at him, struggling with a mixture of anger and fear.

Luke drew in a deep breath. He usually laid it on the line early in the program to the witnesses he was assigned to protect. The people hunting his charges were cunning, crafty, and unencumbered with a conscience. Follow orders or risk getting killed; it was as simple as that. He was unused to softening his approach, yet he could tell he'd shocked Terry. That's what he'd meant to do, to scare her just enough so she'd follow directions that just might save her life. But he couldn't afford to have her fall apart on him.

He scrubbed a hand over his face. "Look, I should have explained last night that we can't have you outside just yet. The possibility that our location has been discovered is remote, but we can't take *any* unnecessary chances."

Every time he changed tactics and became nice, tears welled up in her eyes. Damn, but she was getting weary of this seesaw of emotions. "I know you're just doing your job." She tightened her grip on her arms. "I want to cooperate, but it's so hard to know what to do, what not to do. I . . . I feel so damn confused." With a shaky hand, she indicated the room, the building. "This, all of this, being here, being so *monitored*—it's all so overwhelming. I'm trying, but I'm just not used to things yet."

"I understand."

Her eyes met his. *"Please* don't say that again."

How had she managed to put him on the defensive? Luke wondered. He decided to take refuge in the familiar, to outline what usually took place in the first phase of the protection program, hers in particular. If she hadn't been so tired last night, he'd have told her then, and wished now that he had. "Let me explain a few things. A new doctor's coming this afternoon. When he okays the removal of your bandages, if you feel well enough, we can go shopping. We'll get you fitted with a wig, dark glasses or contacts to change the color of your eyes. Maybe both, and clothes that you can pick out. Maybe things you choose will make you feel more like yourself."

Herself. It was difficult to hang on to a sense of self under the circumstances.

She wasn't responding, but rather staring at her hands as they shredded a tissue. "How's that sound, Terry?" he asked.

"Yes, that's fine." Her voice was low, trembly. "I think I'll go lie down for a while." She turned to leave.

"Sara will be back shortly with groceries. She'll fix something to eat, I'm sure." He stumbled on, hoping she'd cheer up. "That woman sure loves to eat. She chows down more than some truck drivers I know."

The effort was lost on Terry at the moment. "I'll be down later."

He thought she looked pale and fragile. "If I said anything to upset you . . . "

"It isn't you." She had to leave before she lost it in front of him. "It's me." Hurriedly, she ran toward the stairs.

Luke let out a whoosh of air. Fervently, he wished the witness in this assignment was a man.

Sara came through the kitchen door carrying two bulging paper bags. "I hope you're all hungry, 'cause I've got enough here to fill you to the brim." Setting her bundles on the counter, she glanced around. "Where's Terry?"

"She went up to lie down." He didn't meet her eyes. "She's a little on the touchy side, wouldn't you say?"

Sara brushed back a lock of brown hair. "Did you upset her, Tanner?"

For the second time today he felt defensive. "I told her she couldn't go out until I said so. She didn't take it well."

Probably because he'd made it sound like an order instead of a request. "She's got a lot to deal with. You might try going easy on her."

His version of easy apparently wasn't good enough. "You coddle her, if you want. I'm here to see that she stays alive." He picked up the keys from where she'd put them on the counter. "I'll be back in an hour. You got your piece with you?"

Sara patted her shoulder holster beneath her jacket. "Right here."

"Lock up after me."

"Don't you want to eat first?"

"I'm not hungry." With that, Luke left.

Men, Sara thought, especially men in law enforcement. She'd known her share of them. Too much macho pride and too little sensitivity, most of them. Shrugging out of her jacket, she decided to fry some bacon. Perhaps a BLT would awaken Terry's taste buds. The poor thing didn't eat enough to keep a bird alive.

Humming to herself, she unpacked the groceries.

Nick Russo watched his brother walk over to the cubicle in the prison visitors' room. Sam's tan had begun to fade; his face appeared sallow. He'd lost weight, too. Nick could only imagine how a sharp dresser like Sam must feel having to wear the prison issue blue cotton shirts and pants. He pasted on a smile as his brother sat down and picked up the phone on the other side of the glass.

"What do you know, Nickie?" Sam asked, his dark eyes intense.

"You were right, Sam." Nick kept his voice low. "There's been no body turned over to the family. I've got a feeling the Feds are hiding something."

Sam nodded. "I knew it. I'm telling you, that girl's not dead. My gut's never wrong."

The guard by the door shuffled his big feet. Nick shifted uneasily in his chair. "What do you think we should do?"

"You heard from Ozzie?"

"Not a word."

Sam's eyes narrowed. "Why not? You got plenty of money. Why can't you find him?"

Nick hated these visits, hated not having the right answers. "Take it easy, Sam. I got two guys looking. Ozzie's dug in deep somewhere. He'll surface, honest."

Sam leaned forward. "Easy for you to say. You're out there and I'm the one in here."

Nick ran a finger around the collar of his silk Pierre Cardin shirt. They kept it too damn hot in here. "I know it's rough . . . "

"No, little brother. You don't know. I don't ever want you to know. You gotta get me out of here." Sam swiped at his damp forehead. "That girl's alive. Find her, take her out, and their witness will be gone. And so will their case."

"Our snitch at Central tells me the Feds are in on it. They probably got her tucked away somewhere out of state. She could be anywhere—New Mexico, Colorado, California."

"It's up to you to find out where. Watch the old man. He could know more than he lets on. Get pretty boy to help. He owes us. You tell him I'm going to sing if something doesn't happen soon."

"Right, Sam. I'll tell him." Nick could feel the guard's eyes on him, and he wondered if the guy could read lips. Beads of nervous sweat rolled down his back. He wanted out of here. "Anything else?"

Sam shook his head and was about to hang up when he remembered something. "The Feds. You remember that agent you almost took out awhile back? What was his name?"

"Tanner," Nick answered, savoring the memory. The knife had gone in, slick and clean. Trouble was that Tanner had rolled, throwing off Nick's aim. Otherwise, the tough agent would've bought the farm.

"Yeah, right. Check it out. I heard he's on leave somewhere in Arizona. If he's involved, you better get backup. He's mean as shit and he's got a score to settle with you."

He didn't need backup, Nick thought. He needed a couple of minutes alone with Luke Tanner to finish the job. "I'll take care of it," he told Sam, sounding suddenly confident.

Wide-awake, Terry stared at the ceiling. She'd slept most

of the day, awakened only long enough to eat a little and to allow the doctor to remove all the bandages this time. The bedside clock read nearly midnight and she couldn't sleep.

Shoving back the covers, she got out of bed. Since she had to keep her bedroom door open, she'd taken to sleeping in sweatpants and a long T-shirt. Quietly, she walked to the bathroom, noticing as she passed Luke's room that he was stretched out under a light blanket. The man seemed immune to cold weather. In the mirror, she checked her face again.

Hard to get used to this image. There was blotchiness and a little swelling. Overall, her face seemed thinner, her eyes appearing larger. The doctor had said in a couple of weeks he'd like to do a little more repair, depending on how the healing progressed. Terry didn't know if she could go through any more right now. She touched the fuzz on top of her head. Now if only her hair would hurry and grow out.

Maybe a glass of milk would help her sleep. She had no slippers, so she padded down the stairs barefoot, turning on the light in the kitchen. The heavy drapes were drawn over each window, making it pitch-dark without lights. Terry poured herself a glass of milk and took a sip. The first swallow brought a gurgling response from inside. If only her appetite would return. Maybe it would if she could get the knots out of her stomach.

Mid-November out there. Cool, but not cold in this area of California. There was probably a moon. She opened the drape over the kitchen window. Yes, a nearly full moon illuminating the yard. She could almost pick up the scent from the sea, mostly through her imagination. Scarcely a leaf was stirring on the trees out back. Yet she caught a movement along the fence line. Rising on tiptoe, she leaned closer. Yes, there it was, something almost streaking along, low and close to the fence. Terry's heart picked up its rhythm as she ducked to the side, straining to see better.

"You're doing it again," a deep voice from the doorway said. "Exposing yourself to danger," Luke finished.

"Jesus!" Startled, Terry all but fell backward as she came down hard off her toes. Her hand flew to her chest, trying to ease her thumping heart. "You must be part cat to sneak around like that."

"I better not be. There's a big black Doberman out there who thinks he owns the yard." Luke closed the drapes.

"So that's what I saw moving around."

"I went to get him this afternoon, but you didn't make it back down for introductions." His eyes searched her face and saw that the smoky smudges of fatigue were lighter. "You feeling better?"

Terry nodded, then sipped her milk. "Just sort of slept out, I guess." Suddenly aware that she wore only a thin shirt, she hunched her shoulders and wandered into the living room, finally curling up in a corner of the couch as she hugged a pillow close to her chest.

Luke shrugged into the shirt he'd grabbed after stepping into his jeans, and followed her. Instead of turning on a lamp, he opened the flue, struck a match to the fire he'd laid earlier, waited to make sure the flames caught, then sat down at the far end of the couch. Silently he stared into the fire-place, content with the quiet, allowing her to talk only if she felt the need.

Terry drew her legs up and propped her chin on her bent knees. For several minutes, all that could be heard was the crackling of dry wood as it succumbed to the fire. The scent of hickory and pine drifted to her, and she breathed in deeply. "Mesmerizing, isn't it?"

"I could stare at it for hours." And he sometimes did.

She could, too. Feeling a bit awkward, she ran a hand into her hair, feeling self-conscious without her scarf.

"Don't do that," Luke said quietly, turning to face her. "Don't be embarrassed."

"But I look so awful."

He leaned closer, lightly touching the short, blond new

growth. "You couldn't look awful if you tried, with or without hair."

Her eyes widened at his words, at the way his blunt fingers gently caressed her scalp. Then, just as suddenly, he withdrew his hand, as if regretting both the remark and the touch. Terry swallowed, realizing that was the first touch she'd had in weeks that wasn't from a medical caregiver. She hadn't realized how much she'd missed that personal contact.

There were some things that needed to be said between them, she decided. "I'm sorry about getting so emotional on you earlier today."

He shrugged. "You have a right to your feelings." He'd thought about her reaction on and off all afternoon and evening, finally coming to the conclusion that she was most likely going through Post Traumatic Stress Syndrome. He'd seen it before frequently. The roller coaster of emotions, occasional crying jags, temper outbursts followed by contrite apologies. Confusion, a feeling of being overwhelmed, of unreality. People who'd witnessed tragedy or violence often had some if not all of those reactions, usually sometime after the triggering incident. He wasn't sure he knew how to treat Terry Ryan man-to-woman during the weeks ahead, but he knew exactly how to handle someone with PTSS. That would have to be his approach, something he was comfortable with.

"But I don't have the right to lash out at you when you're trying to protect me. I hope you'll bear with me. I'm working on it."

"Some things can't be rushed, Terry."

His eyes were a warm gray tonight, not the cool silver they usually were. "That's what Dad always says." Her curiosity aroused, she studied his lean profile as he turned to stare at the flames again. "Are you close to your family?"

A muscle in his jaw clenched. "No."

The one word bitten off so abruptly seemed bitter, as if a

warning to back off. She decided to try another tactic. "I don't even know if you're married."

Forcing himself to relax, Luke stretched out his legs and leaned his head on the couch back. "No, never took the plunge." He knew a good deal about her from her bio, but he decided to let her tell him in her own words. "How about you? Anyone special back home?" So far, the only person she'd mentioned missing was her father.

Terry hugged her knees. "Not at the moment."

He was glad there was no guy waiting, someone she'd be pining over. That would have made his job infinitely more difficult.

"How did you come to work for the government?"

"Long story. Sure to put you to sleep."

Apparently, he didn't like to talk about himself any more than she did. "I'll let you know when you start to bore me."

He decided to tell her just enough to satisfy her curiosity. "Actually, Bob Jones got me into training. He's a couple years older, but we grew up together. I admired him, so I kind of followed in his footsteps." In essence, that was the truth, but volumes were left unsaid.

He was a master at divulging only the little he didn't mind someone knowing. But she'd had a head start. "You grew up at the Northern California Boys' Ranch with Bob?"

He sent her a sharp look. "How'd you know that?"

"I didn't. George told me that that's where Bob was raised, and since you say you grew up with him, I assume it was there." She could tell he was annoyed. "I wouldn't think it was anything to be ashamed of. Are your parents dead?"

"I don't really know, and I certainly don't care." He rose, his movements choppy as he went to the fire and began poking at it, then added another log. He leaned one hand on the mantel and stood staring into the flames.

So much for a friendly chat, Terry thought. "I didn't mean to pry."

Luke let out a long breath, then returned to the couch.

"You weren't. I'm just not real comfortable talking about my past. Let's talk about you. I understand you're an artist. How'd you get into that?"

A neat segue, she thought. "I've always liked to draw. Caricatures are my specialty. My father often discussed local politicians with me, national ones, too. My sense of humor's a little twisted, I guess, because I started making fun of some of them. On paper with my pen, that is. I had a poli sci prof at ASU who encouraged me to do satirical sketches. I found I liked it. When I graduated, I applied at the *Phoenix Gazette* after reading that their resident cartoonist was retiring. Lo and behold, they hired me." A sad thought ran through her mind. "The man who was killed in the parking garage, Don Simon, helped me get the job."

He'd seen the pictures, read all the reports, yet her recitation interested him more. "Have you remembered any more about that incident? For instance, about the man who never got out of the car?"

She shook her head. "I've tried, but nothing focuses in."

"Don't force it. In time, your memory may open up."

"I suppose." Terry drained her glass, then stood. "I think I'll try to sleep now, though I hate to leave this great fire. We should get some chestnuts to roast. We used to do that every Thanksgiving." And afterward, her mother would add them to the turkey dressing. Hard to believe the holiday season was nearly here, and she was miles from everyone she knew and loved for the first time in her life. What would Christmas be like without her family?

She was about to get weepy again, Terry realized. Time to be alone. "I'll see you in the morning."

Luke got to his feet, noticing that her eyes were shiny with unshed tears. He didn't really know her, but he felt a kinship of sorts. He'd spent a lot of years feeling lost and alone. "Terry?" He stepped to block her exit so she'd be forced to face him. "Do you want to talk about it? Might help."

When she looked up, she realized he was closer than she'd thought. His shoulders seemed a mile wide and his square jaw was shadowed with a day's growth of dark beard. She could see an expanse of bare chest covered with dark hair where his shirt hung open and a medal on a silver chain. He was so big and hard-looking, yet his mouth looked soft, inviting.

*God! What was she thinking?* Surely she was losing her mind altogether.

"No, I'm fine. Really." Giving him a wide berth, she moved around him.

Luke watched her hurry up the stairs, wondering whether she'd have stayed if he'd asked her, if he'd touched her hand. She aroused unexpected feelings in him. He wanted to comfort her, to hold her. How long had it been since he'd felt like that about a woman? Maybe he never had. He usually was more interested in sex than solace.

Not that he hadn't been very aware that she hadn't had anything on under that thin cotton shirt.

Walking to the fire, he shook his head at the direction of his thoughts. It was a cardinal mistake to get interested—sexually or otherwise—in the witness you were protecting, a fact that had been drummed into him since day one. He'd forgotten that once, and it had nearly cost him his life.

Making sure that Terry Ryan walked away whole with as little mental and physical damage as possible was his strategy. Falling for her wasn't part of that strategy.

He'd have to keep that firmly in mind, Luke thought as he sat back down on the couch. Moodily, he stared into the wonderful blazing fire all alone.

"Sam Russo's attorney is screaming, but so far, I've been able to keep the identity of our secret witness under wraps," Bob Jones said into the phone. "Naturally, they're throwing names around, but they're just guesses. How's Terry holding up?"

"She's doing okay." Seated on his bed, Luke glanced at the closed door. "Have you been able to locate Ozzie Swain yet?"

Bob leaned back in his desk chair. "No, and we've got a lot of men on it, as well as the police. Nick's the one who worries me. The word on the street is he's willing to pay big money for information on the whereabouts of Terry Ryan."

"But I thought you said they don't know for sure that Terry was there and witnessed the killing?"

"They don't *know*, but they're not stupid. They know the Feds are involved and they've probably figured we wouldn't be hanging around unless we had something concrete. By the way, I went to see Mac. The sergeant isn't talking." Jones had a gut feeling that Mac knew far more than he was telling, yet he'd refused to answer most of his questions. "There's only one reason I can come up with that neither Sam nor Mac is willing to implicate others."

Luke's mouth was a thin line. "Let me guess. There's a contract out on Terry. If she's taken out, there's no case."

"Right. Is she pretty well healed physically?"

"Yeah. Not much stamina yet, but she's finally eating more." He'd talked Sara into remaining long past the need for her assistance just so she'd cook nutritious meals. "I'm thinking of driving Terry to Monterey or Pacific Grove and getting her a wig. She's real self-conscious about her short hair."

In his Phoenix office, Bob rose to walk to the window. It wasn't like Luke to be so open to a woman's needs. It wasn't that he was insensitive, but more that he was indifferent to anything not directly related to the safety of his witness. Was there more going on with this witness? "Probably a good idea. I don't have to tell you to be careful whenever you have her away from the house."

"No, you don't. Sara's leaving today." They'd been in Carmel ten days and he really couldn't justify keeping her on any longer.

Jones had been expecting that. "How does Terry feel about that?" He'd wondered if the naturally empathetic nurse-agent had bonded with Terry.

"I don't know. I haven't asked her."

That sounded more like the Luke he knew. "Do you need anything from this end?"

"Yeah. I need you to hurry up the trial date, to find Ozzie and put him away, and to keep a steady eye on Nick."

"I hear you. I'll be in touch." Bob hung up, then stared out the window thoughtfully.

Once, as a young deputy, Luke had gotten involved with a woman on a case. Jill Hastings had known how he felt and had used it against him, nearly costing Luke his life. Terry Ryan certainly wasn't that sort of threat. Still, an agent whose feelings were involved lost his perspective, and often his ability to protect.

There'd been something in Luke's voice. Jones couldn't put his finger on just what, but something. Maybe he'd make the time for a quick visit to Carmel. Soon.

Terry pulled down the visor on the passenger side of the van and checked out her image in the mirror. "I've always wanted green eyes." She turned to Luke as he pulled away from the optical store and eased out into traffic. "What do you think?"

He spared her a quick glance. "They look fine."

She frowned at him. "Fine? What kind of a comment is fine? Fine is how you describe your grandmother's hat or your maiden aunt's dress."

"I don't really think of you as either my grandmother or my maiden aunt. What do you want me to say? Your green eyes are terrific. Is that any better?"

Her attention was back at the mirror where her new auburn wig showed her a startlingly different image. "I'm having a little trouble adjusting to this color. I've always been blond. I think my skin's too light for dark hair, don't you?"

"I haven't given it much thought." Luke swung around a pink Cadillac driven by a senior lady who could barely see over the steering wheel. The sun was warm overhead, the sky a cloudless blue. Gulls dipped low over the sea along the coastal road, the air scented with a blend of fish and salt spray. They'd been cooped up for two weeks and he could well understand Terry's excitement at being outdoors. He shared her enthusiasm, but that didn't keep his eyes from scanning every passing vehicle, or checking out the most innocuous-looking tourist walking along.

"Maybe I should have gotten the light brown wig," Terry mused, tugging the hair piece more snugly in place.

"You want to go back and we can pick up one in every color? The neighbors will think I'm living with a harem."

She made a face at him. "Why not, even though the neighbors never see me? Apparently, the government's got a lot of money to squander. Or is all this coming out of your pocket?"

"Expense account." He spotted a row of shops up ahead on the left. "What kind of store are we looking for to get you some clothes? I'm pretty tired of those sweat suits."

"You and me both." Terry peered through the windshield and noticed a boutique sandwiched between a souvenir store and an ice-cream parlor. "We could try over there."

Luke put on his blinker and pulled into an angled parking spot. He handed her the oversize sunglasses they'd picked up earlier. "Put these on." While she did, he checked again to make sure his .38 was firmly lodged at his waistline at the small of his back, then settled his jacket over the bulge.

Watching him, Terry sobered, losing her short-lived euphoric mood. The reminder of the gun Luke always carried and the disguise she would have to wear every time she left the safe house had her smile slipping away. As he opened the van door and held out his hand to help her down, her eyes nervously scanned the area, the faces of strolling tourists, the traffic passing by.

She mustn't forget that a man with a gun was out there somewhere looking for her, one who wouldn't hesitate to shoot her as he had Don Simon. Hesitantly, she looked at Luke.

He thought he knew exactly what she was thinking. "It's okay, Terry. You're with me."

With him, the man who literally held her life in his hands. She had to trust him; she had no other choice. Slowly, she put her hand in his and stepped out.

"I thought you said you knew how to shoot," Luke said, standing back and watching her take aim at the makeshift target he'd put together in the backyard.

"I do. My father taught us all how to shoot as teenagers." She assumed the stance she'd been shown years ago, gripped her right hand that held the gun with her left, and lowered her head as if lining up the target. "What's wrong with this position?"

"Well, for starters, you're stiff as a board and poised as if you're ready to turn and run as soon as you pull the trigger."

"That's because I know it's going to be a loud sound. Dad took me to the shooting range where they have protective ear coverings."

"Out here, we have to rough it a bit." He stepped up behind her, placing his hands on her elbows. "Loosen up. The tension should be in your wrist and hand, not throughout your body." Close behind her now, his hands slid along her arms, adjusting her fingers. "Your left hand should lightly grip your right wrist to steady it, not in a death hold. If you grasp it too tightly, you'll cause the shot to jerk to one side."

She was wearing the navy corduroy jacket they'd bought earlier this afternoon, yet even through the heavy material, she could feel his touch along her arms, the strength of him. Terry swallowed. "I see."

"You've got to leave some play in your stance." Molding himself to her, he touched first one leg then the other with his bent knee, getting her to relax a little. "Now line up your head so your eyes are directly across from the target." Placing his cheek along hers, he aligned their upper bodies.

It was a cool evening, but Terry suddenly felt warm. She could feel his breath on her neck, his five o'clock shadow brushing her still-sensitive skin, his heart steadily beating against her back. The clean masculine scent of him was playing havoc with her concentration. She shifted her feet nervously.

"Are you ready?"

"Yes."

"Then go ahead and shoot."

Terry took careful aim at the empty twenty-eight-ounce can of tomato sauce sitting on a stack of wood about fifty feet away. She pulled the trigger.

And missed by a mile. "Shit!"

Luke stepped back. "Don't get discouraged. It takes practice." He pointed to the glass jar he'd placed next to the back door. "And go put a quarter in the jar."

"I don't have any money, remember? And you're not my father. Besides, how'd you know I'd swear and you'd need the jar?"

"Because I've been living with you for two weeks."

That had an uncomfortably intimate sound to it. "Swearing releases tension."

"Not as well as a few other things I can think of." He held out a closed fist to her.

She chose to ignore his last comment. "What's that?"

He reached for her hand and dropped in a pile of quarters. "I know your father would appreciate it if I'd make sure you clean up your language."

That made her smile. Dutifully, she walked over and tossed a quarter in the jar, then shoved the rest in the pocket of her new jeans before returning to try again. But when he stepped close to surround her again, she lowered the gun. "Look, why don't I try this on my own? You . . . you make me nervous." Which was certainly the truth.

Luke waved his hand, indicating she should proceed.

Drawing in a deep breath, Terry again assumed the stance. She shuffled her feet until she felt just right, corrected her grip the way he'd shown her, and took careful aim. When the bullet pinged off the can, knocking it onto the ground, she let out a victory yell.

He smiled at her. "Okay, hotshot. One hit doesn't a marksman make. Let's see some more." He'd lined up six cans.

She managed to hit two more making it fifty-fifty, not a bad first day out. She hadn't practiced in years. They strolled back toward the back door as the sun slipped into the sea and the breeze picked up. Terry hefted the small gun, gauging its weight. "Dad had me practicing on a Smith & Wesson five-shot snubby, I remember he called it. It was lighter than your .38."

He took his weapon from her. "Yeah, but not much. This is a Colt Special, used by most police. I've got a Magnum locked in my case that would probably knock you on your ass, which is probably the only place you haven't had a bruise lately. We might try it one day. I think it's important that you practice daily."

Her hand on the doorknob, Terry paused. "Why? Do you think we might get into a shootout?" She felt foolish just asking.

"No, but being prepared for anything is what keeps people alive." He touched the ends of the short wig and remembered her file picture, the long blond hair that used to fall past her shoulders. She was right. The color was all wrong. "Does this feel kind of like wearing a tight hat?"

"Yes, it does."

"Why don't you take it off when we're inside? I prefer short hair to fake hair, don't you?"

It seemed to Terry that ever since Sara had left, Luke's remarks tended to lean more toward the personal than before. She didn't answer, but instead opened the door. Prince rushed out, relieved to have his freedom back. She waited until he walked to her, then stroked the sleek black Doberman's coat.

Watching, Luke was amazed that Prince had taken to Terry so quickly. She'd been raised around dogs, she'd told him, but not dogs trained to guard and attack on command. Yet he noted that she was very careful not to move too quickly or to surprise Prince from behind. For his part, the Doberman seemed smitten with her.

Shivering, Terry stepped inside and went to hang up her jacket. The clothes she'd picked out earlier did make her feel more comfortable, more like her own things. And she'd gotten used to the house, the dog, and even some of the restrictions imposed on her, for she knew they were only temporary and very necessary.

A movement outside the kitchen window caught her eye. She stretched on tiptoe to watch Luke throw a stick for Prince to go fetch. What she hadn't gotten used to or comfortable with, Terry realized, was the federal agent she was forced to live with, someone she was having trouble thinking of as a protector instead of a man.

# CHAPTER SEVEN

Neil Manning dropped the stack of papers he'd been studying onto the coffee table and leaned back on the couch. Wearily, he scrubbed a hand over his face. He'd been going through his friend's, Jerry Foster's, papers over and over for days now. There was no getting around what he'd found. Numbers didn't lie.

Jerry had to have been on the take.

A surge of anger had his hands curling into fists. How could Jerry have risked everything—his future, his friendships, his very life—for money? Neil was as fond of money as the next guy. But to look the other way while scumbags manipulated his fellow officers in the city he'd called home all his life—the thought was inconceivable. How had Jerry been suckered into playing along?

He'd worked with the man for ten years, lived with him for two. How was it that he hadn't even suspected? Neil sat up, slamming a fist into his open palm. Because he'd trusted his friend, that's why. He'd turned from the gossip making the rounds at the station, defending Jerry to the point of getting into some near-fights with some of the guys. Not Jerry, he'd told them all. Not his best friend.

Yeah, right.

He'd found the bankbooks in the pockets of Jerry's old suit at the back of the closet when he'd been bundling up the clothes to give away, as Mrs. Foster had asked him to do. Three separate accounts. And crudely sewn into the lining of an old leather jacket, a plastic bag of money. Eighteen thousand, to be exact. Neil stared at the stack of small bills he'd just finished counting, struggling with his emotions.

But that wasn't the worst of it, Neil thought as he picked up the small black notebook and thumbed through it. Coded names, dates, amounts—all recorded in Jerry's neat handwriting. Enough here to end half a dozen promising police careers.

He felt betrayed. How was he going to tell Jerry's blind mother that her son was a thief, a bad cop, a turncoat? He swallowed down his anger, trying to think clearly.

He'd have to report this, of course. A frisson of fear raced up his spine as he wondered if they'd think he'd been in on it with Jerry. Well, they could check his bank account. About seven hundred in savings, maybe two in checking. That ought to prove something.

Neil wished Mac was still around. He'd always been able to talk to Mac. Had Jerry been involved in the same thing that Mac was accused of? Had Jerry been killed by some of his cohorts in crime because he'd been about to spill the beans? But, if it had been a hit, how was it no one had come to check out the apartment? They probably hadn't known about the notebook.

Was *anyone* at Central still clean? he wondered. Who could he trust? The captain was still on the sick list. He probably wouldn't have gone to Marino even if he weren't. He was no longer the man he used to be.

Of course, Neil knew the Feds had been sniffing around. He could call them. But loyalty to the honest cops he knew at Central made him decide to check it out at the local level first. But who should he take all this to?

Best option left was the lieutenant. Remington wasn't

exactly a cop's cop. He'd always given Neil the impression he thought he was a shade better than the other guys. Still, he was a man who got the job done.

Neil scowled with distaste as he gathered the notebook and evidence into a neat stack, then shoved it into a large manila envelope. He had three days off. He wouldn't talk to anyone till after he thought things over. A dead friend's reputation was at stake here, as well as those of several prominent cops at Central, to say nothing of possibly endangering himself.

Should he see a lawyer? No, that would make it seem as if he had something to feel guilty over, some act to defend. Should he call Internal Affairs? Hell, they'd probably call for him once he turned everything over.

Neil rose and walked to Jerry's room, placing the envelope in the top drawer of his dresser. He'd sleep on it. Meanwhile, he'd pack up the rest of his friend's clothes. Disappointment weighed heavily in his chest as he moved to the closet.

Terry adjusted the earplugs of her Walkman, then fiddled with the radio dials until she found the station she wanted. She stretched out under the covers of her bed, hoping the music would lull her to sleep. She'd talked Luke into buying the headset for her yesterday when they'd gone shopping in town, explaining that she was having trouble sleeping. The trouble was that she didn't do enough during the day to wear herself out sufficiently to sleep. Boredom was tiring, but rather than becoming drowsy, she was wide-awake till the wee hours most nights.

"Are you lonesome tonight?" the deep voice of the male singer on the golden oldies station asked. *You can say that again*, Terry thought. Lonely and feeling sorry for herself. A bad combination. And the situation wasn't apt to improve soon.

Physically, she was feeling better. The clavicle was healing, for she was able to move her shoulders with hardly any discomfort. The bruises had faded. Her hair was only about an inch long, but that obviously couldn't be rushed. There were two slashes on her face that, despite the surgery, were still very visible. Apparently the glass shards had been jagged. The doctor who'd checked on her recently had hinted that she should consider more corrective surgery soon, but when she'd grown agitated at the very suggestion, he'd backed off and said she could wait awhile.

The very thought of entering another hospital, of once again being open to that kind of pain and dependency on others, had Terry feeling suddenly warm and sweaty. She shoved aside the covers, glancing toward the open door that faced Luke's room across the hall. He was in there, she knew, probably in one of his half-asleep states. The man was so in control of himself that he didn't seem to allow sleep to totally take him under. No matter what hour she got up to use the bathroom, as she passed by and glanced in, she could see his eyes were open and watchful. At the slightest sound, he was instantly in the hallway, gun in hand, a constant reminder of the ever-present danger she faced.

"Do you miss me tonight?" the singer went on. *God, yes.* She missed so many people. Tomorrow was Thanksgiving, a day she always looked forward to. The whole family gathered at Mom and Dad's, her nephews already excited about Christmas, climbing on her lap and confiding their wish lists. Not this year.

She'd gathered from their spotty conversations that holidays didn't mean much to Luke. Yet he seemed to sense that this time of year was special to her. So he tried, in his way, to fill the void. Since Sara's departure, he'd taken over the cooking until she'd insisted she needed more to do. He'd encouraged her, allowed her to plan the meals and cook her favorites, praising her efforts. Yesterday, they'd bought a turkey and all the trimmings for tomorrow's dinner. She knew he was making the effort strictly for her.

And she wondered why. Surely, his job description didn't include keeping the little witness well fed and happy during the holidays. Was it simply easier than watching her mope and pine away for all that she was missing? Terry had a gut feeling it was more than that. Maybe he ignored the holidays because he hadn't grown up with the traditions that had fashioned her life. Maybe he wanted to enjoy the celebration, yet wouldn't admit to something he'd consider a weakness, even to himself.

Luke Tanner was a hard man to figure. He'd revealed so little about his past that she felt as if she scarcely knew him even though they'd lived under the same roof for weeks now. It was unnatural to be that reticent. Was he hiding some terrible secret? Or had he grown up along with Bob Jones at that boys' ranch in such a miserable fashion that even discussing that time would sadden him too much? It might be interesting to try to find out. It might relieve the boredom somewhat as well.

*Damn, but it's hot tonight. There goes another quarter,* Terry thought as she pulled off the earphones and stood up to remove her sweatpants. Down to only her T-shirt and underpants, she decided that, rules or no rules, she was closing her door. Privacy was something she longed for almost as much as her family. Quietly, she closed the door. She punched up the pillow, put on the earphones, and lay back.

If only she could turn off her mind and invite sleep. Wiggling into a more comfortable position, she concentrated on listening to an old Elton John tune.

She couldn't have said how long she lay there before the door slammed open, the crashing sound drowning out the low music, the overhead light flipped on, and Luke stood in the doorway, his gun aimed directly at her.

"Oh, my God!" Terry jerked upright, scooting back toward the wall, her eyes wide with fright. "What is it?" Her earphones dangled from her neck while her heart felt as if it might burst within her.

"Are you all right?" His left hand still on the flattened door, Luke's eyes surveyed the room before he stepped inside.

"Yes. Why? What's happened?" Odd how the gun she'd used daily for target practice looked much larger and more deadly when it was pointed at her.

"I woke up and saw your door was closed. I knocked—twice—but you didn't respond." He lowered the gun, feeling suddenly foolish. "I didn't know what to think so I . . . "

"So you came charging in here and scared the holy hell out of me again." Terry placed her hand over her still thudding heart. "Jesus, Luke. We won't have to wait for those men to find me. I'm going to die of a heart attack brought on by my protector."

"Why the hell did you close the door? You know the rules." His voice was gruff, more from embarrassment than anger.

For the first time, she noticed that he was wearing only blue low-riding briefs. In the harsh overhead light, she could see the broad expanse of his chest and the medal hanging on a chain that he was never without. On his right side she saw what appeared to be a scar. His hips were lean, his legs muscled and strong. The bulge in his briefs drew her attention a shade longer than it should have before she raised her eyes to his.

"I was warm so I stripped down. I closed the door because I . . . I can't relax dressed in so little when I know you're just across the hall." Her explanation sounded stupid and teenage, even to her own ears. She hugged her knees and dropped her gaze as she felt her face color. The sudden emotional reaction had her trembling again. She closed her eyes, wishing she had better control.

The tension drained from Luke as guilt took over. He'd upset her yet again. He turned off the glaring overhead light and flipped on the bedside lamp. He put the safety back on and set the gun on her nightstand. His first instinct was to comfort, to reassure her, and he didn't stop to question it. Moving to the bed, he sat down and hesitantly touched her shoulder. "I'm sorry I scared you."

The trembling that he'd thought to ease only increased. Slowly she raised her head and opened her eyes. Without her contacts, her eyes were a deep blue and filled with confusion and lingering fear. Luke felt awkward and uncertain as he trailed his fingers down her slender arm. "I always seem to do things that upset you without meaning to."

Yes, like charging into her room nearly naked and making her starkly aware of his masculinity. The clean male scent of him had her struggling with an arousal she hadn't felt in months. How could he sit beside her so casually and not notice? She dropped her gaze to her toes and pretended a nonchalance she was far from feeling. "It's all right. My nerves are on edge, that's all."

He wasn't a man used to explaining or to comforting. He was twelve years older than this fragile woman, and tonight he felt every day of it. Yet he couldn't seem to look on her as a younger sister, which would have been far more appropriate, or even as a stranger he was guarding. Instead, he saw her as a woman who was making him feel things he wasn't sure how to handle.

If circumstances were different, he'd pull that woman into his arms and comfort her in a way that would relieve both their tensions. He'd caught Terry looking at him a time or two in a manner that told him she'd not pull away. But she was entrusted to his care, and he had no business violating that trust, no matter how badly he ached to reach out for her.

Abruptly, he stood, turning his back to her. "Get some rest. And leave the door open." He needed to walk away while he still could. Grabbing his gun, Luke marched to his room.

Terry realized she was still trembling and suddenly cold. Slipping under the covers, she pulled them up close around her. Luke Tanner was a man of icy control, she decided. Apparently he could storm in and view her wearing next to nothing and remain totally unaffected. Awhile back he'd told her she couldn't look awful if she tried, with or without hair, but that comment had obviously been made to placate her. It was apparent that she held no appeal for him whatsoever, for he'd treated her like a kindly older brother just now.

How could he want her? she asked herself, blinking back the tears. She'd lost weight and was too thin. Her face was scarred, possibly permanently. Her once-lovely hair was little more than peach fuzz. What's more, she was angry or weepy by turns. What man would want a woman like that?

Not that she wanted Luke to be attracted to her. God knew her life right now was complicated enough without tackling a relationship. Still, it hurt her feminine pride to watch him walk away from her so casually after he'd set her churning.

Wasn't it enough that she had turned into a frightful mess, that she had to be separated from everyone she loved, that she was being hunted down like an animal by men who would shoot on sight? Did she also have to feel a sensual pull that she was too vulnerable to cope with just now?

Left to his own devices, Luke probably would have broiled a steak for dinner. More truthfully, if he were spending Thanksgiving at his house in Sedona, he probably wouldn't have even taken note of the holiday, for all it usually meant to him. But he'd seen the melancholy look in Terry's eyes when they'd stepped inside the supermarket with all the seasonal decorations and come-ons. So he'd suggested that she pile the basket full of whatever her family usually ate for dinner.

You'd have thought he'd handed her the winning lottery ticket. It was the first time he'd seen her look truly happy in the weeks they'd been together. She'd picked out a turkey with as much care as any White House chef, then proceeded to gather yams and bread cubes for dressing and cranberries, plus the makings for a pumpkin pie. He'd smiled indulgently, surprised at how easily pleased she was. And even more surprised at how good it made him feel to please her.

Now, after finishing two helpings of the marvelous dinner she'd put together while turning down all offers of help, Luke pushed back from the table, sure he couldn't eat another forkful. "Lady, you're one hell of a cook," he told her.

Terry accepted the compliment graciously with a nod of her head. "And just wait until you taste dessert." The only way she'd been able to keep her mind from straying to her loved ones on this family day was to keep herself busy with the meal preparation. But she'd about run out of steam now that they'd eaten.

"I think that'll have to wait awhile." He patted his stomach. "You're going to make me fat. Jones is going to kick me off the Marshals staff, the first one to leave due to obesity."

She'd seen his rock-hard waistline up close last night and knew he was kidding. "I hardly think so." She finished the last of her wine, then leaned forward. "Do you ever think about retiring? This line of work must get to you, on the go so much, always having to live with strangers."

He frowned, wondering how she'd guessed the very thing he'd been pondering lately. "Yeah, it does. I think about quitting, from time to time. This job is better suited to a young man. At thirty-eight, I worry about my reflexes slowing down."

She thought about last night, how he'd appeared in her doorway, his eyes scanning the room in the space of a heartbeat. "I don't think you need worry about that just yet. Have you thought about what you might do when you do quit?"

He toyed with the teaspoon on the tablecloth as his mind focused on his ranch. "I've got a little spread in Sedona. Some acreage, a house I've fixed up, a good-sized barn."

"My family has a cabin up that way, near Oak Creek Canyon. It's a nice area."

"Yeah. Horse country. I've already bought one. I like working with horses."

"You mean Arabians? The market's kind of dried up, or so I've heard."

"No, quarter horses. They're not so high-strung. There's a lot more call for them, too. I thought I might look into breeding." He shrugged self-consciously. "Maybe one day. Who knows?" Odd how she managed to get him to talk about himself without realizing he was doing it. "What about you? Do you miss not working?"

"I sure do." She'd picked up an art pad and some pens and pencils last week, and spent some time sketching. It helped pass the time, but it wasn't the same. "I'm sure I've been replaced."

"Are you good?" He moved around too much to read just one newspaper and hadn't seen her work.

The corners of her mouth twitched. "I'm wonderful."

She was wearing a kelly green silk blouse with cream-colored slacks, an outfit she'd picked up at the boutique. Her face had some color today, probably from the heat of the kitchen. He thought she looked particularly good, but after the unexpected way she'd made him feel last night, he decided to keep his thoughts to himself. "I'm sure you'll be able to find another job, once this is all over."

Once this was all over. If only she knew the date. With a sigh, Terry rose. "I've got some scraps for Prince if you want to take them out while I clean up."

"Oh, no. You cooked, I clean up." He stood and began clearing the table. "Go on in by the fire. You've earned a rest."

"You're sure? I don't mind helping."

He gave her a mock scowl. "Go on. Go sketch something."

Luke found her an hour later curled up in a corner of the couch, her sketch pad propped against her bent knees, her lower lip caught between her teeth as she concentrated. After placing a fresh glass of wine for each of them on the coffee table, he threw another log on the fire and stirred things up, then joined her. The TV in the corner beckoned with football games on all day, but he felt oddly content sitting and watching Terry correct an error with her soft eraser, brush away the pieces, then select another pencil. "Do I get to see?" he asked.

"Maybe." Something wasn't quite right. She pulled back, studying the sketch. The lines at the corners of his eyes. Yes, that was it. She worked in silence for several minutes, then lowered her legs and handed the pad to Luke. "Okay, what do you think?"

He had been expecting a caricature of some sort, along the lines of political cartoons. She'd had him picking up papers whenever they left the house so she could read the news and get new ideas. But this drawing was different.

The man was older, with a round face and a nearly bald head, remnants of thin hair barely visible. The nose was broad, the eyes deep-set, the chin square with a stubborn tilt to it. There were laugh lines around his eyes and, though he wasn't smiling, there was a look about the mouth that hinted of a sense of humor, as if he were about to tell a joke. It was obvious that the drawing was done by someone who cared a great deal for this man.

"Your father," Luke said, taking a guess.

"Yes," she answered softly. She took back the pad, touching the face, wishing it were real. "He calls me Theresa Anne, my real name, most of the time. No one else calls me that."

Such fatherly devotion was foreign to Luke, but she sure sounded as if she meant it. "You ought to save it and give it to him for Christmas. I don't know the man, but he's got to like this."

Terry blinked away a sudden rush of emotion. "Do you think I'll be home by Christmas?"

"I wish I knew, Terry."

"Yeah, me, too." She closed the pad and placed it on the end table, along with the pencils. "What was your father like?" she asked, simply to start a conversation so she wouldn't think about home. He'd said he wasn't close to his family and she'd wondered about what kind of people they were ever since.

Luke stretched his legs out toward the fire. "The last time I saw him I was about six and he was a sonofabitch."

Whoa. That strong a reaction she hadn't been expecting, cold words said so dispassionately. "I take it he walked out on the family."

"Oh, yeah. He left me and my mother and moved to Hollywood to become a movie star." All these years later and there was still so much bitterness, so much resentment.

"You're kidding . . . a movie star? Did he make it? What's his name?"

"Same as mine and no, he didn't make it. I learned later that he was a fairly handsome guy and had everyone telling him he ought to be in pictures. He bought the dream, but didn't have the drive, I imagine. I heard he appeared in some crowd scenes and even had a few bit parts, but nothing more."

"Where is he now?" She doubted that his father had returned since Luke had had to go to the boys' ranch.

"I was in my teens when I read in the paper that he'd been arrested for drunk driving. He was a stunt man by then and couldn't keep that job, either. I have no idea what happened to him after that." Why had he even answered the first question? The wine, Luke thought, reaching for his glass. Too late now. He took a long swallow. "So you see, if I could draw, I wouldn't paint nearly as kind a picture of my father as you did of yours just now."

She wanted to keep him talking, the need to know his background oddly important to her. "What about your mother?"

"Ah, yes. My mother." Luke set the wineglass down. "After dear old Dad left, Mom hung around about six months before dropping me at my grandmother's, then taking off for God only knows where."

"Was your grandmother good to you?"

His hand moved to the medal he always wore, the one thing she'd given him. "She was, for a while. Then she got sick. I probably caused her poor health. I wasn't an easy kid. She finally gave me up when I was nine, made me a ward of the court."

His voice was shockingly unemotional, but Terry felt certain he'd schooled himself to block out his feelings for his family. She could hardly blame him after the story she'd just heard. "And that's when you wound up at the ranch?" At nine. Dear God, he'd been just a boy.

"No. They don't take boys under twelve at the ranch. I bounced around from one foster home to another. Ran away a lot. They found me, dragged me back. Incorrigible, they labeled me." He angled his body until he faced her. "Now, don't you think you had a fairy-tale upbringing compared to mine?"

"I suppose, although no one lives the TV version, you know. My older sister got in with a fast crowd and started drinking in her teens. She was killed while driving under the influence at seventeen. My brother, Sean, had a bad first marriage, but his second seems to be solid. They have two great sons. My other brother, Michael, has diabetes and has nearly died twice. He just got married last year. And my father's had a heart attack. We've had our struggles." She searched his eyes and saw the pain remembering had put there. "But we were raised with a lot of love, and I'm sorry you missed out on that as a child."

Luke made a derisive sound deep in his throat before turning to toss back the rest of his wine. He thought of having another glass, then realized that there wasn't enough wine in the world to make his childhood memories warm and fuzzy. "Don't tell me you still believe in love and happily-ever-after?"

She studied him from under lowered lids. "You know, I had you pegged as a cynic the day we met."

He leaned back, his head resting on the couch, his eyes on her face. "And you're not? You who work for a newspaper, a woman who looks into the lives of our governing body and finds many of them wanting, I would imagine. How can you be a cockeyed optimist after all that?"

"Actually, I think I'm a realist. I believe bad things happen to good people sometimes, my own case a perfect example. But I don't think we need to let those things sour us on the entire world. My parents buried a child and managed to go on. You had a rough upbringing. No doubt about it. But you've become a good person, a caring man, one who helps others. That's the upside. Why dwell on the downside?"

Luke shifted to stare into the flames for so long that she was sure he wasn't going to answer her. Finally, he did, in a voice low and empty of hope. "Why would anyone believe in love when it disappoints you at every turn? People have their own agendas, go about their business and don't much care who gets hurt in the cross fire. Caring for someone just opens you up for another round of pain. Who needs it?"

*You do*, Terry thought. In all her twenty-six years, she'd never met a man who needed love more.


The captain was fuming. If he hadn't been hurting like hell from an infection he developed after surgery, he'd be pacing. If his doctor's warning about his high blood pressure wasn't still ringing in his ears, he'd have reached for one of his cigars. Sucking in what he hoped was a calming breath, he stared again at the newspaper cartoon that had pissed him off royally.

Naturally, the *Gazette* had hired a political cartoonist to replace John Ryan's daughter after her death. Terry had had a caustic pen, but she'd stopped short of throwing barbs at the Phoenix Police, perhaps in deference to her father. But this new kid, Tremayne Boyle, had no such lingering loyalties. What the hell kind of name was Tremayne anyway?

Marino's scowl deepened as he studied the drawing. A large room filled with desks was depicted with various mice wearing police uniforms, all involved in activities that would have gotten them booted off any police force. One officer had a buxom babe on his lap, supposedly interrogating her while feeling her up. Another was placing offtrack bets on the phone. Two were reading porno magazines while still another was upending a bottle of booze.

In the background was the mouse-cop in charge, obviously Lieutenant Remington complete with snazzy suit and his trademark wing tips propped on the desk, oblivious to everything going on around him while he napped. And in the opposite corner was a square showing a wizened old cat wearing a police hat with a captain's badge, all stretched out in a hospital bed eating from a box of candy held by a bosomy nurse. The caption beneath the cartoon read: While the cat's away, the mice will play.

Damn that little shit Tremayne and damn the *Gazette* for ridiculing his department.

Trying desperately to hold on to his temper, Captain Marino snatched up his bedside phone and dialed Remington.

At Central, the lieutenant let his immediate superior vent his ill humor over the *Gazette* cartoon. Of course he'd seen it. The bull pen had been abuzz since he'd walked in and a copy still lay on his desktop. Phil could do little or nothing about Marino's complaints. But he could listen.

Finally, when Marino paused for a breath, he spoke calmly. "It's called freedom of the press, Captain. I could complain to his editor, but that would encourage questions we can't answer."

Marino finished counting to ten. "They lost two of their own. I don't blame them for being upset. Is there any truth to this cartoon? Has the whole damn department fallen apart while I've been out?"

"Of course not. It's business as usual here. If anything, everyone's working twice as hard. We want this cleared up as badly as they do. Maybe more so."

Then why in hell weren't they finding the killer? "Why hasn't that Swain fellow been picked up? Maybe he could shed some light on all this. I can't believe that Russo hasn't talked. He strikes me as the sort who'd make a deal with the devil for a lighter sentence. Go see him. Get something cooking, for Christ's sake." Marino felt the heat rise into his face. How could he stay cool with all that was going on?

Remington didn't think this was the time to remind the captain that Sam Russo had been questioned repeatedly and simply refused to talk. His lawyer had already threatened to charge the police with harassment. "I'll get right on it," he lied. Remington had talked with the captain's doctor just yesterday. It would be awhile before Marino would be returning. Maybe by then something would break.

"You know how I feel about all this, Phil," Marino said, his voice sounding old and weary. "I'm not going to let this ruin my record. I'm not going to retire with my precinct under a cloud."

"Yes, sir. I understand." Phil understood that there wasn't a hell of a lot either of them could do at the moment to change things.

"What about that cop who was killed in the alley? Foster. Anything new on that?"

Phil picked up a phone message he'd received earlier. He needed to get the heat off himself, to protect his future. A smoke screen might just work. "I'm not sure if this is anything, Captain, but Foster's ex-partner, Officer Neil Manning, called me this morning. He's coming in tomorrow to discuss something important, something he needs to talk about in person. It could relate to Foster's death. The two shared an apartment."

"I hope to hell it does. Call me after you talk with him."

"Right. Anything else?"

Marino checked the clock. Thank God it was time for another pain pill. "That's it. Keep in touch." He hung up the phone and reached for his pill bottle.

Remington glanced thoughtfully at the newspaper cartoon on the corner of his desk and then studied the message from Officer Manning. He picked up the phone and dialed a private number. Turning his back to the room, he listened to the ringing until a man answered.

"That matter I talked to you about . . . I'm going to need some help."

"Right," the voice answered, then hung up.

She needed some personal things from the drugstore, things she felt uncomfortable having Luke pick up for her. Tampons, moisturizing cream, deodorant, and a prescription for birth control pills the visiting doctor had written for her. It was time to get her system back on track. Maybe going shopping was just an excuse to get out of the house after being indoors for two days, Terry thought. Of course, he had to drive her. The only time she was ever alone was in her bedroom, door still ajar, and in the bath. It was wearing.

Still, as Luke pulled the van into a curbside space, she had to admit that the thought of driving into town without his protection frightened her. She watched his hooded gaze check out each passing car, each strolling pedestrian, as he helped her down. Walking into the corner pharmacy, he stayed close behind her.

The small store was in the midst of renovation, apparently expanding to include the adjacent space recently vacated. No workers were on the scene on this Saturday afternoon, a floor-to-ceiling tarpaulin hanging along the left section to partition off the area. The place wasn't crowded, only a toddler and his mother examining the Christmas wrappings and an elderly man picking up a prescription at the back counter.

Terry moved down the deserted aisles, quickly gathering her few purchases. Would she ever get over this uneasy feeling of pending danger?

"Stay with mommy, Brian," the mother admonished the little boy as she picked up a huge bag of colorful bows. Ignoring his mother, the boy sauntered past her.

Terry reached for a Chapstick and added it to her pile. Her lips were so dry in this cool weather. She nearly bumped into Luke as she turned around.

They were at the counter paying for her purchases when the lights flickered and they heard a small popping sound. It was followed by a woman's scream.

"Oh, my God!" the young mother yelled. "Brian, what did you do?" She stared at the still form of her child on the floor by the raised tarpaulin. "Help, someone, please! My son! He's not moving!" She dropped to her knees. "Oh, God! He's not breathing!"

Luke's first thought was that someone might be setting up a diversion in order to get to Terry. He grabbed her arm, urging her toward the door. "We're leaving."

The middle-aged clerk who'd been ringing up Terry's items ran around the counter and over to the woman. "What happened?"

The druggist had also left his post and was looking down at the boy, a worried frown on his face. "Did he touch something behind the tarp? Didn't you see the sign? That area's off-limits."

"I don't know." The mother was frantic. "Oh, God, my baby's not breathing. Someone, please help!"

Terry stopped in her tracks, preventing Luke from dragging her out. "We can't leave. He's only a child. This isn't a trick," she pleaded, guessing what he was thinking. "Please, Luke, we have to help that little boy."

Luke paused. Maybe she was right. No one else was in the store. He went over to the boy, still holding on to Terry.

"Stay right here where I can see you," he told her as he knelt down.

By the tarp, he noticed a receptacle hanging out of the wall without a coverplate. By the look of the boy's burned hand, he guessed that the kid—curious as all kids were—had touched the circuit breaker which had sent electrical impulses throughout his little body. An adult might have only received a mild shock, but the small boy had been knocked unconscious.

Quickly assessing the situation, Luke glanced at the child's mother, her face pinched and anxious. "It looks like electrical shock." He looked up at the druggist who seemed stunned and immobile. "Phone 911."

Luke's tone was that of someone used to being obeyed. The druggist came out of his trance, nodded, and hurried to the phone as the others moved aside. The boy couldn't be more than four, he decided, and he was very white and lying very still. Pressing his ear to the child's chest, he listened, then applied two fingers to the pulse in his neck and found it fluttering. He was fibrillating, his heartbeat out of sync.

Luke thumped the small chest and got no response. He tilted the boy's head up and made sure his mouth was clear, then began CPR. Glancing up to make sure no one else had entered and that he could see Terry, he breathed into the boy's mouth, then placed his crossed hands on the small chest, counting softly. "One, two, three, four, five."

Working smoothly, calmly, he repeated the process while the mother held a trembling hand to her mouth and prayed, tears flowing from her eyes. Terry was praying, too. The child was so small, so still.

Seconds later, the siren of the EMS could be heard coming closer. Just then, the boy cried out and coughed, raising his head, squirming to sit up. Luke let out a relieved breath. In a move that was natural and unplanned, he cradled the child against his chest.

"Brian, Brian," his mother wailed.

The boy was crying loudly now, obviously frightened. Luke handed him over to his mother, who hugged the boy to her as if she'd never let go.

"Thank God," the druggist muttered. His concern over a possible lawsuit had him pocketing the pliers and rearranging the tarp as the EMS crew came rushing through the door.

"Come on," Luke said, hurriedly shepherding Terry outside and toward the van.

"Wait," Brian's mother called after them. "I need to thank him," she explained to the clerk who looked after the departing couple.

"We didn't pay for my things," Terry said, holding up the bag of merchandise.

Luke rushed her into the van and jumped behind the wheel. "I'm not going to worry about ten dollars worth of stuff right now. I don't want to have to answer a lot of questions." Seeing a break in traffic, he pulled out and left the scene.

Terry strapped herself in and leaned back, forcing herself to relax. "It was touch-and-go there for a while. You were really great with the boy."

Luke was uncomfortable with praise, especially for doing something he'd have walked away from if she hadn't insisted they stay. "Don't make a big thing of it. Anyone who knows CPR could have done what I did."

"But I don't know CPR and apparently no one else in the store did, either, or they'd have tried. You saved his life."

"The EMS guys would have saved him, too."

"Maybe." She studied his profile, but he was concentrating on his driving. "Can't you accept a compliment?"

Luke scowled. "All right. I was friggin' wonderful."

"You thought for a moment there that the whole thing was a setup, didn't you?"

"It could have been." He didn't want to talk about it anymore. "What do you say we go for a drive?" Without waiting for an answer, Luke maneuvered the van toward the hilly coastal road going south.

Driving aimlessly was a tension reliever. The late afternoon was still sunny, the temperature not quite fifty degrees. In the passenger seat, Terry was gazing out the side window, seemingly as glad to be out of the house as he. The traffic was light on this balmy holiday weekend.

Luke thought that she seemed contemplative and subdued after the excitement in the drugstore. She was wearing jeans, her navy jacket, and a floppy hat she'd picked up earlier and plopped on over her wig. With huge sunglasses covering half of her face, he decided that her own mother probably wouldn't recognize her. However, it wouldn't do to under-estimate the Russo brothers and their men. "We should have come earlier and brought the makings of a picnic," he said, squinting up toward a wooded section off to the left.

"Turkey sandwiches. I wish I'd thought to pack some." Her feelings had shifted again as she'd watched Luke with the boy. He'd been so gentle, yet very much in control. Then he wouldn't take credit or accept praise. A paradox of a man.

She cracked the window, breathing in the sea air. "This Big Sur area is so beautiful. Isn't the Hearst mansion along here somewhere?"

"San Simeon and no, it's farther south."

"I'd love to visit it sometime. I'll bet it's fabulous." Checking out the black rocks covered with green moss clinging to the cliffside where the tidewater tumbled in, Terry was fascinated. "Imagine being able to enjoy this view every day from one of those huge houses way up there."

"You think you'd like to live on the ocean?"

"Sure. However, with the cost of California seaside real estate, I don't think I have much chance of that."

Luke's eyes scanned the traffic, front and back, a sudden instinct warning him that something wasn't right. He knew better than to ignore his instincts. He kept his hands steady on the wheel, not wanting to prematurely upset Terry. "Who knows? You might get syndicated on your next job and become world famous." He glanced over at her. "I'll be able to say I knew you when."

"I'll be happy just to get a job again." They rode along in silence for a while, then she felt the van swerve as Luke changed lanes abruptly. "Is something wrong?"

"I don't know." Luke's eyes shifted from the rearview mirror to the windshield, studying each vehicle.

Tensing, Terry turned to look behind them, but the shaded windows kept her from seeing clearly. "What is it?" she asked, fighting a rising panic.

He watched the dark blue sedan he'd noticed minutes ago switch into their lane, staying two lengths behind them. "Probably nothing," he said in as calm a voice as possible.

Terry leaned closer to peer at the outside mirror on her side. It took her only a moment to spot it. "Oh, my God!"

Luke shot her a quick glance. "Does that look like the car you saw in the garage?"

"Not exactly. But they could have switched cars. Who else would be following us?"

# CHAPTER EIGHT

Luke slowed the van gradually, hoping the dark blue car would pass them. "We don't know yet if that car is really following us. His lane changes could be coincidental."

Terry felt anxious sweat pop out on her face. She gripped her hands together to still their shaking. "Oh, come on. You don't believe in coincidence any more than I do."

The car behind also slowed. No, he didn't believe in coincidence. His eyes darting back and forth, he spoke to Terry. "I want you to unbuckle your seat belt, move behind me, and crouch down on the floor."

"Oh, God, you *do* think it's them!" Her voice was high-pitched with the beginning of hysteria.

"Terry! Get a grip. We don't know anything for sure, but I don't want to take any chances. Do as I say." He knew how frightened she was, but he couldn't take the time to reassure her just now.

She fumbled with the seat belt, finally unlocked it. Glancing out the window nervously, she got out of her seat and moved behind, lying flat on the floor. Gripping the driver's seat, she closed her eyes and prayed.

With Terry out of the line of fire, Luke concentrated on his driving, speeding up again. In moments, the blue sedan picked up speed. He searched his memory, trying to recall the last time he'd driven this route and if he'd seen a road leading off the highway. It wasn't his nature or his training to run or to be a sitting duck. He believed that the best defense was an offense. He wasn't confrontational by design, only of necessity. But there were times when that was the best approach. Still, there was no point in being hasty.

Again, he changed lanes and cruised along, waiting and watching. Sure enough, the sedan followed.

"Are . . . are they still behind us?" Terry asked, hating the weak sound of her voice.

"Yes." The road ahead opened up and Luke saw what he'd been seeking. A narrow two-lane path led off to the left, winding upward into the wooded hillside. A smattering of homes was barely visible through the trees. He'd have to time it just right. Bracing himself for a quick turn, Luke eyed the oncoming traffic.

"What are you going to do?" Terry asked.

"Just hold tight." He was going about forty-five, but he couldn't take a chance on slowing more. They'd see him hit the brake lights. He was almost there. Waiting till the last possible second, he turned the wheel sharply left and heard the squeal of tires as the van bounced onto the dirt path. Dust flew every which way as Luke gripped the wheel, straightening out of the turn.

He was dimly aware that Terry had held on because he hadn't felt her roll to the other side. He headed up, waiting for the dust to settle so he could make sure they'd lost the sedan. Sure enough, no one was following.

Still, he kept on climbing, unable to trust the situation yet. He was rounding a hairpin turn when he spotted the blue car racing after them, speeding to catch up. He felt his gut tighten the way it always did when he knew he'd have to go head-on with someone. Or several someones.

"Are we in the clear?" Terry spoke into the silence.

"Not yet. Stay down. I'll let you know when." The shadows were deepening up here, although it was only late afternoon. Tall evergreens were densely crowded in with cedar and pine, leaving little room for the sun to break through. He'd have to pick his spot carefully, Luke knew. He wouldn't get a second chance.

Moments later, he saw that the path narrowed up ahead, leaving a sheer drop on one side and steep cliffside on the other. It would have to do. Carefully slowing, his eyes flickering from road to rearview, he bided his time. Finally, he reached the deserted stretch where the path hugged the rocky abutment. Now or never, Luke thought as he slammed to a stop, shoved it into park and reached for his gun.

"Don't move until I come back," he ordered Terry, then leaped from the van. There was no room for the sedan to move around them, so it screeched to a halt behind, its bumper nearly kissing his. Gun drawn, Luke rushed the driver's side and yanked open the door. "Get out," he shouted.

Startled, the driver just stared at the gun pointing at his face. "Hey, man, we didn't mean nothing."

Teenagers. Two scrawny teenagers with bad complexions and even worse haircuts. He hadn't figured kids would be driving a big Lincoln. The boy in the passenger seat scurried out, holding his trembling hands up in the air.

"Don't shoot, mister," he whined.

Luke's eyes were as cold as the Pacific as he jerked the driver out and shoved him against the car. "Spread 'em."

The kid obeyed. Luke could feel him twitching as he patted him down. He motioned to the other punk with his gun. "Over here."

The frightened boy joined his pal and leaned against the car while Luke checked him over. Taking a step back, he ordered them to turn around. "Just what the hell did you think you were doing following me?"

The driver swallowed around a huge Adam's apple. "We were just, you know, riding around."

Luke narrowed his eyes. "Uh huh." Gun still trained on them, he reached for his ID and flipped it open, watching their eyes grow wide. "Let me see your driver's license." The kid who'd been behind the wheel reached toward his back pocket. "Nice and slow," Luke warned. "You don't want to make me nervous."

Following orders, the kid held out his wallet.

"Take out your license." When he did, Luke saw that it was a temporary, recently issued. Steve Dawson, turned sixteen last week. He eyed the other boy. "Who's your friend?"

"Danny," Steve offered. "Danny Compton."

"Whose car?"

"My dad's," Steve answered. "Registration's in the glove compartment. He said I could drive it this afternoon, honest. You can call him and check."

"Don't think I won't." Stepping back, but keeping the two in his sight, Luke took his notebook out and copied down the information from the boy's license, plus the plate numbers. He had no plans to do anything with them, unless it became necessary. "What's your dad do, Steve?"

"Insurance agent."

"You live with him at this address on your temporary license?"

"Yeah, sure. All my life." The kid tried for pleasant, unsure just where he stood. "Look, we didn't mean any harm. We were just fooling around."

Luke stepped close to both boys, watched their eyes fill with fear as they stared at the gun rather than him. "You were deliberately following my van, even when I turned off. You couldn't see who was inside. Maybe you thought it was some helpless woman, someone you could force over and rob. Or do worse to, right, boys?"

"No," they both chorused, shaking their heads. "We were just, you know, horsing around," Steve added.

Luke handed the license back to Steve. "Don't you *ever* let me catch you doing anything like this again, you hear?"

They bobbed their heads in unison. "Now get out of here and go straight home."

Steve reached for the door handle. "You going to call my dad?"

"Maybe. Maybe not." He stood back and waited until they both got into the sedan. Then he returned to the van. Shoving it into gear, he moved ahead until he found a fork in the road. Pulling over, he let them pass, watching them speed up and zoom off. Angrily, he turned around and headed back to the highway.

"Who was it?" Terry finally asked. She'd been so frightened, not being able to hear anything but muffled voices. She'd cringed, waiting for the shot that meant that they'd killed Luke, too. Like the wimp she was, she'd stayed hidden, wondering what she'd do if they did kill him. Now, ashamed of her cowardice, she couldn't seem to get up.

"A couple of kids out joyriding." He stopped at the intersection, then swung onto the highway toward home. When she didn't return to her seat, he glanced over his shoulder. "You can come back now. It's okay."

But Terry stayed where she was until they'd pulled into the driveway and Luke turned off the engine.

Luke stood at the bottom of the steps staring up thoughtfully. Terry had been in her room since they'd returned from the drive and the incident with the blue sedan. She hadn't wanted dinner and apparently she hadn't wanted company for she'd gone straight to her room. He'd checked on her several times through the open door and found her lying curled up on her bed, her Walkman earphones in place. She wasn't asleep, but rather staring off into space.

She worried him.

He rubbed the back of his neck, wondering what to do. Should he leave her alone until she got over this mood? Should he take up some food and order her to eat before she made herself sick? Or should he just march into her room and demand an explanation for her sulky behavior?

Luke wasn't happy with any of those choices.

Damn, but women were infuriating, he thought as he walked to the kitchen window and pulled back the heavy drape. A slice of moon sprinkled the backyard with silvery light. Prince was patiently pacing the perimeter as he so often did. Not a breeze was stirring, not a leaf moving. The restlessness was confined to him alone, it seemed.

Earlier, he'd built a fire, and he strolled back to the living room to stare into it. At the time, he'd thought that Terry would come down after resting awhile and join him. At his cabin in Sedona, he'd sat many an evening gazing into his fire after a day of hard work. He'd felt soothed by watching the flames lick at the logs. Why was it that now he couldn't enjoy this fire for worrying about the woman lying upstairs looking so lost?

Unlike Jones, Luke kept himself removed from the personal problems of the witnesses assigned to him after several incidents that had nearly gotten him killed. He'd learned not to take on their troubles, not to turn himself inside out trying to keep them amused until their confinement ended. He was painfully aware that he never should have gotten to know Terry Ryan any better than the others. A protector was most effective when he was detached, impersonal, somewhat distant.

Somewhere over the past weeks, he'd lost that distance.

All right, damn it, enough! He started up the stairs.

Terry felt too weary to move, too bruised to cry. She wanted nothing more than to be in her own bed, to curl up and pull the covers over her head, to escape until she could deal with the world again. Provided that day ever came.

She was so very tired, yet afraid to sleep for she knew that tonight, she'd dream, reliving that nightmare chase. This whole thing was never going to end. She must have angered the gods but good, for she seemed destined to spend the rest of her days and nights running, trembling, frightened.

Setting aside her earphones, she sat up and reached to the nightstand for a tissue and blew her nose. It was then that she saw Luke standing in the doorway, his face stormy. What rule had she violated this time to upset him still again? Calmly, she waited for the explosion.

If he'd come upon her sobbing, he might have walked away, unable to deal with a distraught woman weeping. But he'd stood watching the silent anguish on her face, and she'd gotten to him. Though he felt a shade out of his element, he stepped into the room and walked over to look down at her.

It wasn't like the night he'd charged into her room with his gun drawn and scared her. He saw no fear this time, just sadness and fatigue. She'd removed her contacts and head-scarf, and wore only jeans and a blue sweater, her feet bare. She looked much younger than he knew her to be, yet the awareness in her deep blue eyes was very much that of a woman.

He didn't know what to say to her, so he said nothing. Instead, he sat down on the bed, scooted back to the side-wall, and gently eased her into his arms. He felt her stiffen for a moment, resisting the contact. Then she let out a sigh, wound her arms around him, and snuggled into his chest. Luke let out a breath he hadn't known he'd been holding.

She was so slender, scarcely a hundred pounds, a fragile mound beneath his big hands. He was reminded of a song that spoke of the trembling heart of a captive bird. As the memory formed, Luke frowned, unused to entertaining fanciful thoughts. He certainly didn't consider himself a tender man, yet Terry Ryan moved him to a sensitivity he hadn't known he possessed.

Against his shirt, he could feel her eyelashes as she blinked, so he knew she wasn't dropping off to sleep. Yet she lay against him so still, so quiet. He reacted instinctively, not thinking so much about what he was doing as much as letting his feelings guide him.

His one hand gently stroked her back, his touch one of comfort and nothing else. His other hand strayed to her hair, his fingers exploring the baby-fine texture, letting her know with slow caresses that the short length didn't bother him the way it bothered her. Gradually, he felt her breathing change and knew the instant she began to respond.

She shifted slightly in his arms, her hands on his back subtly drawing him closer. The warm female scent of her wrapped around him and he breathed in deeply. A warning bell sounded in the back of his mind, and Luke knew he was wandering into dangerous territory. He was too smart for this, too well trained to allow his senses to dictate to his brain.

But the message didn't get through. His arms tightened around her as he lowered his head, his cheek resting on her hair. It felt so good to hold her, to feel the flutter of her heart against his. When was the last time he'd simply held a woman, making no demands, expecting nothing? He couldn't remember if he ever had.

If his intention had been to empty her mind of fear, Terry thought, then it was working. Suddenly she could think of nothing but how it felt to be held against that hard, strong body, of how safe she felt for the first time in weeks. He was so big, so solid. And for once, he wasn't issuing orders or being cool, controlled, and standoffish. He was being human.

How had he known how badly she'd needed the touch of another human being? How could this tough, focused lawman have ever seen the need hidden beneath the facade she'd shown him? How could he have guessed that she'd wanted this so badly?

But she couldn't indulge herself too long, couldn't take advantage of his kindness, couldn't take a chance that he'd misinterpret her need for comfort for another more basic need.

Slowly, Terry pulled back and sat away, not meeting his eyes. "I'm all right now. Thanks." She felt awkward, even a little embarrassed.

Luke studied the dusting of golden freckles across her small nose, so common to the Irish. His gaze moved to her mouth, full and soft and inviting. He knew she felt self-conscious about her looks since the accident. He didn't have the words to tell her that she was lovely in his eyes. He'd let his actions speak for him.

He reached to tilt her chin upward so she had to look at him. He saw the need in the blue depths of her eyes, and gave in to his own. In one swift movement, he touched his mouth to hers and drew her back into his arms.

Surprise had her lips parting and he seized the moment to send his tongue in to mate with hers. She didn't struggle, didn't move at all. Then she breathed a soft sigh and gave herself up to the kiss.

He'd expected shyness, hesitancy, a touch of reserve. Instead she kissed him back, fully, completely, her taste exploding on his tongue. His hands roamed her back as he shifted, slanting his mouth more firmly over hers, taking her deeper. She didn't kiss like a wounded bird, but rather like a woman who was making his heated blood race through his veins.

Luke couldn't have said later how long the kiss lasted. But suddenly he knew as surely as he knew his own name that he never should have touched her, that he'd started something he might not be able to stop if he didn't end it right now. Pulling back, breathing hard, he stared into eyes still hazy with passion unexpectedly aroused.

What in hell had he done?

Terry saw the regret on his face, and looked away. "Are you playing games with me?" she asked softly.

"No. I wanted to reassure you and . . . " He rubbed the

back of his neck, disgusted with himself. "Oh, hell. I wanted to kiss you and I did. No big deal."

No big deal. Anger replaced the last vestiges of desire. "Do you kiss all the women you're assigned to protect?"

He almost flinched at that one. "No."

She scooted off the bed, her bare feet cold on the floor, and hugged herself in a classically defensive posture. "No, of course not. Then you must have kissed me because I'm so beautiful, so irresistible, with my perfect face and my gorgeous hair." She watched a frown appear and rushed on. "No, I thought not. You kissed me because you felt sorry for me, the poor little battered, bald waif. Well, I don't need your pity, thank you very much." She whirled away from him, choking back the tears that threatened to fall.

"Pity?" Luke got to his feet, grabbed her arm and swung her around to face him. Before she could react, he yanked her close and crushed his mouth to hers.

This was no sweet, tender kiss, no slow exploration, no tentative mating dance. His mouth devoured, his tongue plundered, and his arms molded her body to his with a ruthlessness just barely held in check. He drank from her, deeply, thoroughly, and finally felt her stunned response.

Terry's hands moved up his back, her fingers digging into his shoulders as she hung on, scarcely able to stay upright, her knees wobbly. She tasted his anger and felt his strength as he held her in a bone-crushing grip. She'd thought him dangerous from the moment she'd first laid eyes on him, but hadn't realized until now how much control he'd exerted over his emotions. She'd made him mad and he'd unleashed the fury that lay just beneath the surface.

Yet she didn't fear him, not physically. Senses swimming from the passionate onslaught, she knew her greatest fear centered around the way he could so effortlessly make her feel. Alive, aware, throbbing with needs she could scarcely put a name to. What defenses did she have against all that?

Just as abruptly, he wrenched his mouth away and let her

go. He watched her take a staggering step backward to maintain her balance, and felt a fresh rush of anger at what he'd done. No, he never should have touched her. But she'd pushed him too far.

"Did that feel like pity to you?" Luke asked, his voice thick. Without waiting for her answer, he left the room and went downstairs.

No, that definitely hadn't felt like pity. Terry walked to the wall mirror and studied her reflection. Her eyes were bright and shining, her mouth swollen from his kisses. She licked her lips and tasted him. The truth was staring her in the face, the truth she'd denied even to herself.

She wanted Luke Tanner and now he knew it, too.

The phone rang at ten that evening, surprising Luke. Only Jones had the number. At this late hour, he doubted if his commanding officer had called for a chat. He'd been sitting staring into the cooling embers of the fire, going over the scene in Terry's bedroom, wondering what he should have done differently. He welcomed the diversion as he went to the kitchen and picked up on the third ring.

"Luke? We've got a problem," Jones said without hesitation.

He listened quietly, taking notes, asking a few questions. Less than ten minutes later, he was taking the stairs two at a time.

The door to Terry's room was ajar and the bedside lamp was on low. She was lying on the bed, staring at the ceiling. She turned to the doorway, a question in her eyes, a guarded look on her face.

"We have to move out," Luke told her. "Get dressed and pack up your stuff."

She sat up, the fear returning rapidly. "Why? What's happened?"

"There's been another killing."

***

Terry sat in the passenger seat of the van trying to sort out her jumbled thoughts as Luke turned onto Highway 1 heading south. They'd left at precisely ten-forty, after he'd piled everything they'd brought with them into the van. Prince was sitting up on the seat behind Luke looking out the window, his ears sharp and alert. She hadn't asked any questions yet, knowing there wasn't time. Luke wouldn't have been rushing them along if there wasn't a real sense of urgency.

She glanced at his profile now and saw that steely control clearly visible. She'd seen him soften only twice, when he'd held the little boy he'd saved in the drugstore and earlier when he'd kissed her senseless. But she didn't want to think about that right now.

"Will you tell me where we're headed?" she began, needing to know. After all, this was her life, too.

"A safe house up a mountain trail in Big Sur. Used to be owned by a millionaire named Higgins as a sort of getaway cabin. He had it built for his mistress, or so I was told. He's in prison for a long stretch. Tax evasion."

She'd told him earlier today when they'd been out driving around—Lord, had that been less than eight hours ago?—that she'd like to live in Big Sur. But she hadn't meant in hiding. "You said there'd been another killing? Who died?"

He'd wondered when she'd get around to asking. He was getting to know her, the way she mulled things over in that sharp mind, then began questioning. "A police officer named Neil Manning."

"What's he got to do with us?"

"Manning was partnered with a cop named Jerry Foster who was gunned down in a Phoenix alley the same night your reporter friend was killed. At first, Jones wasn't sure there was a connection. Then when they started poking around and found evidence of money laundering and corrupt cops, the Federal investigators became fairly certain that Foster was involved and was the one Simon was going to meet that night. So they started leaning on Manning to see if he knew anything." Luke slowed down, realizing that he'd been speeding. This was no time to be pulled over with explanations required.

"And did he?"

"We'll never know. He was roommates with Foster and he was settling the guy's estate. A good guess is that he probably ran across something incriminating in going through Foster's papers. He called Lieutenant Remington and set up an appointment to see him in person. Said he wanted to talk over something he couldn't discuss on the phone. We also know that Manning's new partner told him that the Feds wanted to talk with him. But apparently Manning felt more comfortable with Remington. Then, when he didn't show and didn't report for his shift either, Remington sent a couple of cops to his apartment. They found Manning dead in the shower, the water still running. Coroner said the head wounds were more in keeping with a beating than a fall. The apartment had been professionally searched and stripped clean."

Terry felt a shiver take her. "Then it wasn't an accident?"

"No, that's why I told you there'd been another killing. The Feds couldn't find anything to indicate what Manning felt was so important. The apartment was clean as a whistle, no fingerprints, no papers, nada." He glanced over at her and saw the worried frown. "Do you know this Remington? Did he used to come over to your father's house, too?"

"No, they didn't socialize, but I've heard Dad speak of him for years, and I've met Phil. He's a gentleman cop, as Dad used to say. Didn't start out walking a beat, but came right out of college, then graduated at the top of his class at the Academy. He's good-looking and knows it. He dresses beautifully, but there's something about him that keeps people at a distance. An aloofness, I guess. I understand he's next in line for the captain's job when Marino retires."

"What about Marino? Do you think he's clean?"

"Lord, I don't know. It's not like I hung around the precinct, you know. Most of my impressions are second-hand, through my father's opinions. I'd sure like to know how Dad feels about Mac. That must have been a shock."

"Were Mac and Remington buddies?"

She frowned thoughtfully. "I don't know. They worked together, but they're very different men. They don't seem the type to be friends in their off hours." She peered over at him in the dim light of the dash. "Do you suspect everyone at Central?"

"Pretty much, until this is over and we can clear them. There's Mac and Foster, maybe Manning. I'd be willing to bet there are more."

"You think this Manning was on the take, too?"

"Could be. Or he could've found something and tried fleecing the big boys. When they wouldn't play, he decided to turn them in to Remington. The boys heard about his call and saw to it that he had a little accident in the shower. It has all the earmarks of a professional hit."

"It all sounds so calculated, so cold-blooded."

"That's because it is." Luke turned off the highway, down a side street, and into a Chevron station. He looked the place over, then pulled up next to the rest rooms. "See that green van over there? We're going to transfer our stuff into that on the off chance that someone has made this one. I'm going to check out the ladies' room and, after I do, I want you to wait inside there until I come get you."

"Why can't I help you move our stuff? I don't want to wait in some crummy rest room."

Luke swung his cool gaze to her face, back to being the Federal Agent again. "Will you just do as I say?"

Terry sighed heavily. She wouldn't like it, but she'd do it. "Can I take Prince in with me?"

He nodded as he jumped out of the van.

In twenty minutes, they were on the road again in their

new van. If possible, it was outfitted with even more gadgets than the prior one. Terry was continually amazed at what Bob Jones could accomplish with a couple of phone calls. She glanced back at Prince curled up on the backseat, apparently having decided they'd be spending many more hours traveling through the night.

"How much farther is this Higgins house?" she asked Luke.

He rubbed an old scar near his right temple that always ached when he was tense. Relocating was always the hardest on his nerves. "It's not all that far, but after we leave the highway, the road becomes little more than a path. Big Sur is very much a private community, with some of the strictest building codes and restrictions in California, if not the country. Homes or buildings may not be visible from the highway, so they're all tucked up in the hills among the rocks and trees. Great for our purposes, but the devil to find the first time."

"So you've never been to this place either?"

"No, but Bob tells me it's about as safe and secure as they make them. You might even get your view of the beach from up there." Spotting the sign he'd been seeking, he turned off the highway onto a narrow road that stretched straight up.

A light coastal fog had rolled in, swirling around the bent cypress trees and much taller redwoods and pines. It was chilly out, but warm and cozy in the van with the heater on. As they climbed, Terry became aware of the utter blackness surrounding them, with only the headlights shining ahead. The highway far below was no longer visible nor were there streetlights. If they passed houses, the inhabitants must all be asleep, for it was dark everywhere. It was a decidedly eerie feeling.

Luke drove slowly and with great care, knowing that if he missed a turn up here and crashed, they probably wouldn't be found for a long while.

Terry's thoughts were back in Phoenix with the slain police officers. "Did either of those men killed have families?"

"Manning never married. Foster was divorced with two kids."

"Who do you suppose killed them?"

"Could have been Ozzie Swain, the gunman whose picture you drew. Or Sam Russo's brother, Nick. Or some other scumbag who works for the Russo brothers or the mob."

"I'm not sure I understand why we had to relocate just because this policeman was killed."

It was the question he'd been wanting to avoid. "Just a precaution," he hedged.

Silently, Terry studied his profile. The mouth that had worked such magic on hers was once more a grim line. And suddenly she knew. "It's because I'm the only one who's seen the killers and can identify them, isn't it? Before they had Manning, who *might* have told them something. But now . . ." Her voice trailed off.

Luke felt a muscle in his cheek clench as he gritted his teeth. She was too damn smart for her own peace of mind. And he wasn't about to lie to her. Pausing to downshift at the base of a hill, he turned to her. "Yes, that's why." He watched her swallow hard, then turn toward the side window.

They rode the rest of the way in silence. Even following the map he'd quickly drawn, Luke nearly missed the turn into the winding drive of the cabin nestled under a large natural rock overhang.

"Not very big, is it?" Terry commented, glad to have something else to settle her mind on other than the Russo brothers.

The house wasn't, but the yard was, with a six-foot cyclone fence and lots of trees and shrubs. Luke opened the gate, parked the van in the carport, returned to close the gate, making a note to get a lock tomorrow. "I'm going to leave

Prince with you while I have a look around the grounds."
Getting out, he turned on his high-beam flashlight.

Terry saw that it was nearly midnight. She'd be glad to
get some sleep, and perhaps she could after this tiring day.
There hadn't been a calm moment since the incident in the
drugstore, the chase with the blue sedan, the kisses that had
left her shaken and needy, and now this night run. Not your
ordinary day.

Luke returned and released Prince into the yard, where he
immediately began sniffing around. "I'll help you inside,
then come back for our stuff." He led the way to the front
door and used the keys he'd gotten when he'd picked up the
green van. Shoving open the door, he leaned in, groped for a
wall switch, and turned on the lights. As Terry waited on the
porch, he glanced inside, making sure the rooms were empty.

Returning, he had a look of amusement on his face as he
held the door for her. "You're going to love this place."

Her curiosity aroused, Terry stepped in. Her gaze slid
around the room as her mouth opened in stunned surprise.
"My God! This isn't a house. It's a bordello!"

# CHAPTER NINE

Luke closed the door behind them, then swung around, placing his hands on his hips as Terry strolled around. They were both a little awestruck. The carpeting was plush and very white, the furniture black leather grouped around low glass-topped tables. Mirrors of all sizes framed in gold were hung on all four of the walls covered in shiny red paper that managed to look like patent leather. A bearskin rug complete with snarling head was spread in front of a brick fireplace. The ceiling was painted with something silvery and iridescent, giving the effect of twinkling stars.

Bordello was an apt description, Luke thought, unable to resist smiling at Terry's shocked face. "I guess this is Higgins's idea of a little love nest."

"It's like a movie set," she said, venturing farther and passing a small kitchen area off to the side. There were two closed doors on the left. "I can hardly wait to see the rest." She swung open the first door and began to laugh. "You won't believe this."

Luke came alongside and peered in. The entire bathroom was mirrored, walls and ceiling. There was an elaborate black sunken tub and a glassed-in shower with brass fixtures fashioned to resemble animals' heads. "There's no accounting for taste," Luke muttered as he walked over to shove open the connecting door. His hand found the wall light switch.

Terry walked into a bedroom such as she'd never before seen. A huge heart-shaped bed with a brass headboard dominated the room, with a long couch covered in what looked to be red satin tucked under the high window. A television screen that had to be five feet across was at the far end, and gold Kewpie dolls frolicked along the ornate ceiling border. "This is incredible," she commented, moving inside. "How old is this Higgins fellow?"

"In his sixties, as I understand."

"Must be every man's fantasy, to stash a mistress away in a place like this."

"Not every man." Luke strolled over to glance at the titles on the stack of movies alongside the VCR. As he'd guessed, they were largely porno films. "I'll bring the bags in."

Still looking around, Terry followed him into the main room. "There's only one bed in this house, Luke."

"Yeah, I noticed. Don't worry. I'll take the couch." He stepped outside as Prince ran up to meet him.

After carrying their things in and setting out a bowl of water for the Doberman, Luke went to the Pullman kitchen to help Terry put away the food they'd hastily packed. "We can give it a couple of days, then drive inland to some small town and get anything else we need."

Terry stacked canned goods in the cupboards. "How did Bob Jones activate the electricity and phone from Phoenix, or does he call someone to come up here and turn things on for us?"

"The Feds have connections all over," Luke answered vaguely. He placed the coffeepot on the counter, then picked up the phone. "Not working yet, but probably by tomorrow."

Finished, she walked back into the main room. "I can't imagine why the government would want this place."

Luke shrugged. "Beggars can't be choosers. We take what's available. Besides, who'd think we'd be hiding someone out in this brothel-like atmosphere?"

"You've got a point there." Terry yawned expansively. It had been a long, tiring day. "I think I'm going to turn in." She glanced over at the leather couches by the fireplace. They looked cold and uninviting, but at least they were both long enough. "There must be extra blankets somewhere. I'll help you make up your bed, if you like."

He followed her gaze. "Oh, I'm not sleeping out here. I meant the couch in the bedroom."

"The . . . you're kidding!" She'd figured she'd have trouble sleeping in that odd bed as it was. How could she manage to drop off with him less than four feet away?

"No, I'm not. These couches are too far away. I wouldn't be able to see you." He turned off the kitchen light and waved toward the room. "After you."

There was no point in arguing with Luke once he'd made up his mind, even if she weren't too tired to do so. Silently, Terry marched into the bathroom and closed both doors.

Who in the hell would think to upholster a couch in satin? Luke thought as for the umpteenth time he rescued the pillow that kept sliding out from under his head. The only spare cover he could find was a satin comforter which he barely kept on even when he clamped his legs around it. He hoped Higgins was equally uncomfortable in his jail cell.

He'd left a night-light burning in the bathroom, and the door ajar. It was pitch-black outside, the moon hidden by a heavy cloud cover, so only the dim glow could be seen from across the room. To his right, in the center of a bed that seemed larger than a king despite its weird shape, Terry lay with her back to him. As far as he could tell, she hadn't moved since she'd slipped under her own satin coverlet. Where did a man get sheets for a heart-shaped bed? And how'd Higgins manage to conjure up the nerve to buy the damn thing in the first place?

Luke shifted and the pillow slid off once again. Swearing under his breath, he grabbed it in a death grip and jammed it under his head. He'd stayed in a lot of peculiar places during his years with the marshals office, but this cabin had to be up there among the oddest. He'd watched over many a witness also, yet Terry Ryan stood out from the crowd.

Unbidden, thoughts of the way she'd kissed him back returned to plague him, and his body hardened. A lot of passion locked away inside that small form, he couldn't help thinking. After that first moment of hesitation, she'd thrown herself into the kiss, holding nothing back. He'd been seconds away from slipping his hands under her shirt and closing his fingers over the breasts he'd felt pressing against his chest, warm and womanly.

He'd stopped in time, thank goodness. He'd remembered that he was supposed to be her guardian, not her seducer. He'd felt like a rat, wanting to be her lover when what she needed was a friend. But then she'd turned to him with that wounded look in those big eyes, sure he'd just been feeling sorry for her. Hell, it hadn't been anything near pity. It had been lust, pure and simple. Well, maybe not so pure, but it surely was simple, at least in his book. Put an attractive female into his arms and his body reacted.

Only he shouldn't have let it get that far, not with this female. This one was more vulnerable than almost any he'd run across, and he still felt the heel for having touched her. But even as guilt washed over him, he had to admit he still wanted her. If circumstances were different, he'd leap up off this damnable couch, crawl into that joke of a bed, and make love to her until neither of them could move. Then they'd both sleep far better.

For he knew Terry wasn't asleep. There was just enough light that he could see that her breathing was erratic, not the slow steady rhythm of someone asleep. Was she awake because of the nerve-wracking day she'd experienced? Was it because she wasn't used to someone being in her room? Or was it because *he* was that someone in her room?

In the bed, Terry changed positions, but still didn't turn to face him. Just as well. He hadn't shut his eyes yet and he didn't particularly want her to know that. It had been monumentally stupid of him to pull her into that second kiss. He'd wanted to reassure her that she was still attractive. Instead, he'd revealed that he wanted her. And that knowledge sat between them like an uninvited guest, already getting in the way of everything they did and said.

Sighing, Luke squirmed uncomfortably. He wasn't used to sleeping in his jeans, but he'd thought it best. They were too tight, too confining. With an oath, he threw aside the cover and got up.

"What's wrong?" Terry asked from the bed.

"Nothing. Go to sleep." Grabbing his shirt, Luke left the room and walked to the fireplace. He wished he had a cigarette. He wished he was back at his place in Sedona, where he'd slept like a baby, worn out by a hard day's work. He fervently wished he'd never agreed to take this case.

"I knew you'd come through, Oz," Nick Russo said into the phone. "Sam's going to be pleased."

"Why? Did he think I'd desert?" The voice was hoarse from a chronic smoker's cough.

Nick didn't think he should say that that was exactly what he and his brother had been thinking. "Nah, nothing like that. Where are you now?"

"Over the border. That's all you need to know." Swain wasn't sure he trusted Nickie. Sam was the one who usually gave the orders. The younger brother was the nervous sort and trigger-happy. He needed seasoning. That's why Ozzie meant to do everything he could to spring Sam. Then the Russo brothers would owe him, big time.

"How about the girl? You got a line on her whereabouts?"

"I'm working on it. I'll tell you this much, my California sources say she's there and you'll never guess who's with her?"

Lighting a cigarette, Nick thought he knew the answer. "Luke Tanner?"

"You got it."

"Shit!"

"You got anything new to tell me at your end?"

Nick blew smoke at the ceiling. "I wish. The Feds are all over the place, investigating the reporter's death, Foster, and now Manning."

"They didn't buy the accidental death, eh?"

"No, but they got no proof. You're in the clear."

"Yeah, sure, except word is they want me real bad. I took a big chance coming back in town. I hope Sam knows it's going to cost him."

"Oz, you know Sam takes care of his own. Find the girl and you'll be the golden prince. Know what I mean?" Nick was itching to do it himself, but the cops were watching his every move. He'd gone to the track the other day, and one followed him into the men's room. They didn't even bother to keep their distance. It was getting on his nerves, making him jumpy.

"Yeah, I know."

"The man says you got to move fast on this. Mac's threatening to call a news conference."

Ozzie stuck a toothpick in his mouth and shoved it to the corner. "Tell the man to quit stewing or he's going to blow this wide open. I said I'd take care of it and I will."

"Okay, Oz, but we ain't got a lot of time left. Prosecutor's aiming for a trial date shortly after the holidays, probably mid-January. We drew Carmichael on the bench. That's why Mac's sweating. That judge'll lock him up and throw away the key. You know Mac. He ain't going down alone."

"Tell Mac to sit tight and keep his lip buttoned. There's worse sentences than prison, you get my drift?"

"Yeah, right. Stay in touch."

The line went dead in Nick's ear. He hung up, took out his handkerchief, wiped his sweaty face, then drew deeply on the stub of his cigarette before crushing it out. Damn but he wished this whole thing was over and Sam was back. Running the operation alone was no breeze. The guys were getting nervous, antsy. He could put off the big boys only so long. Nick desperately wanted to put it all out of his mind, to go to Vegas for a couple of days, get a couple of broads, and just have fun.

But first, he had to get Sam out.

He ran a worried hand over his black hair. Maybe they shouldn't trust Ozzie so much. Maybe he should go himself, find the girl, take her out. Maybe he should lean on the old man, see if he knew anything.

Luke Tanner's image popped into his mind. He'd had a gut feeling ever since Sam had mentioned his name that Tanner was involved. So he'd tracked the wily agent to Sedona and learned that he'd bought a ranch, but Luke hadn't been there in weeks. Now, with Sam's hunch and Ozzie's pals reporting a sighting, he was sure Tanner was with the Ryan girl somewhere in California. Nick grinned. Maybe he could get two birds with one stone.

Why should Ozzie get the prize, be a hero to Sam? Ozzie was chickenshit. Nick was number two man, and he intended to stay second-in-command. Squaring his shoulders, he grabbed his car keys. Whistling, he went out the door.

The ax cut into the bark of the Douglas fir with a satisfying crack. Luke pulled back and repeated the swing, chopping into the same groove. He'd already made a small vee on the opposite side. It wasn't a very big tree. A couple more whacks and that should do it. He took aim again.

From a safe distance, Terry watched the tree-cutting ceremony with mixed emotions. On the one hand, she was pleased that Luke had suggested they find a Christmas tree and take it back to the cabin to decorate with whatever they could find. On the other hand, she wasn't sure that the contrast of this makeshift tree with the ones she remembered from her past might not be her undoing.

Hard to believe that tomorrow would be Christmas Day. She'd managed to keep her spirits, if not joyful, at least not despondent over the past two weeks that they'd been staying in the bordello bungalow, as they called it. But as the twenty-fifth approached, she'd had to struggle to keep the tears at bay.

To his credit, Luke had left her alone when she got in those moods. And he'd surprised her with his perception when he'd suggested cutting down a tree this morning. Because of his effort, she was determined to keep a smile in place. She wouldn't be having a Christmas as usual, but at least she'd be having one. Unlike Lynn, who was gone forever.

She could only imagine what her parents and Aunt Julia, plus her brothers and nephews would be going through this holiday. They couldn't possibly miss her more than she missed them. Having to stay in this ludicrous house with still no word on when the trial would begin and her exile would end was definitely taking a toll on her.

As was being in such close quarters with Luke Tanner.

Though he slept—or tried to sleep—on the couch next to her bed every night, he otherwise had kept his distance from her ever since the night they'd shared those powerful kisses. She knew he remembered, as she did, for she'd turn and catch him looking at her in a way he couldn't disguise quickly enough. He rarely touched her even by accident, and he kept his remarks studiously impersonal. He spent much of each day outside with Prince or by the fire whittling figures from pieces of wood he'd found nearby.

She also kept busy separately, cooking time-consuming

recipes to eat up the hours, drawing enough sketches to fill two art pads and reading every paperback she could pick up on their rare visits to nearby towns for supplies. They talked, of course, and the tone was friendly even. But it was as two barely acquainted coworkers in the same building might.

Yet there was a tension between them as real as their independent efforts to deny it.

"Timber!" Luke sang out as the fir hit the ground. Up the hill confined behind the fence, Prince's sharp ears picked up the sound and he barked in response. He'd decided not to let the dog run loose on their occasional walks along the trails for the big Doberman had a tendency to wander.

"Now what?" Terry wanted to know. "Surely you aren't planning on carrying that big tree back yourself?"

Luke hefted the trunk up with one gloved hand and hoisted the ax over his other shoulder. "Now, we drag it back."

"Aha! I guess I never would have made it in the wilderness." She fell in step with him as they headed back to the cabin, thinking that he looked every inch the outdoor woodsman. Since their arrival at this cabin, he hadn't shaved and he hadn't had a haircut since joining her nearly two months ago. She rather liked his new look, though the change made his lean face appear even more dangerous.

"Does your family open gifts on Christmas Eve or Christmas morning?" Luke asked.

"Christmas Eve after dinner. Then we all go to midnight Mass." She felt uncomfortable discussing the holiday, not just because she was away from her family, but because she couldn't help but wonder what Luke and Bob Jones had had in the way of Christmas celebrations spending years at a boys' ranch. Not much, she imagined.

She had a face that expressed her every emotion, Luke thought, studying her as they strolled together. "We used to open ours on Christmas morning," he said softly, giving in to an odd need to reassure her that those years hadn't been all bad. He caught her surprised glance and shifted his gaze to the clouds in a darkening sky. "Different churches would collect things and distribute them to us. Gloves, slippers, scarves, hand-knit sweaters. Cookies and homemade fudge. Footballs and secondhand bikes. We did all right."

Sure they did. Her heart went out to the boy he'd been, the one who'd known neither a father's love nor a mother's. She searched her mind for a change of subject. "I don't suppose if you were back in Sedona that you'd be bothering with a tree. Thanks for going to the trouble for me."

"It's an experiment, really. I want to see what you can come up with in the bordello bungalow to decorate this thing."

Terry smiled up at him. "Just you wait and see."

She surprised him with her inventiveness. She'd strung together popcorn on one line, cranberries on another. She'd clipped pictures with unusual shapes from magazines and fastened them to the branches with bits of thread from a sewing kit she'd found. She'd cut strips of red satin cloth found in the same kit and made them into streamers for the tree. She'd found a holly bush and added sprigs from that. And she'd fashioned a big silver star from aluminum foil for the top. In lieu of lights, she'd propped his high-beam flashlight so that it shined on the tree.

"There, what do you think?" she asked, standing back.

Hands crossed over his chest, he surveyed all sides of the tree, his brow furrowed. "Best damn tree in all of Big Sur. Maybe in all of California."

Terry gathered up the remnants of her decorations. "You're making fun of me."

"No, actually, I'm not." He stopped in front of her. "I like it far better than those professionally done trees. Your tree has meaning. It has . . . " He paused, searching for the right word.

"Heart," she offered, because that's what homemade trees meant to her. "My mother's tree has all these ornaments all four of us made in school when we were little. Rice Krispies dyed and glued together in the shape of stars and wreaths. Reindeer made from pipe cleaners. Cotton pasted on as a beard for Santas cut out of red cardboard. She saved them all."

His eyes warmed as he looked into hers. "Yeah, that's what I mean." He took the trash from her and went outside to dump it.

Terry stood looking after him, wishing she could have gotten him a Christmas gift, something small but meaningful. She had a feeling Luke hadn't had many meaningful gifts in his lifetime. He was a paradox, this hard man who would deny having any soft feelings. Yet he had them and he craved them in return, she was sure of it.

But would he ever acknowledge what he thought of as a weakness?

Emily removed John Ryan's shoes and heard him grunt a response as she maneuvered his legs up onto the bed. Gently she pulled the blanket up to cover him, then stood looking down at her husband of over thirty years.

Ten-thirty on Christmas Eve and he was passed out drunk. This hadn't happened on a holiday since the year Kathleen had died. Emily knew why John drank these days. But she could do little to lighten his sorrow. She had her own fair share to deal with.

John let out a deep snore and shifted in his sleep. Would he ever be the same, either way? Emily wondered. This stress wasn't good for his heart. Would another attack take him before long? He hadn't been drinking, at least, not until tonight. He also hadn't been eating well and he'd lost weight.

With a heavy sigh, Emily switched off the bedside light and left their bedroom. She'd sent the kids on to mass, telling them she'd be along. Wearily, feeling older than her fifty-four years, she went to the closet for her coat.

Only in prayer, it seemed, did she place any hope or find even temporary peace.

It would come over her at the oddest moments, Luke noticed. Terry would get that faraway look in her eyes and he knew she was remembering. Her family, her friends, the life she'd had to give up. Sometimes she'd go to the bedroom and listen to her Walkman until the mood passed. Other times she'd curl up on the couch, unaware he was watching her, and the trembling would take over. She'd hug her knees tightly while she stared into the fire, seeing other scenes, he was certain.

All were symptoms of Post Traumatic Stress Disorder. He'd been taught how to help someone through those episodes, by talking soothingly to them until the spell passed, or holding them until they could fight their way back, and even walking with them with an arm around a shoulder, letting them know someone understood. But, except for that evening she'd let him hold her, Terry didn't appear to want his help.

That was his fault, more than likely. The one time he'd reached out to comfort, he'd soon been touching her in a way that had nothing to do with comfort. Probably she was afraid of allowing him too close for fear she'd find herself in a situation she was too bruised to be able to handle. He couldn't blame her.

She'd managed to make it through the holidays, but two days after Christmas, he noticed she was pacing in that restless way that preceded a bout with her disturbing memories. He'd spoken with Bob Jones earlier, hoping he'd have some good news that he could pass on to Terry. But, although a judge had been assigned, the trial date was yet to be decided. That news had depressed her. But maybe he could come up with a diversion and get her mind off her troubles.

He walked over to where she was standing looking out the window. "What do you say we pack a picnic lunch and go for a hike up one of the mountain trails? I think we're both getting cabin fever from being cooped up so long."

Terry shoved her hands into her jeans pockets. "I don't know." She frowned at the distant hill dotted with shrubs and manzanita. What if someone was out there waiting for her with a high-powered rifle?

"It's a beautiful day. Come on. The exercise will do us both good."

She watched a blue heron land in the top of a pine tree, its wingspan awesome. She'd always enjoyed nature, enjoyed hiking the trails in Phoenix, though the California mountains were much higher and more rugged. Back then, she hadn't been afraid of anything. Now she jumped at shadows, cringed at sudden noises, cried out in her sleep. "I'd like to, but . . . "

Luke turned her to face him. "Terry, I won't let anything happen to you. Do you trust me?"

She did, as far as that went. But no one man could think of everything, be everywhere. And did she trust herself not to fall apart up there if the fear took over? "Yes, I trust you. And I am tired of being inside, but I can't help being afraid. You told me any stranger might be a hired gunman."

He had told her that to keep her from being careless, to get her to follow orders. But what good would staying alive be if her mind cracked from the strain? "We're not apt to run into anyone up this almost-deserted mountain. I'll be armed as always. We won't go far, just up around the other side, where we can see the ocean. All right?"

In the end, she agreed, and later, as they sat on a plaid blanket from the van and drank coffee from the thermos and nibbled on cold chicken, Terry was glad she'd allowed Luke to talk her into going. Her hands curled around the warm mug, she drew in a deep breath of clean, salty air and watched the distant waves bounce against the rocky shoreline. "It is beautiful up here. The sea's more hypnotic than staring into a fire."

Stretched out and braced on his elbows, Luke watched several pelicans prance along the frothy water. "I can't blame you for wishing you lived up here." His glance took in the area surrounding them. "I wonder where all the homes are." They hadn't passed but one on the way up, and that one was near their own cabin. Through his binoculars, he'd seen an older man wearing overalls outside that sprawling house. He'd been carrying what looked like a BB gun that he used to take pot shots at a flock of noisy crows.

"You couldn't wish for a more private area." She watched a sandpiper land in the golden grass near a scrub California black oak and begin scavenging for food. "It's so peaceful up here. You can almost forget that that highway leads to all manner of rotten people just waiting to hurt others."

Luke shifted to study her face and saw the unmistakable signs of stress. He saw also the two areas of scar tissue that would need more plastic surgery. He'd tried to bring that up again recently, but Terry had refused to consider anything to do with doctors right now. He'd wanted to press, had been told by her last doctor that there would be less corrective work necessary if she didn't wait too long. But he also understood her reluctance to face more pain after all she'd been through. It would be easier once all this was over.

He searched for words that might make her feel better. "Terry, I know you don't think so now, but one day, all this will be in the past, a terrible nightmare but one you got through. You're a survivor. You'll be all right. I know because I've been through this with a lot of other people."

She turned to look at him. "And they all came through with flying colors, all walked back into their former lives and picked up the threads as if nothing had happened?"

"I didn't say it would be easy, but in time, it will be over."

"Did anyone you had in the program ever just decide to drop out, to take their chances?" She'd been wondering about this for some time.

Luke sat up, the image of Jill Hastings appearing in his mind's eye. "Only one that was under my protection, a woman."

"Had she been on the run with you like me, moving from place to place at a moment's notice?"

"Yes."

"How long?"

He poured more coffee into his mug. "About four months."

Terry angled her body around so she could see him better. "Did she just decide to walk away one morning?"

"Not exactly. It's a long story." One he didn't want to tell nor even remember.

She touched his arm, something she rarely did. "Please tell me. I need to know."

Under the circumstances, she was a hard woman to refuse. He took a sip of his coffee, wondering where to begin. "Jill Hastings was her name and she was a registered nurse on private duty at the home of this wealthy California politician, Charles Greenway. She was in her late twenties, blond, attractive. He was considerably older, had had a mild heart attack, and she'd been hired to nurse him back to health.

"Everything was fine until the day she overheard Greenway congratulating a couple of his men on killing a zoning inspector, who'd refused to cooperate, at his orders. Jill ran out and got away, calling us from a phone booth. Like with you, we took down her statement and put her in protective custody because Greenway had a lot of powerful people in his pocket. We'd been watching his activities for a long time, but couldn't pin anything on him. But suddenly, we had him."

"And you were assigned to protect Jill?"

"Right. I was green, on my second assignment. I was young and stupid, despite all my training. We were on the run and it was exciting, adrenaline pumping, living on the edge, you know?"

"You fell in love with her," Terry guessed. He was quiet so long, staring out to sea, that she wondered if he was going to continue.

"I thought I did, I suppose. Since then I've decided it was probably hormonal."

"Are you just saying that because she hurt you?"

He looked at her, a little surprised at her astuteness. "Maybe. At any rate, it never would have worked out." He saw no point in detailing the actual involvement. "Jill hated being confined, became restless quickly, threatened to walk away countless times. Finally, she made good and left one night after dark when I thought she was asleep. We were staying in a cabin in a remote area of Colorado. It wasn't snowing, but it was damn cold. I called HQ for backup and went looking for her."

This was hard for him, she could see, so she waited and let him tell it in his own way.

"It was early morning, scarcely dawn, when I finally spotted her on one of the trails some distance from me. But what I didn't know was that one of Greenway's men had located us, too. I also didn't realize that the backup the home office had sent, Bob Jones and another agent, had caught up with us. The area was thick with fog and visibility wasn't good. I called out to Jill, telling her to stop, that we'd go down the mountain together. She turned and I know she saw me, but she kept on going. I ran after her. I'd just rounded a bend when I spotted this guy with a gun behind a tree, taking aim at Jill. I yelled to her and lunged forward. But Jones was closer to her, his reaction faster. He threw himself in front of Jill and took the bullet meant for me."

She frowned at his face, grim from the telling. "The bullet had been meant for Jill, not you or Bob."

"But Bob took it when I should have been there protecting Jill. She'd been *my* assignment, my responsibility. If it hadn't been for Bob arriving at just that moment, I would have taken the bullet that hit him."

Terry shook her head. "That's crazy, Luke. It was circumstances, that's all. And obviously, Bob's wound wasn't fatal."

"No, but it could have been."

She wasn't going to debate that with him. "What happened to Jill?"

Luke drained his tepid coffee. "She was taken back and eventually testified. And we picked up the gunman as well, so the case was wrapped. But it's always left a bad taste in my mouth. I should have watched her more closely. I shouldn't have had to call for backup. And I never have since then."

"I guess sometimes we have to learn our lessons the hard way." Terry got to her feet, shivering in the cooling air. "It's getting late and getting cold. Let's go back." She gathered the rest of their things into the picnic basket.

Luke rose and folded the blanket. "You see how much trouble Jill Hastings caused by leaving the program too early?"

Holding the basket in front of her with both hands, she angled her head and met his eyes. "I wonder if you're upset because she left the program or because you lost someone you cared about?" She held his gaze, trying to ascertain what was going on behind those pewter gray eyes. "Or are you too stubborn to admit you loved her?"

"What makes you think I did? You weren't there."

"No, but your reaction even years later reveals a great deal. And because I know that the worst part of loving is the void it leaves when it's over."

He raised a questioning brow. "Then you've been in love?"

"I haven't exactly lived my life in a vacuum. And yes, he hurt me, too. But I got over it."

His interest was immediate. "Who was he? Did you care a great deal for him?" The thought of her deeply involved with someone bothered him more than it should have.

Terry drew in a breath, not really wanting to go into all that. "He was a lawyer. The *Gazette* was doing a feature on him and I went along because the editor wanted several sketches instead of pictures. Up-and-coming mover-and-shaker and all that. Did I care a lot? I must have. A month later, I moved in with him."

Luke was annoyed at the disappointment he felt. "But he's not in the picture anymore?" He saw her shake her head as she shifted the picnic basket to her other hand. "What happened?"

"We had a quarrel. I left." She glanced up at the darkening sky. "We'd better go." She turned, starting back.

He didn't want to react, but he couldn't help it. "You left him after a quarrel, just like that? You walked out after a minor little disagreement?"

She heard the change in his voice and knew exactly what he was thinking. Slowly, she swung back to him. "It wasn't a quarrel over whose turn it was to take out the garbage or who left the top off the toothpaste. You're certainly quick to judge without knowing the facts, aren't you?" She could see his mind working behind that hard, immovable face. He was lumping her with his mother, his grandmother, and this Jill person—all women who walked away from him. How could he think like that?

"All right," Luke said in what he thought was a very reasonable tone. "What *are* the facts?"

She cocked her head at him. "It's none of your business, you know."

"I know that. But I just told you about Jill and . . . " He stopped, knowing he had no right to press her, wondering why he wanted to.

He was like a dog with a bone. She could refuse, just turn away. But maybe he needed to know that men weren't always in the right and that there are some damn good reasons why women leave. "We quarreled because he wanted me to quit the paper, to stay home. He said he was making enough money for both of us and I didn't need to work. But I *enjoy* working and I was just getting somewhere. I refused." She waited, watching him.

He was trying to understand. He really was. "So the first time you didn't get your way, you walked out."

"Damn it, no! It wasn't like that. You're so blinded, so sure you're right. You don't know shit." Furious, she whirled around and started to march off.

Luke sucked in a gulp of mountain air. "Why are you so angry? You did leave, didn't you?"

She halted, waiting until she could catch her breath before swinging back to glare at him. "Yes, I left. But not until he hit me. Twice, across the face, both sides. Hard. Happy, now?" She turned, wondering how in hell she'd allowed herself to be drawn into such a reaction.

He was at her side in seconds, turning her around, calling himself six kinds of a fool. "I'm sorry. Jesus, Terry, I'm sorry. Sorry that bastard hit you, sorry I jumped to conclusions. It's just that I . . . "

"It's just that you think all women are the same, all walk away when the mood strikes, for whatever frivolous reason." She felt drained, weary. "When are you going to stop judging every woman by the few who've hurt you?"

He dared touch her face, his palm cupping her cheek. "I was wrong. You were right to leave him. You should have had someone beat the hell out of him."

Now, years later, she could almost smile. "That's just about what happened. I asked my brother, Sean, to get my things. Chuck came home while Sean was packing my bag. Sean told me later that he beat him up pretty good."

"I don't know how you managed to get past that and still . . . still trust men."

"I don't trust very many of them. It takes me awhile. But I can't judge all men by that one jerk." She hoped her words were sinking in. "As they say, sometimes you eat the bear and sometimes the bear eats you. That's life." She turned and started back down the mountain.

The hike back was quiet, each of them lost in their own thoughts. It wasn't until they rounded the final curve and the cabin came into sight that Luke's internal antenna picked up the scent of danger. He stopped, moving Terry behind him with one arm as his gaze swept the property perimeters.

"What is it?" she asked, her heart beginning to pound.

A small wisp of smoke was still curling out of the chimney from the fire they'd built earlier. A light they'd left on in the front window was still burning. Dusk had deepened the shadows and a chill wind rustled the surrounding tree leaves and bushes. The van was still parked in the drive exactly as he'd left it, the fence gate closed.

"Something's not right," he whispered, reaching for the Luger he'd brought along as double insurance. Removing the safety, he started down. "Stay close behind me."

She did, unable to see around his wide shoulders but glad to have him as her shield. *Please, not again*, she prayed.

They were some ten yards from the fence line when Luke spotted what had set his senses on alert. His eyes scanning in all directions, he inched closer. He stopped near the gate and stared down at the deathly still Doberman, blood oozing from a wound in his head.

"Oh, God!" Terry gasped, peering around him. "Someone's shot Prince."

# CHAPTER TEN

Gun drawn, Luke quickly unlocked and examined the van. It was clean. He helped a trembling Terry inside and handed her his .38. "I'm going into the house. If you need to use this, do it." He studied her face. She looked stunned, but he could see that she understood. "Lock the door after me." He stepped out.

Moving cautiously, he went to the front door and listened. Not a sound. He entered, shoving back the door, assuming a shooting stance. He saw nothing out of the ordinary. One by one, he searched the rooms, the closets, everywhere. Nothing disturbed. Hands on his hips, he looked around. The whole thing was very odd.

Perhaps Prince had been killed by someone other than the men after Terry. They hadn't heard shots, but then they'd been some distance away. Still, the sound of gunfire usually carried a long way. Professionals used silencers. Hunters wouldn't. Could have been a stray bullet from a man hunting quail or wild pheasant. But he couldn't take the chance.

It took him minutes to gather up their things and carry them to the van. Because of the frequency of relocating, they'd learned to travel light. Still, it was dusk by the time he had the van loaded and ready to roll. Terry was belted in the

166

passenger seat, though her nerves were in evidence and she still held the .38.

As Luke pulled past the first bluff, he glanced up the hillside where the only other house they'd seen for miles around was situated. In a shaft of light from the open garage door, he noticed the same man in overalls that he'd seen before standing watching them, the long barrel of his gun resting over his forearm, his expression unreadable at this distance. Prince had done quite a bit of barking, especially nights when wild rabbits and squirrels could be heard scurrying just outside the fence line. Could that cantankerous neighbor have waited until he and Terry had left the house, crept down the hill, and shot the dog because the barking had gotten on his nerves?

They'd probably never know, Luke decided as he shifted into gear and started down the road.

Once they reached the highway, he swung north, wondering where on earth he should go. Maybe the best thing to do at this late hour would be to drive to some small town, find a hotel and check in, then call Jones. It might take some time to find another safe house. It wasn't as though there were dozens in California, and they'd already been to three.

Luke scanned the cars in the light traffic and saw nothing suspicious. Noticing that Terry still held the .38 in a death grip, he ran the possibility of the neighbor shooting Prince by her to ease her mind.

She didn't buy it. "Why would he do such a thing? He'd never even come to the door and asked us to keep our dog quiet."

"He didn't look like the polite type." To his trained eye, any search of the inside of the cabin would have been detected. Besides, if the Russo thugs had found them, they wouldn't have silenced the dog, then taken off. They'd have stayed around, knowing that the occupants wouldn't be far from the place without the van. Shooting them on that remote mountainside when they returned wouldn't have presented a problem to trained killers. With silencers, no one in that isolated neighborhood would have been the wiser for days, perhaps weeks. Not until Jones would have called to check on them.

With each passing mile, Luke became more convinced that he'd reacted to an old man's mean justice rather than any real threat. No matter. They were probably better off out of that garish cabin. It was time for a change. The problem was he knew of nothing available without calling in and having Bob set something up. When they were settled somewhere, he'd make another effort to convince Terry that they'd not been in any real danger.

His mind racing, Luke drove carefully. Maybe he should consider driving to a slightly larger city, where there'd be more people. The old adage about getting lost in a crowd still worked. Up ahead was the turnoff from Highway 1 to 101 that wound inland heading north. Numerous cities could be reached from that route. He'd choose one that seemed particularly crowded.

On the road to San Jose, he slowed the van. The little town of Beachside was hosting some sort of a winter festival, with banners flying and billboards urging residents and visitors to attend opening ceremonies on the upcoming weekend. There would be marching bands, amusement rides, booths offering crafts for sale, and a huge potluck supper.

Exactly the type of local diversion he'd been seeking, Luke thought as he spotted the Seafarer Inn up ahead. Now if only they had a vacant room with twin beds. He was greatly relieved to get rid of that damn satin couch and more than ready to stretch out on a real bed.

"I think we'll check in here, then call Bob and update him," he explained to Terry as he pulled the van into the inn's parking lot. She'd turned her thoughts inward on the drive and hadn't spoken a word. But he saw her turn toward him now, looking confused.

"Here?" She saw the crowds of people milling around on the streets, window-shopping, licking ice-cream cones, jostling one another. It was cool, but clear and pleasant, a nice evening for strolling. Yet every face looked suspicious to her, every person posing a threat. "I thought we were going someplace away from people, where they couldn't find us so easily."

"There's safety in numbers." He took the gun from her and put it in his waistband. "Come with me to the front desk." He hopped down and went around to open her door.

Adjusting her wig, Terry stepped down, wondering how many more places they'd have to stay in before she could go home.

"I've got a gut feeling the dog was killed by someone other than Russo's boys," Luke said into the phone. Seated in a captain's chair at a small desk in the nautically decorated room they'd been given, he glanced over at Terry already curled up on the twin bed against the far wall. For her benefit as much as to inform Bob Jones, he went into great detail about searching the house they'd vacated and finding it undisturbed and of the odd neighbor up the hill with a gun.

"I can't be certain, of course," he wound up, "but I don't believe that if Russo's men had tracked us that far, that they'd have left until they'd gotten us, too."

"That sounds plausible," Bob said from his home in Phoenix. He had a private secure line that only his agents used. "However, I do have an upsetting piece of news for you."

"Go ahead," Luke said, revealing nothing by his expression since Terry was watching him.

"Nick Russo gave our tail the slip. We believe he's in California."

"Along with the other one?"

They were used to one another, of speaking in coded phrases. "We're not sure where Ozzie Swain is, although he might be. He hasn't been spotted since this all began. Something else you should know. Our man trailed Nick to

Sedona last week. He asked around and located your house. Our man visited with one of your neighbors who told him that he'd talked with the fellow in the picture he was shown, and he'd told the man that the new owner of the ranch had been there remodeling all summer, then left abruptly and hasn't been back in weeks."

"Shit." The oath was out before he could check it. He turned his back to Terry. "How the hell did he pick up the scent?"

"Nick's a lot of things—cocky, brash, unpredictable. But he can be cool under pressure when the need arises. We know the Russos have a lot of connections. Once they knew the Feds were on the scene, they took things to their logical conclusion. I also have a feeling that Nick wants to finish the job he started on you."

"The feeling's mutual. Well, forewarned and all that. He may not recognize me. The beard's back. Unless the neighbor told him that, too."

He might have guessed he'd let himself go shaggy, Bob thought. Luke had always disliked the clean-cut look. "How's Terry holding up?"

"All right. Some days better than others." He kept his voice low, chose his words carefully.

"I have a suggestion, one I doubt Terry's going to like. But we've discussed it at this end and we agree that it's the best shot she has. I can set it up along with another safe house if she agrees."

"Let's hear it."

"You mentioned she needs more corrective plastic surgery. We feel she should give serious consideration to allowing the doctor to alter her features somewhat. I talked to a doctor here. It can be subtle, yet cause a dramatic difference. Change the cheekbones, adjust the angle of the jaw, alter the nose a bit. Then with a good wig and colored contacts, she'll look like a different person. If you're bearded and wearing Western clothes, which I assume you are, staying in the rural places you've been, you'd both have a different look."

Yes, but his changes could be shaved off in minutes and hers would be permanent. He'd seen pictures of Terry before her accident. She'd been lovely, with high cheekbones, big blue eyes and beautiful blond hair. Except for the shorter hair and the two small scars, she was lovely now. He was certain she could hardly wait to get back to being exactly as she once was.

"I don't know, Bob." Terry hadn't even wanted to discuss the minor surgery required to remove the two remaining scars on her face. Despite Bob's assessment, the procedure he was suggesting sounded pretty major to Luke. And probably fairly painful. Terry had already been through so much pain, and her mental state was still very fragile.

"We can't force her to do it, of course," Bob said into the silence. "You know I hate to even have to suggest it. But we want her alive and this is her best chance."

"It's a long shot."

"Well, see what you can do to persuade her. Meanwhile, I'll get in touch with the doctor I have in mind up that way. You feel you'll be okay at the inn for a day or two?"

"I think so."

"Good. I have a safe house up near Truckee that I feel would be perfect for Terry's recovery. I'll set it up. I can even call Sara Baines and send her up to help."

"No, don't do that. We can manage."

Luke had nixed the nurse quickly. Too quickly. Bob hesitated, wondering if he sensed a problem. "Is everything all right otherwise?" he asked, his tone solemn and questioning.

Luke bit back a sharp retort. "Yeah, everything's just dandy."

Tanner was getting touchy. Not a good sign. As soon as Terry's surgery was over, he'd make it a point to pay them both a visit, Jones decided. "The trial won't take place until either the end of this month or sometime next." He could almost feel Luke's frustration ripple over the phone lines.

"Swell."

"Call me tomorrow. Hopefully you can talk her into the surgery. I'll have more answers for you then."

"Right." Luke hung up and scrubbed a hand over his bearded chin. How in hell was he going to get her to agree?

He swung around to face her and saw that she'd heard every word and, while she didn't know what Jones had said, she knew something was up. Bracing himself, he walked over to sit across from her on the other bed.

"No!" Terry swung her legs over the side of the bed and sat up. She'd listened quietly while Luke had detailed his conversation with Bob Jones. She hadn't reacted externally, hadn't yelled or sworn as she'd wanted to. Now she faced him just as calmly. "I don't care what you and Bob and the entire marshals office suggest. I *won't* go through any more extensive surgery. Period."

Her quiet anger went deep, he knew. Luke couldn't blame her. But it was his job to convince her, for her own safety's sake.

"This isn't just a whimsical suggestion, Terry."

At her sides, her hands curled in the bedclothes. "No, it's a command cloaked in gentle words and for-your-own-good reassurances. But it's a command nonetheless."

"No, it isn't. The truth is, we can't make you do this. I'm trying to explain that it's in your best interest to change your looks just slightly so that you'll be more difficult to recognize."

"That's bullshit!" She rose and began pacing. "All that pain and helplessness to be changed into something I'm not. And for what? For a couple of weeks. Then I testify and what becomes of me? I'm no longer who I was." She stopped near him, her eyes filled with anguish. "I've already lost so much. How can you ask me to give up even more of my identity?"

He went to her, took her hands in his. "No one can change what you are, Terry. If the accident had marred your face beyond recognition and they'd have had to reconstruct it from scratch, you'd still be you. Your face doesn't define you." He softened because he couldn't help himself. "I don't want anything to happen to you. That's why I'm asking you to seriously consider this."

"I thought you said you could protect me. I thought you asked me to trust you. I did and now you want more. Have you all gotten mixed up? I'm not the criminal here. *I'm* a victim and I've paid enough!" Tears she'd fought to control all but choked her.

"All right, all right." Despite everything that told him he shouldn't, he reached for her and gathered her close.

Her body was almost rigid with tension, her fingers bunching in the material of his shirt as she struggled not to give in to her need to cry out her frustration. He didn't understand. No one understood.

His hands caressed her back, trying to soothe her. "I was only trying to protect you in the best way I knew how, but I can see now that it was a mistake." He felt awkward in the face of her torment, uncertain what to do. "Forget it." She was small and vulnerable. He hated what all this was doing to her. "We'll be all right."

He meant well. She believed that. But the powers that be were incapable of seeing things as she did, and Luke had to follow their orders. There was only one way to handle this. She should have known it would come to this.

She longed to give in, to let him hold her, let him make love to her so she could forget everyone and everything. She'd had one taste of him and knew he could distract her as no one before him had. But she couldn't remain in his arms. It would be too easy to allow his comfort to trigger the desire always there, making her restless and needy. She was so damn tired of being needy.

Terry moved out of his hold and turned, walking to the window. Two stories below, people were still wandering the streets, people with no life-threatening problems, no men with guns searching them out. Carefree, laughing, uncomplicated people with happy lives. Like she once had been.

"Maybe Bob Jones is right," she said softly. "Maybe the only way this nightmare will end is if I just do what he says. I told myself when I woke up in that Phoenix hospital that I'd do whatever was necessary to make sure the men who caused Lynn's death and murdered Don Simon in cold blood were put away. I told myself I could stand anything as long as I knew it would one day be over." Slowly, she turned around and met his eyes. "You can tell Bob I'll do it."

The abrupt turnabout worried Luke, but he didn't let her see. "Are you sure? I don't want you to do anything you feel isn't right."

"I'm sure I'm doing what's right for me at this time." She covered her flushed cheeks with both hands. They felt warm to the touch. "I hope I'm not coming down with something."

Luke frowned. This was no time for her to get sick. "Why don't you lie down? You look tired. I think I'll grab a quick shower. I feel a little grungy. After your nap, we can go get something to eat."

Terry gave in to a yawn. "All right." She'd slipped off her shoes earlier. Now, she pulled back the covers and slid under. She felt cold all over, yet her face was on fire. She closed her eyes, wanting to blot out the world.

Luke took his time in the bathroom, letting her rest. This ambivalence she was feeling was probably related to the stress disorder, he realized. He only hoped that later she wouldn't regret changing her mind about the surgery.

Stepping back into the bedroom, he saw that she was lying as before, only she'd put on her Walkman headset. Music seemed to calm her frayed nerves. From the dresser, he gathered his loose change and wallet, put on his watch and grabbed his jacket. It was eight in the evening and his stomach was reminding him it was long past dinnertime. He walked to her side and touched her arm.

Terry's eyes flew open and she removed the headset.

"Time to get up and get something to eat," Luke told her. "You can rest more afterward."

She shivered. "I'm not that hungry. You go ahead."

"I don't want to leave you here alone, Terry."

"I'll be fine. Lock the door and I'll put on the chain. And leave me your gun."

"But you need to eat. You'll feel better."

She closed her eyes and sighed. "Please, Luke. I just can't make myself go. Bring me back a sandwich, if you insist."

He hesitated. He'd spotted a coffee shop next door and a Burger King across the street. One of them would do and neither was far. The room faced the street two stories up. No one would have access that way. He was uncomfortable about leaving her, but he'd be gone ten minutes tops.

He looked into her drowsy eyes. "All right. Come put the chain on and *don't* open the door under any circumstances unless you recognize my voice."

Sleepily, still shivering, Terry got up and padded after him to the door.

"I'll be back as quickly as possible."

"Okay." He stepped through the door. "Oh, Luke?" She waited until he turned back. "Thanks. For understanding."

He stared at her a long minute, nodded finally, and hurried down the hall toward the elevators.

He was in Burger King, standing at the counter, opening his wallet as the clerk set down the sacks of food when he realized that something was very wrong. His wallet contained not a single dollar.

It took a moment for the shocking truth to hit Luke.

Muttering a foul oath, he turned on his heel and sprinted out the door, ignoring the surprised clerk calling out after him.

He hit the street running, dodged several cars crossing, raced through the lobby and took the stairs up two at a time, too impatient to wait for the elevator. The key turned in the lock and there was no restraining chain to keep him from opening the door. And he knew even before he stepped into the room.

Terry was gone.

Out on the street in front of the inn, Luke forced himself to breathe deeply as his eyes scanned the sidewalk, wondering which direction to try first. She had a scant ten-minute start on him at the most, and he could walk much faster. There were more people to the left, the block cluttered with storefronts housing a small boutique, a movie theater, a camera shop, a drugstore and so on. She'd probably figure she could be less easily spotted in a crowd. He started walking.

He tried to remember how much cash he'd had in his wallet. About sixty dollars, to the best of his recollection. It wouldn't take her far. Not enough for much of a plane ticket and the closest airport was San Jose. She scarcely had enough for bus fare. Where would she head? he asked himself, trying to think as she might.

He'd already guessed why she'd taken off, or at least he thought he knew. Too damn much pressure too steadily applied. Fear had ruled her life since the moment she'd awakened in the hospital bed in October. Here it was January, and the fear was still a constant companion, a daily reminder that someone was stalking her. She'd seen what that someone could do when she'd looked at Don Simon's bleeding body and heard about her cousin being burned alive in the wreckage. Who could doubt that the killer meant business?

The pressure of knowing she still had to testify, of trying to keep one jump ahead of the gunman, of staying alive long enough for the authorities to apprehend all of them. The pressure of living with strangers, of having to relocate because the pursuers might be getting closer. Then, the final pressure that caused her to blow: the heavy-handed suggestion that she undergo facial reconstructive surgery.

Damn, what had they been thinking of to put this woman through even more? How much was one individual supposed to take? Her only crime had been being in the wrong place at the wrong time, and her life as she once knew it had been ripped from her, taken, changed, forever gone. Who wouldn't crack under those circumstances?

His eyes narrowed as he walked briskly, searching the shapes and sizes and faces of people on both sides of the street, glancing behind him occasionally. What had she been wearing? A navy turtleneck, jeans, white Reeboks, and her corduroy jacket. He hadn't taken the time to check the closet to see if she'd changed, but he doubted it. She'd probably taken the money while he'd showered, lain there making her plans, then slipped out as soon as she heard the elevator door close.

Luke ground his teeth, angry with himself. He should have seen this coming. She'd been so adamant about not having the surgery, then suddenly she'd done an about-face. He'd thought that strange, but he'd let it go. Hadn't she asked on their hillside picnic if anyone had ever voluntarily left the program? Yes, he'd described the only case he personally knew of and it had ended badly. But Terry was distraught enough to believe her situation was different.

It was, very different. She was in even more danger now that he knew that Nick Russo was somewhere in California, and probably Ozzie Swain, too. She hadn't ever seen Nick, except the picture he'd shown her. She might not recognize him if he sat down beside her. God, how could one innocent, naive woman elude those two pros?

He glanced in stores he passed, his eyes flicking over shoppers, strollers, anyone in blue. She'd probably worn her wig, maybe that floppy tan hat she sometimes wore. He stared through the hardware store doorway noticing a woman with auburn hair at the counter with her back to him. But when he stepped closer and she turned, he didn't find the face he sought. He walked on.

Where would she go? he asked himself again. Surely she knew the money wouldn't last very long. Would she hole up in another hotel room until she had a plan? Would she make the cardinal mistake of phoning her family or a friend? That would really upset the applecart. She had to have figured out that Russo's men were watching them back in Phoenix. Surely she wouldn't risk that.

But then, she wasn't thinking too clearly just now. And neither was he. He'd come to the end of Beachside's main shopping district. Angrily, he crossed the street and renewed his search, all but breaking into a run. She had to be somewhere. Panic was an unfamiliar feeling, one Luke seldom experienced because he rarely let things get out of his control. The one time he'd stepped more than twenty feet from her in weeks and it had to be at her weakest moment.

He glanced into the darkened windows of a beauty shop, berating himself with every step he took. His fault. This was all his fault for bringing up the surgery against his better judgment. He'd *known* how she felt, and he'd still done it. If something happened to her, if Russo's people found her before he did, he'd never forgive himself. He hurried around a strolling threesome and marched up to the ticket booth of the theater.

A blond teenager who looked barely sixteen was standing with his back to the street, flirting with a short redhead with large dimples. Luke knocked on the window. Quickly, he described Terry to the kid, asking if he'd sold her a ticket recently.

"Hey, man, the show's packed, you know. I was too busy to notice anybody. Sorry." He turned back to the girl.

Dare he take the time to go into the theater—the darkened atmosphere an ideal place to hide—and run up and down the aisles, searching for her? Luke asked himself. Probably not.

The streetlights were on and businesses closing, one by one. The crowd was thinning, the night breeze cooling and picking up. Still, he walked, searching, fuming, hoping.

At the opposite end of the main drag, he spotted a motel sign. He rushed into the small lobby and found a tall, husky man badly in need of a shave seated behind the counter watching "Seinfeld" on a small television set. He glanced up as the bell over the door clanged, his pale eyes none too friendly. Slowly, he got up and moseyed to the counter.

"I'm looking for a young woman," Luke began as he flipped out his ID. "She's about five-five with auburn hair, slender. Wearing jeans and a navy corduroy jacket. Has anyone like that checked in recently?"

The man's eyes slid from the ID to Luke's face where he took his time looking him over. "Nope. What's she done?"

"Nothing. We think she's in danger. Are you sure you haven't seen her? It would have been within the last half an hour."

"Yup, I'm sure." The man sat back down, his attention already on the sitcom as he scratched his belly.

"I'm going to leave my card here on the counter. I'm staying at the Seafarer Inn across the street. Would you please call me if you see her? You could save her life."

The clerk didn't even look up. "Yup."

Damn backwoods jerk, Luke thought as he slammed out of the office. Probably wouldn't recognize Madonna if she strolled in nude. He crossed the street again.

Only a handful of people were out now. It was ten and most residents were in their homes, visitors back in their rented quarters. Where could Terry be? It was cold and dark.

He remembered fragments of their last conversation. *I'm sure I'm doing what's right for me at this time*, she'd said. That had to have been when she'd decided to run. Then, at the door, she'd said *Thanks, for understanding*. Had she been trying to tell him that she was aware the surgery hadn't been his idea, that she knew he wanted to protect her? Or was his guilt over letting her get away making him see things differently?

He wanted to hit something with savage force. He wanted to blame someone and could only wind up blaming himself. He wanted to find her, whole and unharmed and ready to return. Grim-faced, Luke reached the inn and went inside to question the desk clerk there. Moments later, he was back outside, having been told that no one had seen anyone looking like Terry's description. She had to have come through the lobby. Were they all blind? Had she vanished into thin air?

Hurrying to the parking lot, Luke unlocked the van. He'd cruise the streets, and, if that didn't work, he'd hit the truck stops in both directions and see if she'd hitched a ride out of town. He thought she might be too frightened to do that. But then, he'd thought she would be too frightened to leave him, too.

Apparently some fears took precedence over others.

# CHAPTER ELEVEN

The movie was about to end. Scrunched down in her seat in the middle of a row of people, Terry strained to see her watch. Nearly eleven. This had to be the last showing. The people would be filing out, the ushers and clerks closing up. Then where could she go?

It was warm in the theater and yet she felt chilled. Fear did that to her. She'd left the inn hurriedly and without time to formulate a plan, escape the only thing on her mind. She'd huddled in her seat for two hours trying to tune out the inane comedy on the screen and trying to think, yet she still hadn't come up with a viable plan.

What was she going to do?

Lost. She felt utterly lost without Luke beside her. Never mind that he'd been her protector for ten weeks now; he was also the solid presence who'd been there for her. Leaving him had been one of the hardest things she'd ever done. But she felt certain in her heart that it had been the right thing. Because he was a man who'd sworn to follow orders, and he'd been ordered to get her face altered. Oh, he'd said that it was her decision and that they couldn't force her to have the surgery. But they both knew that the Feds held all the cards where she was concerned.

She simply couldn't handle that. She'd hated deceiving Luke, hated taking money from his wallet, which she fully intended to repay. But she'd seen no other way out. It wasn't that she thought she was so all-fired beautiful. But it was *her* face, *her* identity, the way she perceived herself. She'd lost so much that the thought of changing the way she looked was unbearable.

The audience around her was laughing and several people nearby were putting on their outerwear. The movie was ending and she had nowhere to go. She'd half-expected Luke to come charging into the theater, having persuaded the manager to stop the show and turn on the lights, then thundering down the aisle and dragging her out bodily. He was undoubtedly searching for her this very minute. In her present agitated state of mind, could she outwit him?

Terry noticed that the credits were rolling and people were straggling out into the aisles. Pulling the collar of her jacket up, she shuffled out, insinuating herself into the midst of a trio of chattering teenage girls. If Luke was in the lobby watching everyone who walked out, perhaps she could somehow be swallowed up in the crowd.

Her eyes darted every which way as she scanned the lobby for the tall, lean figure. He was nowhere in sight, thank heaven. The teenagers strolled in the direction of the ladies' room. She followed along. Inside, she went into the last stall and locked the door behind her. She listened while a young mother insisted impatiently that her cranky daughter wash her hands. The teenagers were freshening their makeup and discussing whether or not to stop at Burger King before heading home. Terry sat down and waited.

Did the cleanup crew work after the last viewing or did they come in before tomorrow's first showing? Maybe, if she sat cross-legged on the seat, if the manager made a swing through the lavatories to check for anyone lingering behind, he wouldn't spot her. When she heard the last of the girls leave, she wiggled into position and waited, praying silently that no one would find her.

It seemed like hours and she could still hear voices coming from the vicinity of the nearby lobby. The counter girls were closing up, the young man at the ticket machine was talking about counting and bagging the money, and a deep-voiced male whom she guessed to be the manager was giving a few clipped instructions. Feeling stiff and tense, Terry bent her head over her crossed arms and wished they'd hurry.

Suddenly, she heard the bathroom door swing open and brisk steps march in. Seconds later, apparently whoever was checking was satisfied, for the light went off and the door swung shut. It was pitch-dark. Terry listened to the hammering of her heart.

A final round of good-byes drifted in from the direction of the lobby. Then there was only silence.

She was afraid to move, afraid that she'd missed the arrival of a night watchman or a janitor who'd catch her the moment she stepped out of the ladies' room. So she waited for what seemed an eternity, until her legs were numb from remaining in the same cramped position for so long. Finally, she dared untangle herself and stealthily unlock the stall door.

It was too dark to see much, but a faint light leaked from beneath the swinging door. Moving carefully, she crept out, blinking in the light of the Coke machine, which apparently stayed on all the time. There was also a low fluorescent glow behind the candy counter reflected in the mirrored back wall. It wasn't much, but it was enough that she wasn't completely in the dark.

Terry stood back, away from the double glass doors leading outside. That was the only way someone could see in, should they be walking by. Peering around the window's edge, she peeked out. From where she stood, she could see only one young couple strolling hand in hand across the street. As she watched for several minutes, two cars drove by. She decided to take a chance and scoot past the glass doors.

Reaching the far side of the lobby, she breathed a sigh of relief. Her throat felt dry and scratchy. She eyed the Coke machine, but she had no loose change. Stepping behind the counter, she opened a drawer and found only papers. The next one apparently was petty cash, the key still in the lock. She opened it, took out four quarters and shoved in a dollar bill from her pocket.

She flipped the tab on the Coke can and drank deeply. Her limbs ached from tension and she felt drained and tired. Carrying her drink, she walked past the curtains into the darkened theater. Two red exit signs glowed above rear doors on either side of the screen, affording the only light in the large room. It was enough.

Terry made her way into the second from last row, sat in one seat and swung her legs over the arm. It wasn't ideal, but she was safe and warm. She took another swallow of Coke, then placed the can on the floor. Wearily, she scooted down and laid back her head. Maybe if she could sleep a little, she'd awaken and a plan would occur to her. With an expansive yawn, she closed her eyes.

Three o'clock in the morning and he was wide-awake. Luke turned over restlessly in the narrow twin bed, unable to turn off his mind. He was exhausted from walking, driving around, asking about, searching a second time along the same route. Tired but too wired to sleep.

Where in hell had Terry gone?

He'd been over every conversation they'd had yesterday, every action and reaction he could recall. And he still came up with the same conclusion: that she'd left because of accumulated pressure and the fear of more surgery. Yet not in anything she'd said in all their time together could he find a clue as to where she might go if she left him. Probably because, arrogant fool that he was, he'd never dreamed she would.

She had to be scared to death, wherever she was. Even with him beside her, she'd jumped at every little unexpected sound, cringed at sudden movements, flinched at passing shadows. Of course, she was damn gutsy when she had to be. She'd endured pain he could scarcely imagine without complaining.

Still, this was different. Men with guns and live ammo were hunting for her, and she knew it. He had to find her and he didn't have much time. If Jones was right that both Nick Russo and Ozzie Swain were somewhere in California, it would only be a matter of time till they tracked her. He had to find Terry before those killers did.

Another hour passed slowly before Luke gave up on sleep, rolled out of bed and quickly showered. Dressed again, he reached for the phone. Though it was the middle of the night, he needed to talk with Bob. He knew that his commanding officer was used to receiving calls at all hours.

Bob Jones listened to Luke's terse recital of the events of the past few hours, and struggled not to groan aloud. He'd personally selected Tanner for this important assignment. How could he have taken his eyes off the girl, even for ten minutes? It wasn't at all like his best agent to be careless. He waited to speak until he was certain his voice didn't betray his disappointment. "What's your plan on finding her?" he asked quietly.

"Go over the same ground at first daylight. I've talked to a few people. I need to question more. The problem is, I'm hesitant to reveal much about her, not wanting anyone else to pick up the trail."

"I understand. I'll check with men in the area to see if anyone's spotted Nick or Ozzie. Of course, they may not be together." Bob paused, thinking. "Is there a private airfield there where she could have chartered a plane?"

He'd asked that same question of the desk clerk on one of

his several sessions with the taciturn man. "Nothing until San Jose. She doesn't have enough money to charter a plane."

"An attractive woman can sometimes talk her way into free passage."

"That's true, but I think Terry's too frightened to speak to very many people."

"She wasn't too frightened to set out with only sixty dollars. She's feeling desperate, apparently. She won't be acting in character." Jones wondered if he should bring up a possibility he'd been toying with, then decided to plunge in. "Did the two of you quarrel? Is there something more to your relationship than you've told me?"

Luke swore under his breath. "Damn it, Bob, I've kept this strictly business." Except for that one mind-blowing kissing session, but he'd had the good sense to back off. "I tell you she took off because she can't face another operation right now. I sensed that and I didn't think I should bring it up to her. But I did. It was a mistake."

Jones could sense Luke's temper about to boil over. He was blaming himself, which Bob would have done, too. Bob was also remembering the time another woman Luke had been protecting had run away. Altogether different circumstances, but Bob knew that the memory stung. "All right."

"I'm going to check some bed-and-breakfasts around here. Maybe she just holed up, needing some time to think. And the bus station, the car rentals."

"She has no credit card so she couldn't rent a vehicle," Bob reminded him.

"Unless she told a good enough story. Like she lost her wallet, remembered her VISA number, had them check out her driver's license with DMV in Arizona. Could be done, and she's clever."

"You have a point. Think she might hitch a ride?"

"Possibly, though that can be dangerous and she's skittish. I checked an all-night truck stop outside of town, think-

ing big rig drivers might appear safer to her, but no luck."
Luke stared out the hotel window at the dark main drag
down below. Not a soul out, the streetlights still on. He could
see a faint light inside the diner not yet open and the mar-
quee of the darkened movie theater. He thought of something
else. "Can you get a police artist to alter Terry's file picture?
You know, remove the blond hair and replace it with a short,
curly auburn wig, change the color of her eyes from blue to
green and thin her face down a bit? If you could fax a copy
to me here at the hotel, I could show it around and maybe
someone would remember seeing her."

"You'd have to be really selective. If Nick Russo or one
of his men saw one . . . "

"I'm aware of that. Oh, and Bob, don't go through the
Phoenix police. Let one of our guys do the sketch work. I
don't trust anyone in that Central Division until we get this
cleared up."

"Nor do I. All right, you get going and keep me informed.
Let me know if you change your base."

"Right." Luke hung up. He hadn't quite apologized to the
chief for screwing up. He couldn't come up with the words.

Her legs slipped off the arm of the theater chair, causing
Terry to be startled awake. It took a moment for her to orient
herself. Heart pounding, she rubbed circulation back into her
knees as she listened intently. No other sounds. Gingerly, she
stood, moving carefully until feeling came back to her numb
limbs.

Peeking around the front doors of the theater, she saw
that the gray light of dawn was lightening the sky. After
freshening up in the bathroom, groping around in the dark,
she went back to the refreshment counter. Her stomach
growled, reminding her she hadn't eaten in a long while, but
there was nothing but stale popcorn and candy bars.
Unfortunately, this theater didn't sell coffee. Maybe a little
sugar would jump-start her.

She selected two candy bars, then thoughtfully stuffed two dollars into the drawer in payment. She'd already stolen from Luke and didn't want more thievery on her conscience. She shoved one bar into her jacket pocket and unwrapped the other, taking a bite as she wandered the lobby, mindful of the glass doors.

On a chair off to the side, she discovered a knit cap in pale blue with a white tassel, either lost or discarded. Moving to the mirrored side wall, she tried it on over her wig. Not bad. It would make her even more anonymous, she hoped. Yes, it would do, although her scalp was screaming for air. Plenty of time for that when she got to a safe place.

Luke. Her mind kept returning to Luke. Where was he? Was he still in town or had he left, possibly searching for her elsewhere? Had he called in the cavalry and were reinforcements from the marshals office already preparing to flood the area with agents, all carrying her picture? There was a pay phone at the far end of the lobby. Maybe she should phone the inn and see if he was still in town. No, if he hadn't checked out, the desk clerk would likely catch him going in or out and tell him there'd been a call from an unknown woman asking about him. People tended to cooperate with the law. That would surely raise Luke's suspicions, for what other woman would be inquiring about him? It wasn't worth the risk of having him learn she was still nearby.

Chewing her unconventional candy breakfast, she studied the posters on the wall, one advertising a new Kevin Costner film. Terry cocked her head, gazing up at the nearly lifesize photo. With his hair cropped close, a stern, unyielding expression, and a combative stance, Kevin resembled Luke more than a little. Before he'd grown the beard. She could just imagine what Luke would say if she pointed that out to him.

If he would ever talk to her again after all this, that is. Somehow, during the restive night, she'd come to a rather unsatisfactory but necessary conclusion. She'd have to go into hiding, go underground, change her identity. Go to another city, do different work than she usually did, live among strangers. All the things she'd been resisting in the marshals' program. But, just until she could think things through, she could do it. Her first priority had to be to feel safe.

She couldn't risk calling her family, though she longed to with a pain that was almost her undoing. Perhaps the marshals office could find another way to nail the men responsible. If not, they'd just have to let them go. If no one found her, they'd all assume she'd died somehow. Then the Russos would call off the search for her and the authorities would have to give up, too. Later, when she got her head straightened out and she was stronger mentally and physically, she'd go back and testify. If she was lucky, they'd all forget about her.

Except maybe Luke. Or would he give up, too? It didn't seem his nature. But then, did she really know him? She knew he didn't care about her nearly as much as she'd come to care for him. She hadn't let him know, of course. She wasn't even certain if her feelings were that of a woman for a particular man, or merely for the secure way he'd made her feel when they were together. She guessed that he'd probably be angry with her by now for tricking him. And frustrated when he couldn't locate her and had to admit it to his superiors.

Then again, he may have simply flown back to Phoenix, let others take over while he'd gone home to his ranch in Sedona. No one would bug him there, or thwart his plans or confront him about his feelings. He was perfectly suited to the solitary life. And he was well rid of her.

Only she'd thought he was getting better lately. The last two weeks, he'd chosen to spend more time with her rather than being outside with the dog or chopping wood. He'd opened up a bit more, too, not turning away from conversations, even starting a few. A temporary respite, most likely. Luke Tanner seemed to pride himself on needing no one.

Too bad because she really needed him right now. Finishing her candy, Terry blinked back a rush of self-pitying tears. She couldn't afford to think along those lines. Yet if only he'd indicated that he'd stand up with her against Jones and the marshals office about refusing the surgery, she never would have left him. But he hadn't. And there was no use crying over it.

Another wall poster caught Terry's eye and she stepped back for a better look. A serene drawing pictured Safe Harbor, a shelter for women and children in San Jose. The location and phone number were printed below, along with a list of organizations that helped sponsor the shelter and the fact that they were always looking for donations of food, clothing, small appliances, used furniture.

Why hadn't she thought of that before? But how would she get to San Jose before Luke or someone else found her? Was this small town on the Greyhound bus line? She didn't know, but she knew how to find out.

Excited now, Terry went to the wall phone and picked up the telephone book dangling on a chain. She found the number and checked her watch. Seven in the morning. She hoped someone was in the Greyhound offices as she used one of her quarters to call.

Moments later, she hung up with her first smile in a while. The Greyhound bus stopped alongside the corner drugstore which, the phone agent had told her, was just two blocks up from the Seafarer Inn. The bus to San Jose left at eight-ten and the fare was twenty-eight dollars. Now all she'd have to do was to make sure no one looking for her would spot her before she got on that bus.

Don Simon had done a series of articles on shelters for battered women in the Phoenix area last spring. Terry had read them and remembered that they refused no one in need and asked few questions. They even helped women find jobs. Exactly what she needed.

It wasn't much of a plan, but it was the best she could come up with under the circumstances.

Luke bolted down the rest of his milk shake, the burger he'd hurriedly eaten lying like an undigested lump in his stomach. Couldn't be helped since he couldn't spare more time for lunch. But he'd had to stop at the inn's coffee shop for something since it was two in the afternoon and his breakfast had consisted of a large takeout coffee.

He'd spent hours walking the streets, checking in stores and restaurants and questioning people at the carnival being set up in the town square. He'd talked to truckers and taxi drivers and waitresses. He'd spent way too much time at a small family-owned bed-and-breakfast run by a loquacious little woman named Sadie who'd told him a young woman resembling Terry's description had rented a room from her last night, then gone for a walk. When he'd finally tracked her down, the woman had turned out to be a good head taller than Terry, thirty pounds heavier and years older.

His head hurt, his eyes stung, and his stomach churned. All that and he was no closer to finding Terry than last night. Luke paid his check and stepped outside into bright afternoon sunshine. He glanced up and down the street, wondering where else to check. Someone had to know something.

As he stood considering, a Greyhound bus lumbered around the corner and stopped alongside the drugstore. Luke walked over.

The bus discharged a thin older man and no one else. Through lightly tinted windows, he could see half a dozen passengers waiting patiently to get back on the road. The driver went inside to check with the druggist, who was the only one working the counter. Luke followed along.

"No passengers for me this afternoon, Curt?" the bearded driver asked.

"Sorry, Bud." The short, overweight druggist straightened his rimless glasses on his broad nose. "Slow day, I guess."

Bud placed some loose change on the counter and picked a bottle of fruit punch from the cooler. "Okay, see you later."

Luke approached. "Have you been on duty all day?" he asked.

Curt frowned, his breathing somewhat wheezy. "Yes, why?"

"Have any other Greyhounds left from here today?"

"There's an eight-ten morning run stops here."

Luke flipped out his ID. "Did you happen to notice if a young woman with reddish brown hair wearing a navy jacket and jeans got on this morning?"

Curt puckered his thick lips as he studied Luke's ID, then looked up. "What's she done?"

Funny how that was always the first question. "Nothing. I need to talk with her. Did you see her?"

"Might have been her. Young woman was sitting out on the bench waiting for me when I opened this morning. Little thing wearing a knit cap and looking kind of nervous."

Luke tried not to let his excitement over this possible new lead show. "She got on the eight-ten?"

"Guess so. She bought a ticket to San Jose."

From his pocket, he removed a copy of the fax that Jones had sent to the hotel and held out the artist's picture of Terry for Curt to see. "Did she look like this?"

The druggist peered through his bifocals. "Sure looks like her. Seemed nice. I thought she was a runaway. I offered her a donut, but she wouldn't take it. Finally took a Styrofoam cup of black coffee, but she insisted on paying me. Hope she's not in any trouble."

Luke hoped she wasn't, too. "Thanks for your help."

San Jose. About twenty-five miles north on Highway 101. What was Terry planning to do in San Jose? Luke wondered as he rushed to the inn to check out.

\*\*\*

Risa was a large woman with warm brown eyes and an overbite that should have been corrected years ago. She had a face that inspired trust, Terry thought as she approached her desk in the reception room of Safe Harbor Shelter for Women & Children on a side street near downtown San Jose.

"What can I do for you?" Risa asked, pinning her name badge on the lapel of her gold blouse. Darn thing kept falling off.

"I need a place to stay," Terry said. The room smelled heavily of lilacs, as if a deodorizer had been sprayed to mask the smell of disinfectant and fried onions. She felt a queasiness in her stomach, already jumpy with nerves.

The older woman's smile was warm and welcoming. "How long will you be staying with us?"

"I'm not sure. I just need to get on my feet." Through the arch, the sound of a baby crying could be heard. What if they were full up? Where could she go from here?

Risa's shrewd eyes appraised the young woman. She was obviously wearing a wig in what she probably thought was a good disguise. Her features were fine, almost patrician, but there were dark smudges beneath her green eyes and two scars on her cheeks. Probably a battery case runaway. No matter. There was always room for one more in need. "We have a bed available."

Terry relaxed fractionally. "Just until I get a job."

"Maybe we can help you find work. What kind of experience do you have?"

Terry thought quickly. She could hardly go to work for the local paper. "Waitressing." She'd worked summers at Garcia's Mexican Restaurant in Phoenix while in college. It hadn't been all that long ago.

"Plenty of those available this time of year. What's your name? We use only first names here."

"Emily." Her mother's name was the first that had popped into her mind.

Risa rose to her full five-eight and came around the desk. "All right, Emily, let me show you to your cubicle. You got any more things?"

"No . . . no, I don't have a bag."

Poor kid, probably had to leave in a hurry. Running from some damn man, no doubt. Bastards, all of them. "We have some donated items in the back if you want to look through to see if anything fits." She moved through the archway, limping heavily, a permanent souvenir from her second husband.

The large room was partitioned off with curtains hung between the beds to afford the occupants a small measure of privacy. Terry saw that there were six cubicles on each side and a larger arch led into another room where more beds could be seen. As she followed Risa, she saw a painfully thin woman curled up on a cot asleep, another younger woman changing a wiggling baby, and a third one with scraggly hair and a black eye sitting in a rocker reading the newspaper and marking ads.

Risa stopped at the last partition. "This be all right?"

It was a single cot with a pillow, pink sheets, and a blue blanket, plus a hardback chair. It was a far cry from home, but it was clean and safe. "Yes, just fine. I don't have much money, but once I get a job . . . "

"You don't have to worry about that for now. Margaret Mary's in the kitchen fixing lunch. Should be ready soon. You get some rest. You look all in."

Tears sprang to Terry's eyes at the woman's kindness. "Thank you."

"One thing more I need to know," Risa said, pausing. "Is there a man after you?"

She wouldn't mention Luke, for if he found her, he'd never harm her. But the other two posed a very real threat. "Yes," she admitted, her voice low and suddenly wary. "Two men."

"I thought so. Don't worry. They won't get past the front door, honey." With that, Risa limped on toward the kitchen.

How ironic that she should wind up in a shelter for battered women, Terry thought. She'd almost been one once, but she'd had the good sense to walk away from Chuck at the very first hint of violence. The women she'd passed on the way in looked as if they hadn't been that fortunate.

It was not yet noon, but she lay down gratefully and closed her eyes. She couldn't remember ever being so tired.

It was four by the time Luke checked in at a Best Western Motel on the outskirts of San Jose, then set out to find the Greyhound bus station. Most weren't in the best sections of town, he knew. Of course, it would have been broad daylight when Terry arrived. But still, she was so small and defenseless, and she looked about seventeen in jeans and sneakers. She'd be easy prey for the type of men who often lurked around bus stations.

His mouth a hard line, he parked in the lot alongside the station and hurried inside.

Ten minutes later and no wiser for information gathered, he set out on foot. No one had seen any young girl arrive today from any location. Right. No one had paid attention was the problem. He supposed he couldn't blame the ticket agents and washroom attendants. It wasn't their job to monitor arrivals.

Terry undoubtedly would have been walking, scared and tired, he decided. Where would she have gone from the bus station? Did she have a destination in mind, or was she just hoping to find something? It was sunny and cool with the sun lowering in a pale blue sky. Not much to recommend this area of town, Luke thought. A seedy-looking hotel, an Indian restaurant, a boarded-up building. Across the street, a burger joint, a check-cashing establishment, a sleazy bookstore. Good God, he hoped she hadn't lingered long around here.

Still, he'd have to check them all. Desperate people did desperate things.

Luke found his hands forming fists as his frustration mounted. He wanted desperately to find Terry. Not just because he knew that Jones was pissed that he'd let her get away, although he hadn't said as much. Not even because she could be found by Russo's men or by other unsavory characters, although that was his primary concern. Aside from all that, he wanted to find her because he had feelings for her.

He wasn't about to put a name to those feelings. Not ever. He'd heard words like love and caring and commitment bandied about all his life. Wives swore to love their husbands for all time. Men vowed till death do us part. What a crock!

Forever was a joke. His father's forever had lasted till some stronger need had drawn him away. His mother stayed true a few months past that. Both had spoken words of love, to each other and to him, but had walked away with incredible ease. His grandmother had said she loved him. And she had, until the burden of raising a sad, confused, antagonistic little boy had become too much for her. The foster families—shit! They'd all been in love with the state's monthly check.

Then there was Tim Rogers, the guy who'd run the boys' ranch. Thank God, love hadn't been part of Tim's vocabulary. He'd preached discipline, hard work, and clean living. That Luke had finally bought into. Something solid to believe in. Not sentimental shit like love and forever and always.

No, he wasn't going to muddy up the waters by labeling his feelings for Terry Ryan. He wanted her, he liked being with her, and he cared what happened to her. But that was it. Hell, he loved no one, not even his dog.

He stopped at the first storefront, a twenty-four-hour coffee shop, ordered a cup at the counter and started a conversation with the middle-aged man with a patch over one eye who poured his coffee. Two refills later, he'd learned nothing new. Luke moved on.

The wind picked up and he pulled up the collar of his jacket. He was chilled and hungry, grumpy and tired. But he couldn't quit. If there was one thing Luke Tanner wasn't, it was a quitter.

If it took the rest of his days, he'd find her, by God.

She'd forgotten what hard work waitressing was. Only two days and her feet ached, her back hurt, and her stomach churned with nerves. Butch, the short-order cook behind the counter, signaled that it was her break time, and Terry sighed gratefully.

She got herself a glass of milk and moved to the last table in back, where most everyone took their breaks. Wearily, she sank into the chair and took a sip, hoping the milk would ease the burning. She was back to being unable to eat without stomach cramps.

The Metropolitan Café had been serving San Jose residents for over twenty years, or so Stefano, the mustachioed owner, had told her when he'd agreed to take her on. Stefano hailed from Athens and his heart was almost as big as his stomach, or so Risa had informed her. He'd given work to quite a few women she'd sent over, providing them with uniforms and asking few questions. His parents had immigrated years ago and had faced tough times. Stefano knew what it was like to get by on the edge. Terry didn't know how he managed to fudge the paperwork. She didn't want to know.

Lighting a cigarette as she walked over, the older waitress named Phyllis sat down opposite Terry. Or Emily, as she was known here. She hadn't chatted much with anyone, although they all seemed friendly enough. Phyllis had a sixty-year-old face, platinum-colored hair, and a size twenty-four uniform. But she'd been with Stefano since he'd opened and was the self-appointed mother hen to all the younger women.

"You want something to eat with that?" Phyllis asked. "Stefano told you, it's on the house, two meals a day. You should eat more, Emily. You're too skinny."

Terry gave her a small smile. "Thanks, but I'm not hungry." As always, her eyes were scanning the passersby strolling along the street outside the large plate glass windows of the café. Would she ever be able to stop looking over her shoulder?

Phyllis blew out a cloud of smoke, studying Terry through the haze. "Honey, you got someone after you?" she finally asked, her raspy voice lowered.

Terry's eyes widened. "What makes you ask?"

Phyllis's chuckle was throaty. "The way you act, kind of jumpy and nervous, for one. The way you're always looking out the window. And because there was this guy in yesterday evening asking Stefano if he'd hired on a young woman. The description fit you to a tee."

Terry gripped the glass, the pulse in her throat beginning to throb. "What . . . what did Stefano tell him?"

Phyllis took another deep drag. "Hell, you got nothing to worry about with him. He told the guy everyone here been with him for years."

She relaxed fractionally, but only for a moment. "What did the man look like?"

"Tall, broad shoulders, dark hair, good-looking. Had a beard."

Terry almost spilled the rest of the milk. She looked down into the glass, trying to get herself under control before she gave herself away to this kind woman. How had Luke tracked her? Far better that he had than one of Russo's men, but still, if he'd come this far, he wouldn't give up. It was just a matter of time before their paths would cross.

The thought of moving on had Terry sagging back in the chair.

"Honey, you're white as a sheet. Is that guy after you? Let's tell Stefano. He's got friends. They'll get him to back off, that's for sure." Phyllis ground out her half-smoked cigarette in the small ashtray, then placed her freckled hand on Terry's arm. "You in trouble, Emily?"

"No." She nearly choked on the lie. "Yes." Running a hand over her face, she sat back. "I don't know," she finally confessed.

Phyllis leaned closer, her lined face concerned. "Tell Stefano, honey. He'll help you."

How could she? She couldn't involve that good man in her problems. Besides, she didn't want anyone to harm Luke. And as for the others who might find her, she wouldn't think to let Stefano go after those killers. She was stuck in a trap of her own making. She'd left Luke, put herself at risk, and now was exposing others to a possible threatening situation. She had no doubt that if the man she'd seen gun down Don Simon found her here, he'd open fire, killing anyone who got in his way. Yet if she went out on the street and let Luke find her, he'd take her straightaway to a hospital where they'd whisk her into surgery.

What on God's green earth could she do?

Phyllis was still staring at her. Terry took a deep breath. "Please don't say anything to Stefano. I've got to think this through."

"Are you sure? You don't want to take a chance on getting yourself hurt."

A hysterical laugh almost erupted from Terry. No, she didn't want to get herself hurt. But she'd done a damn fine job of setting up just that. "I'll be okay. Thanks, Phyllis."

"Okay, honey. I'm here if you want to talk." Lighting another cigarette, Phyllis rose and headed for the ladies' room.

Terry drained her milk and hoped it would stay down. Her stomach was still burning. Maybe the best thing would be if she finished out her shift, quit the job, and holed up in Safe Harbor a couple of days until Luke and any others looking for her gave up the search. Risa wouldn't let them know she was there even if they stumbled into the shelter. Then, when things died down, she'd either move on or find a job where she didn't work with the public. She wasn't sure exactly what that might be, but there had to be something she could do.

Terry saw Butch signalling from behind the counter that he needed her back on the floor. Shakily, she got to her feet and went back to work.

The rain began around two, turning into a real deluge by three. Outside the windows of the Metropolitan Café, the street was nearly flooded, the traffic thinning as dark clouds overhead warned of a greater storm building. Inside, Terry shuddered as a clap of thunder reverberated throughout the old building.

Thankfully, her shift would end at four. She'd opened at seven with Phyllis and wondered why the older woman seemed to handle the work more easily. She'd be glad to get off her feet, though the weather had cut down on the number of customers. The problem was that Safe Harbor was six blocks away and she had no umbrella.

Oh, well, Terry thought ruefully, she'd survived worse. Compared to all she'd been through, what was a little drenching rain?

She'd already had a talk with Stefano, telling him as little as possible to make him understand, and he'd regretfully accepted her resignation. Though he could have held it up, he paid her for the two days she'd worked. With tips, she had eighty-one dollars. Not a fortune, but she could at least pay Risa something. She couldn't keep sponging off the kindness of Safe Harbor.

She and Phyllis were the only waitresses working the slow time between lunch and dinner except for Robbie, the counterman. Only two booths were occupied, an older couple having a late lunch and two younger tourists lingering over coffee as they pored over maps and guide books, both in Phyllis's section. An older woman carrying a shopping bag came in and took a stool at the counter, ordering from Robbie. Terry's tables were all unoccupied, giving her a chance to catch her breath as she stood by the short-order counter, watching Butch build a club sandwich.

Suddenly three chattering women walked in, dripping wet and complaining about California rain. They seated themselves in one of Phyllis's booths, causing the older waitress to roll her eyes in Terry's direction. Despite her own fatigue, Terry felt sorry for the poor soul having to be on her feet for hours at a stretch at her age, so she grabbed a tray.

"I'll get their water and setups, Phyl. You go take their order." She caught the woman's grateful smile and turned to the service area.

Terry had just lifted the tray and turned toward the front when the door swung open. She froze in her tracks as she watched the man step inside, shaking rain from his tan London Fog. He was of medium height, built stocky with a swarthy complexion and pockmarks on his face. A toothpick was stuck in the corner of his mouth. It bobbed as his small, dark eyes met Terry's and he smiled.

*Ozzie Swain!* Her senses went on red alert and Terry gasped out loud, dropping the tray, sending water spritzing in all directions, followed by shards of broken glass, napkins and silverware clattering to the floor noisily. Everything happened in a matter of seconds.

Startled, Butch leaned over the counter. "Hey, what happened?"

Phyllis swung around, her mouth open in surprise as all the customers in the café looked toward the back. "You okay, honey?" she asked, walking toward a white-faced Terry.

Poised for flight, Terry narrowed her eyes at the newcomer and belatedly realized that she'd been mistaken. This man was taller, with a kind face and shocked expression. He stepped forward, glancing around, wondering what to do.

Nerves, Terry thought. Her nerves had caused her to

overreact. Embarrassed, she bent to pick up the broken glass as Butch came around with a mop to clean up the water.

"Slipped out of your hands, did it?" Butch asked, trying to be helpful. She looked pale as a ghost and he wondered what in hell had caused her to freak out.

"Yes, I guess so." In her haste, Terry cut her finger on a sliver of glass and cried out. It was the last straw. She sucked on her finger, fighting tears.

"Honey," Phyllis said, coming over and easing Terry upright. "Why don't you go into the back room and sit a spell. You're maybe coming down with something."

"Hey, lady," the man in the London Fog said, walking closer, his hand sliding into his inside pocket, "don't I know you? You look kind of familiar."

Terry tensed all over again, wondering if she'd been right the first time. After all, she'd only caught a glimpse of Swain in the parking garage that evening. What was he reaching for in his coat pocket? Oh, God, she had to get out of there, now.

Shoving at the hands trying to help her, Terry turned and ran toward the back door. The man in the raincoat holding a pack of cigarettes stared after her with a puzzled frown, but she didn't look back. Hitting the crossbar, she set out down the alley, unmindful of the rain, her need to escape to safety uppermost in her mind. She heard footsteps behind her and Butch calling her Emily and beseeching her to stop, but she didn't even turn around.

At the corner of the building, she emerged onto the street, glad to be out of the narrow, deserted alley. There weren't many people out in the rain and few cars, but the street was less threatening. Hardly breaking her stride, she ran toward Safe Harbor, her sneakers sloshing on the damp pavement with every pounding step. She had to get away, had to.

After only a block, she became aware of footsteps still following her. Why was Butch still after her? She picked up her pace.

It was then that her pursuer yelled out. "Terry! Wait!"

*Oh, God. Someone knew her real name. Someone had found her.*

# CHAPTER TWELVE

Terry's blood ran cold as fear clutched at her heart. She had to know, had to chance a look. Swiveling her head around, she barely slowed her pace as she glanced over her shoulder.

It took but a moment for her to recognize the tall, broad-shouldered man wearing a black leather jacket and sporting a dark beard running toward her. Her relief at not seeing Ozzie Swain or anyone who resembled him was so great that her steps slowed and she turned.

Luke. Thank God. Suddenly drained of energy and hope, she stopped, waiting for him to catch up. It was over.

She was through running, too tired to fight. She couldn't do this alone. He'd won.

Luke didn't notice the dispirited look on her face or the surrender in her eyes. He saw only Terry, saw that she was whole and unharmed. He'd taken a hell of a chance when he'd spotted the sprinting figure and thought he'd recognized her a block back. He'd called out her name, praying no one who wanted to hurt her would be within earshot. And miraculously, the woman running in a downpour had been Terry.

Reaching her at last, he crushed her to him, burying his

face in her neck. "Thank God I found you," he said into her ear. "I was afraid I'd lost you."

Had she heard right? Terry didn't dare trust the hope that flared. After a moment, she eased back from him, ignoring the rain that was soaking them both, capturing his eyes. "What did you say?"

He spoke from his wary heart, his relief at finding her greater than a lifelong reluctance to reveal his feelings. "I thought you didn't want to be found. I looked everywhere for you. I've been going crazy."

She still hesitated to believe him, though his tone more than his words held the ring of truth. Luke Tanner was a cool professional whose major focus was his work, his job, his responsibility to the marshals service. Surely he couldn't feel more than that for her, the need to recapture an important witness and keep her safe until such time as she testified in court. Could he?

Her wig was sodden and lopsided on her head from the rain and the chase. She'd run off without her jacket and the thin waitress uniform was soaked, her shoes sopping wet. She was chilled to the bone and trembling. She noticed none of it, noticed only the intensity of his eyes on her. "You're in trouble with the home office about my leaving, right? The case is in jeopardy, so you're naturally upset. That's why you were anxious to find me, right?"

Luke didn't blame her for not believing him. She'd told him that it took her a while to trust a man. "No, because of this." Action. He was always more comfortable with actions than words. His arms tightened, his head lowered, and his mouth took hers.

Days of frustration, nights of distress, hours of worry boiled over into the kiss. He was none too gentle, none too patient. His mouth ravished, conquered, claimed ownership of hers. His hands at her back molded, crushed, kneaded. And finally, after an instant of shock, she responded in kind.

He was kissing her the way every woman wanted to be

kissed, Terry thought—masterfully, possessively, thoroughly. He left no doubt in her mind what he wanted. He wasted no time on the niceties, on romancing her, nor had she expected as much. His beard rubbed along the tender skin of her face and even that felt good. He was a rugged man in a dangerous line of work, and his rough edges would never all be smoothed out. It shocked her to acknowledge that he was exactly what she'd been seeking.

She tasted different, wild with need, giving as good as she got, unapologetic in her desire as she sent her tongue to tangle with his. Hunger raged through Luke's system and had his head reeling. Her slender arms wound around him and his heart thundered a welcome.

This, this was what he'd almost lost. This seemingly fragile woman who'd taken over his mind, his senses, his life. This was the one who might very well bring him to his knees, Luke knew. And he must not let her realize it.

Breathing hard, he pulled back as thunder shook the leaden sky, underscoring the turbulence he felt. "Do you understand now?" he asked, the hoarse words dragged from his throat.

She saw far more than he guessed, Terry thought. "Yes," she whispered.

He had to ask, had to know if he'd been right. "It was the surgery, wasn't it? That's why you left." He wanted to hear that it wasn't him she'd been running from, but the situation.

"Yes," she answered instantly. "Please don't let them operate on me. Please, Luke."

"I won't. I promise you." He kissed her again, fiercely, to seal the vow.

Relief flooded Terry, reflecting in her eyes.

He saw it and swore he'd never let her down again, never let anyone hurt her. "Where are your things?"

What did she have but a few tired pieces of clothing? Terry waved a dismissive hand. "Never mind them."

He picked her up into his arms and hurried to where he'd left the van.

The room he'd taken at the Best Western was perhaps fifteen by twelve with a king-size bed, oak veneer furniture, blue tweed carpeting a bit worn in places, and a cheerless dark drape hanging crookedly on the single window. The presidential suite couldn't have looked better to Terry as she entered and removed the leather jacket Luke had draped over her shoulders.

Despite the van's heater, she'd shivered during the entire ride over, more from nerves than cold. Luke hadn't spoken much on the drive, hadn't even questioned her about the last several days, but rather he'd concentrated on the rush hour traffic in a downpour. She watched him lock the door behind them as she slipped out of her soaked shoes, wondering what he was thinking, wondering if the kisses they'd shared, the words they'd said, had had as much impact on him as on her.

He stepped closer and pulled her snug against himself. The ride over had been torture. He bent his head, nuzzling her throat, nipping her earlobe. He was rock-hard and hurting, unable to recall a time when he'd wanted a woman more. This woman.

She felt him pressing into her, aware of his arousal, aware of her own. "I really need a shower," she said, as a shiver raced along her damp spine.

He let her go, but his hungry eyes stayed on her face. "I could use one myself."

They stood in the wide tub enclosed by the white plastic curtain dotted with silver and blue fish while steaming water spilled over them. She'd been reluctant to reveal her body with its faint scars in the harsh overhead light, but when Luke had bent his head to kiss each one, she'd felt her heart turn over. Beneath the spray, he washed and shampooed her short hair, then his hands went exploring. There was no reluctance on his part, no hesitation, as he worked up a soapy lather and smeared it along her back, over her shoulders and onto the pale slope of her breasts.

Terry was helpless to do anything but feel, absorb, immerse herself in the sensations buffeting her. His hands were rough, callused, yet gentle on her sensitive skin. His mouth was on hers, stealing her breath, her very will. His fingers slid down her rib cage and around to linger on her breasts, causing them to swell, to ache. She braced herself on his strong shoulders as her knees threatened to buckle. Then he slipped the bar of soap lower, between her legs, caressing silkily until she moaned out his name.

Turning off the faucets, Luke stepped out, ignoring the water dripping from him. Too impatient to dry off, he picked her up and carried her to the waiting bed. He yanked back the spread and blanket, then, in the dim light of the bedside lamp, he followed her down onto pale pink sheets. He paused, his eyes roaming her body in a way they hadn't been able to in the shower.

Terry felt the flush begin, the knowledge of her imperfections coloring her skin. There was nowhere to hide. This thorough inspection was what she'd been dreading. She wanted desperately to look her best for him and knew she didn't. Frizz for hair, a scarred face, her body too thin and marked by barely healed cuts. She raised one knee in a protective gesture and brought her arm up to shield her breasts as her eyes dropped to his chest. "I know I'm not much to look at . . . "

His gaze had traveled down her but seconds, yet it had been long enough for all her insecurities to return. "Are you fishing?"

"No, it's just that I . . . "

Needing to silence her, his hands framed her face before his mouth devoured hers in a stunning kiss, his tongue dominating hers. When he drew back, he saw the haze of passion tinting her skin, replacing the heat of embarrassment. The

accident and her injuries had robbed her of her feminine con-
fidence. He wanted to do his best to give it back to her. "How
many times do I have to tell you how terrific I think you look,
how beautiful you are? Inside. Outside. Everywhere."

Her eyes wide and wanting to believe, she watched him.

He took her hand and guided it to his erection, and heard
her gasp. "Can you tell how much I want you? Can you feel
how much I need you? Is this enough proof?"

Beneath her quivering fingers, he throbbed with life. An
almost-painful need rose deep within her as her lower body
leaned toward his heat. "Oh, Luke," she whispered, touching
her forehead to his chest as her hand caressed him.

She hadn't consciously planned nor hardly allowed herself to imagine how he'd feel, how she'd feel touching him.
But she'd wanted him almost from the start. She needed his
strength, the safety net of his arms. And she desperately
needed to know she wasn't longing alone. The proof that she
wasn't was in her trembling hand.

All the warnings he'd been given, all the cautions he'd
lived by echoed in the back of Luke's mind. It was too late.
He wouldn't listen to them, unable to turn from her.
Responding to his need alone would have been wrong, but
the hunger, the invitation in her touch was his undoing.

Tenderness. This fragile woman who'd endured so much
deserved tenderness. He would have to curb the need to rav-
age, to plunge, to take her quickly, though that was exactly
what he wanted to do. This kiss was longer as he took her
deeper, letting the giddy sensations swamp his already foggy
brain.

He took his hands down her sides and back up again,
feeling her skin jump and quiver.

"Luke, I . . . " She shifted restlessly, her fingers reaching
but missing the mark as he deftly evaded her. Frustration had
her hands bunching the sheets. His mouth trailed along her
jawline, her throat, pausing at the pulse that pounded in double time. She drew in a quivery breath that ended on a moan.

His hands were on her breasts, and then he bent to take a nipple into his mouth. She arched spontaneously as he brought first one then the other to life. Again he returned to kiss her hungrily while he skimmed his hair-covered chest along her swollen breasts, the tingling sensation causing her to shiver.

His breathing ragged, Luke buried his face in her neck, murmuring hungry, hot, exciting things in her ear. Her eyes were half-closed as she lay back, absorbing each new sensation, as with lips and teeth and tongue, he pleasured her.

No longer content to be a languid recipient, Terry shifted and they rolled together on the tangled sheets, panting now. She raised herself and touched her mouth to his, her tongue taking possession, her hands diving into his hair, her face buried in the softness of his beard. She drew in the dark male flavors, glorying in her freedom to touch as she had only in her restive dreams.

She moved lower, her lips trailing kisses along the solid planes of his chest, shoving aside the silver pendant and chain. The rain slammed against the window, the sound almost drowning out a groan he couldn't suppress. Her hands learned him, as curious as his had been to know her, to know everything.

Luke knew he was close to losing control. Again, he shifted positions, kissing her eyes closed, the small scars she fretted over, and always returning to her mouth that drew him like a magnet. While his tongue dueled with hers, his fingers found her, warm and wet and welcoming. Unable to resist watching her, he lifted his head and began to stroke her.

Terry knew it couldn't be so, yet his hands felt as if they knew her body better than she, knew what she needed and when. Her own hands fluttered, then gripped the sheet as she closed her eyes. She felt a whimper build as her body demanded the release not yet within reach. Unashamed, oddly uninhibited, she gave herself up to the increasing rhythm. When the first hard wave hit her, she cried out, stunned at the intensity that swamped her.

Head reeling, breath coming in spurts, she opened her eyes and saw more than his passion. In the warm gray of his gaze she saw a compassion he would probably deny. It was precisely then she knew she was in love with Luke Tanner. And knew that it was probably a mistake.

Luke watched her slowly return to herself, reining in his own raging need with iron control. In the back of his mind was the nagging thought that he'd never before been so concerned with a woman's pleasure. To admit that would be to admit that she'd become more of a part of him than he was comfortable acknowledging.

He smoothed back her soft, damp hair. "Was that, as they say, good for you?" he asked, his voice husky with just a touch of amusement.

Terry smiled, then licked her dry lips, aware that her tongue tasted him on her bruised mouth. "Oh," she began, sounding breathy, "it was all right, I guess." She watched a slow smile form. "But I want more. I want you."

A frown skittered over his features. She was so small and he knew how much heavier he was, how easily he could injure her delicate form. "I don't want to hurt you. Maybe you should come on top."

She knew what concerned him. She'd been recovering from the accident ever since they'd met. "Luke, I'm not fragile. I won't break. Nothing hurts anymore and I need you so much." Again, her hand caressed him intimately and she felt him jerk in response. "I want you inside me, now."

He hadn't been waiting for permission as much as assurance that she could handle his weight. Removing her hand, he braced himself above her. Then he was on her, slipping inside as easily as an old lover might. He shifted her hips, delving in deeper, starting out slowly.

His gaze fastened on her face, he picked up the tempo. Her eyes were huge and a little glazed, her cheeks damp with perspiration. His own skin was slick, his concentration total, his breathing more raspy with each rapid plunge. He gritted his teeth, exerting every ounce of control he could muster as he watched her climb back up, his own body screaming for release.

Terry had never felt so much a part of someone as she watched him holding off, his thrusts steady and deep, patiently taking her where he knew she wanted to go. She gave herself up to him entirely, letting him set the pace, emptying her mind of everyone and everything except Luke.

Luke, who was joined with her more completely than any man ever had been. Luke, who wouldn't leave her wanting while he sailed off the edge alone. Luke, who was the hardest man she'd ever known, and the most tender. She tried to speak, to tell him, but didn't have the breath to utter a word. And then she felt herself spinning away.

He saw it coming, saw the wild, pounding wind tunnel take her and whirl her away. The strength of her orgasm had her muscles tightening around him, sending him flying and finally shattering. His braced arms folded and he collapsed onto her while the waves continued to ripple through him.

"I found her." Seated on the bed, Luke shifted the phone to his other ear as he glanced over his shoulder. Terry was asleep, lying on her stomach, her short blond hair tucked into the pillow. She was exhausted from her days on the run alone, a story he'd gotten out of her as she'd lain in his arms afterward. In sleep, her face was untroubled and as innocent as a young girl's. But she hadn't made love like a girl.

"Is she all right?" Bob Jones asked, his voice tinged with both relief and concern.

"Tired but otherwise fine."

"Where did she go?"

He repeated Terry's story about the first night spent in the movie theater, the bus trip to San Jose, taking a bed at Safe Harbor Women's Shelter, and her job at the Metropolitan

Café. "This afternoon, a customer came in resembling Ozzie Swain, complete with pockmarked face. He reached into his pocket and she freaked out, dropping a tray of drinks. The guy had been reaching for his cigarettes. She was afraid to trust her memory of what he looked like, so she bolted out the back door. That's when I saw her running down the street and recognized her."

"Lucky you happened along," Bob stated, listening hard, trying to read between the lines.

"Luck, hell. I'd been walking those streets night and day, stopping in every hotel, motel, coffee shop, fast-food joint. I must've talked to two hundred people."

"And did she say why she took off?"

"Just like I'd told you, she can't face more surgery right now." He and Terry had talked about that again and he'd renewed his promise to take her side against Bob on that issue. She'd fallen asleep then, trusting him. He felt the weight of that trust sit heavily on him now.

"Damn it," Jones said softly. He wasn't a man to raise his voice, his anger more the quiet, deadly kind. "I'd hoped you could change her mind. As long as she has that face, she's in danger. We can't change her height or her body shape. But . . . '

"Forget it, Bob. We'll take our chances."

Jones heard the finality in Luke's voice. He also heard more. *We. Our.* Two against one, against the world. When had his best agent begun to side with the witness instead of the chief? Something had happened to shift things, and Jones thought he knew exactly what had transpired. "You've fallen for her," he said, and it wasn't a question.

"Hell, no." Swearing more inventively under his breath, Luke got up, dragging the phone wire across the room as he walked over to the window. "You know better than that. I don't buy into that crap."

Everyone buys into that crap when the right person comes along, Bob thought. He, too, had been a loner all his life until Laura had come along and made him want more. Now, married six years, he wouldn't have it any other way. He'd suspected that one day the same thing would happen to Luke. Ordinarily, Bob would be pleased for his friend, despite the denial he was professing right now. But caring for a witness he was assigned to protect could make an agent careless. As the chief, he couldn't afford to lose a good agent or the only witness in an important case.

There was only one thing to do. He'd have to pay a visit to Luke and his charge as soon as they were resettled and see for himself. If, in his judgment, the case was in jeopardy and lives at risk, he'd replace Luke. There'd be hell to pay, for Tanner wasn't an easy man to confront, but Bob would have to pull rank.

There were days, more than a few, when he hated his job.

"Are you still there, or did you fall asleep?" Luke asked, knowing full well that Bob had lapsed into silence only because he was trying to assess the situation.

Jones ignored the prod. "Are you sure the man she saw at the cafe wasn't Ozzie?"

"Yes. I had her go over everything that happened. If that had been Ozzie, he'd have had ample opportunity to take her out. No one else was following her when I ran after her. A case of mistaken identity brought on by nerves."

"All right. The cabin outside Truckee is all set, electricity on. When can you leave?"

Luke moved the drape aside. It was evening and a steady rain was still coming down, apt to last all night. Terry needed a good night's sleep. And he needed to hold her. "In the morning."

"That'll give me time to fax to your motel a map of how to find this place. It's way up there, almost to the Donner Pass, off Highway 80. Weather report says the rain you're getting down there may well turn into snow up that way soon. Elevation's about eight thousand feet. You might want to get chains for the van and pick up some supplies. You could get snowed in."

The way he felt right now, that would be the best thing that could happen to them, Luke thought. Car tracks and footsteps could be spotted more easily in snow. He'd visited that area west of Reno before and knew that many of the roads could be difficult to navigate in winter. That could only help them if someone got wind of their whereabouts and tried to reach them. "Sounds good to me."

"How's the money holding up?"

"I got a cash advance on the card just yesterday. We'll be all right."

There was that *we* again. "There's a secure phone line in the place. Call when you get there."

"Will do." Luke hung up and listened to his stomach growling. He turned around and saw that Terry was awake, the sheet tucked in around her body. He wondered how much she'd heard.

She smiled at him lazily. "Hey, officer. There's a naked man in my room." And what a naked man. Tall, weathered, strong. Imperfections, sure. More scars than she had along that long, lean torso. But unabashedly male as he strolled back to replace the phone. She drank in the sight of him as warmth spread through her.

Luke lay down on top of the covers and rolled to face her. "Shall I have him thrown out, miss?"

She trailed her fingers along his chest, loving the feel of the soft hair, the smooth skin, the hard muscles beneath. "Mmm, I think I have something else in mind for him." Leaning over, she touched her mouth to his.

No going back, Terry thought as he took over the kiss. Once a man and woman crossed the line in their relationship, there was no going back. Not that she wanted to. But what, she wondered, did Luke want?

Easing back, he saw that the short nap had done some good. She looked a little less tired, less strained. Her lips were still a little puffy from his kisses and her eyes still contained the remnants of sleep. She looked lazy and contented and very beautiful. He felt the stirring of fresh desire. "Do you feel better?"

Stretching languidly, she all but purred. "I don't know how I could feel any better than I do right now." Perhaps if this whole thing with the Russo brothers was behind them, if she could come out of hiding, put them away with her testimony and get on with her life, maybe then she'd feel permanently better. But maybe then, she'd lose the only good that had come out of the whole tragic mess: Luke.

She distracted herself from that thought by picking up the medal he always wore and studying the disk. Silver-and-black flames were superimposed over a Celtic cross. "This must hold special meaning for you."

Luke nodded. "It does. My grandmother gave it to me to keep me safe. She considered the piece a good luck charm. It's a St. George's talisman, named after a channel linking the Irish Sea and the Atlantic Ocean. I don't know anything about its origin."

Sitting up, he removed the chain from around his neck. "I want you to wear it so it'll keep you safe."

She wouldn't have guessed he'd believe in such things. "I can't take your lucky piece."

"Yes, you can. I want you to have it." He tugged her upright and slipped the chain over her head. The medal fell to hang between her breasts. "Beautiful," he whispered.

"Thank you." She kissed him, then fell back onto the pillows.

Slowly, he trailed the backs of his fingers along her stomach, watching the muscles quiver at the contact. "Maybe if we put some hot food in there . . . "

"Ah, I guess you're hungry." Only she saw his attention shift back up to her breasts, his eyes darkening.

Leaning down, he blew his warm breath on them and saw them pucker in invitation. "Hungry? Yeah, I think I am." He kissed the full curve of one breast and heard her draw in a quick breath. He looked up and saw the surprise in her eyes. "What?"

"I'm just still amazed at how you make me feel. Here with you now, I feel safe. I feel not so lost." Her hand moved to stroke his hair.

"Maybe you need to stop playing Wonder Woman and let someone help you. Sometimes being strong means asking for help."

"I never claimed to be strong. That's a man thing."

Turning her toward him, he nuzzled her breasts with his bearded face. "You're definitely not a man."

She smiled, realizing that a serious conversation at this moment was impossible. Did she really want to talk or did she want . . . ? She sighed out loud as he tossed back the sheet the rest of the way and pulled her to him.

"I want you again, Terry." The admission felt as if it had been wrenched from him, but that didn't make it any less true. "Again and again and again."

"No more than I want you," she confessed in a hoarse whisper, then turned her face into his throat and gave herself up to the magic of his touch.

Three A.M. The bewitching hour, or was that midnight? Terry didn't know. She did know that awakening in the middle of the night in a dark, unfamiliar room and being unable to go back to sleep was becoming an all-too-familiar feeling. She stared at the ceiling, wondering how many strange beds she'd slept in since this whole nightmare began. Too many.

The motel's parking lot lights drifted in faintly over the top of the sagging drape covering the window. It was enough so that she could make out the time on the bedside clock. And the features of the man sleeping beside her.

She was afraid to move, knowing what a light sleeper Luke was. She wanted to study him at her leisure when he wasn't aware of her. He lay on his side facing her, one arm extended under the pillow, the other resting atop the sheet that covered him only to his narrow waist. Even in sleep, it seemed as if his features weren't entirely relaxed. There seemed an almost indiscernible tenseness about him, a readiness to leap up at the slightest sound or movement.

He probably needed his rest more than she, for she knew that he'd been walking the streets searching for her for days, scarcely sleeping, hardly eating. She'd never meant to put him through that. Thankfully, he didn't seem to hold her little escapade against her. He hadn't even asked her to promise she'd never do anything that foolish again, although she'd vowed to herself that she wouldn't.

And oh, the glorious way he'd made her feel when they made love. After they'd made love again, he'd ordered dinner sent up from the motel restaurant, which had turned out to be better than she'd expected. She hadn't really eaten a solid meal in days with her nervous stomach acting up. Perhaps she'd felt better because she was being watched over by Luke again. Or perhaps good sex, which she hadn't had in many months, had increased her appetite.

At any rate, they'd eaten steak sandwiches and fries and hot coffee. Then they'd watched the news on television from bed, becoming drowsy together. It had felt so wonderful falling asleep in his arms after they'd made love again. He'd managed to keep her fears at bay, to cause her to relax until she'd felt lethargic and contented.

She noticed the scar on his right side, the one he'd told her earlier was a knife wound put there by Nick Russo. He had another smaller one on his face near one temple, and he couldn't even recall who'd put that one there.

Ah, but he was still beautiful. Such a strong face, such a determined, focused man. Thank God he hadn't given up and left her to fend for herself. She'd been mistaken about the man in the restaurant being Ozzie Swain. But perhaps the next suspicious man she saw might be the real thing. She couldn't have hidden out at the shelter forever, going from one entry-level job to another. And it didn't seem as if the Russo men were going to give up, either.

How long were the police and the courts going to drag this thing out? Why couldn't they set a trial date and stick to it? Surely the prosecution of police officers and mob criminals accused of brutal murders ought to take precedence over more minor crimes. In every major city, Terry was aware, court dockets were full to overflowing. Justice was no longer a speedy thing, if it ever had been. It crept along slowly, leaving a lot of gaping loopholes that clever attorneys discovered daily.

But how long could she be expected to remain in hiding? How long could one man, as finely trained as Luke was, be expected to be able to keep her safe from harm? The criminals were many in number and he was but one. Jones had said that Ozzie Swain and probably Nick Russo were searching for her. But they could also have put a price on her head, enticing even petty criminals to hunt her down and score with the big boys. What chance, no matter where they hid away, did they have against the mob, men with no scruples to get in the way of their methods?

"You're doing it again," Luke's voice said, startling Terry.

She turned toward him. "What am I doing?"

"Obsessing. Conjuring up scenarios that could happen. Getting yourself worked up over what might happen." He shifted to a more comfortable position, punching up his pillow, then taking her hand in his. "Am I right?"

Terry let out a ragged breath. "You know me too well."

Apparently she wasn't aware that her expressive face revealed her emotions so clearly, especially when she thought no one was looking. "Don't obsess. It'll only upset you."

"Yeah, well, I guess I have a right to be upset from time to time." She watched her thumb trace the blue veins on his hand as she spoke. "The mob never forgets, do they, Luke?

What I'm really afraid of is that even if I testify and the men in jail are convicted and sent to prison for a long while, Sam's brother will never let up until he finds me. There's nowhere I can go, nowhere to hide. And he can hire others who'll look, too. I'll never be safe, never be free."

Luke knew it was a legitimate fear. He didn't know if he could ease her mind, but he had to try. "That's not true. We have ways. If necessary, we can change your whole identity, set you up in another city of your choice far away from here, and they'll never find you."

"That doesn't sound very appealing. I don't want a new identity." Again, she'd be away from her family, her friends. She'd have to start all over.

Discouraged, Terry sat forward, drawing her knees up and hugging them. "You know, all I ever wanted was to be the best political cartoonist in the state. Maybe to get syndicated. I couldn't do that with a new identity. My style would be recognized and I'd be identified." She let out a sigh. "Oh, well, it was a stupid dream anyway."

He sat up with her. "Dreams are never stupid. Unrealistic sometimes, but not stupid." He touched her chin, forced her to face him. "I'm going to do everything in my power to see that you realize that dream, Terry. Do you believe that? Do you trust me?"

She searched his eyes and could see he meant every word. She was as aware as he that he could only do so much, but that wasn't important. What was was that he *wanted* to help her in every way at his disposal. "I trust you," she whispered, and handed him her heart with that simple statement.

# CHAPTER THIRTEEN

"Oh, my. Listen to this." In the passenger seat of the van, Terry folded the newspaper so she could read the article written by Carlos Dunahee, the *Phoenix Gazette* reporter who'd been like a one-man crusade needling the police to do more about finding Don Simon's killer.

"Is he poking jabs at Central again?" Luke asked as he swung onto Highway 580 north, which would intersect with Interstate 80 leading to Truckee. It was a sunny morning after yesterday's rain, for which he was grateful. They had a full day's journey ahead.

Terry had been following Dunahee's articles for several weeks. He'd been relentless in calling for public support of police reform in light of the arrest of several cops accused of heinous crimes. Her friend, Andy Russell, had joined Carlos at a public forum, calling for a citizen's committee to investigate the happenings at Central Precinct since Internal Affairs and even the county attorney were dragging their feet. She didn't know Carlos, but she wished she could talk to Andy to find out how things really were.

"He sure is getting people worked up." Terry took a sip from the Styrofoam cup of coffee she'd picked up along with the newspaper while Luke had gassed up the van. She began to read. " 'This reporter feels a decided coolness at Central Division these days, and it's not difficult to figure out why. Since Don Simon was found slain in the parking lot across from the *Gazette,* even police beat reporters are made to feel unwelcome in the precinct, as if somehow our very presence might precipitate another murder.' "

"He's feisty, isn't he?" Luke commented as he signaled before moving into the left lane of the highway.

"We're just getting to the good stuff." Terry took another hasty sip before continuing. " 'Speculation runs rampant nonetheless throughout the precinct. From Homicide to Missing Persons, from Burglary to Records, in every department cops are nervous, conjecturing under their breath, trying out theories on one another. Overheard in the men's room was the most believable hypothesis, that Terry Ryan, thought to be the only witness to reporter Simon's brutal slaying, is still alive and well, stuck away somewhere under protection of the Feds.' "

Luke glanced over and noticed that her expression had closed in. "They're only guessing. Rumors like that circulate at every precinct."

She looked up. "I suppose it was only a matter of time till someone put that in print. They'd be fools not to have thought of it." She returned to her reading, silently now. But the next paragraph had her gasping aloud.

"What?" Luke asked, frowning. Maybe he should see to it that she couldn't get ahold of newspapers from now on.

"My father. He's had another heart attack."

Just what they needed right now. "Read it to me."

Terry swallowed around a lump. " 'Retired Officer John Ryan, Terry's father, naturally has been following the case more closely than most. A day hasn't gone by that he hasn't been at Central, bothering the big boys, demanding answers. As with the rest of us, Ryan's pleas fell on deaf ears. Which is probably one reason he was taken to Good Samaritan Hospital last week with severe chest pains. Ryan retired sev-

eral years ago with a heart condition. Having a daughter's
fate be unknown for months wouldn't be easy on a well man.
Officer Ryan also lost his eldest daughter, Kathleen, twelve
years ago in a drunk driving accident.'"

Terry lowered the paper, blinking back a rush of tears.
*Oh, Dad. Please be all right.*

"Chest pains, it said, Terry. Not a heart attack."

"That's how the first one started out, too."

"I'll call Jones when we get to the cabin and have him
check out your father's condition, okay?"

She nodded before turning to stare unseeingly out the
side window. Questions raced around in her mind. Was her
father still in the hospital? If it was serious, as bad as last
time or even worse, he would be. Oh, God, she'd give anything to talk with him, to hear his voice, to let him know she
was all right so he wouldn't worry. She knew how much
John Ryan worried, about money, his children, his job. If
only she could remove at least one concern from him, she
would in a heartbeat.

Maybe, if she asked him, Luke would let her call home,
talk with her mother and reassure them she was safe. After
all, wasn't the phone at their destination supposedly secure?
Didn't that mean that no one could tap the line and listen in
or trace a call from the number? Given their new closeness,
maybe he'd grant her this small wish.

She glanced over at Luke's profile, saw that he was concentrating on traffic in that focused way he had. Studying the
hard angles of his face, the grim expression, her doubts
returned. He wouldn't let her call, citing a dozen reasons
why she shouldn't phone. She'd have to be content with
hearing news thirdhand from Bob Jones to Luke and then to
her, each of them editing along the way. She didn't even
know exactly where they were headed.

"I don't suppose you'd tell me where we're going?" she
asked, thinking it was worth a try.

At this point, he saw no reason not to. "Bob and his wife
own a cabin somewhere between Grass Valley and Reno

near Truckee. He gave me directions. No one knows about this place, so it's particularly safe."

What did it matter where? Terry thought. The real question was how long would they be there, and that Luke couldn't answer. She slid on her sunglasses, leaned her head back and closed her eyes.

"Get some rest," Luke told her. "You'll feel better."

She had rested, but she hadn't slept much. She'd been too stimulated by Luke's lovemaking, too worried about her future, too saddened by the prospect of one day soon having to give up what she'd just found. Life so rarely was fair, she decided as she heard Luke snap on the radio.

Willie Nelson's gravelly voice began with "On the Road Again." *You can say that again*, Terry thought.

It was early evening when they stopped outside of Sacramento at Pomeroy's Country Store. Luke decided it was as good a place as any to stock up on supplies they'd need for an indeterminate stay in the mountain cabin. The air had turned much colder as they'd driven north. Radio weather predictions were for snow on the way and colder temperatures. As he stepped out, he spotted the first snowflakes.

He walked around the van to help Terry down, but she'd beat him to the punch and jumped down herself. She'd been quiet most of the day since reading the upsetting newspaper article, leaning back, hiding behind her sunglasses and pretending to sleep though he knew she hadn't. He'd decided it would be best to leave her to her thoughts. They'd talk things out once they got to the cabin and were safely entrenched.

He fell in step beside her as they walked toward the door. "Pick up everything you think we may need. If a storm hits, we may not be able to get to a store again for a while."

Wordlessly, Terry went inside and grabbed a basket.

It took half an hour for them to push the cart through all the aisles, piling in food and staples that they'd need. They had no way of knowing just what the cupboards at the cabin held, if anything. Terry added a few personal items, including hair dye. Her wig had pretty well been ruined yesterday and she was tired of wearing it anyway. She chose a warm light brown shade and decided that the cuts on her scalp were healed enough to handle the dye. Then she could leave off the knit cap she'd been forced to wear today.

At the register, Luke reached for his wallet as Terry shoved the loaded cart within reach of the cashier. He glanced out the window and saw that the snow was picking up. "Maybe we should pick up a couple of sandwiches and eat them in the van. We have another two hours to go and I'd like to be there before the storm worsens."

"Fine with me." The short-order counter was off to the side. "I'll go put in an order. What would you like?"

"A sub with roast beef, Swiss cheese, lettuce, and mayo. And a real Coke, not that diet stuff." He handed her a twenty.

Taking it, she gave him a look of disapproval. "If the cholesterol won't kill you, the sugar will."

He grinned. "Gotta die of something. Might as well enjoy the trip."

Shaking her head, Terry went to the counter.

She accepted the sandwiches and drinks from the slim blonde behind the deli counter as Luke joined her with the bagged groceries. She handed him the change then glanced around, finally spotting what she wanted. "I need to make a stop at the ladies' room. I'll be out in a jiffy."

He saw the two rest rooms side by side in a small corridor past the deli counter. "I'll wait for you in that hallway."

He was back to dogging her every step, Terry thought as she walked to the rest room. Just doing his job or because he didn't trust her not to take off again? Remembering her fear when she'd thought she'd seen Ozzie, she supposed she should be grateful, but moments like this, that smothered feeling returned. Shoving the door in, she saw that the room was unoccupied, both stalls empty. She hurried into one.

Finishing, she came out and stopped at the sink to wash her hands. It was then that she spotted the wall phone just under the closed window. Her heart leaped into her throat as she dried her hands.

Terry glanced toward the door. Was Luke just outside? Could he hear her? She had left the money she'd earned at the Metropolitan Café in her suitcase and she'd returned the sandwich change to Luke. But in her jeans pocket were two quarters from the night she'd been in the theater.

Making a quick decision, she pulled out a quarter and lifted the receiver before she could change her mind. She inserted the quarter and dialed the long-distance operator as she checked her watch. Seven in California, which would mean eight in Arizona, with the winter time change. In a hushed voice, she told the operator she wanted to make a collect call, and recited her parents' number. With heart pounding, she waited.

"Hello?" The voice was male, sounding faint and somewhat fuzzy.

The operator came on. "Collect call for anyone at this number from Terry. Will you accept charges?"

"Terry? Did you say Terry?" The voice seemed stronger, as if the man had been asleep and now was wide-awake.

"Yes, sir," the operator said. "Terry. Will you accept charges?"

"Yes, yes," John Ryan said impatiently, sitting up in his easy chair in his Phoenix living room. "Terry, is that you?"

Tears sprang to Terry's eyes as she heard the operator click off. "Yes, Dad, it's really me."

"Oh, thank God you're alive. I wasn't sure until this very minute."

Terry huddled toward the phone, speaking softly. "How are you? I read you were hospitalized again with heart problems."

"Me, I'm okay. Just some chest pains, not another heart attack. What about you? Oh, God, I can't believe it's really you." He suddenly remembered. "The accident. Are you fully recovered?"

"I'm all right." She paused to swallow, choking with emotion. "Don't worry about me, Dad, please. I'm okay."

John Ryan ran a trembling hand over his thinning brown hair. "Where are you, Theresa Anne?"

"I'm not sure exactly where, but don't worry. We're headed for a safe house. It's owned by the head man's family."

"He's with you?"

"No, I'm with a federal agent who never leaves my side. You know, the Witness Protection Program."

"Why? Why did they take you away? If they only knew what it was doing to your mother and me." His voice broke on a sob.

"You know why, Dad. I only called to make sure you're not sick again."

"Your mother's not home. Give me a number where I can call you back. She'll want to talk to you."

Terry felt her heart squeeze. "I can't, Dad. They don't know I'm calling. Please, you mustn't tell anyone or I'll get in trouble. Please, be patient and I'll be home. One day soon." She heard voices in the hallway outside the rest room and realized time was running out. "I have to say good-bye. It's beginning to snow and we have a two-hour drive ahead of us. Luke wants to beat the storm so we have to get started. I love you, Dad. Please don't worry."

"Wait, Terry. Don't hang up. Are they treating you all right?"

"Fine, Dad, really. Good-bye for now." Hastily, she hung up, struggling to hold back the tears. Taking a deep breath, she moved to the sink and splashed cold water on her face. She was patting herself dry with a paper towel when the door swung open.

The slim blonde from behind the counter stood in the doorway. "Your husband wants to know if you're all right?"

Terry nodded. "Yes, thanks." She followed the woman out into the hallway and found a frowning Luke waiting.

"Is anything wrong?" he asked, his voice concerned.

She placed a fist on her stomach. "Cramps, but I feel better now. Ready to go?"

He narrowed his eyes thoughtfully as he took her arm, but finally turned and walked her outside. "Don't scare me like that, will you?"

"Next time, you'll have to come in with me," she said with no small amount of sarcasm as she hopped up into the passenger seat, praying her little performance had fooled him.

Better. She felt better. Her father was home, he hadn't had a heart attack. She leaned back as Luke finished loading their supplies, then climbed in.

He started the engine, still watching her. "You drink too damn much coffee. That's probably what's got your stomach all upset."

She smiled to herself. "You're probably right."

Less than an hour into their trip, the storm began in earnest. Luke pulled into a gas station and had chains put on the tires, a requirement at the higher altitude when a heavy snowfall was predicted. After that, the four-wheel-drive seemed to barrel through and over even the heavier drifted snow. Visibility was the problem, especially when they left the main highway and started up the mountain, following the map Jones had faxed him.

"It looks like a picture postcard or a scene out of a movie," Terry said, gazing up at bare tree limbs balancing snow accumulations.

"It may look pretty, but it's damn treacherous to drive in," Luke commented, his hands tightening on the wheel as they eased around a narrow curve. Unfamiliar roads, darkness and a snowstorm. Not ideal traveling conditions. He turned the windshield wipers on high.

"I've never been out in snow," Terry confessed.

"You're kidding? You mean you never drove up into northern Arizona in the winter? Great ski country."

"No, I never went. My brothers used to go and even my sister. But none of my friends ski so I never bothered to learn."

He wished he had time to teach her, but he didn't mention the thought aloud. It would lead to suggesting that he might one day, which would indicate they had a future together. And Luke knew they didn't.

His own future was unsettled at the moment. He was uncertain whether he wanted to continue with the marshals service or stay on his ranch and raise horses. His house was paid for, the renovations nearly complete. His needs were few, so he wouldn't have to make a lot of money. He'd be truly independent, with no one over him telling him what to do and when. Perhaps the time had come to hang it up.

Still, although he'd been a loner, he'd always been among people. At the ranch, he was truly alone and though he'd preferred it that way so far, would he want that for the rest of his days? He truly hadn't known anyone he wanted to share that solitary life with.

Until Terry Ryan came into his life.

Luke turned the wheel sharply to the right, then around to the left, tensing as he maneuvered a hairpin turn. Suddenly, the road straightened a bit and he relaxed.

Yes, he could picture Terry on his ranch. In one of their talks, she'd told him she liked horses and rode well. But that would be far from the only requirement. What about that large, loving family she had, the one she missed more each day? She'd want to be with them and he didn't think he could handle a steady stream of Ryans invading his space.

And what about his love of danger and excitement, which he rarely admitted out loud, but was astute enough to acknowledge quietly. Being free of the pressure of his work would be a plus, but would he miss the thrills, the satisfaction of a job well done? Would he feel tied down if he wasn't free to go when he felt the urge, which was the way he'd lived his life for as far back as he could remember?

He wanted Terry in his life, but he couldn't imagine checking in constantly with someone, explaining his need to take an occasional job for Jones or maybe just setting out with his truck and Yuma for parts unknown until the need passed. What woman would put up with that?

Luke downshifted, then glanced over at Terry. In the dim light of the dash, he could see a look of almost childish delight on her face as she peered out at the winter landscape. In many ways, she appeared very young. After all, he was twelve years older than she. But in other ways, she showed a maturity beyond her years.

And in the bedroom, she matched him superbly, unapologetically making her own demands, then letting him set the pace, open and enthusiastic about each new thing they did together. He didn't want to lose that rare bonding, but he didn't know if he was willing to pay the price for keeping it. There were times when he caught her looking at him and knew she was weaving forever dreams around him. He'd have to straighten her out about that and soon. Luke Tanner and forever were distant cousins, not even on speaking terms.

The van suddenly lurched sideways before Luke got the vehicle under control again. He heard Terry's quick gasp of fear. "It's okay. We just hit a slick spot." To prove his point, he slowed even more and crept around the next bend. "It shouldn't be too much farther now." A drive that he'd estimated would last two hours was now well into the third. However, he didn't dare go any faster.

"I trust you," she said, more calmly than she felt. This sort of outing in a snowstorm always looked like more fun in the movies than it was in reality.

*I trust you.* Luke hoped her words wouldn't haunt him.

The cabin was tucked into the side of the mountain, the snow camouflaging it so well that they nearly drove on past. The yard had a cyclone fence with barbed wire along the top and a heavy iron gate. Standing on the wooden porch after Luke had checked out the interior, Terry shivered. He'd picked up a heavy jacket for her that morning since she'd left her other one behind, but they hadn't thought to get boots and her Reeboks were wet, her feet cold in the short walk from the parked van.

"I should have carried you," Luke commented as he held open the door. "I would have if you'd have waited for me to help you down."

He couldn't seem to understand that she didn't like sitting like a good girl and waiting until he came to fetch her. "My shoes will dry," she said, moving inside.

The interior was comfortably rustic. The large living room had paneled walls, carpeted floor, and a huge stone fireplace. The kitchen was big, too, like a country kitchen, with Mexican tile on the floor and another fireplace, smaller and made of red brick. Both bedrooms were good-sized and they also had fireplaces.

"Doesn't this place have a furnace, or do they rely strictly on fireplaces for heat?" she asked as Luke brought in their bags.

"I've never been here before, so I'm not sure." He put both suitcases in the largest bedroom. "I'll check it out in a minute." He went back outside for their supplies.

"I hope there's a good supply of wood," Terry commented as Luke carried bags into the kitchen.

"There's a big pile out back. One more trip and we're moved in." He left her opening cupboard doors and checking out their contents.

By the time they explored the place, put everything away,

and unpacked their clothes, it was nearly midnight. Luke had found the furnace and although it was a vintage model, it did work. Still, he built a fire in the bedroom because he liked the coziness of it.

Pomeroy's Country Store offered more than merely groceries for sale since it was one of the last markets before the turnoff to mountain roads. Clothing, hardware, some automotive supplies, and drugstore items were in a separate section.

Terry had picked up an old-fashioned, long-sleeved flannel nightgown that she put on after her shower and found that it fell to her ankles. Luke had picked up a black knit cap and matching fur-lined slippers for both of them. Looking at herself in the floor-length mirror on the back of the bathroom door with her short curly hair, the pale blue granny gown and the fuzzy moccasins, she laughed out loud. A real glamour girl, she thought, wondering what Luke would think.

She felt the flush of guilt when she thought of Luke and the conversation they'd had a short time ago. When they'd finished in the kitchen, he'd walked with her to the bedroom doorway and paused. He wanted them to sleep together in this room, he'd told her, but he didn't know how she felt, despite last night. He would put her things in the other bedroom if that's what she wanted.

There'd been very little interplay between them during the long day's drive, especially since leaving Pomeroy's. No soft words, no lingering touches. Terry had been thinking about her father, wondering if she'd done the right thing by phoning. And she felt guilty about deceiving Luke. But she knew she wanted him in her bed. "I want to be with you," she'd said, looking up at him.

She'd been surprised by the quick flash of pleasure on his face before he'd pulled her into an openmouthed kiss that told her more than any words could have. Now, leaving the bathroom, Terry again struggled with the guilty knowledge of having gone behind Luke's back. How could she make love with a man she'd lied to?

Entering the bedroom and seeing him standing by the blazing fire wearing only his briefs and holding two brandy glasses, she swallowed hard. She prayed he couldn't read the truth in her eyes. She'd never been a very good actress, even as a child trying to keep small infractions from her parents.

Luke stared at her, more than a little surprised that she could look sexy in a gown that covered her from neck to ankles. Even from where he stood, he could smell bath powder and the scent of the moisturizing lotion she used. He held out the snifter of amber liquid. "This will warm you."

She took it, bringing it up to her nose and inhaling the intoxicating bouquet. As if she needed further warming after seeing him standing nearly naked with the firelight dancing on his bronze skin. "Thank you." She took a small sip and felt the heat trail downward.

Luke tasted his. "I called Bob and told him we made it."

"Did he have anything new to say?"

"No, just that he'd keep us informed. I asked him to check on your father's condition."

"Thanks." She turned away, unable to meet his eyes. She searched for a less disturbing subject. "Did this place once belong to another drug lord or whatever?"

"Bob never told me and I didn't ask." He drained the brandy and set the glass on the mantel. Terry seemed jittery and nervous, and he wondered why. He wondered what he could say to put her at ease. "Your hair's really looking good." Three months had brought about a marked improvement. It was still short, of course, but so much better than the wig. "I didn't know you had curly hair. In the file pictures I saw, it hung straight down to your shoulders."

"That's because I used to blow it dry using a brush to straighten the natural curl. I really don't like the curly look, but I don't have much choice right now."

"I like it." He watched her turn aside and give in to a yawn as he eased back. "Tired?"

"Kind of." Terry carried her brandy over to the bedside table and set it down. She noticed that he'd removed the spread and turned down the covers. "Oh, look. A feather bed. My grandmother used to have one of these." Smiling, she stepped out of her moccasins, slipped under the warm coverlet and stretched out. "Ah, this is heaven."

Luke joined her, staying on his own side but turning to look at her. "Since you're tired, I should probably let you get some rest."

Enormously relieved that somehow he understood, she let out a relieved breath. "I know I'll feel better after a good night's rest."

Something was wrong. She had her back to him, as if she didn't want to look at him. Luke's mind quickly scrolled back over the brief conversations they'd had during the long drive, but he couldn't come up with anything that might have upset her. Maybe he was making a mountain out of a molehill. Perhaps she really was just tired. He stretched to kiss the back of her head. "Sleep tight."

Curled away from him, Terry felt remorse flood her. He wouldn't understand if she confessed her call. He wouldn't accept the fact that she'd simply *had* to make sure her father was all right. She'd just have to live with her deception. Closing her eyes, she willed sleep to come.

She'd never been snowed in before, but Terry found she rather liked it. The cabin had everything they needed. It was warm and cozy inside while the snow continued to fall outside for two days. Standing at the window watching the wind rearrange the drifts, she smiled. Yes, she could easily go on like this for days, weeks. Marooned high up a mountain and all but buried in snow, inaccessible to outsiders, safe for the time being, at least.

She turned to watch Luke sitting on the stone hearth

whittling and carving still another small animal from the wood he'd brought along. He was quite good really. She'd lined them up on the mantel—a deer, a rabbit, a horse, an elk. He was currently working on an owl.

She listened to the fire crackling and felt a contentment she was sure she'd never known before. She'd painstakingly pushed her guilt to the back of her mind, convincing herself that no harm had been done and nothing would be accomplished if she confessed. They were getting along well. Why rock the boat?

Why couldn't life always be like this? she asked the Fates. With a sigh, she moved back to the plaid couch and picked up her sketch pad. She was doing a pencil drawing of Luke in profile, and this was a good time to catch him unawares as he concentrated on the owl taking shape.

Since the night she'd shown him the drawing of her father, she'd done dozens of others, mostly political cartoons based on news she'd read in papers she'd picked up along the way. Some she felt were good enough to be published and wished she could send them to the *Gazette*. But, of course, she knew she couldn't. So she'd concentrated on other subjects as the mood struck her.

She'd done several of Luke, but this one was by far her best. It had taken some time to capture the steely strength, yet allow the tenderness to show through. Finishing the final few strokes, she held up the pad, trying to view it critically.

"Can I see?" Luke asked, sitting down beside her on the couch.

Lost in her art, she hadn't heard him cross the room. She could refuse, Terry supposed. But she was more than a little curious how he'd view himself seen through her eyes. She handed him the sketch.

He hadn't known the drawing was of him and he hadn't known what a talented hand could do to transform what he considered an ordinary face into one of far greater interest.

"You flatter me," he said, studying the sketch from several angles.

"That's how I see you," she said softly.

She'd put more than her skill into the drawing, Luke decided. She'd drawn a portrait seen through the eyes of a woman in love. Struggling with the realization, he tried to keep his expression even as he stood. He'd let things get too far, get out of hand. And he had only himself to blame.

He handed the pad back to her. "Can I have it?"

Something was wrong. There was a sudden tension about him. "Sure."

"Sign it, would you please?"

She hesitated as he walked away. "You don't seem as if you like it." She was at a loss for words.

"But I do. I want to hang it from the mantel. Maybe there are some thumbtacks in the kitchen." He left the room.

Numb with foreboding, Terry signed the drawing and felt like weeping.

Moments of happiness and feelings of well-being lasted only briefly, it would seem.

You can't have everything, not ever, Terry reminded herself. She was in a safe place with a man she'd fallen in love with. But there the fairy tale ended. Luke didn't love her and probably never would.

Two days after she'd given him the sketch she'd drawn, she again stood looking out the window at the blanket of snow. It had stopped coming down, but there was plenty piled up and some very high drifts. Earlier, Luke had gone out and cleared the porch and a short path with a shovel he'd found in the storage room. It was a serene, peaceful scene. Yet she didn't feel serene or peaceful.

Nothing had changed, outwardly that was. Luke was quiet and polite during the day, talking whenever she began a conversation, friendly even. And nights, he was the lover she'd always dreamed of having, insatiable, considerate, thrilling. Yet nothing was as it should be.

She should have known better, Terry chided herself. Hadn't she warned herself not to fall in love with a man who always moved on? Perhaps he did care, in his own guarded way, but not enough to make their arrangement permanent. Whenever he felt that she was getting too close, he'd back away. She'd be better off not to let herself think about the future. He was married to his work, despite his occasional discontent with some aspects of it. And he wasn't about to change his lifestyle for her, nor anyone else most probably.

Luke Tanner depended only on himself, trusted only himself. He was incapable of sharing the deepest part of himself with anyone. She would have to accept that, to be content with loving him while she had him, then letting him go without making him feel guilty. He hadn't lied to her, had never promised her anything. It was she who had taken things a step farther. And that had to stop right now.

What she needed was some physical exercise. This sitting around with too much time to think was making her crazy. Walking to the hall closet, she ducked inside and began to rummage around. In minutes, she found some things she could use. While not exactly ideal, the oversize boots and gloves would do. Eager for some fresh air, she sat down to pull on the boots.

Strolling in from the kitchen, Luke saw her hunched over. "What are you doing?"

"Going outside."

She looked pleased and he was glad to see that. It was far easier to keep his distance when Terry wasn't looking so lost and alone as she sometimes did. "What for?"

"To play in the snow. I've never had the chance before. I'm tired of being inside."

"Play? You want to play?" He hadn't played in years, if ever, feeling as he did that he'd been born old.

She stood to put on her coat. "There are more boots in the

closet. Why don't you join me? Or are you too old to play, Grandpa Tanner? I thought you government types were supposed to keep in shape. Think you can help me build a snowman? That's pretty mild work." She pulled a blue knit cap over her short hair.

A snowman. He remembered one winter he'd spent at the boys' ranch. They'd built two forts a dozen feet apart, pummeling each other with snowballs. The roughhousing had worked off a lot of excess energy. "Maybe I will." He poked around in the closet, taking out several boots and holding them up to gauge the sizes.

Hiding her grin, Terry stepped outside, then realized the sun on the white snow was too bright for her. She went back for her sunglasses and saw that he'd finished dressing. "Come on. Last one to roll a mound big enough for the snowman's body gets his face washed with snow." She dashed out ahead of him.

They worked at their masterpiece for the better part of an hour, fashioning snow arms and fat feet, using a dry twig for the slash of mouth, digging down and finding stones for his eyes and nose and buttons. Luke couldn't help but notice how happy Terry looked, her cheeks red from the cold, her blue eyes bright. It was hard for him to believe this was her first exposure to snow.

Finished, he stood back to inspect their creation, which was nearly as tall as he. "Not bad."

Terry reached up and grabbed his black cap and stuck it onto the snowman's head at a jaunty angle. "Hey!" he protested. "Why didn't you use *your* hat?" Turning, he saw that she'd moved out of reach. Intent on pulling off her cap, he went after her.

Laughing, she evaded him, dashing around the side of the snowman, nearly slipping but regaining her feet, stopping to scoop up handfuls of snow. Slightly ahead of him, she stopped long enough to toss off a snowball that caught him on the left shoulder. She scooted to the side of the house, knowing he'd follow.

And the chase was on, Luke reaching for her and missing by a scant inch as she skidded away. He increased his stride and watched her feint left, then run to the right, her laughter ringing out in the clean mountain air. "When I catch you, you're going to eat snow, young lady," he called out.

Moments later, she lost her footing and went down in a belly flop. He dived for her, landing alongside, then flipped her over. She giggled up at him, defiant to the end. He held up a snowball threateningly. "Say you're sorry or this is it."

"Never," she said.

Beautiful. She looked so damn beautiful that he forgot all about wanting to shove snow in her face. Instead, he dropped the snowball and removed her sunglasses. The laughter left her and her features softened as awareness registered. He lowered his mouth to hers, erasing all remnants of her smile.

Terry had seen his eyes change and knew moments before he did exactly what he was going to do. She felt her heart constrict at the rush of desire that made her feel boneless. He deepened the kiss and just before her mind went blank, she wondered if she could ever get enough of this man. They didn't see eye to eye on so many things, yet her need for him always took over. Lost in him, she gave herself up to the wondrous feelings.

Quicksand. He wasn't in snow, but rather quicksand, and going down for the third time, Luke thought. She was dragging him down more each time they kissed, snaring him more surely each time they made love. And yet it was he who instigated each new bout, he who couldn't stop reaching for her. He shifted the angle, tasting the by-now-familiar sweetness of her mouth, becoming more demanding.

He knew his body had to be heavy on hers, yet she only drew him closer. He forgot the cold, the wind picking up and dusting them with a light powdering, the dampness that had crept into his ill-fitting boots. He forgot everything but this minute, this woman in his arms, in his blood. He forgot it all and took from her.

Then he heard the unmistakable sound of a car engine slowly climbing up their snow-covered road.

# CHAPTER FOURTEEN

Terry had never seen Luke move so fast, not even when he'd been running after her on the streets of San Jose. He scrambled to his feet, pulled her up and got her inside the house in what seemed like two heartbeats. "Go into the bedroom," he ordered as he grabbed his Luger from the mantel.

"No." If she heard shots, she didn't want to wonder who'd dropped and who'd been left standing. "I'll stay down and out of the way, but I won't leave you."

Swearing silently, he didn't want to take the time to argue with her. He pulled the heavy drape closed across the front window, then stationed himself at one corner, his Luger cocked, his .38 in his waistband.

"How could someone have gotten past that heavy iron gate?"

"The lock's broken." Not that any lock would keep out someone truly determined. Chances were this was nothing since he was certain that neither Ozzie Swain nor Nick Russo would be dumb enough to drive up to a cabin they suspected Terry to be hiding in in broad daylight, with the car engine announcing their arrival. Sneak attacks were more their style. Still, he doubted if it was someone out for a

Sunday drive in this weather, either. Eyes narrowed, he waited for the vehicle to come into his line of vision.

In minutes, the nose of a late-model, four-wheel-drive Ford Explorer came bounding over the snowy path. Earlier, he'd brushed the snow off his van and now watched the Explorer pull in behind it, bold as you please. He relaxed fractionally, thinking this had all the earmarks of an innocent visit. When the driver's door opened and a tall man wearing a black leather jacket similar to his own stepped out, he was sure of it. "Sonofabitch," Luke muttered, setting the safety on the Luger and opening the front door.

"Who is it?" Terry asked, peering around the archway.

"Bob Jones," Luke said, stepping out onto the porch.

Relief had her sagging against the wall. "Thank goodness. I'm going to get out of these wet things."

Luke squinted into the sun bouncing off the snow as Bob slammed the door of the Explorer. "You could have called and warned me you were coming. I damn near blew your head off."

Jones saw the Luger dangling from Luke's right hand. A warning was exactly what he'd hoped to avoid. He'd wanted the element of surprise on his side. The last couple of conversations he'd had with Luke had set him to worrying. He'd come ostensibly for another purpose, but also to see just what in hell was going on with his best agent.

"Sorry about that, but I only got word this morning that Dr. Ward was available." Bob glanced toward the Explorer and saw that the doctor was walking around the vehicle somewhat gingerly, holding on, afraid of falling in the slippery snow. He also glanced over at a very large snowman wearing a jaunty black cap. Interesting.

Frowning, Luke tried to remember who Dr. Ward was. He waited until both men made it to the porch.

Carrying his briefcase, Bob stomped the snow from his shoes. "Luke, this is Dr. Rufus Ward. You may recall he's the certified hypnotist we use occasionally. I thought maybe Dr.

Ward could free Terry's mind and she might be able to tell us something more. Doctor, you may already have met Senior Agent Luke Tanner."

"Yes, we've met," Dr. Ward said. "Five or six years ago, I believe."

Dr. Ward was short and more than a little portly, with a thick white mustache and coal black hair, a startling combination. Rimless glasses sat on his wide nose. Luke vaguely remembered seeing the face before. He shook hands. "Good to see you again." He said it, but he didn't mean it. In fact, he wished neither of them had shown up.

But neither would have guessed from his closed expression as he ushered them inside where a fire was burning. "Make yourselves comfortable," he said, taking their coats and removing his own jacket. He bent to throw another log on the fire. "That must have been quite a drive up."

Dr. Ward sat down in the easy chair at an angle to the fireplace, but Jones opted to stand, rubbing his hands together. "It wasn't bad on the highway. It was plowed and sprinkled with gravel. But after we turned off, it was damn scary. I was sure glad the rental company insisted on chains."

Buying time, Luke used the poker to stir up the logs. "You flew into Reno?"

"Yes, that's the closest route in."

Luke straightened. "You've got a real nice place here."

"Laura and the boys love it up here. I wish I had more time to get away. It's a great change from Arizona's heat." His eyes roamed the room, looking for he knew not what. Some clue, something that would convince him that Luke was as he'd always been. "Where's Terry?"

"Changing clothes. We were out in the snow." He offered no further explanation. Damn, he didn't need this visit right now.

"I'm right here, Deputy Jones," Terry answered, coming out from the bedroom. She was wearing the kelly green silk blouse and the cream-colored wool slacks, her hair softly curled, her skin glowing, and the two small scars scarcely noticeable. On her feet were the furry moccasins. She walked over to the fireplace, giving Bob a shy smile.

Jones wasn't a smiler, as such, but he smiled down at her. "I must say, Terry, you look much, much better than the last time I saw you." That had been in a Phoenix hospital and she'd been bandaged and hooked up to all manner of tubes and machines.

"I *feel* much better." She turned to the man who'd risen from the chair while Jones introduced them. "Nice to meet you, Dr. Ward," she said, while she silently wondered what kind of a doctor the shorter man was. Surely Jones hadn't brought a plastic surgeon here to try yet again to talk her into surgery.

Sensing her sudden unspoken unease, Luke hurried to explain. "Dr. Ward's a hypnotist who's helped us out on occasion. Bob thinks you may have seen something that night in the garage that's buried in your subconscious."

Jones, too, recognized her hesitation. "Only if you want to, Terry, but I'd like you to help us out by allowing Dr. Ward to hypnotize you. The most insignificant fact might be a case breaker, and we still don't know the identity of that fourth man in the car."

Terry looked up at Luke and caught his almost-imperceptible nod. "All right, if you think I can help." She relaxed then, once more assured Luke wouldn't let harm come to her. "But first, let me put together some lunch. It's nearly noon and you must have set out pretty early."

"That would be nice of you," Jones said, strolling over to admire the small carved animals on the mantel. The drawing at the far end caught his eye and he moved over for a closer look. It was Luke most certainly, drawn by a talented hand. He'd made it a point to look up some of Terry's political cartoons in back issues of the *Phoenix Gazette*. She had a distinctive style. He turned to look at his old friend, wondering when she'd sketched him.

Luke wouldn't meet his eyes. "I think I'll change out of these wet pants. Enjoy the fire." He went into the bedroom.

Watching him go, Jones noted that it was the same bedroom that Terry had come out of after freshening up. Of course, he knew there were two bedrooms, yet they were apparently sharing one. So that's how it was. His instincts had been on target, Bob thought, with no small amount of regret. Would Luke never learn?

"Nice place you've got here, Jones," Dr. Ward commented, leaning back and looking around.

"Yes, isn't it?" Bob answered distractedly.

In the bedroom, Luke slipped out of his wet jeans and socks, then pulled on tan cords. He shoved up the sleeves of his black sweater and stepped into his moccasins, then walked into the connecting bath and towel-dried his hair, surprised at how long it was getting. He knew how much Bob hated the scruffy look, though years ago when he'd been out in the field, Jones had opted for casual more often than not, trying not to stand out in a crowd as a Fed.

Luke grimaced at his mirrored reflection, rubbing the towel over his beard. No one would mistake him for a Fed these days. Alongside the neater-than-neat chief, he resembled the criminals they were chasing more than a federal marshal. But maybe Bob would be so intent on what he could learn from Terry under hypnosis that he wouldn't comment on Luke's appearance.

Fat chance, he thought, entering the kitchen from the back way.

Terry looked up from plugging in the coffeepot. "I'm heating the soup I made yesterday. And I fixed a batch of corn bread that should be out of the oven in another twenty minutes. What else do you think we'll need?" She looked nervous, worried.

He moved to her side and slipped an arm around her waist. "That's plenty." The soup, a rich beef vegetable, was a meal unto itself. He pulled her to him, tilting up her chin. "Are you really all right about this hypnosis thing?"

"I think so. You'll be there the whole time?"

"Absolutely." He placed a light kiss on her mouth. "Don't worry. It'll be okay."

Finally, she visibly relaxed and even smiled. "Thank you."

Luke squeezed her hands, then left to join the men.

The lunch went well, with conversation centering around the unpredictable winter weather, the cozy little cabin, and John Ryan's health which, Jones assured Terry, was just fine after his brief hospitalization over chest pains. While Dr. Ward had a second helping leaving no one to doubt why he had such a generous waistline, Terry hardly ate a thing. Yet she seemed poised and self-assured, although Bob noticed that her hands trembled slightly when she raised her coffee cup. Luke called on his steely control, keeping his expression free of emotion. Yet his gaze wandered frequently to Terry, seeming to reassure her in the silent communication of lovers.

Bob's intelligent brown eyes missed nothing as Terry and Luke responded to his artfully disguised questions, carefully studying the give-and-take between them. That there was intimacy between them, he'd already determined. Whether or not their feelings, acknowledged or not, were getting in the way of Terry's safety and Luke's judgment, he had yet to decide.

Afterward, Dr. Ward closed the living room drapes, leaving them with only the light from the fireplace, and instructed Terry to lie down on the couch.

Jones removed his tape recorder from his briefcase. "Terry, I'd like to record this session. Your recollections could be crucial to our case. It wouldn't be admissible in court, but it could convince a judge that he needed to sign an arrest warrant if, in fact, you can identify that fourth man."

She sent Luke a quick glance. "I have no objection."

Jones set up the recorder, placing the microphone near Terry's head, then turned it on. He moved out of her range of vision to listen with Luke.

Pulling up the footstool, the doctor sat alongside the couch at about Terry's waist. "Have you ever been hypnotized, Terry?"

"No."

"There's nothing to worry about. Just try to relax." He held up a gold pendant picturing a dove. "I'm going to set this to swaying gently. I want you to concentrate on it and nothing else. Empty your mind of everything. Just look at this pendant, watch the rhythmic movement, let it capture your interest totally." He watched her focus in as he'd asked.

The firelight danced off the pendant as it swung slowly. Terry truly wanted to help these men, to give them more to work with in order to catch all the criminals who'd been involved in killing Don and Lynn. She narrowed her gaze, her eyes following the gentle movement.

After several moments, Dr. Ward spoke again. "Now, start counting, Terry. Backwards from a hundred. Speak slowly, softly. One hundred, ninety-nine . . . "

"Ninety-eight, ninety-seven, ninety-six . . . "

Terry opened her eyes and saw Dr. Ward's round face first thing. She blinked in the shadowed room. The last thing she remembered was counting and that seemed just seconds ago. She didn't even recall closing her eyes. "I guess I don't hypnotize. Sorry."

Dr. Ward smiled. "You did fine, my dear." He pocketed the gold pendant, then turned to Jones. "You ready to take over."

"You bet."

Luke went to Terry as she sat up, joining her on the couch. "How do you feel?"

"As if I missed something." She ran a hand through her

hair, and straightened her blouse. "Apparently I went under. What did I say?"

Bob sat on the stool that the doctor had vacated and took over. "Terry, how well do you know the officers at Central Precinct, the men your father used to work under?"

"Some I know fairly well because they used to come over often. My folks are Irish and they have this big old house off Central Avenue. Almost every weekend, there were family gatherings or some kind of holiday celebration. Mac, for instance, was there a lot. Even Captain Marino came for Dad's retirement party."

"So if I described a couple of the men to you, you'd be able to put a name to the description?"

"A physical description, you mean, or a psychological profile?"

Jones thought that over a moment. "Let's start with the physical."

"That one's easier. Sure, if I know them, I probably could come up with a name."

"All right." Jones had a thick file on every officer at Central and had spent time interviewing most of them. "This man's in his fifties, tall, on the thin side, with very little hair that he can't seem to stop stroking. He always looks a little rumpled. He gives the impression of being unsure of himself."

Halfway through the recitation, Terry began smiling. "That sounds like Earl Bates. I believe he's a detective now." A thought struck her and she frowned. "Don't tell me Earl's involved in all this?"

"Don't second-guess me. Let's try another one. This man's in his forties, good-looking, divorced with no children. He's got sandy hair barely beginning to gray, but it's styled and he never *looks* like he needs a haircut. His clothes are well tailored, conservative, spiffy enough to be on a magazine cover."

Terry nodded. "Stop right there. There's only one man at

Central that fits that description. Lieutenant Remington. The men always talk about how he looks like someone out of *GQ,* behind his back, of course."

"Did he ever come around to your father's house?"

She thought back a moment. "Not regularly. Probably at the retirement party, but I don't remember seeing him much, except occasionally when I'd drop by the station to meet Dad."

"Can you tell me anything specific about Phil Remington, about his manner, his wardrobe?"

"I've only had a couple of conversations with him over the years, though I've seen him at least a dozen times. His manner is very professional, very competent, but he's not a warm man. You mentioned his clothes. He has excellent taste. His ex-wife's family has pots of money and I guess Phil got used to buying quality things." Something came to her and she smiled. "He gets kidded a lot about these import- ed Italian wing tip shoes he wears, but it doesn't faze him. He keeps on wearing them." She saw Bob raise his eyes to Luke. A knowing look passed between them. "What?" she asked, looking from one to the other. "What did I say?"

Jones braced his elbows on his knees, his eyes on her. "When you were under hypnosis, you said you couldn't remember much about the fourth man in the car except that he had a razor-sharp crease in his pants, wore wing tip shoes, and had a briefcase on the floor by his feet. The initials in gold were P.R."

Terry's hand went to her mouth as she gasped. "Oh, no. Not the lieutenant, too."

Walking over to gaze into the smoldering fire, Jones looked lost in thought. This revelation of Terry's had far-reaching ramifications as Remington had been acting chief since the captain was out on sick leave. If the man cur- rently in charge was arrested for participating, or even being present, during a cold-blooded murder, subsequent cover-up, and endangerment of the only witness, there was a great deal more at stake here than they'd originally suspected.

Stooping to shore up the fire, Luke glanced up at his superior officer. "Think her testimony under hypnosis is enough to arrest Remington?"

Bob scrubbed a hand over his face. "Doubtful. But if we can verify that Remington was out that day at that hour, if he can't prove his whereabouts, if we ask around and get lucky, finding someone who saw him returning or stepping out of that gray sedan. Then if we question the lieutenant and he sweats a lot or gives us vague answers, we'll talk him into a lie detector test. If he flunks that, we'll play the tape for a judge. We're looking at more than one murder here and police corruption at a very high level. I think a judge will give us some leeway."

"More than one murder?" Terry questioned.

Jones turned to her. "More like four, most probably. Lynn Hartley, certainly, since we have proof that your car was tampered with. And we strongly suspect that the deaths of Officer Jerry Foster and his partner, Neil Manning, are directly related. We just can't prove it all yet."

Lynn's smiling face floated into Terry's mind, and she swallowed hard. "I hope you can prove the case, that you can put them all away."

Luke captured her gaze, saw the sadness in her eyes. "We will, Terry."

"Yes," Bob agreed, "with your help, we will." He checked his watch and saw that it was nearly three. He picked up the tape recorder and looked over at Dr. Ward. "I think we'd better get going, Rufus. We have a plane to catch and quite a drive to the airport ahead of us."

Luke went to get their coats. He returned wearing his shoes and jacket. "I'll walk out with you," he said, handing each man their outerwear.

"It was good meeting you, Miss Ryan," Dr. Ward said as he buttoned his coat and opened the front door.

"The same here, Doctor." She watched him step outside, then glanced at Luke, obviously waiting for Bob by the door.

"I'll join you in a minute," Jones told Luke. He waited until the door closed behind both men, then turned to Terry. "Thank you for helping us, Terry." He searched her face, searched for the right words. "Is there anything you need, anything you want to talk about?"

She knew what he was getting at, but decided to let him ask. "Naturally, I'd like this to be over, to at least have a court date set soon. I don't suppose you have any idea how much longer?"

"Unfortunately, I can't just waltz in with this new evidence and get an indictment. I have to build the case. This takes time."

"I understand. Otherwise, I can't think of a thing, thank you. I have everything I need, under the circumstances."

Hands in his coat pockets, Bob studied her. She seemed to be handling things with a calmness that surprised him, considering all she'd been through. And it wasn't over yet. If Luke had given her that sense of security, what would happen to her when he took it away, which Bob firmly believed he would?

He glanced toward the master bedroom door pointedly, then back to meet her steady gaze. "You and Luke are . . . "

"Close friends, yes." She saw no reason to fence with him. Her chin came up a notch. She had nothing to be ashamed of. They were both free, unmarried. "I take it you don't approve."

"It's not for me to approve or disapprove, except as it affects your safety and the resolution of this case." His loyalty to his friend and his heartfelt duty to warn this young woman warred with one another. "Have you thought about what will happen when this is all over?"

Folding her arms over her chest, Terry strolled to the fire, needing some distance. "At first, I took everything one day at a time, surviving being uppermost on my mind. But later, of course I've spent many hours wondering about the future."

Bob was well aware they weren't discussing the case, and knew she was, too. "You're in love with him," he stated, wondering if she'd deny it.

Terry turned back to face Chief Jones. "Yes, but I'm not naive or stupid. I'm not sure Luke's ready to trust someone completely." A sad smile came and went. "But you see, I can't just turn off my feelings, even if I wanted to."

She'd made her point and Bob could see it cost her. She wasn't the sort to talk about such deep feelings with veritable strangers. "I can see that he's told you some about his background." He drew in a thoughtful breath. "It isn't that Luke's incapable of caring or trusting. I happen to feel that he's got a great many emotions stored up inside. But, because of things that happened to him years ago, he's unwilling to let himself care too much for fear that person will walk away, as others have in his past."

"I think you're right."

"Under other circumstances, I'd urge you to bide your time, that eventually he'll come around. But you two have been thrown together under stressful circumstances, and it may get worse. That has to play a part in all this. I worry about your safety if Luke's concentration is impaired."

She knew that Jones had the power to replace Luke. She didn't want that, couldn't imagine adjusting to a new agent until the trial. And she didn't want what little time she might have left with Luke to be shortened. "His concentration's as keen as ever. We were outside in the snow before you came. He had me inside and safe in less than a minute after hearing the sound of your engine, long before your car came into sight. I trust him. I know he won't let anything happen to me."

Love had definitely colored her judgment. However, she'd run once and if he replaced Luke now, she might take off again. Terry Ryan wasn't your average frightened witness. She was spirited, stubborn, smart. He needed her cooperation in order to get her testimony. Then he could stand back and let her work out her problems with Luke. "All right, Terry. I'll call as soon as we know something positive."

Outside, Luke was stewing. He doubted if he was going to get off scot-free without a lecture from Jones. Pulling up his collar against a chill wind, he squinted up at a cloudy gray sky. "Looks like we may get more snow," he commented casually to the doctor, who was shivering by the Explorer.

"Get in, Rufus," Bob said, coming out and walking over to where Luke stood. "I'll join you in a minute." When he heard the car door close, he turned to Luke. "How's Terry been acting since you found her? Any signs she may bolt again?"

Luke thought he'd give a lot to know what had been said inside. "Not a one. As I mentioned, she took off because of the surgery suggestion."

"The two scars on her face aren't as bad as I thought they'd be."

Luke scuffed the toe of his shoe at the hard-packed snow where they'd rolled the snowman's body. "She says when this is all over, she'll have those taken care of on her own."

Bob supposed there was no good way to say what was uppermost on his mind. No matter the approach, Luke was bound to get defensive. Since he'd heard Terry's version, he wanted now to hear Luke's. "Do you know what you're doing?" he began.

Luke wasn't going to insult his old friend by pretending he didn't understand. "I think so."

"I imagine you remember Jill?"

A muscle in Luke's jaw twitched. "This is different. I was young then, and inexperienced."

"True, but did you learn your lesson?"

Luke turned away, his anger rising even though he knew Bob had every right to call him down. Jones missed nothing.

Even if the bedroom arrangement hadn't been obvious, the intimacy between him and Terry was something a green rookie could have spotted. The surprise visit had caught him off guard, with no time to brief her. "The cardinal rule, never fall for the witness you're protecting," he recited, then swiveled back, his expression inscrutable. "You're wrong. I'm not in love with her."

"Maybe not, but she's in love with you." If ever a man needed a woman in his life who cared deeply, it was Luke Tanner. But not this woman, not at this time.

"I've made her no promises, told her no lies. She looks young, but she's a big girl. She knows this is a . . . an interlude. That when it ends, we'll go our separate ways."

"Does she?" Bob Jones rarely lost his temper, seldom raised his voice. He was about to do both now. "Damn it, Luke, you can't see the forest for the trees. What if this case gets messed up because our only witness is too emotionally involved with her protector? I don't want to see that girl get hurt."

"That won't happen. Terry's stronger than she looks. She'll testify and I'll keep her in one piece until she does. Nothing else is relevant."

Jones decided to push just a little harder. "I can take you off the case, replace you."

Luke's eyes were flinty as he looked at his chief. "Yeah, you can. But you won't. You have my word. There'll be no screwup. If something goes wrong, you won't have to remove me. I'll personally turn in my badge to you."

"By then, it may be too late." Bob studied Luke's stony silent reaction for another few seconds, then nodded. "All right. Don't let me down. This is too important. We've got a great deal riding on this, several lives, hundreds of man-hours, lots of money." He opened the driver's door.

"Don't you think I know that?" Luke asked quietly.

"When a woman becomes all-important to a man, very often his good judgment flies out the window. I'd hate to see you blow your career." He got behind the wheel, then looked up before pulling the door closed. "You never should have touched her, Luke."

Clenching his jaw tightly, Luke watched Bob turn the Explorer around, then start down the snowy path. For long minutes afterward, he stood staring after them, his thoughts murky. Finally, he turned and slowly walked back to the cabin.

Inside, Terry let the drape fall back into place on the window and walked over to the couch. She'd watched Luke and Bob argue for some time alongside the rented Explorer. Two tall, guarded, implacable men. The casual observer might not have thought from where she stood that they were arguing. But she knew the signs—the rigid stance, the subtle shifting of weight from one foot to the other, the intense eyes that could intimidate so easily.

They'd been arguing about her, she was certain. Perhaps about the incident where she'd run away. Or maybe on how to handle her as their only witness, how to keep her from leaving again before that nebulous court date. But more likely, they'd been arguing about her relationship with Luke. She'd seen Luke's back stiffen out there, seen his defensive look. Bob had probably been even more blunt with Luke than he'd been with her.

Luke came in, stomping snow from his shoes, then stepping out of them. He tossed his jacket onto the chair and walked to the fire, rubbing his hands together. "Damn cold out there." He turned and saw the speculative look on her face. "Are you all right?"

"Fine." She watched him sit down beside her, wondering if he'd tell her what he and Jones had talked about if she asked.

Her cheeks were flushed from the heat of the fireplace. To his annoyance, Luke found himself wanting her desperately just that quickly. It had been hours since he'd held her in his arms out in the snow. Do you know what you're *doing*? Bob had asked. Hell, no, came the answer, more truthfully now. He turned to scowl back at the fire.

"I guess your conversation with Bob wasn't too cheery," Terry finally said, hating the sudden tension in the room. When his frown deepened, she decided she'd hit the nail on the head. Perhaps she could distract him, seduce him out of his mood. "Why don't you kiss me?"

"I'm all cold."

"I don't care. Kiss me anyhow."

He knew he shouldn't, yet he couldn't resist her. He pulled her close, both pleased and frightened that she seemed to want him every bit as much as he wanted her.

Long, breathless moments later, Terry pulled back to look at him. She saw a hunger in his eyes that was as deep as her own. Then he frowned again, and she saw caution overshadow his need. "Maybe we should talk," she suggested, which wasn't at all what she really wanted to do.

"About what?" He bent to nibble on her neck. God, she smelled so good. He didn't want to think, didn't want to talk. He wanted to lose himself in her while he still could.

"You got a lecture out there, didn't you? From Jones. About me."

He'd caught her determined look and knew she wasn't going to drop this. "He worries too much." Luke sat back, thrusting his legs toward the fire. "He's like an old woman, always fretting."

"Please don't joke about this. Am I a problem for you, Luke?"

The biggest one he'd ever tackled. "What did he say to you? What did he ask you?"

"He didn't ask in so many words, but he guessed that we're more than just friends."

Luke felt his temper rise. "I hope you told him to go to hell for prying."

"I told him the truth."

"Shit!"

"Should I have lied? He's worried that I'll keep you from doing your job, that I'll distract you and we'll both be hurt."

Luke swallowed down his temper and tried to put things in perspective. Nothing had really changed. "If you knew Jones better, you'd realize he worries about everything from the ozone layer to the national debt to the escalating cost of orange juice. Don't you know that most things we worry about never happen? It's the things we never give much thought to that knock us for a loop."

"You can say that again, like leaving work and witnessing a friend's killing that changes your entire life." Terry sighed. Always, it came back to that.

He hated that haunted look that took over her eyes. "That pretty much threw a monkey wrench in my plans, too. There I was, happily puttering around my ranch, fixing sagging porches, laying tile on the patio, talking to my faithful dog when along came Jones and begged me on bended knee to take on this case. To interrupt my vacation to watch over this beautiful damsel in distress."

Terry had to smile at that. "Oh, and wasn't she beautiful? Battered, beaten, burned, and bald. No wonder you dropped your life for this knockout of a woman."

"Damn, there she goes, fishing again." He scooted over, turning her into his arms. "I happen to like bald women. Would you shave your head if I asked you real nice?"

Nearly nose to nose with him, she decided to let him elevate her mood. She slid her hands into his thick hair. "No, but I think if we don't cut yours soon, we'll have to put it in a ponytail. Or braid it. Something."

"Do you know how to cut hair? It's not exactly as if I can leave you here and run down the mountain to find a barbershop."

"I've been known to whack away at mine a time or two. Want me to try yours?"

He shivered as her fingers massaged his scalp. "Maybe

later. Right now, I have more important things in mind." He dipped his head and tasted the satin smoothness of her throat.

She let out a sound, half sigh, half moan as his lips moved up to capture her ear. "What are you doing? It's broad daylight, the middle of the afternoon. We're in the living room. Shouldn't we at least move into the bedroom?" Perhaps it was Jones's visit that had her feeling so suddenly proper.

"Stop being so Catholic school conventional, Theresa Anne. Who cares what time it is? Who needs a bed?" He slid onto the floor, taking her with him, cushioning her slide onto him before he rolled her over and looked down into her surprised eyes. "No one's watching. It's okay."

"But what about Bob's warning?" She dared him to deny it.

Instead, he chose to ignore it. "Screw Jones and the horse he rode in on." Moving down her, he settled his mouth on the peaks of her breasts through the silk of her blouse.

She felt the urgent rush of heat, but her practical side was still in charge. "Hey, this is the only decent blouse I presently own."

Leaning back, Luke gripped the front of her blouse and gave a powerful tug. The buttons went flying and she was exposed to his hungry eyes.

Terry cried out a shocked protest. "You've ripped my favorite blouse."

"I'll buy you another one." Working quickly, he yanked off the ragged blouse and the rest of her clothes. Wearing only firelight and the St. George's medal, she lay before him, breathing hard and looking beautiful. Her eyes were deep blue pools, aroused and aware, watching his every move. "You're incredible and you damn well know it." If only that's all it was, her looks, his lust. He could get past that. But it was far more than that that he couldn't let go of. The essence of her, this surprising woman who'd so effortlessly turned his world upside down.

He placed his hands on hers and stretched her arms upward, then lowered his head to feast on her breasts, circling and tasting each erect peak until her skin was flushed and her body shimmering with need.

Bob's words echoed in his fevered brain. *You never should have touched her.* The chief was absolutely right. Only now, he couldn't stop. She was like an addiction, a craving, an obsession. He wanted to kick the habit, knew that the best thing for him and for her would be if he could. Yet he couldn't turn away from her.

His hands moved down her, skimming over heated flesh. She was moving restlessly now, soft sounds coming from low in her throat. His lips trailed lower, a dizzying journey. Guessing his motive, her body arched as his mouth settled on her.

In moments, she cried out with the power of it, the swift intensity of it. She closed her eyes as the afterwaves buffeted her and her pulse pounded with the force of her release.

Slowly, Luke moved back up, wanting to read her reaction in her eyes. The fact that they were filled with shocked pleasure shouldn't have pleased him so damn much. He stood and quickly pulled off his clothes, lowering to her moments later.

Her chest still heaved as her breathing slowly normalized. She had never known anything quite like this with another man. She reached up to touch his face. "How can I fight the way you make me feel?" The question was a husky whisper.

"Why do you have to?" he asked, kissing her eyes closed.

"Because one day you won't be with me anymore." It wasn't whiny, or accusatory or complaining. It was stated as fact.

He had no answer he could give her. Instead, he knelt, then slipped slowly inside her. He took her mouth in a kiss filled with passion, charged with need, tinged with sadness.

He moved with gentle care, with infinite tenderness, giving her physically what he couldn't give her otherwise.

He held back, watching her give herself up to the sensations, needing to see the changes he could bring about in her. This time she climbed slowly, yet he knew the second she was about to explode. Finally, his vision blurring, he let himself join her.

It wasn't until long minutes later when he raised his head that he noticed her cheeks were damp with tears.

# CHAPTER FIFTEEN

Nick Russo was wet, tired, and hungry. He'd been driving back from California in a blinding rainstorm after weeks of a fruitless search for some sign of Terry Ryan or Luke Tanner, only to get a frigging flat tire on Highway 10 just outside of Phoenix. He'd pulled off on the shoulder and tried to get someone to stop and give him a ride to the nearest gas station. But at six on a dark, chilly February evening, car after car had whizzed by him, the drivers anxious to get home and not giving a damn if they splashed dirty road water all over him.

Finally, three farmhands in a rickety truck had stopped and told him he could get in the bed of their pickup with their dog if he wanted to. Cursing elaborately and fighting off the stinking dog and coping with a tailgate that threatened to open for the interminable half an hour it took to find a station, he'd almost cheered when he jumped off. From there, he'd paid the attendant to tow in his car and service it, then made a call to one of the guys to come get him. By the time Gino had deposited him at his apartment, Nick was already sneezing.

It took him over an hour to warm up in a hot shower, get into dry clothes, have a big plate of spaghetti with clam sauce, and calm down. Now, looking at the phone, he was feeling nervous again.

He hadn't been in touch with Sam since he'd left town. He'd intended to drive straight through to Florence and visit his brother on his way back as they'd arranged, but the unexpected storm had slowed him and soaked him. The average guy would understand normal delays. Sam Russo wasn't your average guy.

Nick emptied his wineglass, lit a cigarette, and picked up the phone, wondering if they'd even call Sam to the phone this late. The minutes dragged on, but finally he heard Sam's terse hello.

"Hey, Sam, it's me, Nick."

"Where the hell are you?" At the wall phone in Corridor C where the call had been transferred, Sam's cool gaze stayed on the guard waiting and watching him less than ten feet away. He listened to his brother's explanation of why he hadn't shown up, and snorted. "Must be nice, driving for hours in the sunshine, enjoying the view, probably with some broad draped over your lap."

Nick blew smoke toward the ceiling and swallowed down his temper. "Didn't you hear me? It's raining like crazy. I was alone and I got soaked through to the skin." As if to emphasize his point, Nick sneezed.

"I wouldn't know, little brother. My hotel room don't have no windows."

Feeling bad, Nick shook his head. "I wish I could get you out of there, Sam. I tried, for weeks, but nothing panned out in California."

Sam's fist hit the wall with a thud. The guard straightened, sending him a stern look. "Sorry. I slipped." He turned his back on the guard and spoke low into the mouthpiece, his voice muffled. "You tell the man he's got two weeks, till the fifteenth of February. Nothing happens by then to spring me, I start singing."

"That ain't gonna get you out, Sam."

"Maybe not, but I'll go down with company. Either he does something or you locate the lady. My final offer."

"What? Tell me what else I can do." Nick's voice had become high-pitched in his anxiety. He drew deeply on his cigarette, trying to calm his nerves. Fleetingly, he wondered if the phones the prisoners used were bugged.

Frustration coiled in Sam's stomach, turning his dinner sour. "You seen Ozzie?"

"We can count him out. Says he tried, but he's sick and tired. He's back south of the border."

"Shit! That tears it." Sam turned and saw the guard motioning that his time was up. "Fourteen days, Nickie. Find her." He slammed the phone down. Eyes bitter, fists clenched, he marched back to his cell.

Nick replaced the receiver, got up, and poured himself a generous splash of Jim Beam. He tossed it back, then grimaced. He could make another call or two, but would it get him anywhere? Feeling chilled despite his warm robe and the booze, he sat back down and riffled through the messages the boys had taken for him while he'd been gone.

One stood out, making him sit up straighter. The idea came to him slowly, but surely. He smiled. Yeah, it just might work. No, it *had* to work. He had to get Sam out of that hellhole. Thoughtfully, he crushed out his cigarette in the glass ashtray.

Getting up, he went into his bedroom, feeling better than he had in hours. Tomorrow, he would make his move.

"So, what do you think?" Terry asked, holding up two packages of hair dye. "Should I go light brown or dark?"

Luke looked up from the kitchen table where he'd been cleaning his guns. "I don't think you should bother with either. Your hair's growing out just fine."

Terry's brows raised in question. "Just a few days ago, everyone wanted me to surgically alter my face. Now you don't even want me to change the color of my hair? What's going on?"

Luke went back to his oily rag. "I don't plan on taking you off this mountain until the trial date. And then we'll probably get a helicopter in and fly home that way. So there's no need." He'd made this decision in the middle of the night, lying in bed holding her. He was taking no chances he didn't have to take.

"You mean we can't even go into town, to have a meal or to shop, until this is over?"

"What for? We have enough supplies here to last quite awhile. It'll be over soon. I talked with Bob and he's working on getting the case moved up on the docket."

She pulled out a chair opposite him and sat down. "What if someone drives up here and sees me?"

"They won't get close enough to see you." Squinting, he peered into the barrel of the gun, checking for clearance. "I'll blow them away before they get too near."

"You're kidding, I hope."

His eyes slid to hers. "You think so?"

Hers widened. "You mean you'd actually shoot someone to protect me?"

"In a New York minute, honey. That's what this is all about." He gave her a tight smile. "But don't worry, because no one will come up here."

The shock of it had her reeling. "You mean someone like Nick Russo or Ozzie Swain, or one of their men, right? You wouldn't shoot a stranger who wandered off course, would you?" Did she know this man at all, this man she'd been sleeping with, sharing her body with, giving her heart to?

"Depends." He held the Luger, balancing it in one hand as if testing the weight. "If I couldn't persuade him to leave, I might have to use one of these to convince him."

He sounded so cold-blooded, so menacing. Even in bed, she'd noticed that the predator in Luke was held in check only by his iron control. She remembered the incident in the drugstore, when the distraught mother had called for help with her small son. Luke's first instinct had been to grab Terry and run. She'd had to persuade him that there was no devious plot, that they had to try to save that child. At times, they were miles apart in their thinking. Where she sensed mostly good, even after all that had happened to her, he always saw something sinister.

He'd lived his entire life on the edge with danger a constant companion, even in his early years. Terry sensed an ever-present, dormant anger in him and wondered if it was something Luke could ever overcome.

From the beginning, she'd suspected nothing permanent would ever come of their relationship. Instinctively, she'd known that loving a man like Luke Tanner, who thrived on a violent profession, was something most women would have trouble adjusting to. Brought up in a devoted home and knowing only kindness and affection all of her life, his way was foreign to her.

Yet, Lord, how she wanted him, how she loved him, even though, if a miracle happened and things worked out, she wondered if she could accept his way of life.

A moot question, for it wasn't going to happen, she reminded herself, watching him slip the .38 back into his beltline. Wearing a gun was as much a part of him as the color of his eyes. "You're never going to give up this line of work, are you, Luke?" she asked softly.

He shrugged, wondering what to say since he wasn't sure of the answer himself. "You're thinking I'm addicted to guns and issuing orders and playing cops and robbers?"

"Aren't you?"

"Only on assignment. I'm different at my ranch. I'm relaxed there, no responsibilities, no one to guard or criminals to watch out for. Only me and my dog and hard physical work."

She didn't buy it. "Tell me, do you have a gun on your person even as you're working around your ranch?"

Slowly, his eyes met hers. "I've pissed off a lot of people in my day, put a lot of guys behind bars, some of whom serve their time and get released. Anyone persistent enough could find me. Should I be a sitting duck for every dirtbag who wants to settle a score?"

Terry shook her head. "No, of course not. But you see what I mean? Even when you're not officially on a case, you're always on guard. You have to be. The danger never ends."

He placed the Luger in the shoulder holster he rarely used, then leaned back. He saw an opportunity and knew he'd be a fool not to take it. "That's right, it never ends. Never will. That's why I live alone, why no one could live with me. That's why everyone I've ever known who tried to live with me left. They were smart to do so." He stood, picking up the holster, his eyes cool as he looked at her. It was time he laid it out for her, time he set her straight. Wanting her with him wasn't enough, wasn't right for her. He'd have to let her go and there was only one way. "Let that be a lesson to you, Terry. Don't build your dreams around me."

She blinked against her first reaction, not wanting him to see how deeply he'd plunged in the knife. "What if I already have?"

Luke huffed out a sigh. "You shouldn't have. You don't know me, not really. I come with a ton of baggage, all of it bad. There's a reason why all those people left me. If you lived with me long enough, you'd find out why. And you'd leave, too. It's just a matter of time."

She frowned, truly astonished. "Is that really what you think, that I'd leave, too?" It was a thought that hadn't occurred to her full blown until now. "Is that why you're pulling back? Your job isn't the real reason for this, is it? It's your background, your past. But you forget that I've lived with you for months now, under the worst possible circumstances. What more could I discover that would turn me away?"

He shook his head, annoyed that he'd somehow lost control of the conversation. "You wouldn't understand if I told you."

"I won't understand or you can't think of a good explanation?"

That made him mad. "All right, I'll explain. I'm probably more like my dear old dad than I like to think. Walk away from commitments without a backward glance. Pursue my own agenda and to hell with what anyone else wants. I'm selfish, egocentric, and self-indulgent. And I'm not about to change."

His assessment was way off. "That's not so. You help others in everything you do. Daily, you risk your life for the person you're protecting. You give up being at your ranch which you enjoy to help others. You . . . "

"Are you going to let me continue? You asked for my explanation, remember?"

She sat back. "All right, go ahead."

"Then there's my mother. What kind of a child must I have been that my mother—and we all know that mothers are supposed to love you no matter what—walked away without a backward glance? What kind of a nasty little boy couldn't win over his own mother?"

Terry heard his voice falter just a little and felt her heart break for the child he'd been, unloved and unwanted for so long that he'd begun to shoulder the blame. "That's her loss far more than yours. We all know that all mothers aren't what they're supposed to be."

"How about my grandmother? And Jill? Two more women, both claiming to care, both taking a hike when they got tired or the going got rough. Say what you will, I'm not good for the long haul. I'd be stupid to try again."

For long moments, Terry stared at him as he thrust his hands into his pockets, his eyes downcast. Then she gave in to a burst of anger that had been building slowly as he'd stated his case. "How dare you judge me by the way others treated you." She saw his eyes raise to her, a scowl forming. "What makes you think you know me so well? Did you ever ask, did you ever question me? They all left and so it stands to reason in your warped little mind that I would. How very fair-minded of you."

Unable to sit still, Terry jumped up, pacing as her outrage grew. "You don't give a damn about my feelings. You've never even inquired how I feel. You took one look at me and, in your infinite wisdom, came to the only conclusion, the one you always come to: you're unlovable, incorrigible, impossible. Therefore, no one, including me, would stay with you. So, to protect yourself from being hurt again, you build a damn wall around yourself and you don't let anyone in. But I got in, didn't I, Luke? I broke through, I got close and now you're really scared. This has nothing to do with your job or the danger involved. You want to strike first, to say good-bye before I do, because you're so certain I will."

Luke was gritting his teeth together so hard he thought they might crack. He glared at her silently, unable to come up with a good response.

"You didn't take into account *my* background, the kind of person I am or . . . or . . . "

He felt weary to the bone. He just wanted to get this over with. He hadn't had the faintest idea how difficult it would be when he'd started. "Or what?" he demanded.

"Or the fact that I love you." Shocked that she'd said the one thing she'd vowed not to, Terry stood with hands on her hips, her lower lip trembling.

Stunned to hear her say the words, Luke swallowed. "What did you say?"

"Oh, shut up!" She turned, hurrying to the bedroom, needing to get away from him, wanting to curl up and die.

Luke watched her leave, heard the bedroom door slam. The sadness in her eyes, there beneath the anger, was something he'd probably never forget.

Jones had been right. He never should have touched her.

She was too damn good for him, too sweet. He didn't deserve her. But she was wrong. She'd have found him out and left him, in time. Better to hurt her now than later, he thought. She'd get over it, over him. She was too lovely to be alone too long.

And he'd have yet another regret in his life. Only this one, he doubted he'd ever get over.

Phil Remington sat down at his rolltop desk in his beautifully appointed Phoenix apartment, and let out a weary sigh. Swiveling his leather chair in a half circle, he gazed around. He loved this room. He'd decorated it himself in restful shades of blue, brown, and ivory. The antique clock on the mantel chimed the half hour melodiously. He gave the chair another half turn and looked out the window as the streetlights came on in the park three stories below. A peaceful neighborhood, a prestigious apartment building where many of the movers and shakers in the community lived. To a person, they admired him, respected him, sought out his company.

And now it was all over.

Phil turned back to glance at the arrest warrant on the desk top. He'd been so sure he could bluff his way through, that he could pass the lie detector test by sheer force of will, that even if he didn't, they had too little on him to make a case. Circumstantial evidence was rarely enough. But that damn tape recording of Terry Ryan under hypnosis revealing that he was in the gray sedan had turned the tide. The Feds had been able to persuade a judge to sign the papers.

At least they hadn't humiliated him by arresting him right in his office, perhaps because he'd been acting chief, a further embarrassment for the department. Chief Deputy Bob Jones had personally served him his papers and allowed him an hour to go to his home and attend to a few personal matters before his lockup. Jones was waiting outside the door for him to finish up. Phil glanced at his Rolex. Twenty minutes left.

He'd put his house in order, so to speak, then sat down with the phone. But he had no one he wanted to call. Not even Sharon, though she'd probably unknowingly started it all.

Remington wasn't the name he'd been born with. It'd been Ramon and he'd always hated it, hated being thought of as a spic when he didn't even look Mexican, taking after his blond mother. The Ramons had been dirt poor, his high school dropout father a maintenance man, his mother a maid at one of the posh hotels in Scottsdale. With six kids, there was never enough money. They'd all married young, but not Phil. He'd worked three jobs, sometimes four, to get through college. Then top graduate from the Police Academy, the fair-haired boy expected to move up quickly in the ranks. And he had.

Along about then, he'd met Sharon Ames, with her blond good looks and her moneyed family. Phil had been dazzled and, against her parents' wishes, they'd been married. That's when he'd discovered the wonders of being wealthy. A beautiful apartment, expensive clothes, fabulous trips, a new BMW every year.

Only the marriage hadn't worked. Sharon wanted children and Phil didn't. He'd grown up in a house full of kids and never wanted to live like that again. Sharon wanted him home more, but he had to keep his job or lose his identity, the one thing he had going for him on his own. Even old man Ames respected him as a police lieutenant. But he hadn't counted on petulant and spoiled Sharon filing for divorce. Stubbornly, he'd let her, sure she'd change her mind.

She hadn't and Phil discovered what it was like to have to live on a cop's pay again. Sharon had given him a taste of the good life, then snatched it away. Phil decided he hated scraping by.

That's when it had all really begun. Slowly at first, so much money for just looking the other way. His good friend, Mac, had shown him how easy it was. By then, there'd been others in on it also. It wasn't as if they were covering up killings. It was just a little harmless smuggling, a few dummy companies shifting money around. Hell, those dealers would have managed to transport that stuff across the border anyway. Who cared if the money filtered through a few dummy companies? Why not get in on the payoff?

He honestly hadn't known Swain was going to blast that reporter that evening. Scare him a little, sure. But not kill him. Then there'd been the incident with the girls' car, then Foster and Manning. In too deep by then to get out.

Leaning back, Phil closed his eyes. He'd been so certain that Nick or Ozzie would find the Ryan girl. He'd visited Mac and gotten word to Sam, begging them to hang in there. The only witness would be taken care of. Neither man had believed him.

He'd had it all figured out. Moreno would retire and Remington would take over. He'd planned to ease away from the Russos, to get clean and stay that way. With what he'd put away and on a captain's salary, he'd do just fine.

But it hadn't worked out that way. And now it was all over. His family would be shamed. Sharon's father would finally be able to say, I told you he was no good. All his plans down the tubes, all his dreams up in smoke. He was once again Felipe Ramon from the wrong side of the tracks.

He heard the discreet two knocks on the door, and Jones's voice. "It's time, Lieutenant."

"Right away," Phil answered. Straightening, he picked up his service revolver. He knew how dirty cops were treated in prison. There was no other dignified way out.

Sticking the barrel in his mouth, Phil pulled the trigger.

Terry stood at the kitchen sink, looking out the window at the snow flurries that had been falling for the past hour. Each hour since her argument with Luke had dragged on, seeming like two instead of one. He'd moved to the second bedroom that night and had slept there since. Days they'd been scrupulously polite to one another, but cool and impersonal. She felt bruised, disappointed, heartsick.

She prayed daily for a call telling them the court date was at hand so this maddening politeness, this enforced imprisonment, this torture, much more soul wrenching than her earlier confinement, could end. She felt listless and lethargic, unable to distract herself from her heartache.

For his part, Luke seemed determined to keep occupied. He chopped wood until the pile was far greater than they'd use up if they stayed the entire winter. His way of coping, she believed. He'd found a fairly new lock in the storeroom and installed it on the gate, replacing the broken one. But she knew that wouldn't keep out the Russos and Luke must have known, too. It had been something to do, something to pass the time, busywork to wear himself out so he could sleep.

Terry wasn't sleeping all that well. Funny how quickly she'd gotten used to curling up in his arms, drifting off with her head resting over his heart, the steady rhythm so reassuring. Now, she tossed, turned, pounded the pillows, wrestled with the covers, unable to get comfortable, or to turn off her churning mind. Over and over, she tried to recall the details of their last discussion, every word, each look, all the nuances. And for the life of her, she couldn't come up with a way she could have avoided walking into the trap he'd set so beautifully.

For she was convinced that, after Luke's conversation with Bob Jones, he'd decided he'd made a mistake—a procedural mistake and a personal one—by letting her get too close. He was, first and foremost, a company man. Perhaps he'd even promised Bob he'd make amends, pull back from her, return to being the cool federal agent overseeing a witness who meant no more to him than any others he'd guarded over the years. And he'd done a magnificent job of doing just that.

But in her heart, Terry was convinced it wasn't his job that drove people from Luke. It was what he'd allowed himself to become because of his past. It was how he perceived himself as unworthy of someone's love. It was his deep-rooted fear that history would repeat itself that had him withdrawing before anyone could leave him high and dry and hurting again.

She understood how he felt, but he was dead wrong. However, she despaired of ever convincing him. And, after the cold way he'd dismissed her, after the way he'd all but recoiled from her stupid, spontaneous proclamation of love, her pride wouldn't let her try. Somehow she'd make it through the following days, or weeks if it came to that. She was made of tough stuff, as her father used to say. She'd survived so far and she'd make it the rest of the way. And then, when it was all over and Luke was no longer around, she'd have plenty of time to mourn the loss of the only man she'd ever truly loved.

The shrill ringing of the phone startled her into dropping her coffee mug into the sink. Her nerves were back to edgy and jumpy. She spilled out the coffee she didn't want anyway and rinsed the cup as she heard Luke answer the phone in the other room.

If only she could sleep, she'd go take a nap. She'd tried reading one of the few books in the cabin, and hadn't been able to concentrate, the words blurring on the page. She didn't even want to sketch, a pastime that had filled her empty hours for years. Her art usually absorbed her so completely that the world around her, including her troubles, would disappear. Not anymore.

She wished she was hungry so she could occupy her time putting together a hearty stew or a pot of soup. But she had no appetite and noticed that Luke seemed to have lost his as well. They ate separately now, each opening a can of soup or fixing a quick sandwich at odd hours so as to avoid the other. Hard to digest anything when you swallowed it down with a huge dose of tension.

"Get your coat on," Luke's deep voice said from the archway.

Unnerved by the unexpected request, Terry swung toward him. "Where are we going and why?" Hadn't he said they wouldn't be leaving until the helicopter ride back to Phoenix? Could it be that the end was in sight and she was going home?

"Into town, and I want to get going before the snow gets worse. I need to pick up something." He walked to the store-room off the kitchen and bent to pick up his leather boots.

"What is it that's so important?"

Luke pulled on his right boot. "Dogs. I just called a guy from the yellow pages, runs a kennel. He's got a couple of German shepherds he's trained for police work." He pulled on the second boot and straightened. "If they're as good as he says, I want to get them for the yard."

"You called him? I thought the phone rang."

"It did." He grabbed their jackets, handed hers to her. "The call was from Jones."

She watched him shrug into his jacket. Something wasn't right about his face. She knew he was a master at masking his feelings, but it wasn't working. He was worried and she had to know why. "What did Jones say that suddenly made you decide to get the dogs?" she asked quietly.

He could have kept it from her, but saw no reason to. How much lower could she feel than she had been lately? At least, this would give her something else to focus on, something other than what could never be between them. "Remington committed suicide earlier today."

"Oh, God," she whispered. Another death. When would it end? How many more would die? "I suppose this means he was guilty, in on the police corruption at Central?"

"That's how it looks." He glanced out the window and saw the sky was darkening, the gray clouds heavy with snow. "Will you get going?"

"But I thought you didn't want me to leave here?"

He sucked in a breath, knowing she wasn't going to like what he was going to tell her. "I'm going to fix a pallet on the floor behind the driver's seat. I want you to lie down there and I'm going to cover you so anyone looking in would only see some blankets and a tarp." He saw her frown and hurried on. "Terry, it's the only way you'll be safe. The guy's going to meet me in his yard with the dogs. The van won't be more than a few feet from me at any time."

"But the windows are tinted."

"Not that much. And not the windshield."

Good grief, what else? "And if you buy the dogs, are they going to be all over me on the way back?"

"No. He's got cages for them that I'll also get. And some stuff so I can build a dog door. I want them to sleep in the storeroom, yet be able to get out in a hurry if they hear something."

Terry pulled on her coat. There was never any use arguing with Luke. "I don't understand what this has to do with Remington's suicide."

Luke walked with her toward the front door. "Jones believes that Remington was the direct contact for both Sam and Nick Russo, and the big boys they deal with. He doubts if the corruption has gone higher, which means he was their main man, their best source. Now, they probably have no one with enough authority on the force to give them information they need to figure out what we're doing. It's just one more reason for them to eliminate you."

Although she'd known for months now that she was in danger, every time she heard it spoken aloud, it jarred her anew. At the door, she leaned against the frame for a moment, closing her eyes, trying to push back the rush of fear.

Luke wished it didn't affect him so, seeing her turning pale each time she heard another piece of truth. He believed in keeping his witnesses informed. After all, it was their lives at stake, as well as his. But somewhere along the line, Terry's pain had become his.

He touched her arm. "I won't let anything happen to you."

She opened her eyes and looked at him. Without a word, she turned and walked outside.

Luke swore ripely. She didn't believe him, no longer trusted him. With his backing away from their personal involvement, she'd apparently decided he'd also abandoned his professional responsibilities. Not altogether, of course. But that he wasn't as deeply committed as before. It wasn't true, but how could he convince her without starting another discussion that would only lead them in circles?

Damn, but this job sucked more often than not, he thought as he locked the door and followed her.

At eleven o'clock that evening in a rundown section of Phoenix, an older man with thinning hair sat in a corner booth of a dim bar nursing a beer. The man he was waiting for was late, as usual. Nick Russo liked to keep people waiting. It was a power play, designed to show that he was more important than they, a way to intimidate. Too bad most people weren't convinced.

Nick was a poor imitation of his brother, Sam. If Sam was sent up, Nick would never be able to keep things together. The whole organization at this end would fold because Nick didn't command the respect he so sorely sought. He was a flashy dresser who liked to play the ponies and surround himself with cheap women. He hadn't bothered to learn the business because he'd always had Sam taking care of him, cleaning up his mistakes, alibiing his weaknesses.

Still, Nick was a man to be feared, mostly because these days he was running scared. Frightened men made stupid mistakes when their backs were to the wall, as Nick's now was. And he had a hair-trigger temper, a man who acted first, then thought about it. His eyes on the tavern door, the old man ran an unsteady hand over his head and wondered why Nick had called this meeting. He had a gut feeling it wasn't going to be good news.

Ten more minutes passed before he saw Nick come through the door, a cigarette dangling from his lips. He shook down the collar of his tan Burberry raincoat as his dark eyes scanned the bar's occupants. Spotting the old man, he signaled to the bartender, who waved back, then he made his way to the back booth.

Nick hated this seedy joint, but used it often for meetings he didn't want to be seen having. Mickey behind the bar kept a sharp eye out for the law and never watered Nick's drinks or charged him for them. It was a form of insurance. He slid into the booth opposite the old man, noticing the strain on his face. "How are things, Pop?"

"You know damn well how they are." He put the bottle to his mouth and drank, pleased that his hand was steady. It wouldn't do to let this punk know that inside he was shaking.

"You hear anything I might like to know?" Nick asked as Mickey set a chunky glass filled with golden liquor and one ice cube in front of him, then quickly left them alone.

"That's my question. You got far more sources than me." Nick had on a cologne so strong that it overpowered the beer smell that permeated the place. The old man took out his handkerchief and blew his nose.

Nick put out his cigarette, tasted his Jim Beam, then sat back. "You sure you didn't hear from her, Pop?"

Eyes on the bottle he toyed with, he shook his head. "They're not going to let her call. You know that." He couldn't know. No one could. He hadn't even told Emily, afraid she'd go to pieces and tell someone. Surely this cheap hood couldn't have tapped his phone. If Nick knew for sure, he'd be all over him. He was fishing, that was all.

Nick's eyes narrowed thoughtfully. "You better not be lying to me, old man. Because if you are . . . "

John Ryan's temper flared. "*I'm* not the liar here. You guys promised me no one would get hurt, and look what's happened. My niece is dead, that nice reporter kid. Those two young cops. And now Remington. You heard?"

Nick waved a dismissive hand. "He was a fool. I told him to hang tough. He was weak, impatient. He deserved exactly what he got." He leaned forward, his elbows on the table. "If you know something, you better tell me. Sam's about ready to sing and that's not going to be good news for you, now is it, Pop?"

Ryan ran a nervous hand across his chin, surprised to find he hadn't shaved today. He was getting sloppy, careless, just like Emily had told him. Because he no longer cared, about himself, about anything. "I don't care what happens to me. I just don't want anything to happen to Theresa. If she gets hurt in any way, I'm going straight to the commissioner."

Like hell he would. "Now, Pop, let's not be hasty. I got a deal for you. You contact Terry, tell her I'll fix her up anywhere she wants to go. A house, new ID, money. Whatever she wants. But she's got to act now. Word is that the trial date's coming up fast."

"I tell you I don't know where she is." Which wasn't exactly true.

John Ryan was no one's dummy, though the department had passed him over time and again for promotions. Terry's call had been collect. It hadn't taken a genius to find out from the phone company where the call originated. Pomeroy's Country Store. She'd told him that that evening they were expecting a snowstorm and that Luke was anxious to get going because they had a two-hour drive ahead of them. That had to be Luke Tanner.

Terry had also mentioned that the cabin they were headed for was owned by the top Fed. From his visits to the station, he knew that was Chief Bob Jones. Using his police ID, John had called the Registrar of Deeds office in both California and Nevada, and finally tracked down the address of the

Jones place that same day. But the last thing he would do would be to tell this punk anything he'd figured out. "What makes you think I do?"

Nick took a long swallow of bourbon. "Because you stopped pestering downtown for some action. Because you been lying low, making yourself generally unavailable."

"I've been sick. Chest pains. I was in the hospital." And this conversation wasn't helping him a bit. As if to show he was speaking the truth, he removed a small tin from his shirt pocket, dug out a nitro, and stuck it under his tongue.

Everyone knew the guy had a heart condition. Personally, Nick couldn't have cared less, but he didn't want the old guy to keel over, not yet. He needed him for one last thing. "Well, if I was you, I'd find a way to contact your daughter and tell her about my offer. I know the Feds have probably told her they'd set her up, but my offer's better. Comes with a lifetime guarantee of cash. Otherwise, if she don't take it, well, I can't guarantee nothing." Nick drained his glass, watching the old man over the rim.

John Ryan was trembling, inside and out. Nick's offer was about as good as his word, which stank. "You promised she wouldn't be hurt." He blinked his watery blue eyes, hoping he wouldn't break down in front of this smarmy shit.

"You worry too much, Pop. Bad for your heart." With a small, mean smile, Nick slid out of the booth. "I'll be in touch, day after tomorrow. You better have good news for me."

Nick waved to the bartender on the way out, his mind distracted. Ryan knew something. Nick could smell it. He'd put a man on him, maybe two. Better yet, he'd tail the guy himself.

The old man watched Nick Russo leave with a grimace on his face. If only he were thirty years younger, and well. He'd clean up the sidewalk with that creep. Gripping the edge of the wooden table, he closed his eyes on a pain that sliced through his chest.

He'd gambled and lost, thinking he could beat the system. He'd bought into a fool's dream because he'd been a desperate man. It was already too late for him, but not for Theresa Anne, not for his young, beautiful daughter. There was only one thing more he could do for her.

Opening his eyes, he rose slowly and shuffled out of the bar.

# CHAPTER SIXTEEN

Luke checked the heavy plastic flap covering the opening of the dog door's metal frame, which he'd installed into the storage room's outside door. It swung both ways easily and there was a metal plate that secured the opening when he wanted it locked. Rising, he gauged the size through squinting eyes. He'd had to cut a fairly large entrance since both German shepherds were full grown. Could a man squeeze through that opening? With difficulty, probably. Certainly a small woman could. But neither would risk it if there was a snarling dog or two on the inside.

He opened the door to the windowless room, gave two long whistles, then shut the door and waited. It wasn't half a minute before first one, then the other German shepherd came barreling through, each giving a short, curious bark when they saw him. "Good job, Rogue. Atta boy, Duke." He rubbed each large head in turn, scratching behind the ears, pleased at their intelligence.

Barney, the man who'd raised and trained the dogs, had said they were two of his best. That was what Luke had wanted. He watched as Rogue found the pan of drinking water and helped himself. Just then, a clump of snow fell from the slanted roof of the add-on storage room, the sound causing Duke to rumble low in his powerful chest. He rushed out the dog door with Rogue following close on his heels. Barking furiously, they roamed their new domain, warning anyone that they were on the prowl.

Satisfied, Luke walked into the kitchen. And was greeted by the silence he'd come to expect lately.

He hated it. There was a time when he'd thrived on silence, longed for it when he'd been out daily in the noisy world on assignment. But ever since Terry had shown him the difference between comfortable shared silences and tension-filled hours, he'd begun to hate the stressful quiet since their quarrel. He'd initiated it, knowing he had to rebuff her before they were so involved that they wouldn't know where one began and the other left off. But that didn't mean he enjoyed it.

Luke walked to the stove and poured himself a cup of lukewarm coffee. He was drinking way too much of the stuff, especially since he was no longer eating the terrific meals Terry used to cook. She'd cut back on cooking, and on smiling, on talking, on everything that had mattered to him. Funny how he hadn't realized how much the little things she'd said and done had pleased him until she'd withdrawn them.

He took a sip and tasted bitterness, which had nothing to do with the state of the coffee. He'd dug a hole for himself that there was no climbing out of. The fact that he firmly believed he'd done the right thing didn't make him feel one bit better.

The hard-to-swallow truth was that, after some middle-of-the-night soul searching, he'd come to believe that some of the things Terry had thrown at him that day had been right. He did find it hard to trust anyone. He was suspicious of everyone who seemed to care for him. He did feel that, based on past experience, most people would leave when circumstances suited them.

Maybe Terry Ryan was different. He'd learned to judge

folks from the things they did rather than what they said. But he'd steeled his heart against believing too quickly in the good of others. More often than not, people let you down. That wasn't cynicism talking, it was reality.

But Terry hadn't. At least, not yet. And she'd made the unbelievable declaration that she loved him. Did she, or had she just romanticized this whole thing? A man and a woman, thrown together in dangerous circumstances, on the run, against all odds. It was the thing movies were made of. But the reality was, there were real bullets in his guns, and that fact had her scared silly.

Luke stared out at the falling snow unseeingly, remembering instead her white face when he'd said he'd blow away anyone who came near her. That was a reality Terry had trouble living with. Even later, when all this was behind them, could she live with the fact that that was what he was, a lawman, someone who felt undressed without a gun, a man always watchful, forever on guard? Growing up the way he had, Luke hadn't had a problem adjusting to the life of a cop. But even though her father was a cop, Terry had come from such an opposite background—suburban peace and quiet, no threats, no violence, caring parents, a home filled with love and laughter.

Something he'd never known.

He drained the coffee and set the mug in the sink. Then she'd come along and given him a taste of that life. And he'd lapped it up like a desert walker finding a watering hole. Helping her in the kitchen and sharing the first real Thanksgiving dinner he'd ever truly enjoyed. Sitting by the fire and just talking, holding her close, sipping a glass of wine. Laughing with her in the snow, kissing her wet face. Lying in bed with her, her legs wrapped around him, the soft sounds she made when he joined with her. What man raised on scraps of affection could resist the banquet of warmth she'd showered on him?

Maybe he'd been more than a little wrong. Maybe he'd

found the one person who could change his mind, change him. Maybe Terry could mend his shattered faith and make a believer of him. But was that what he really wanted? He'd bought his ranch so he'd have something of his own, and taken this job because he owed Jones. But what did he *really* want to do when this ended?

Would the ranch, raising horses, and having Terry in his life be enough to keep him happily homebound? Could he stay committed to one person, which was the only thing a woman like Terry would accept? Would she even have him, believe him, if he were to tell her he'd like to try? Would he be enough for her?

Turning from the window, Luke thrust his hands in his jeans pockets. Too damn many questions and too few answers. Through the archway, he could see Terry curled up in a corner of the couch, reading a book. Or was she merely pretending to read, for he knew that she was as miserable as he? No amount of feigning fatigue or simulated absorption in a book could fool him. All the signs he himself possessed—nervousness, short temper, that haunted look—were present in her.

Yet he couldn't react to her silence, couldn't retract what he'd said. He'd have to play this through in order to keep her safe, to lessen the hurt, until he could figure things out. It would be wrong to start up again only to bow out later. Somehow, from somewhere, he'd have to find the answer.

The ringing of the phone was a welcome interruption of his troubled thoughts. Luke walked to the end table and picked it up, noticing that Terry didn't even glance over. Must be a hell of a book. "Yes?"

"I've got some good news and some bad news," Jones began without preamble.

"Lay it on me," Luke answered.

"Two pieces of good news. We have a court date, a week from tomorrow."

"Great. What else?"

"The word on the street is that Nick Russo's called home his men who were looking for Terry and you."

Luke frowned. "Something must have happened."

"You're right. Nick's cagey as a fox. We have two guys on him, yet he manages to lose them regularly and often. Damn frustrating. However, we learned something today, but you aren't going to like it."

"Say it."

"We've kept a check on his bank accounts. He used an ATM in Reno about an hour ago."

"Great. I don't suppose he's there to try his luck at the tables?"

"Damned if I know."

"Are you sure it was him?"

"Pictures don't lie. The camera got him withdrawing two hundred."

What in the hell was going on? "We've got a leak somewhere."

"That's my guess, too."

"Do you have a tap on Nick's phone line?"

"Can't get authorization. No just cause."

"Shit!" Luke's mind raced, considering possibilities. "This house. Is it listed in public records in your name?"

In Phoenix, Bob rubbed at a headache that had been throbbing awhile. "In my wife's name. Jones is pretty common."

"Yeah, right." Luke rubbed at the back of his neck. Too late to run, and where would they go anyhow?

"You want me to send backup?"

"We don't know anything for sure, right now. Nick may not find the place, or even be in the area to try." More agents on the scene would probably just get in the way. He could always call if it became necessary. "Let's hold off for now. I've got the dogs and we've got snow a foot high and still falling. We've got sturdy locks, two guns, and plenty of ammo." Behind him on the couch, he heard Terry's gasp and turned to see her wide-eyed stare. "I'll phone if I need anything," he said into the phone, wishing he'd taken the call in the bedroom.

"You do that. How's Terry holding up?" Jones wondered if they'd discussed what he'd said to both of them.

"As well as can be expected. Talk with you later." He hung up and walked to the couch, sitting down beside her.

"It's bad, isn't it?" she asked, her voice unsteady.

He told her all of it. She had a right to know.

A court date at last. But the other news diminished her pleasure. "Nick Russo's in Reno and he could be headed here?"

"I didn't say that." Although that's exactly what Luke thought. "He's in Reno, that much we know. But, assuming he's somehow discovered we're up this way, is he smart enough to look up the records of homes in this area, recognize the name on this one, and tie it to Bob? Jones is a pretty common name."

Terry gripped her hands together tightly. "How in the world did he learn we were in this area? What leak were you talking about?"

"We don't know how he found out, and he may not have. He may be coming up this way on a hunch, having searched all of southern California. Or he may be there just to gamble. He's a regular in Vegas."

She knew that probably wasn't so and she thought that Luke did, too. Too upset to sit, she got to her feet and walked to the fireplace. "You're just saying that to pacify me. Don't patronize me, Luke."

He stood and moved to her. "I told you everything I know. The rest is just conjecture."

"Is it?"

She'd turned as pale as the white sweater she wore. "Yes." Setting aside their recent differences, he pulled her to him, pressing her head to his chest, rubbing her back. "I'll take care of you, I promise."

There it was again, the pleasure of being in his arms. But she'd have to do without it soon enough. She'd better not get used to his touch again. She pulled back. "I . . . I need to be alone." Moving around him, she walked to the bedroom they'd once shared and closed the door.

Luke wanted to throw something, hit something, anything to get rid of the rage inside him. Rage at Nick Russo, the system, his own inadequacies. If it was the last thing he did, he'd put that bastard behind bars for all the torment he and his brother had put Terry through.

Grabbing his jacket, he went outside to chop more wood.

In her room, curled up on the bed, Terry felt renewed guilt churn in her system like undigested food. Had Nick Russo somehow gotten to her father? Had her call to Dad been the thing that would allow that gangster to find them? Had he hurt her father, made him talk? She was certain that John Ryan wouldn't have exposed her to harm any other way.

She put her hand to her mouth to keep from crying out. If she told Luke about her call, he'd be furious, and it would accomplish nothing. The court date was close at hand. She'd just ride it out. The cabin was really isolated. Perhaps Nick Russo wouldn't be able to locate them. *Please, God, don't let that man find us.*

It was the middle of the night and he couldn't sleep. Had he heard something or had it been his imagination? Luke pulled on his jeans and slipped his feet into the fleece mocassins. As always, he jammed the .38 into his waistband. He heard the furnace go on and left his room, wandering along the hall. Only ashes smoldered in the fireplace, but the woodsy smell lingered. The cabin creaked and moaned and a winter wind whistled through the eaves.

Terry's door was ajar, something he'd insisted upon, despite their separate room arrangements. He glanced in and saw she was finally asleep. He'd heard her restless turnings long after she'd switched off the lamp, leaving only a small night-light burning.

In the dark in the kitchen, he opened the blinds. Moonlight flooded the yard, reflecting on the stark white snow. One of the dogs was silently patrolling the yard. He could hear the other one snuffling around in the storage room on the other side of the folding door. Nothing seemed amiss, yet he was edgy with nerves.

It was Jones's call, Luke decided as he closed the blinds. Knowing that Nick Russo was probably in Reno tonight. When had he arrived and why was it that *two* federal agents hadn't been able to track him leaving Phoenix? Had he driven or flown? Had he already had someone look up the county records for deed ownership in California, or was he going to do that tomorrow? Was Reno as the city with a major airport closest to the cabin a lucky guess or information he'd gotten from a paid snitch?

Luke walked to the front window and looked out. Nothing and no one stirring. His imagination on overtime. He walked back down the hallway, pausing at Terry's door. But a peek wasn't enough, so he stepped inside and stood looking down at her. She was on her back, one hand curled on the pillow next to her, her face turned toward him. She looked young, troubled, vulnerable.

She'd shifted the covers down to where they lay bunched at her waist. It was then that he noticed that she was wearing his blue denim shirt, the sleeves rolled up on her pale arms. He'd been wondering what had happened to that shirt since he didn't have a lot of clothes with him. She had a flannel gown, but she preferred this. So she wasn't over him, not really.

And he was far from over her. Despite all his fine speeches to her and to himself, he wanted this woman like he'd wanted no other. Lightly, he trailed the backs of his fingers down one shoulder, over the rise of her breast, moving lower. She shivered, making a soft sound in her throat, then shifted slightly in her sleep.

Luke knew every man had to pay for his sins, but God help him, he couldn't stay away from her a moment longer. He would pay, gladly, for one more night with her. Quietly, he placed his gun on the nightstand, stepped out of his mocassins, and folded back the feather bed. Watching her face, he skimmed his hand up the smooth skin of her inner thigh. In seconds, he inched higher, touching her, stroking her.

Terry went from sleepy to stimulated in an instant, her eyes flying open, wide with shock, then suffused with swift desire as she made a sound, half protest, half plea.

"Shhh, honey, don't fight me, please," he whispered as he eased onto the mattress alongside her. "I need you so much."

And, oh God, how she needed him, Terry thought as she went boneless under his clever fingers that knew her so well. She couldn't fight him, couldn't move, couldn't think as his assault on her senses drove her up, drove her crazy. When the explosion came, she felt herself shatter into a million pieces, clinging to him for support. And he was there, holding her, murmuring to her, kissing her.

Falling back onto the pillow, she felt limp, exhausted, yet wonderfully alive. She wanted more, wanted him. She wouldn't think about the problems between them, the madman chasing them, the cloudy future awaiting them. There was only now, this minute, this man who could make her forget, if only for a little while, all the evil and uncertainties in the world. "I need you, too," she confessed.

He needed no further urging. Gathering her to him, he kissed her, deeply, erotically, lengthily. Her hands on his bare chest explored, caressed, aroused. He eased back and with more patience than he thought he had, he slowly unbuttoned the shirt she was wearing. "This never looked this good on me," he said as he spread the folds, exposing her to his hungry eyes. Then he shoved the material from her and dipped his head to taste every square inch of her.

A rush of emotions clogged Terry's throat as she felt her pulse thunder and her breath hitch out through trembling lips. She was steeped in him, drowning in him. Slowly, tenderly, he touched his lips to her throat, the slope of her shoulders, the soft underside of her breasts. No spot was too large or too small for his avid attention. Here was the gentle lover a woman might dream of, might long for, yet found so rarely.

Impatiently, his hands fumbled at the snap of his jeans. He shoved them off along with his briefs before turning back to her. Unable to stop herself, Terry held out her arms, welcoming his return, reaching for his kiss.

He was a man who'd killed and would kill again, but only to save lives, to protect others. She knew that, knew him. He would deny his gentleness though it was there, just as he would deny how much he cared. But she could feel that, too. This wasn't sex they were sharing, but love they were making.

Because Luke loved her.

She felt it, knew it deep inside herself. Still, she doubted if he'd admit it, even to himself. Yet she knew and the knowledge made her tighten her hold on him, trying to let him know that she loved him in return. He didn't want to hear the words, she knew, but he needed this, needed her to show him in every other way that mattered.

Single-mindedly, he set about giving her pleasure, shoving his own needs aside. The taste of her, the scent of her, had him half-mad, as he pressed his lips to the quivering peak of one breast. His greedy mouth closed on her and he heard her gasp. As he shifted his attention to her second breast, his hand skimmed down and moved into her heat again.

Buffeted by the maelstrom, Terry's breath sobbed from her and her eyes fluttered closed as the storm waves hit her.

Dear God, she hadn't dreamed it could be like this. She'd known satisfaction before, but never this mindless bliss, this fierce eruption. And only one man had been able to bring her to this. She opened her eyes and saw him watching her, his eyes darkly intense.

"Not that I'm complaining, but are you ever going to join me?" she asked, her hand caressing his bearded face.

"Do you want me to?"

How odd that he would need the words, this man who'd turned from them just a few days ago. "More than the next breath I take." She saw the change in his face and knew that he believed her.

He moved over her and in her, a sense of peace overwhelming him instantly. He was home, where he was meant to be. His fingers laced with hers, his eyes locked with hers, he began to move. Slowly, absorbing the feelings, enjoying the intimacy of being skin to skin, heart to heart, climbing together. Light drifted in from the hallway and he saw color infuse her cheeks, felt heat move into his face. Though she fought it, her eyes finally closed as she arched, taking him deeper.

His mouth took hers as the pace quickened. He wanted it to go on forever, wanted her locked with him for all time. But when he heard her cry out in stunned pleasure, his control finally snapped and he let go. Holding her tightly, he emptied himself into her.

Things had shifted again. More than the euphoria of the first night they'd spent in the same bed, last night had been a revelation. An admission that they couldn't seem to do without the other, though neither had spoken the words aloud.

They hadn't slept much, time and again reaching for each other, silently reaffirming the depth of their feelings. Toward morning, wrapped in Luke's strong arms and astonishingly replete, she'd finally drifted off. And she'd awakened the same way, something that was in itself a remarkable pleasure.

They'd showered and dressed, made coffee and eaten breakfast, never mentioning the fierce quarrel that had brought about their devastating estrangement nor the reunion that had introduced this truce. But she noticed that he found reasons to touch her, to brush her cheek, to pull her into a kiss that spoke volumes.

The feelings they shared were not simple, nor would they be easily dismissed, for they'd tried that. The trial was a week away. After that, seemed to be the unstated mutual plan, they'd reexamine their relationship and see where they stood. For now, they would just be. They would take comfort in one another while devoting their energies toward watching out for intruders.

If ever there was a topsy-turvy alliance, it was theirs, Terry thought as she bent to the refrigerator drawer, digging through for vegetables. She'd decided to make a pot of soup. Gathering an armload of carrots, celery, onions, and potatoes, she set them on the counter alongside the stewing beef she'd defrosted.

It was a gray day outside, already looking like evening though it was barely four. It had snowed all night and the wind had blown snowdrifts everywhere, making the overgrown shrubs and barren trees look ghostly. Luke had been out shoveling a path for Duke and Rogue several times, making sure their doggie door was clear. He'd come in a short time ago and gone to sit by the fire, saying he felt chilled to the bone. He'd accepted her offer of a cup of hot coffee, then stretched out in the lounge chair wearing a heavy sweater and the fleece moccasins. He'd even left on his silly black cap. She'd kissed his cold, red cheeks and left him to thaw.

Glancing out the window over the sink, Terry noticed that even the dogs didn't want to be out in this weather since she couldn't catch sight of them patrolling. The big shepherds were probably huddled together in the warm storage room.

They likely couldn't pick up a scent in the freshly fallen snow anyhow, so they might as well stay in.

Humming to herself, Terry rinsed and chopped the vegetables, then took out the big Dutch oven and placed it on the front burner. She poured in a tablespoon of oil, then dropped in the meat to brown. She flipped on the burner, and that's when the kitchen light went out.

Frowning, she wondered if the stove going on had somehow shorted out a wire. Probably just blown a fuse. Going to the doorway, she saw that Luke must have fallen asleep. She hated disturbing him. Fortunately, the big high-beam flashlight was on the hearth. She picked it up and decided to go check the fusebox in the storage room.

Turning on the flashlight, she turned the knob of the storage room. She stepped inside and turned to the left wall where she'd seen Luke checking the fuse box when they'd first arrived. Absorbed in examining each fuse, she didn't hear the rustle of clothing behind her until it was too late. A hard arm came around her neck, pressing against her throat, effectively blocking her air supply and making even a gasp impossible. She caught a fleeting glimpse of someone wearing a ski mask as she dropped the flashlight, her heart drumming in her chest.

"Where's your boyfriend, sweetheart?" a deep male voice asked, speaking directly into her ear.

She made a gagging sound and he decreased the pressure slightly. He was a good head taller than she and he was forcing her body tight against his. Her frantic mind raced, wondering if this strong intruder was Nick Russo or one of his henchmen, worrying what had happened to the dogs, hoping Luke had somehow heard him enter.

Nervously, Nick pressed the Magnum's barrel to her head. He could kill her now, then look for Tanner. But he knew it was smarter to take out the most dangerous one first. Besides, in case something went wrong, he could use the woman as a bargaining chip. "I'm going to give you a little air so you can talk, but don't you do anything stupid."

He yanked off his ski mask and pulled her backward so he could look into her wild, frightened eyes. He loved this, having her at his mercy. He grinned down into her face. "You healed up pretty good, didn't you, sweetheart?" Maybe, if things worked out really well, he'd take the time to have a little fun with her. Serve her right for what she'd put Sam through.

Terry stared, recognizing him from pictures Luke had shown her. Sam's brother, Nick. The loose cannon, as Bob had once described him. Good God, what chance did they have?

Nick kept his voice low. "All right, enough. Tell me where Tanner is."

Terry felt the gun press into her neck as she tried to swallow. She had to make a pretense of cooperating or he might just shoot her right here. She didn't want to endanger Luke, but she had no leverage. "In there," she managed. "Asleep." She doubted that he was. Luke, with his keen hearing, was probably crouching with his gun, waiting for the right moment.

Nick didn't believe her. The Luke Tanner he knew wouldn't have napped in the daytime, nor would he sleep through someone's breaking in. Holding on to her, the gun still in place, Nick dragged her just far enough into the kitchen so he could see through the archway.

Damned if he wasn't asleep, the big tilt-back chair facing away. He could see a black cap sticking up and slippered feet on the footrest. The guy had gone soft. He smiled to himself. It would only make his job easier. He'd take him out while the bastard slept on like a baby.

It was then that he heard a sound at the back door. His arm still around Terry, he swiveled them about.

"Let her go, Nick," John Ryan said. Looking pale and exhausted, he was leaning against the doorframe, blood on his jacket, a police revolver in his hand aimed right at Nick's head. "I told you I didn't want her hurt."

"Dad," Terry managed, the word barely a croak. What was he doing here? How had he traced her? And how was it he seemed to know Nick Russo?

Cursing silently, Nick realized he should have made sure the old man was dead when he'd shot him by the gate. Now he had no choice but to finish the job before Luke came lunging at his back. He shifted the Magnum from Terry's neck and aimed it at Ryan. "You should have stayed home, old man."

John Ryan was past listening. He couldn't take the time to inspect his beautiful daughter and make sure she was all right. He'd have to be content with trying to save her life after he'd somehow slipped up and allowed this son of a bitch to track him here. He'd come to warn her, to take her somewhere really safe. But he hadn't been able to outsmart Nick.

John took two steps forward, then another, the gun in his hand steady even if his legs weren't. The pain in his left shoulder from Nick's shot was burning like fire, but he forced himself to ignore it. "Go ahead and shoot me, Nick. But I'll get you at the same time. I'm not afraid of dying, but you might be."

Nick felt the sweat on his forehead and more trailing down his back inside his shirt. This wasn't how things were supposed to have gone. Thinking fast, he shifted the girl in front of him. "If I go, she dies with me."

But he hadn't counted on the fact that in maneuvering Terry, he'd loosened his hold on her. Seizing the moment, she slammed a hard elbow into his rib cage and, as he bent in pain, she dived for the floor out of the line of fire, giving her father clearance to get off a good shot.

Only John Ryan had lost a lot of blood and his reactions had slowed. As he tried to take aim, he heard a noise behind him.

Just as Nick raised his gun, Luke came barreling through the back doorway, knocking John aside and tackling Nick. They hit the floor in a tumbling heap as Nick's gun went off, a shot going wild into the ceiling before the Magnum dropped to the floor. Crazily, it spun around and skidded under the stove out of reach.

Watching the gun whiz by her and disappear, Terry wanted to scream out in frustration at not being able to grab it from where she huddled in the opposite corner of the kitchen. She kept her eyes on Luke as he slammed a fist into the hoodlum's handsome face. She'd been thinking it very odd that he would sleep through all that was happening. She should have guessed that he'd left the living room, setting up a ruse with his hat and slippers, then slipped around the cabin and come in the back way. He'd promised he wouldn't let anything happen to her.

As the two younger men fought, John Ryan tried to find the gun he'd dropped when he'd been pushed to the floor by the federal agent he knew had been protecting his daughter. His vision blurring from his gunshot wound, he couldn't seem to focus. Blinking, sweating profusely, he finally spotted the revolver on the floor near the sink and, on hands and knees, he crawled toward it. His fingers closed around the handle just as Nick kicked Luke a good one in the groin, then swiveled and dived for John's gun.

He had so little strength left, but John Ryan had to do something to rescue his daughter, to redeem himself just a little in her eyes. He could hear Luke Tanner trying to stand up through a pain he was certain would sideline most men. He hung on with all his waning strength, trying to get the barrel aimed toward Nick, who was gripping his wrist with iron force. They struggled another few seconds and then the gun went off.

John felt the searing heat in his chest as he fell backward onto the kitchen floor, the agony all but blinding him. He'd failed yet again.

Frantic now, knowing he was running out of time and chances, Nick tugged the revolver from John's hand and whirled around. But as he turned, a shot slammed into his gun hand, sending the revolver flying, then another bullet barreled into the right side of his chest. With a high-pitched cry, he fell to the floor, bleeding profusely. He lay slumped on his side, motionless.

Luke stood across the room, relieved that he'd finally been able to recover enough from Nick's vicious kick to wrest his gun from his waistband and end the melee. When he'd run around back and entered the storeroom, he'd put away the .38, worried he might hit Terry, thinking a surprise flying tackle would work until he could get in position. Thank God, the impromptu plan had worked.

Still reeling from the pain in his groin, he saw Terry scoot over to where her father lay, blood seeping from two wounds. Questions whirled around in Luke's head—how John Ryan was involved, how he'd gotten here—but answers would have to wait. As Terry bent over her dad, he went to the phone to call for two ambulances and the police, knowing it might take them awhile to get up the snowy mountain road.

Terry stroked her father's stubbled cheeks, fighting tears. "How did you know where to find me?"

"Your phone call. I . . . I figured it out. Nick must have been . . . been following me." The pain made each breath feel like a stab in the heart.

Terry clutched his hand. "Hang on, Dad. Luke's calling for an ambulance." Guilt settled heavily on her shoulders. If only she hadn't called him, her father wouldn't have come looking for her, wouldn't have gotten shot.

"Too late, honey." His eyelids were so heavy, each breath he took a fresh burst of pain. It was over for him, and John knew it. "I never meant to hurt you . . . or the rest of the family." He felt a dribble of something leak out of the corner of his mouth and he knew it must be blood. "I got caught up in it, you know."

Shocked at what he was saying, Terry squeezed her father's limp hand. *What did he mean? Oh, God, surely not what she was thinking. He was out of his mind with worry and pain, that was all.* "Don't try to talk anymore, Dad. Save your strength."

He didn't have much time left and he had so much he wanted to tell her. She had a right to know. In his hazy peripheral vision, he saw Tanner handcuff Nick even though the man wasn't moving, then stoop alongside Terry, sliding an arm around her waist. But John's eyes were only for his daughter. "I was a good cop, Theresa Anne, for a lot of years. But after Kathleen died . . . so many bills . . . I couldn't keep up. Mac said he knew of a way I could make some easy money. It was wrong, I know, but I looked the other way."

She couldn't say a word, couldn't get past the huge lump in her throat. Not her beloved father, the one who'd taught her right from wrong. She willed her strength to seep into him.

"I hate what I've done to you . . . to the others." John heard a rattle in his chest and knew what was happening. Hadn't he heard it from dozens of victims he'd bent over as a cop? "Tell your mother I'm so sorry." With a coughing gasp, he went limp.

Silently, Terry bent her head and wept.

# CHAPTER SEVENTEEN

In downtown Phoenix, Terry sat in the front row of Courtroom B in criminal justice court, presided over by Judge Carmichael. In front of her was Prosecutor Amos Wood's table and seated alongside her was Chief Deputy Bob Jones of the U.S. Marshals Office. Absently, she toyed with the St. George's medal hanging on a silver chain around her neck. Her eyes were riveted to Senior Agent Lucas Tanner on the witness stand in the trial of the State -vs- Police Sergeant Fred "Mac" McCarthy, Sam Russo and Nick Russo, who'd survived two gunshot wounds. The defense had lost a motion to try the defendants separately. An arrest warrant was out for Ozzie Swain, but as yet, he hadn't been apprehended.

The three men seated with their counsel at the front table on the other side of the room were on trial for the murders of Don Simon and Lynn Hartley. Although the deaths of Officers Jerry Foster and Neil Manning were thought to be connected and attributable to the defendants, no proof had been found. "It's enough that we got them on two counts," Bob had told Terry. Now she had only to pray that the jury would convict them.

Her mother, pale and looking much older these days, sat

in the back of the courtroom with Father Tim O'Malley on one side and Aunt Julia on the other. Terry had asked them not to come, but they'd insisted that they had to hear the details, had to be there when they led away the murderers.

Terry glanced back at Emily Ryan now and saw that she was listening intently to the prosecutor's questions and Luke's testimony. Her husband's death had diluted the joy of her daughter's safe return. But that hadn't been the worst of it. Discovering that John had been on the take for years had crushed Emily's spirit and put a disappointed sadness into her eyes that Terry knew would never fade.

And poor Aunt Julia, having to listen to the vivid details of Lynn's death. The testimony of the two officers first on the scene of the accident and the mechanic's report about the tampering of her VW were difficult for Terry to sit through. She could only imagine what her aunt was feeling.

So much heartache caused by those vile men and their insatiable greed. And there were others, the drug dealers who'd used the Russos to launder their dirty money, and who'd so far escaped being named. Even if the Russos worked a deal, which she wouldn't put past them, their sources from Mexico and Colombia were long gone, probably setting up shop in some other state. The main players, the big boys, were as evasive as the morning fog. One crime syndicate broken up, but others would surface.

It seemed to be the nature of so many to want more than they'd rightfully earned, no matter who got hurt along the way. The whole experience had taught her that it's truly an unsafe world out there and that anyone can become a victim.

In a way, her father had been a victim, too. While no one had held a gun to his head and forced him to turn dishonest, to look the other way and accept payoffs, life had slammed him once too often and made him vulnerable to the pros who knew just whom they could entice into their illegal activities. Perhaps if he hadn't been passed by for promotions so often no matter how hard he worked, John might have had the strength of character to refuse to participate. Maybe if Kathleen hadn't died as she had, leaving John and Emily with staggering debts, things might have ended differently. Perhaps if John hadn't had that heart attack that forced him into an early retirement with too small a pension, he wouldn't have been susceptible.

No one would ever know, Terry thought. Ultimately, the decision had been his and the strong man she'd known had turned weak. Her father's funeral had been huge, despite the cloud that hung over his memory. He'd been loved by many. She blinked back a rush of tears, already missing him so badly. She deeply resented that she'd been robbed of the last few months of his life because of this whole thing. She was convinced that John Ryan, with his ailing, grieving heart, probably wouldn't have lasted very much longer even if he hadn't made that trip to California.

Terry listened with half an ear as the prosecutor led Luke through some dry details. Since he'd been the federal agent who'd wounded Nick Russo, finally stopping him, he'd naturally had to testify. So much had happened since that fateful day when she'd walked out of the offices of the *Phoenix Gazette* and crossed the street with Don into that parking garage. Just over four short months ago, yet it seemed as if years had passed. She'd been physically and emotionally battered, changed from a happy, secure young political cartoonist into someone she scarcely recognized these days.

Who wouldn't be affected by all she'd witnessed? After the kitchen shootout, the ambulances and police had finally arrived at their California mountain hideaway. Her father's body had been driven to the morgue, while Nick Russo had been dispatched to a hospital. Later, they'd both been flown back to Arizona. The memory of that day would forever be a part of her. She wondered if Luke was troubled by the same haunting dreams.

Terry studied him on the witness stand with his once again clean-shaven face, his regulation haircut, his navy pin-striped suit. He looked so good, so in charge, so authoritative. She wanted to run up there and throw herself at him, to force a reaction, to break down that iron control. Irrationally, she wondered if he'd even pause in his testimony.

She'd broken through his reserve a time or two, in the bedroom. But otherwise, Luke did things his way. They hadn't had too much to say to one another flying back to Phoenix. She'd been too numb mourning her father to think about much else.

On the plane, she'd finally confessed that she'd called her father that night from Pomeroy's, in case Luke hadn't overheard her last conversation with Dad. She'd expected a reaction—anger, disappointment, perhaps a lecture. But Luke had merely nodded and continued jotting notes for the report that Bob Jones had requested.

Then there'd been the reunion with her family and friends, and later, the funeral. She felt drained, adrift, lost. She was back home, yet nothing was the same. She'd moved in with her mother, who was now alone, and they'd clung to each other, trying to handle their sorrow. Emily and Julia had long ago closed up the apartment she'd shared with Lynn, a fact for which she was grateful, for she didn't think she could have managed that.

Luke had shown up at her father's funeral, even dropped in at her mother's house for the reception. He'd experienced his first Irish wake, and had seemed a little overwhelmed. She'd introduced him around and he'd received a hero's welcome from one and all. But he'd been cool, almost remote, and hadn't stayed long, taking her aside before ducking out. They'd had a very disquieting conversation.

He'd told her that he was going up to his ranch in Sedona and that he'd like her to go with him. He'd even gone so far as to say he wanted her in his life. She'd waited, hoping for some words she could hang her hopes on. Not a marriage proposal, but something that told her he cared. When she hadn't answered, he'd shrugged and said to think about it, that she'd be welcome to visit anytime. A half-assed invitation that was less hurtful than the usual kiss-off, but just barely. She hadn't seen him again until today.

He'd said a lot of things to her during their time together—that he wanted her, that he needed her. There'd been a time when she'd been so certain he loved her. But he'd never used the L word, the one he feared above all others. So be it. She couldn't see herself just living with him, although she might have if love had been part of the picture. But without an emotional commitment, without hearing the words and knowing he truly meant them, she knew she'd start to lose her self-respect.

He would probably take a little time off, Terry guessed, putter around his ranch, then let Bob coax him back with another intriguing case. He was drawn to the thrill of danger like a moth to a flame. Stroking the medal that she'd worn since he'd put the chain around her neck, she decided she'd have to give it back to him. He'd need it for protection on his next assignment.

The sound of the gavel ending the testimonies for the day brought Terry out of her reverie. She stood as people around her rose, and they all waited while the judge left. She said a few words to Chief Jones and the prosecutor. Then she glanced around the courtroom, but she couldn't see the tall, broad-shouldered man her eyes had been seeking.

Luke had left without saying good-bye.

The last days of March in Sedona can be cold, days in the forties and fifties, nights often below freezing. Luke didn't mind. He was in his barn, rebuilding the last of four horse stalls. Next he planned to tackle the hayloft. He'd read in the local paper that there was going to be an auction of purebred quarter horses in a couple of weeks. He planned to bid on a couple to keep the stallion he'd be bringing home soon company, and he wanted his barn ready.

Luke glanced over at Yuma asleep on a small pile of hay in a dribble of sunshine. The mutt had it made, he thought as he placed the plank board across the sawhorses and started cutting along the pencil line he'd drawn after measuring. There was always plenty to do on a ranch. Once he had livestock, there'd be even more. He could also go riding whenever he felt like it. Maybe he'd read up on breeding, try his hand at that. Lots to do, lots to keep him tired, to get him exhausted so he could sleep.

Not that it was working all that well, not yet. But in time, he'd get used to it again. He'd stop thinking about the things he couldn't have, stop wanting changes that weren't good for him or her.

Her. Terry Ryan, to be specific. God, she'd looked beautiful up there on the witness stand in court. Her hair was a light blond, still short, but looking good, curling softly about her face. He'd never seen her with makeup and dressed up before. She'd worn a long white double-breasted jacket over a short black skirt and heels. She was a knockout in any man's book.

But he was the one man she definitely didn't want. She'd scarcely looked at him, hardly spoken to him since their return from California. He'd wanted to talk with her, wanted to tell her that he'd thought over some of the things she'd pointed out to him the night of their quarrel. But after the funeral, she'd seemed distracted, grief over her father's terrible death and awful revelations consuming her. Later, he'd thought. But later hadn't come.

He wasn't a man who would beg. So he'd left. He'd told her he wanted her in his life and she hadn't responded. When that hadn't worked, he'd invited her to drop by and visit him sometime, hoping when she had time to recover they could talk. She knew she could get directions to his ranch from Bob. She was familiar with the Sedona area since her family had a cabin up here somewhere. The trial had ended a couple of weeks ago and he hadn't heard a word from her nor had she shown up.

What more could he do?

He sawed clean through the board. Luke put both pieces on the stack he was forming, and picked up another plank. He wasn't one who had to be hit over the head to get the message. She wanted no more to do with him. Fine. People had walked away from him before. He'd survive. He always had.

Yuma's bark and belated gallop to the barn door had Luke looking up just before a voice spoke. "Hey, Luke."

His hand was already on his .38 when he swiveled around. He saw Bob Jones walking toward him and relaxed. Perhaps his state of mind could best be judged by the fact that he hadn't heard a car engine approaching. Of course, there'd been the noise of the saw. But still . . .

"Keeping busy, I see." Jones stopped in front of Luke, noting his scowl.

"Yeah. Always something to do." He turned to frown at Yuma. "Some watchdog you are, not barking till the guy's practically on us." Taking the scolding to heart, the Labrador slunk back to his spot of sunshine. Luke finished sawing the second piece, then stepped back. "What brings you up my way?"

"I had some errands to run, so I thought I'd see how you're doing." Bob strolled to the next stall, looking it over. "Nice work. You bought any new horses?"

They discussed horses for a few minutes, but Luke was sure that Jones had an ulterior motive for his sudden appearance. "Don't tell me that you've got another *special* case you need help on?"

Bob shook his head. "No, not right now. I think you deserve some time off." Luke didn't look rested, though he'd had plenty of time to rest. The worry lines around his eyes had deepened. He stepped on the bottom rung of the ladder leading up to the hayloft, testing its strength. "The conviction for all three came as no surprise to any of us. Judge Carmichael's set sentencing for next month."

"I hope he throws the book at them." Luke returned to his sawing. He'd made it a point to pick up the local paper regularly, following the rest of the trial after his own testimony had ended. "So everyone's happy now, I guess."

"I think so. I know Terry is." From under lowered lashes, he watched Luke for a reaction. Apparently, none was forthcoming. Jones cleared his throat. "Something happen between you two?"

Luke set down his saw and began stacking the cut planks by the stall he intended to repair. "Weren't you the one who told me that I never should have touched her? So I stopped touching her." He straightened the boards, taking his time.

Bob rubbed along the back of his neck, wondering why in hell he'd stuck his nose into this. Because he cared about Luke, that was why. "Yes, well, that was then and this is now. The case is over. You're no longer watching over her. Naturally, it's your business, but I visited Terry after the trial in the hospital and . . . "

Luke's head shot up. "The hospital? What was she doing in the hospital?"

"She had surgery to remove the scars on her face."

"Was she . . . is she all right? I mean, I know she was really afraid to go under the knife again."

"She dreaded it, but she didn't want to go through life with scars on her face. She's doing fine, healing well. Another week or so and you won't be able to see a sign of what happened to her."

Sure, on the outside. But what about inside? Was she still hurting, was she scared? Did she sometimes cry at night and there was no one to hold her? Damn, maybe he should have played his hand differently. "I'm glad to hear that," he said, turning back to his woodpile. He hoped his feelings weren't written all over his face.

"And she's getting counseling for Post Traumatic Stress

Syndrome, learning how to handle her memories and feelings."

"That's good."

Bob studied his friend closely. "She still loves you, you know."

"Yeah, right. That's why I haven't heard from her in over a month."

"Luke, I . . . "

"Leave it alone, Bob." He tossed the last of the planks into the stall and pulled off his gloves. "Come on in and have a cup of coffee. It's cold out here."

The inside of the house was looking good, too, Jones thought as he sat on the big leather couch while Luke took the Barcalounger. He took a sip from the mug Luke had handed him. "I guess you plan on staying here and working the place, eh?"

"For a while. I'll probably get bored with it in time." The days were already too damn long, the nights even worse. It wasn't just that he was alone once more. Hell, he'd been alone most of his life. It was more like he was empty inside. "I'll let you know when and maybe you can put me back to work."

"Sure thing." Bob took another swallow, then set down the mug, not really wanting more coffee. He stood, fished his keys out of his jeans pocket. "I've got to run. I took the day off and brought Laura and the boys with me. They're up wandering around the shopping center. I promised I wouldn't be long. They've found this Western place they want to go to for dinner."

A rush of unexpected envy hit Luke, for the family Bob had, the fun times they apparently had together. Funny but he hadn't thought much about Bob's home life, how he always seemed eager to return to his family. He'd met Laura, of course, many times, and had even spent a weekend with all four of them. The two boys were spitting images of their father. "Marriage really agrees with you, doesn't it?"

"I never thought it would," Bob confessed, "but, yes, it does. When I left the field, things changed for me, Luke. *I* changed. Inside. I *like* knowing Laura's home waiting for me to come back to her, just like I'm waiting until I can be with her again." Flustered at speaking so openly about personal feelings, Jones shrugged. "It's hard to explain."

There was no explanation necessary. Luke thought he understood perfectly, though probably he wouldn't have before meeting Terry. He could have had that kind of life, he realized, if he could have swallowed his pride and told Terry how he really felt. If he hadn't rushed off, if he'd insisted they talk things out.

Something still nagged at him at the oddest moments: was it possible for a man like him to love, to have a normal life? Bob had made the transition. Could he?

Luke shoved out of the chair and stood. "Nice of you to drop by." He walked outside with his friend, the lingering coffee a bitter taste in his mouth. Yuma came dancing over, sniffed at Bob a moment, then shot off into the woods, chasing something only he could hear.

Jones opened the door to his blue Buick, then turned to the man he'd spent his teen years with. "You know, Luke, working hard is good for any man. You and I both know that. But nobody on his deathbed ever wished he'd spent more time at work. Especially if he was dying alone. You might want to keep that in mind."

From somewhere, Luke found a tight smile. "Sage advice from my superior officer. I'll surely mark that down. See you, pal."

He watched Jones back up, swing the car about, then disappear down his dirt road. For a long time, he stood there staring after him, frowning, his hands in his pockets.

What the hell was wrong with him and what was he going to do about it?

Detective Andy Russell held Terry's chair for her, then

sat down across the table. "Have you ever eaten here before?" he asked as she accepted the menu from the waiter. Shadowlands was a new restaurant in Scottsdale offering a varied menu and a breathtaking view of the mountains off to the west. Andy had asked Terry out to a welcome back dinner, their first real time together since her return, the trial, and her surgery.

"No, but I've heard a lot about it." She glanced at the menu as she patted the back of her head self-consciously. She'd had her hair trimmed and shaped this morning and she wasn't sure she liked it. It wasn't bad, but she was impatient at how long it was taking to grow out to a more decent length. Maybe if she looked more like she used to, she'd *feel* more like she used to feel.

"I can order for us, if you like," Andy suggested.

Terry closed the menu and smiled at him. "That would be fine." She really didn't care what she ate since her appetite was still sporadic.

The waiter returned and she folded her hands, listening to Andy order a bottle of wine, a special cut of steak, and a baked potato that was a house specialty, so large that they'd have to split it. While the two of them discussed the salad, Terry studied Andy.

He was attractive enough, with his longish blond hair and chocolate brown eyes. His height of six-four was a little intimidating, but he was a gentle man who smiled easily and often. He was five years older than she, a man who invited trust. Although they'd dated for several months a year or so ago, the attraction had been low-key and both had decided that friendship was preferable to a botched romance. She'd accepted Andy's invitation tonight because she felt that an evening with a man who was no threat to her emotions was what she needed.

Andy waited until the waiter brought their wine and went through his little tasting ritual before he raised his glass to Terry. "To you, lady. Welcome back."

"And to you for your invaluable help. Thanks, Andy." She clinked her glass to his and took a sip.

Andy crossed his arms and leaned forward. "Is it true, that they wanted you to come back to the *Gazette,* but you turned them down?"

"How'd you know that?"

"Hey, lady. I'm a cop. I've got spies everywhere." He smiled at her, wondering if she'd ever again be the spirited woman she'd once been.

Terry turned to gaze out the window at a spectacular sunset dripping gold and red on the distant mountains. Even that lovely sight didn't cheer her. "Well, you heard right." She shrugged as she brought her attention back to Andy. "I seem to have lost my enthusiasm somewhere along the way."

He reached over, placing his big hand over hers. "Don't rush it, Terry. You've been through a lot." He'd attended a couple of days of the trial and been shocked at all she'd weathered. That bedlam in the kitchen alone would be enough to traumatize someone, to cause nightmares for some time, to say nothing of watching the father she'd placed on a high pedestal take such a plunge, watch him die. And John Ryan had taken several with him. Internal affairs was still investigating the Central precinct.

She blinked, still struggling with tears that threatened to fall at the slightest kindness. "So they tell me."

"Your surgery, at least, was a success. You're as lovely as ever. Maybe more." The maturity that her experiences had carved in her face made the difference.

"Thanks." She needed to switch the focus. She hated talking about herself and her problems. "How are things going with you? Do you enjoy being a detective?"

He leaned back as the waiter placed their salads in front of them, then picked up his fork before answering. "I sure do. It beats car patrols or the bicycling I did at first. Great for the legs, bad for the disposition."

She knew that the beat cops such as her father had been

in the early days had been replaced in Scottsdale and Phoenix by officers on bicycles roaming certain neighborhoods, and car patrols in others. The rougher sections had two to a squad car. "Are you working on anything interesting right now, anything you can tell me, that is?"

Always pleased to talk about his work, Andy told her about a case that they'd just wrapped, able to speak freely about something that was over, the convictions in. He finished his salad and saw that Terry had scarcely touched hers before the waiter showed up to ask if they were finished.

Maybe it was time to cut to the chase, Andy decided. "How's Luke Tanner doing?" he asked, watching Terry.

"I wouldn't know." She took a sip of wine.

Again, Andy leaned forward. "Look, Terry, I know this is none of my business, but I got to know both Bob Jones and Luke fairly well when they were putting this case together. I got permission to sit in on a few sessions with the prosecutors, too. Luke's quite a guy and a hell of a lawman. Correct me if I'm wrong, but aren't you and he more than just friends?"

"*Were* more than friends. Past tense." Carefully, she set down her glass.

"I hope you realize I'm only bringing this up because of our friendship. Good friends are allowed to meddle, you know."

She managed a smile. "Are they?" The waiter brought their dinners. Terry wondered if she'd be able to swallow.

"You had a quarrel?" Andy persisted after the waiter left.

"Not exactly." She picked up her fork and poked at her steaming potato half, which was huge and loaded with all sorts of goodies.

"All cops are difficult to live with, difficult to form a relationship with." Cutting into his steak, he waited for her response. When there was none, he went on. "All right, I'm going to just jump in here. Do you love him?"

The food on her plate began to blur. She cleared her throat. "Andy, I don't think I can talk about this."

"I don't mean to upset you, but I *know* you, Terry. Can I just tell you what I think?"

She reached for a tissue from her purse and dabbed at her eyes. "I don't suppose I'll be able to stop you, meddling friend that you are."

"I've always been a persistent devil." Andy chewed a bite of steak, trying to come up with the right words. "Sometimes, when people go through a rough time, where they've had to call on reserves of strength just to survive, it almost seems as if they were unafraid to die. They're not, of course, but it seems that way. Lawmen are like that. Every day, facing possible death, but surviving."

Terry tasted her potato. "What's your point?"

"That sometimes those very people are afraid to live." He saw her wrinkle her brow in confusion. "They're afraid of what *might* happen down the road—in their lives, in their relationships, constantly worrying about the future. They miss out on today because they're too busy worrying about tomorrow and agonizing over mistakes they made yesterday."

Perhaps Luke was a little like that. "You think Luke walked away from me before I could reject him? I thought of that, too, and even told him that's how he felt."

"I'll bet he didn't agree with you. I know a lot of cops who're afraid to commit in their personal lives." He made a derisive sound. "Hell, I'm one of them." He let that sink in, let her eat while she thought that over. After a moment, he began again. "Maybe you're like that, too."

She raised questioning eyes to his. "How do you mean?"

Andy'd had a talk with Bob Jones about several things after the trial, and Luke and Terry's names had come up. All the chief had said was that both of them were too damn stubborn to admit they cared, even though it was obvious to everyone who knew them that they did. "It's a hell of a risk,

going to someone, sticking your neck out, saying those three
little words before we've heard them from the other person.
Risking embarrassment. Risking getting hurt. Risking finding out if they care as much as we do.''

Thoughtfully, Terry picked at her dinner.

"Make any sense to you?'' Andy finally asked.

She set down her fork and took another sip of wine. "I
guess it does make a crazy kind of sense.'' She looked into
his serious brown eyes. "Are you through playing Ann
Landers or Geraldo or whatever this is?''

He grinned. "Yeah. You can hit me now or later.''

Terry shook her head. "I don't want to hit you. I should
probably thank you. Again. It takes a real friend to climb out
on a limb and tell you a difficult truth.''

"I was hoping you'd see it that way. I only want you to
be happy, to see you smiling again.''

She rewarded him with a smile. "I want that, too. I'll
think over what you said.''

"Terrific. Now, would you please eat? Most men like
their women with a little meat on their bones.''

"Chauvinist.'' But she picked up her fork.

She had her excuse all rehearsed. She was returning his
St. George's medal to him. If he was cool or rude, she'd
hand it to him and leave. If he was receptive . . . well, she'd
improvise.

Driving her brand-new Mazda RX7 north on I-17 heading for Sedona, Terry ran through half a dozen scenarios in
her mind. But as she neared the turnoff to Luke's place,
according to the directions she'd taken down after calling
Bob Jones, her heart wouldn't stop pounding.

It was a lovely April day, cold but sunny. She turned onto
the road shaded by trees on both sides. It was hardly more
than a dirt path, which didn't surprise her. Luke would
choose a place that would make it difficult for people to find
him. Bob, when she'd phoned him, had told her that, to the

best of his knowledge, he was the only visitor Luke ever had. Luke Tanner wore the tag *loner* like a badge of honor.

Of course, Bob had seen through the weak reason she'd given for her visit. It was obvious that she could have mailed back Luke's medal. In his awkward, halting way, Bob had told her he was glad she was taking the initiative, that any fool could tell that Luke cared about her. Perhaps, but would he admit it? The man was as stubborn as a mule and could be just as cantankerous.

Slowly, Terry followed the curving path, mindful of the potholes and jutting rocks on her low-slung car. After several more sleepless nights, she'd decided that Andy had been right. She'd faced death a couple of times, and come out a winner. But was she strong enough to face life?

She'd chided Luke for that very thing. Yet she was afraid of risking her heart, her feelings, too. Everyone was, she supposed. But, no pain, no gain, as the saying went. If he sent her packing, she would at least know she'd tried.

The cabin came into view as a big yellow Labrador came bounding toward her, barking. But the bark seemed more a welcoming greeting than one meant as a warning. He had to be Yuma, the dog Luke had mentioned picking up on his travels. Terry stopped the car behind a white pickup truck and turned off the engine.

As she opened her door, the Lab cocked his head at her, then came over to sniff at her shoes as she stepped out. "You're a big guy, aren't you?" She bent to smooth the big head, but he angled back and began licking her hand.

"Hell of a watchdog I've got there, don't you think?" Luke asked, pulling off his work gloves as he walked toward her. "I had a package delivered last week and he damn near slobbered all over the mailman."

"He must have picked up his friendly manner from his owner," she said, straightening and squinting in the sunshine that haloed his dark head.

"His first owner, maybe."

Her heart skidded around in her chest as she looked him over. His boots were scuffed, his jeans well washed, the denim jacket worn over a tight black T-shirt was faded. He was growing another beard as she'd somehow known he would, and his hair was longer since the trial over a month ago. She liked him better this way. Truth be known, she liked him either way.

A hammer dangled from his one hand. She wondered if his .38 was tucked into his waistband. "I guess I'm interrupting you."

Luke pointed with the hammer toward the open barn door. "I was in there reinforcing the hayloft." He narrowed his eyes, wondering just why she'd come. He wanted her to leave so his nerves could settle. He wanted her to stay till the end of time.

He wasn't going to make this easy. "I've never seen a hayloft. May I?"

"Sure, why not?" He walked around the Mazda. "Nice wheels."

"Insurance company bought it. I rather like it myself. Goes a lot faster than my VW did." Small talk when all she wanted to do was touch him, hold him, kiss him.

Luke entered the dim barn as Yuma ran ahead, following Terry inside, inhaling her special scent, the one he'd tried to forget. She had on leather boots, black jeans that skimmed her slender legs, and a boldly striped silk jacket over a white T-shirt. She had no business looking so damn good, making him sweat.

What now? he asked himself. She was here, where he'd been wanting her to be, where he'd been dreading she'd show up. But why had she come?

Terry wandered over to examine the four horse stalls, obviously recently reconstructed. "You do nice work. Are you planning on getting more horses?" He'd only mentioned the one stallion when he'd told her about his ranch.

Luke placed a hand on the gate of the first stall, as if testing for imperfections he'd overlooked. "I thought I might get a couple more."

She turned, looking up at him. "So Domino won't be lonely?"

His eyes narrowed. Is that what she thought, that he was like his stallion, lonely and pining away? "Stallions don't get lonely. They just need a mare for breeding."

Well, that was telling her. Terry moved off, glancing up at the hayloft, wishing she'd never come. It had been a mistake. Luke was letting her know he didn't need her any more than Domino needed company.

He trailed after her as she wandered over to gaze out the window tucked under the eaves. "What brings you up this way?"

"Trying out my new car," she improvised.

"Is that so?" He came up behind her, the urge to bury his face in her hair making his palms damp. Cursing silently at how quickly she could get to him, he jammed his hands in his pockets.

"It's a nice day for a drive, don't you think?" Terry looked out at his cabin, out past the trees, and still couldn't see the road from this isolated location. That's what Luke needed—isolation, privacy, seclusion. No people around to make him think, to make him feel. Just a dog and some horses, demanding nothing from him but food and shelter. She'd thought she could join that list, but she'd been wrong. "How many acres do you own?"

"Ten." Enough with the games. "Why'd you really come, Terry?"

She was ready for him. She removed the envelope from her pocket and turned. But she hadn't realized quite how close he was. Their eyes locked and she could feel her heart slip into her throat. Why was it that he could weaken her so quickly while he remained unaffected by her arrival? She swallowed with difficulty as she held out her hand. "To return this."

He frowned at the envelope. "What is it?"

"Your medal, the one you gave me to keep me safe. I want to thank you. It worked. But you're going to need it again when you go out on your next case, so I brought it back."

Did she want nothing of his around to remind her of him? Or was returning the only thing he'd ever given her just an excuse to come visit him? Luke wished to hell he knew. He took it from her, stuffed it in his jacket pocket. "Thanks. You could have mailed it."

She dropped her gaze to the hay on the floor so he wouldn't read the disappointment in her eyes. "I could have. I guess I wanted to see how you were doing. And you did invite me to drop by."

"So I did." If he didn't turn from her, he'd be reaching for her. He swung around, ostensibly to adjust a harness hanging on a wall hook. "As you can see, I'm doing just fine."

A dismissal. There was no mistaking his tone. She'd stuck her neck out and he'd chopped it off, neatly but surely. "I'm glad, Luke. I guess I'll be going then."

His chest felt as if a lead weight were pressing on it. He cleared his throat. "All right. Thanks for stopping by. And take care." He moved away, placing both hands on the stall gate, his back to her.

She would not cry. Not now. There'd be plenty of time for tears later. "You, too." She turned and started for the double doors.

"Terry?"

She stopped. His voice had cracked as he'd called her name. She swung about. "Yes?"

Luke swallowed around a huge lump in his throat and took the greatest risk of his life. Was he afraid of embarrassing himself by asking her to stay? Yes, but the greater risk was that he'd let her walk away, out of his life. "Do you care about me?"

She heard more than he'd intended in that short question. She took a step closer. "Is that so hard for you to believe?"

He didn't move for a long minute, then finally turned, struggling to keep himself under control. "Yes, it is. Do you?"

Terry blinked back tears that gathered on her lashes. She'd told him once in anger; now she'd tell him again. "I love you, Luke." She watched his face change, saw a glimmer of hope spring into his eyes. "I've been so unhappy without you."

"No more than I."

She wanted to rush to him, but he seemed to have more on his mind as he ran shaky fingers through his hair. "I told myself you can't want what you've never really had. Something you've only occasionally glimpsed—someone who cares about you for all time, a home, a family." He thought of Bob and Laura and the boys. Just like he hadn't known he wanted a place of his own until he'd seen the ranch, he hadn't known he wanted someone of his own until he'd met Terry.

"I was wrong," he went on. "I do want you, and the rest. I realize that nothing comes with a guarantee, certainly not a relationship. I've always been ready to put my life on the line in my job, but I've been unwilling to risk being hurt again. It was pretty cowardly of me."

"Cowardly, you? Never." She moved to him finally, unable to hold back. A breath away, she looked up at him. "You're the bravest man I know."

His arms slipped around her then, pulling her close. "No, I'm not. You scare me to death." Easing back, he looked into her eyes. "One small woman and you brought me to my knees. How did you manage that?"

"The bigger they are, the harder they fall?" She smiled then, blinking away the tears. "Do you have any idea how scared I was, coming to you like this?"

"Yeah, I do. About like I felt when I saw you drive up."

He tightened his arms, lowering his head to hers. He kissed her long and passionately. A sense of rightness settled over him, a feeling he couldn't remember having before. He looked again into her shimmering blue eyes. "Tell me again, are you really here for the long haul, for better or worse, whether I stay with the Service or stay here and raise horses?"

"For all time, Luke. I love you. I'll never leave you."

"Would you be willing to swear to that in front of witnesses, maybe that chubby little priest you're so fond of?"

Her smile widened. "Absolutely."

He could smile, too, now that he had her back. "I love you, Theresa Anne Ryan. For all time."

Luke kissed her again, but it wasn't enough. His hands slipped under her jacket as he glanced over where a ladder led upward. "Ever make love in a hayloft?"

Terry smiled. "No, but I'm a quick study. Show me."

And so he did.

THROUGHOUT THE NEXT YEAR, LOOK FOR OTHER FABULOUS BOOKS FROM YOUR FAVORITE WRITERS IN THE WARNER ROMANCE GUARANTEED PROGRAM

FEBRUARY
*HOT TEXAS NIGHTS*                MARY LYNN BAXTER

MARCH
*SWEET LAUREL*                    MILLIE CRISWELL

APRIL
*PASSION*                         MARILYN PAPPANO
*THE LISTENING SKY*               DOROTHY GARLOCK

MAY
*BEHOLDEN*                        PAT WARREN
*LOVERS FOREVER*                  SHIRLEE BUSBEE

JUNE
*GOLD DUST*                       EMILY CARMICHAEL

JULY
*THIS LOVING LAND*                DOROTHY GARLOCK

AUGUST
*BRIDES OF PRAIRIE GOLD*          MAGGIE OSBORNE

SEPTEMBER
*SUNSETS*                         CONSTANCE O'DAY-
                                  FLANNERY

OCTOBER
*SOUTHERN FIRES*                  MARY LYNN BAXTER
*BELOVED*                         STELLA CAMERON

NOVEMBER
*THE DECEPTION*                   JOAN WOLF
*LEGACIES*                        JANET DAILEY